Katie Mettner wears the ~~[obscured]~~ her leg after falling do ~~[obscured]~~ decorating her prosthetic leg to fit the season. She lives in Northern Wisconsin with her own happily-ever-after and spends the day writing romantic stories with her sweet puppy by her side. Katie has an addiction to coffee and dachshunds and a lessening aversion to Pinterest—now that she's quit trying to make the things she pins.

Jennifer D. Bokal is the author of several books, including the Mills & Boon Heroes series Rocky Mountain Justice, Wyoming Nights, Texas Law and several books that are part of the Colton continuity. Happily married to her own alpha male for more than twenty-five years, she enjoys writing stories that explore the wonders of love. Jen and her manly husband have three beautiful grown daughters, two very spoiled dogs and a cat who runs the house.

Discover more at millsandboon.co.uk

DEADLY SECURITY BREACH

KATIE METTNER

COLTON'S FINAL SHOWDOWN

JENNIFER D. BOKAL

MILLS & BOON

First Published in Great Britain 2025
by Mills & Boon, an imprint of HarperCollins*Publishers* Ltd
1 London Bridge Street, London, SE1 9GF

www.harpercollins.co.uk

HarperCollins*Publishers*
Macken House, 39/40 Mayor Street Upper,
Dublin 1, D01 C9W8, Ireland

Deadly Security Breach © 2025 Katie Mettner
Colton's Final Showdown © 2025 Harlequin Enterprises ULC

Special thanks and acknowledgment are given to Jennifer D. Bokal
for her contribution to *The Coltons of Alaska* series.

ISBN: 978-0-263-39740-6

1225

This book contains FSC™ certified paper and other controlled sources to ensure responsible forest management.

For more information visit: www.harpercollins.co.uk/green

Printed and Bound in the UK using 100% Renewable Electricity at
CPI Group (UK) Ltd, Croydon, CR0 4YY

DEADLY SECURITY BREACH

KATIE METTNER

For the real Walter and Zafar.
You got your wish! Thank you for being a friend.

Chapter One

The snick of the ventilation system engaging woke Rebecca Roth from a deep sleep. She'd always been a sound sleeper but a light sleeper—meaning she was well rested, even if the slightest sound woke her too early. A glance at the clock told her it was barely 4:00 a.m., but there was no way she was going back to work on that vaccine before 6:00 a.m. and at least two cups of coffee.

She snuggled back into the pillows and tugged the blankets around her neck. Fall had arrived in North Dakota. While it hadn't snowed yet, it was late October, and the temperatures dropped at night to nearly freezing. With her bedroom in a concrete bunker below ground, it made for a cold start to the day. She had started her tenure here in May and wasn't looking forward to the winter temperatures, if the last few weeks were any indication.

When she got her PhD in cell, molecular, health and disease biology, she had no plans to make her home in the middle of nowhere North Dakota. Still, when the opportunity came up to work as the head scientist at the Research Center of The Advancement of Biogenics, she couldn't turn it down. Not when it gave her invaluable experience creating vaccines for new viruses and was the feather in her cap that she'd need to get a faculty position at a university. She planned to work here for a year, make some inroads on vaccines, and then apply for positions nationwide. Once she started publishing papers about her work at the research center, the possibility that someone would come looking for her was very real.

Currently, she worked with a limited number of people due to an incredibly deadly virus residing in her lab. Only the head of the research center, Dr. Walter Hoerman, and their lab tech, Zafar Zimmer, spent time in the center with her. Other than the people who made deliveries of food and supplies, she saw no one else during her days here. It was essential to keep their team small and protect themselves and the rest of the world from the deadly pathogens hidden within their walls. Her mind's eye immediately zipped to Ignis Cerebri, the scientific name for the deadliest virus she'd ever encountered. The brain-burning virus, as she called it, went straight to the brain, where it slowly and painfully burned brain cells until the patient died.

Rebecca had finished the vaccine and was now moving into the testing phase of the process. It was imperative that she finish each step as quickly as possible so it could be tested on live subjects, since each failure would send them back to the starting line. Without a vaccine for this virus, the world would have a pandemic on their hands unlike anything they'd ever seen. A shudder went through her, and she flipped to her back to stare at the grating on the ceiling. At thirty-five, she had enough money and experience to be anywhere but here. She'd left home at sixteen and had only gotten this far in life because of the kindness of strangers, so she wanted her work to matter to those who stepped up to help her when she needed it.

She supposed most people would say they were doing it for their family, but she was dead to them the moment she came out as gay at sixteen when her *Rumspringa* began. Being Amish and gay meant her options were limited in the community: she could remain in the closet, marry and raise kids while hating every second of her life forever, or break out during *Rumspringa* and accept that she could never go back. Neither were easy choices. Not when your formal education ended in the eighth grade. At fourteen, boys were taught vocational skills to learn a trade while the girls continued learning about running the home and farm. What little science she'd learned in school intrigued her and made her want to know more, so when *Rumspringa* hit, she went straight to the public library and read all the books about science and how science impacts the world that she could find. That was the moment she'd made her decision, knowing full well it would be difficult. But she couldn't live a lie forever. That's not living, and she wanted to experience all the wonderful things the world offered, including love.

With a deep and heavy sigh, Rebecca—Bec as her friends called her—tossed back the covers and sat up. She wasn't going back to sleep, so she might as well make that coffee and get started on her workday. Dr. Hoerman had a house outside the research center, so he wouldn't be in until at least nine, and then he'd work until three or four and waltz back out to carry on his life elsewhere. She'd been the head scientist for five months, and it was easy to see why they couldn't retain one for much longer than that. The scientists weren't the problem. Management was the problem. She had contemplated leaving at month four but needed the win of a properly performing vaccine on her résumé. She hoped she'd have that by this time next year, at the latest. The isolation here could get to a person, and she hadn't even experienced a winter in North Dakota. If things kept going as they were, she might have to leave sooner rather than later. Dr. Hoerman was nice but did nothing to help her with the research. It was hard to think about devoting years of your life to a cause no one else seemed interested in.

Even through her thick wool socks, the concrete floor was freezing, so she hurried to the adjoining bathroom to prepare for the day. Her biggest fear, and the only reason she stayed, was that if she left, no one would finish the vaccine, and the world would suffer because she couldn't hack it. Guilt had no place in the life of a scientist, but this virus was unlike anything she'd ever seen, so for the good of humanity, she had to stay. A hot shower, hotter coffee and warm oatmeal was her plan, and then she'd get down to the business of the day—saving the world.

"JUST CHECKING IN, BEC," Dr. Hoerman said when he entered the office and research space.

Rebecca gasped and turned to the doctor, dressed in khakis and a flannel shirt. There was no sense in dressing up when no one saw you anyway. They only wore business attire when they had conference calls with other labs. Today was not one of those days.

"Walter, you scared me," she said, her hand to her chest.

"I'm early," he said with a wink. He reminded her more of a lumberjack than a doctor but had been a brilliant mind in science for years before becoming the admin of this research center. "Couldn't sleep, so thought I'd get some work done."

It was nearly 7:00 a.m., and she was just getting started with work. Her earlier resolve to get up and work had been curbed by the hot shower that had relaxed her, and she'd fallen asleep for a few hours. She'd needed the extra rest, but now she felt great and hoped today would be the day she could concentrate on the next steps to bring the vaccine to the testing phase.

"I couldn't sleep, either," she said, lowering herself to her chair. "It must be in the water."

Walter snorted. "More like the attitude of a teenager. My sister called and wanted me to talk to my nephew."

"That doesn't sound fun," Bec agreed. "But family is everything, so you have to be there for them." She said it as though she had any. That was the most challenging part of her decision to part ways with her community. Knowing she now had nieces and nephews that she would never meet and siblings she would never see again. Looking back over the last nineteen years of her life, she knew she'd made the right decision by leaving, though. There was no way she would have survived in that community living the life she was expected to live when it would all be a lie.

"You say that like you understand family on a different level," Walter said, sitting at his desk.

"It's an easy lesson to learn when you live more of your life without family than with it. That's the breaks, though. All I can do is hope they're doing well. I know that the people I've met along the way, those who helped me succeed when they didn't have to, are my family now."

Walter nodded as he turned on his computer, so with a sigh, Bec did the same. It was a melancholy morning. Thinking or talking about her family always made her feel that way. What she said was the truth. She'd been gone from the Amish community for longer than she'd been in it, and those people were a memory now. She did hope they were all well, but she also understood she was only alive and well because she left them to be herself.

"Are you seeing this?" Walter asked, and his tone of voice told her there was a problem as her computer flickered to life.

All her attention was on the screen now, and she froze with her hands over the keyboard. The screen was black with a white ace of spades filling it. Quickly, she gave the computer several commands, and when that didn't work, she tried to pull up recovery mode.

"Should I restart it?" Walter asked from his desk.

"No!" Bec exclaimed, her heart hammering in her chest as she turned to him. "I think we've been hit with malware. If you restart your computer, it could brick all the devices."

"Brick them?" he asked, his head tipped in confusion.

"Render them useless. If we lose control of the systems that the main computers run, and somehow the containment system goes down, everyone is dead."

Walter froze as the implications of this hit him. "This is bad."

"This is catastrophic," Bec whispered, her gaze drawn back to the computer where a message appeared as though someone was typing it one letter at a time.

Stay tuned... More to come! 4C3

"Who is 4C3?" Walter asked, his voice relaying the same shock and fear coursing through her.

"A phantom, and if we aren't careful, that's what we'll be."

"Can you fix this?" Walter asked, coming around his desk to face her.

"No, but I know who can. They won't be cheap."

"The time for sparing expense is over," Walter said, squeezing her shoulder. "We have to protect the lab's assets to protect the country. Call them."

Rebecca grabbed her phone and clicked the home button, half expecting that to be bricked. When it wasn't, she let out a breath and opened a browser tab. There was only one team that she could think of who could get them out of this jam. She just had to pray she could help them understand the magnitude of the problem and get them here quickly.

Chapter Two

Iris patted around on the bedside table for her glasses until her fingers wrapped around the frames. Once she slid them onto her face, everything came into focus again. Her double vision prevented her from doing anything without them, but it disappeared once she had the prism lenses on. Just another little gift the traumatic brain injury had given her. That happened when she was seven, so after twenty-six years, she was used to everything required to keep herself going in a world that didn't understand her.

Something had woken her, but she had sworn she'd shut her phone off before bed. The clock by her bed said it was barely 7:30 a.m., which meant she'd only been asleep for three hours. She'd been working on tracking down someone from a client's past last night and hadn't wanted to stop and break her momentum. By the time 3:00 a.m. rolled around, she'd found the guy responsible for stalking their client, and the last she'd heard, he was being arrested. If there was one thing she loved about her job, it was keeping people safe. She wished that she'd had someone doing that for her all those years ago. That was probably why she found so much joy in her work here at Secure Inc. The company encompassed her employer Secure Watch, along with the personal security company called Secure One. She could use her computer skills to protect people in a way her friends at Secure One couldn't—even with their fancy guns and bodyguards.

There was satisfaction in knowing the messed-up pathways in her brain that resulted from her injury had helped her as much as they'd hurt her. Her mother used to say everything in life was a trade-off, and she wasn't wrong. It was a struggle to remember that when dealing with the result of her injuries, but getting wins like she did last night helped keep her going.

Iris grabbed her phone and swiped it open, surprised to see an all-call alert from her boss. Something big must have happened in the past three hours because Mina, her boss at Secure Watch, didn't use that alert unless it was an emergency. Since moving to Secure Inc., Iris had finally found the place that played to her strengths and understood her weaknesses. Speaking of weakness, she grabbed her foot drop braces and strapped them on before slipping into her shoes. That was yet another gift from her TBI. Some people could walk short distances without braces, but she hadn't won that lottery, either. When she walked without her braces, her toes dragged along the floor, often tripping her up until she face-planted. She didn't have time to worry about that today since Mina had only given her ten minutes to meet everyone in the conference room. She didn't have much time to prepare.

After quickly using the facilities and taking time to run a brush through her hair and across her teeth, she grabbed a clean shirt and a pair of pants. The idea of everyone gathering in one room always made Iris nervous. She didn't do well in large groups due to her anxiety. Not to mention, she struggled to follow conversations that involved a lot of voices all at once. Her brain couldn't sort it all out, making her even more anxious. Maybe she should text Mina and tell her she was sick. After grabbing her phone from the side of the bed, she opened the app, but her fingers were shaking too much to type.

There was a rap on her door, and she jumped, a short scream leaving her lips. "It's me, Iris. You're okay," Mina called through the door.

Iris rushed to the door and threw it open to see her boss standing there with Hannah Grace, her three-year-old daughter. "Iris!" Hannah squealed and threw herself around her legs in a hug.

Iris dropped to one knee and gave the little girl a proper hug. From the moment she'd met Hannah, they'd been best buds. She found so much joy in watching the little girl learn and grow each day, and it reminded her that childhood can be innocent and joyful instead of traumatic and scary. "Hi, sweetheart. You're up early."

"Mommy and Daddy have to work, and Aunt Sadie is making breakfast, so I had to stay with Mommy. I'll be really quiet in the meeting."

"You're always a good girl, Hannah," Mina assured her daughter, ruffling her hair. "The meeting won't take long, and then you can have your French toast. I need to talk to Iris for a minute, okay?"

"Okay, Mommy," Hannah said, running to the corner where Iris kept a doll and a few other toys for her to play with.

"I was just texting you," Iris said, not making eye contact with her boss. After the accident, she struggled with many things, including social skills that most people could do without thinking.

"I figured," Mina agreed. "I know all calls make you nervous, but there's nothing to worry about. It's just you, me and some of the guys from Secure One. We have an imminent situation, and we need your help."

"You would probably be better at whatever it is. You're one of the best hackers the FBI ever had," Iris said, staring at the floor.

Mina tipped her chin up, so Iris had to make eye contact. She didn't like it, but she did it because Mina was her friend. "Iris, we need you. It's not about hacking. It's about securing assets. We need your expertise. You're the only one we trust to get the job done. Are you in?"

"You can do it, Iris!" Hannah said, walking over from where she'd been playing. "You're the best at catching the bad guys, just like Daddy!"

Iris couldn't help but laugh as she glanced down at the blond-haired beauty. "Thank you, sweetheart, but your daddy is much braver than I am."

"Everyone in this building would disagree with that, Iris," Mina said. "Bravery comes in many different forms and definitions. You are one of the bravest people I know, so harness that because we need you. Okay?"

Iris forced herself to hold her boss's gaze. She'd been practicing with Hannah since kids made that easier, and now she could do it with adults for longer, too. She nodded. "I'm ready."

Iris took Hannah's hand, and they walked to the conference room together, where Cal and two of his men, Zac Wells and Declan Moss, were waiting for them.

"Hi," Iris said, staring at the floor. "Are we late? I didn't mean to make anyone late."

"Good morning, Iris. Remember, you're fine being

yourself here," Cal said, which he said a lot when she was in the room.

She nodded and slid into a seat next to Mina, allowing Hannah to hop up on her lap to color on a pad at the table while the team talked. The sweet little girl had been born in the med bay and raised in the building all her life, so to her, this was a regular Tuesday morning. To Iris, it was anything but that. Her belly was full of butterflies, and her anxiety was rocketing as Cal worked the remote to get something up on the large screen in the room.

"We got a call this morning from the Research Center for Advanced Biogenics," Mina said to begin. "From what I understand, the research center is privately owned by a group of investors but run by a scientist who obtains quotes and jobs for different types of research from other labs, government agencies and universities. There's also a lead scientist who works on those projects. Their system has been compromised due to malware, and they need help restoring their programs. We have a recording of a call I had with Dr. Rebecca Roth, the lead scientist at the center, about the situation. We'll play that for you and then make our game plan."

Cal clicked the remote, and a woman wearing a white lab coat filled the screen. Iris quickly took in the space around her and noted the laboratory rooms, high stainless-steel tables, and several rooms separated by sliding glass doors. A man sat behind her in a flannel shirt and jeans. He was older, easily in his sixties, and nervous, if the way he tapped his thigh with his fingers was any indication. Whoever he was, he was letting Dr. Roth do the talking. When Iris focused on Dr. Roth, her heart paused in her chest and then resumed in a rhythm that was as atypical as her brain. For the first time in too long, it felt…normal. Slow. Unhurried. Confident. Peaceful. Iris hadn't felt that way since she was seven years old.

"This morning, the lab computers were attacked," Rebecca explained. She was beautiful, with long wavy brown hair and the most bottomless brown eyes Iris had ever seen. They were filled with a pain she knew all too well, and maybe that's why she was instantly drawn to her. It was the pain of knowing you didn't belong anywhere or to anyone. "The system is locked, and this message is on all the computers." Rebecca turned the camera to show a screen that revealed an ace of spades and the message, *Stay tuned… More to come! 4C3*

Cal paused the video and turned to the assembled group. "Here comes the part about why it's imperative we do this job quickly and efficiently." He clicked Play on the remote again.

"Our facility currently harbors the deadliest virus on the planet. Ignis Cerebri, sometimes called the brain-burning virus, will make COVID-19 look like the common cold, and we all know how brutal that virus was. Unfortunately, with Ignis Cerebri, the victims wouldn't know they came into contact with it until they died, and by then, they could have spread it to many more people. There's no way to slow the progression of the disease or treat it that we know of yet, so my job was to develop a vaccine, which I recently completed. I was ready to move into the testing phase and start writing and publishing documentation of the process. What that means is, I don't know if the vaccine works on humans, nor is there enough for a widespread outbreak of this disease. If the containment room security is compromised and the virus escapes through the center's air exchange, there's no way to predict what will happen. Worse yet, if Ignis

Cerebri were to fall into the wrong hands, it could be a biological weapon of Armageddon proportions."

Transfixed by the woman on the screen, Iris knew she had to help her. She'd utilize every tool in the command center and work every second of the day to fix this without even meeting her. Rebecca Roth was captivating from a distance, and she appreciated how in control she was during the report. She had a scientific mind, which Iris could appreciate beyond anything else. It wasn't until Cal cleared his throat that she realized he'd paused the video. Turning slowly with her cheeks heating, she waited for him to continue.

"We need all hands on deck with this one. Dr. Roth says they're locked out of the labs since they don't have access to the program that runs them. That means she doesn't know if the containment system still holds the viruses."

"Does this 4C3 guy have access?" Zac asked. Although he was a relatively new hire to Secure One, he had a mile-long résumé protecting people.

"Ace," Iris mumbled. "4C3 is his call sign online, but you call him Ace when it's converted."

"That's all Greek to me," Zac said, shaking his head. "I'm not up on all the lingo."

Declan and Zac sometimes did double duty for Secure Inc. They worked as security guards on large jobs but could also install security systems, which gave them rudimentary computer skills, at least in comparison to her own. Iris liked and respected them as the kind of guys who could do everything and make it look easy.

"The lingo," Cal said with haste, "will only get worse in this case before it gets better. I don't understand much of what Dr. Roth told me other than 'the deadliest virus' and 'it can't fall into the wrong hands' part. Do we all agree on that?" Everyone's heads nodded.

Mina took over from there. "Good, then the plan is as follows. The research center is in the middle of no-where North Dakota, to protect the general public, but that makes it difficult to get there quickly. Cal will fly the three of you to the research center to shave hours off your travel time."

"Wait," Iris said, "that would include me, right?" Mina nodded with a brow up, and just as quickly, Iris was shaking her head no. "That's not—no. I can't do that. You know how I work, Mina!" That peaceful rhythm she had enjoyed for a few moments was gone, replaced by the banging of her heart against her ribs as she tried not to hyperventilate. The very idea of leaving Secure Inc. and traveling to someplace unknown would send her into a panic attack if she thought too hard about it, so she wouldn't. She wouldn't think about it. Couldn't.

Deep breath, Iris. That inner voice reminded her she was still safe at Secure Inc.

"You think you can't do it," Cal said before Mina could speak. "But I disagree. You can do anything you put your mind to, which you've proven repeatedly."

Mina turned to her and leaned in on the table. "We all know you need things done a certain way, but not only does Dr. Roth need you, but the country needs you. Maybe even the world. There's no question in my mind that you can do this."

"But you could do it," Iris repeated, just in case Mina had changed her mind. "You could go, and I could run interference here for you."

"While that sounds like a good solution, it's not," Mina said gently. "We're in the middle of some other cases here, and I'm also needed for those. You are the only person who can put their entire focus into helping the research center gain control of its system and, therefore, the viruses. You're the person for this job."

"We got you, Iris," Zac said, turning to her but avoiding direct eye contact as he knew that was the best way to make her comfortable. "We'll run security outside the center while you work through the program to get the system back online. Declan will be there if you need an extra hand with a computer issue, but for the most part, our job is to support you by keeping the center safe."

"He's right," Cal said, his voice firm. "Once you get there, you'll be working in an environment not that much different from here. The only people you'll deal with will be Dr. Roth and Dr. Hoerman, but that will be on your terms as you need information or help regarding how the system works. We need you, Iris."

"Will I lose my job if I say no?" She glanced at the two people in the room who controlled her fate in an attempt to read their expressions, but they were stoic.

"Absolutely not," Mina said. "We'll just have to make a different plan."

She might not lose her job, but Iris could tell they'd be disappointed with her if she disagreed. The deep brown eyes of Rebecca Roth floated through her mind again, and a shiver racked her. Dr. Roth needed help, and for a reason that Iris couldn't explain, she wanted to be the one to offer it.

"Time is of the essence, and I'm fast at what I do. I don't like to travel, but I'll do it for you and Cal," she finally said, stroking Hannah's long blond hair. Maybe she was also intrigued enough by Rebecca to want to meet her. "I'll have to take an extra dose of my medication, though, so I'll be dependent on you."

Cal gave her a finger gun with his prosthetic hand. "You think you're not a team player, but you always come through for us. Just remember that we've got you, and we all know how to protect and keep you safe. I know you're worried, scared and nervous, but you have nothing to fear. We got you."

It was always easy for someone else to say that, but it was more complicated when she lived with a brain that had pathways that didn't link up the same way neurotypical brains did. Her therapist always told her that was okay because the world needed people whose pathways were different, or we'd never solve a problem. She was right in theory, but those misplaced pathways made her life more difficult in practice. Still, she trusted Cal and Mina. They wouldn't ask her to do a job they wouldn't do themselves if they had the skills. Did Mina have the skills? Yes, but she was right—she'd be pulled in too many directions to do the job quickly and efficiently. On the other hand, Iris was skilled at shutting out everything but the keys under her fingers and the code flying across the screen. Despite the welling panic in her chest, she was the best person for the job.

Mina's computer started ringing out of the blue, and when she answered it, Dr. Roth's face filled the screen. Iris noticed how terrified her eyes were right before she noticed the streaks of blood on her face and the cuts on her cheeks. "Dr. Hoerman was just kidnapped! I need help!"

Chapter Three

Bec paced the lab, wishing they had more space for her to stretch her anxious legs. Normally, she'd go outside for a walk, but she didn't want to leave the building in case something else happened or another message came in from this 4C3 guy. Unable to access his computer, Dr. Hoerman sat in his office, tapping his fingers. She had suggested he call the investors of the facility, but he wasn't ready to do that yet. He had said that until they had more information about what 4C3 wanted, there was little he could tell them. She figured he was hedging his bets, hoping that this was a little hiccup rather than something more extensive. Her gut feeling was that he would be disappointed. For some reason, they'd been targeted, and now it was up to them to save the world from these highly deadly diseases.

"I thought this couldn't happen to the computers at the center," she said on a trip past Walter's office.

He leaned forward and clasped his hands together on his desk. "That's what I was told," he agreed.

"By the board?"

"And the team that wrote the programs for the center. They said no hacker could take it over."

"How long ago did they say that?" she asked as she paused by his door.

"Why would that matter?"

"Because when it comes to computers, one you buy today is outdated before you take it out of the package. There has to be an IT team keeping the system running smoothly, right?"

"You're asking the wrong guy," he said, giving her the palms up gesture. "I would have to assume the investors employ someone who keeps things running. We've never had a problem before."

"Before today," Bec added, starting her pacing again. "All we can do is hope Secure Watch can fix this disaster before we have a bigger problem. I still think you should notify the board, Walter. We don't want to blindside them if a ransom comes in."

"A ransom?"

"What do you think that is?" she asked, motioning at the message on her computer. "That's ransomware. At some point, 4C3 will request money in exchange for unlocking our systems."

Walter shook his head with an exasperated huff. "I don't understand a thing about this stuff, Bec."

She walked into his office and leaned on the edge of his desk. "Understand this, Walter. If we don't pay a requested ransom, we will never be able to use these computers again and will have no way to access or control what's behind those doors!" Her arm flung out to point at the labs behind her.

He held up his hands as though to ask for calm. "Okay, as soon as nine o'clock rolls around, I'll reach out to them. I don't have home numbers, only the office number."

"I can accept that," she said, leaving his office to return to her computer. The message on the screen hadn't changed.

Secure Watch was on the way, but they'd be a few hours yet, and Bec was on edge since she hadn't heard anything more from the faceless person who had taken their data hostage. Walter didn't seem to understand the gravity of the situation, but that didn't surprise her. His computer skills were second to none with the programs necessary to run the lab, but computer science wasn't his forte. He was never on the ground floor of computer science as it developed, which is why they'd hired someone to protect their system from hackers. Fat lot of good that did. Her opinion was that no amount of money was too much if it meant keeping the viruses inside their lab from reaching the general public.

What scared Bec the most was that she'd been working at the research center for months and had been led to believe that their cybersecurity was second to none. She was told a cyberattack could never happen to them due to the highly contagious viruses housed in the facility. She was angry that the man who was supposed to be in charge of the center didn't know a hill of beans about it. If she survived this, she'd be rethinking her employment here. Part of her worried she'd accepted this job with her ego instead of considering it from all angles. It may have been about proving that her *lifestyle* didn't mean she couldn't make massive contributions to the world. She may have left the Amish community two decades ago, but there was that little girl inside her who still felt like she had to prove she was worthy of being loved and respected even though she was gay. Those were the words her parents had used. They said she could remain in the community even though she was gay as long as she didn't tell anyone else.

She blew out a breath and forced her mind back into the game. Before she took the job here, it was confirmed that few people knew this building in the middle of the North Dakota plains was anything more than a facility for common scientific research, but now she couldn't be sure. The fact that this hacker had hit them with a computer virus told her they knew where to look.

A door slammed, and she spun around on her heel, only to be thrown backward into the glass from the force of something so deafening the world went silent other than a ringing in her ears. All she could see were bits and pieces of the room around her, and she realized the bright light had partially blinded her.

A man. A mask. A gun.

Barely able to see through the lacelike haze across her vision, she watched the man put the gun to Walter's head. He hooked his arm around her boss's neck and hauled him from the chair, leading him backward through the office and down the hallway. She tried to stand, but the glass behind her shattered and she hit the ground, sure a bullet had slammed into the glass. Her neck was wet, and she swiped at it, stumbling to her feet when she saw the blood covering her palm. She tried to run but felt like she was moving through quicksand, bumping and falling into tables and chairs as she tried to make it down the hallway to save her boss. Her head hurt, and her arm burned, but she had to get to Walter. When she reached the hallway, no one was in sight, which told her it was too late. All she could do was lock down the facility and pray.

THE CHOPPER'S SKIDS touched the ground, and Iris's anxiety ratcheted down one notch as they arrived safely. She'd taken a dose of diazepam before they left since there was no other way she'd ever get into the death trap despite knowing she had to get to the research center. She had to help Dr. Roth get control of their systems before things got worse than they already were. That didn't mean she wanted to make the trip to do it. The fear of unknown places was just one of the things she dealt with after her traumatic brain injury. Traveling didn't bother her as long as she knew what she'd be facing and was traveling in a way that didn't terrify her. Neither was the case today. When she got the job at Secure Watch, she'd been surprisingly excited to move to the property. Within a few weeks, she knew why. The energy there was accepting. No one was better than anyone else, and they understood that everyone had different physical and mental idiosyncrasies that they needed to play to for the team to work cohesively. Somehow, Cal and Mina made everyone feel they were imperative to the team, and today's events showed her why. Sometimes, lives were on the line in this business, and specific team members needed to step up. Today, she was that team member, and because they'd fostered a give-and-take relationship with her over the years, she could trust them and do just that.

After releasing a pent-up breath, Iris grabbed her bag and tossed it over her shoulder, knowing Zac, Declan and Cal would unload her equipment and bring it to the center. Once everything was unloaded and jobs were defined, Cal would head back and leave them to do their work while Mina offered support from Secure Inc. Despite trusting their skills, Iris could tell Cal was nervous about leaving them. Who wouldn't be? In this situation, he was dropping off team members he may never see again if something terrible happened. All the more reason for him not to stay. The fewer people here for her to stress about the better when trying to fix this situation. Besides, she worked better and faster when she was alone. Considering what happened to the other doctor here, time was definitely of the essence.

She tumbled out of the old behemoth of a helicopter and glanced around. There was nothing but pastureland as far as the eye could see, and a mountain range was visible in the distance. The summer wheat blew as a light breeze swept across the stalks, and the rustling of the grain was a reminder that life went on around them, even if they were faced with their own little hell. Something told her Dr. Roth felt that way after what she'd been through this morning, and Iris just wanted to get to the center and help her. She walked around the back of the chopper where Zac and Declan were loading bins and equipment into a UTV. She knew for a fact some of those bins held hazmat suits, but she also knew those wouldn't be enough to protect them from what they'd be dealing with if something from inside their home away from home managed to escape.

Cal spoke to three men in a smaller UTV before he waved as they headed across the field toward the mountains.

"Where did you get these?" Iris asked, staring at the ground. "Who were those guys?"

"A couple of army friends of mine," Cal answered as he approached her. "They loaned us the UTVs for the duration of the stay."

"I don't think we're in the right place. There's nothing here, Cal."

His laughter was gentle when he patted her back. "We're about five miles away from the facility, Iris. We couldn't land close to it and draw attention there. It's better to take the UTVs in. They're so common around here it won't seem out of place."

"Did Dr. Roth call the police?" she asked as he motioned for her to climb into the back seat of a UTV. The vehicle was as big as a Jeep, but it was open to the elements, so she kept her head tucked down out of nervousness as Zac fired it up.

"I'll explain when we're there!" Cal said over the roar of the motor.

Head down and eyes squeezed shut, Iris did her box breathing to keep her anxiety level in check as they bounced and rattled through the wheat to a road. The ride smoothed out considerably then, but she didn't look up. Cal had his hand on her back, which made her feel infinitesimally better about the situation. On the inhale, she pictured Rebecca's face covered in blood, and while she held her breath for four counts, she remembered the fear in her voice as she described what had happened. When she exhaled, she pictured herself at the keyboard, bringing the safety protocols back online to protect everyone from an unseen evil. The imagery allowed her to square her shoulders and lift her head slightly just as Zac slowed the vehicle.

Across the road, a building was half buried inside an earth dome. "You'd never know the terrors of the world are held inside there," she said, noting that Cal nodded from the corner of her eye.

"Which is the point, but obviously, someone knew it was here. And that someone has plans we need to put a stop to. Are you ready?"

"Not even a little bit, but I know I'm part of the solution, so let's do this."

"That's my girl. I'm proud of you every day, but today even more so," he said as Zac rolled the UTV around to the side, where there was a small loading dock. Zac jumped out to start unloading while he waited for Declan to catch up in the other UTV. Cal punched a button by a side door and spoke into the speaker, announcing their arrival to the only person inside—Rebecca Roth.

The door clicked open, and Cal motioned her forward, leaving the guys to deal with the supplies. They walked into a cavernous space that defied the outside dimensions.

"Where are we? I thought this was a lab," she said, and Cal nodded.

"We're in the loading bay. The lab is upstairs."

He pointed at a door marked Stairs, held it open for her and joined her as they went up a flight of stairs that opened into a hallway. Cal turned left, and she followed, noting an employee break room on the right, along with several restrooms.

When they left the hallway, on their right were glass partitions separating multiple labs with sliding doors that opened into the large center workspace. Inside each lab was equipment Iris had no idea how to use, as well as rows of test tubes and hanging ventilation fans.

In the center of the room were large tables for standing while working. That was where a disheveled and nervous woman stood wringing her hands. She'd cleaned the blood off her face, but the cuts were copious and dotted her beautiful alabaster skin. It didn't steal from her essence, though. An essence that drew Iris in and made her curious to know more about the woman. "Thank you for coming so quickly." It was easy to hear the fear in her words as she shook Cal's hand. "I don't know what to do next. My ears are still ringing, so you'll have to speak up."

"That's why you called us," Cal assured her in his even yet commanding tone, slightly louder than his normal voice. "Dr. Roth, let me introduce you to Iris Knowles, our cybersecurity expert, who will work with you to resolve this situation."

Iris stuck her hand out to shake while staring at the doctor's shoes. That made it easier for her to make physical contact with strangers. Rebecca slid her hand into Iris's, and the sensation was difficult to describe. Iris knew she was supposed to speak but struggled to form words as Rebecca's touch overwhelmed her. When her warm palm caressed her skin, all she could think of was sunshine on a rainy day. Iris knew she was here to do a job, so as the doctor released her hand, she lifted her head and made eye contact with the woman for an instant. Rebecca imprinted on her soul in that short moment, sending an unexpected shockwave through her.

"Nice to meet you, Iris," Rebecca said, her voice softer, calmer. "I can't thank you enough for coming."

"It was a lot of work to get here, and I didn't want to come, but I did." Iris grimaced as she stared at the floor. "I'm sorry for saying that."

"Iris has lingering effects from a traumatic brain injury," Cal explained. "She finds traveling to new places overwhelming. She'll need a few minutes to adjust."

"He's right, but I promise it won't interfere with solving your problem. Fair warning that I don't know how to lie or be anything but honest and straightforward, or what some might consider blunt. It's an unfortunate result of having my brain scrambled."

"I understand," Rebecca said, but not in the kind of

pitiful voice Iris was used to. Those two words were said with respect, which she proved with her following sentence. "If I can do anything to make it easier for you, don't hesitate to tell me what you need, and I'll make it happen. I prefer honesty over lies anyway, even if the delivery is blunt. We must contain this situation, which will require us to work together as a team."

"Social skills have been difficult for me to learn, and I've tried, but unfortunately, my brain often forgets how to do that, so honest and straightforward is what you'll get from me. Sometimes to a fault, as Cal says," Iris admitted.

"But she always means well," Cal added with a wink.

Rebecca laughed, lifting the mood and Iris's head. "In this situation, be honest to a fault. We're going to need it to get through this."

Iris noted the woman's full lips pull into a thin line as she glanced around the room at the labs. "That is also my assessment," she agreed. "Don't worry, though, Dr. Roth, I won't sleep until you have control of your lab again. My brain is already messed up, so the last thing I want is to feel it burning."

Cal and Rebecca snickered in response to her sentence, which lifted Iris's lips into a smile for the first time since the call sounded this morning. She'd made a joke, and people laughed. A new skill unlocked!

"Please, call me Bec," she said as she motioned them toward a desk where a computer sat. "All my friends do."

"But I'm not your friend," Iris said before she could stop herself. Cal gently grasped her forearm to remind her to be calm.

"Yet," Bec said with a wink. "I have a feeling that will have changed by the time we finish this project. As you can see, all the computers have the same screen and message. It's been hours since we found the message, but nothing has changed, and there have been no ransom requests."

"Unless kidnapping the other doctor was the message," Cal said, motioning at her face.

Iris followed as they walked toward an office strewn with papers and shards of glass. The scene was terrifying, and she hadn't lived through it with a flash-bang and kidnapper. Her heart went out to the woman whose hands shook as she described what happened to her colleague. Iris could only think of one thing to do. She walked over and put her hand on Bec's shoulder. Without pausing her story, Bec laid her hand on hers, and she noticed the scientist's hands stopped shaking immediately.

It was then that Iris realized she could help this woman in more ways than one.

Chapter Four

Rebecca stood around one of the tables in the center workspace with Cal, Iris, Declan and Zac. They were going over the kidnapping step-by-step and making a plan for how to proceed.

"You don't think I should call the police?" Bec asked again. "Won't they hold me responsible for not reporting a crime?"

"They might," Cal said with a nod. "But you can make a case that the message on the computer said more was to come, so you waited to hear from them. We don't know who took Dr. Hoerman. If the people responsible for his kidnapping are watching the property and suddenly it's swarmed by police, they may very well kill him. We should wait for their communication before bringing the authorities in on this, but you'll have to make the final call."

"Like a ransom?" she asked, eyeing everyone around the table. "That would make the most sense, right?"

"I've been doing this job for many years, and it's what my gut tells me," Cal agreed. "I expect it to come in twelve hours or less. They kidnapped him for a reason, and there are only two that I can think of. Money or power. Whoever took him thinks he has control or information about the lab that they can use to their benefit."

"He does," Bec agreed. "He's the one who worked to procure the Ignis Cerebri at this lab."

"So, this is a government facility?" Declan asked, but Bec shook her head.

"No, we're a privately funded research facility with clients from private and public companies and organizations. My job as head scientist is to do whatever is asked scientifically of the client, while it's Walter's job to do all the administrative tasks."

"Do you know who requested that you create a vaccine?" Cal asked, and again, Bec shook her head no.

"That's not my wheelhouse—it was need-to-know information that I didn't need to know."

"Didn't need to know *then*," Zac said. "Now that you do, it's too late."

Bec bit her lip with a nod. "I agree, but he couldn't have told me even if I'd demanded it. I could find out if I logged into his computer, but I can't. Since he had his phone in his hand when he was kidnapped, I can't even look at that."

"Which means Walter is worth ransoming," Zac said.

"Honestly, I'm worth more to them than Walter," she said, rubbing the back of her neck. It was sore from falling earlier when the flash-bang threw her backward. When she dropped her hand, Iris's replaced it. That surprised her but she tried not to let it show. Iris massaged her neck gently, and the warmth of her hand helped Bec focus better on the conversation.

"Because you made the vaccine?" Cal asked, and she nodded.

"Maybe they didn't know that, or it was more of an opportunist kidnapping?" Iris asked.

"Whoever they could take would be better than no one at all?" Cal mused, and heads bobbed around the table.

"The funny part is, they wouldn't have to kidnap any of us if they knew what was inside those labs," Bec said, motioning to her left. "Taking control of the system was enough. We'd have paid anything to get control of it again."

"Let's hope Walter doesn't tell them that," Cal said dryly.

"He won't," Bec assured them. "The only thing he'll do is clam up and say nothing because he works with too many agencies to do anything else."

"The kidnappers will be in touch then," Declan said. "They'll want money in exchange for his life. What we have to decide is if they're working with Ace or if we have two different ransom situations. What other reason would they do this?"

"As long as that ransom isn't the virus," Iris said as she met Bec's gaze. "If it's what you say it is, that's a weapon of mass destruction someone might want to auction off to the highest bidder."

Bec's laughter surprised the other four. "I was hoping none of you would consider that. I should have known that was a pipe dream."

"After the Spiderweb case we worked on a few years ago, nothing would surprise me," Iris said with a shrug.

Bec remembered the case and shuddered. Someone on the dark web had written a program to look like a video game that was anything but that. Had it gone mainstream, the "game" would slowly give the coder the data from every public camera in the free world by planting malware in their operating system. It was a terrorist's dream, and the coder knew that. Unfortunately, the government hadn't yet caught Savant. Fortunately, the woman who discovered the program, Kenley Mason, now a Secure Watch operative, had helped the government write a malware patch to prevent Spiderweb from getting the data from the cameras.

"The Spiderweb case taught us people are always after money, power or both. In this case, I could see them wanting the virus they could sell as a weapon of mass destruction. Unless Walter can convince them that you already have a working vaccine. If he can do that, then they may demand money instead. Declan is correct that we could also be dealing with two different groups looking to get money out of the center, though the odds are high that it would happen all on the same day if they weren't working together. That said, all we can do is wait and see. In the meantime, Iris can work on getting the ventilation system back online," Cal said.

"What about Walter's sister? Should we notify her about the situation?" Bec asked.

"He has a sister?"

"Yes, and at least one nephew, but I don't know her name or where she lives," Bec explained.

"Are they close?" Cal asked.

"I know he talks to his nephew on the phone whenever his sister calls for backup. He doesn't talk much about his family, so I can't say more than that."

"I'll have Mina look into it. I want to keep his family out of it until we get a ransom request, if possible."

"And if Ace does reach out with a ransom request?

Then what do I do?" Bec asked, holding Cal's gaze. She had no idea how to navigate her world now but hated depending on someone else to answer her questions.

"Iris will call Secure Watch immediately, and we can make a plan from there. Trying to do that now is a lesson in futility. Instead of wasting time, we'll be proactive by securing the building while you work on getting the most important aspects of the lab back online. Declan and Zac will patrol the building. If you need anything, radio them using this," he said, holding up a black walkie-talkie. "Unless there's a fire, do not try to leave the building without notifying them. We don't need any unintended casualties."

"We'll be too busy to leave the lab," Iris said, eyeing her equipment. Bec could tell she was aching to set it up. "Give it to me straight, Cal." She turned to her boss. "Are we safe here?"

"As safe as any of us can be right now, Iris," he assured her, his hand on her shoulder. "Declan and Zac have your back with security, and we know you'll get all the important aspects of the lab up and running again quickly."

"I'm glad you have confidence in me."

"We do, or you wouldn't be here," he said, his brow raised. "I also know you'll stop at nothing to protect the entire nation from this virus. Your job is to help Bec do just that and keep Mina updated on each step as you go. If you need help, she's available anytime, so don't hesitate to call her."

"Are you really returning to Secure Inc.?" Declan asked.

"Yes, but not for long," Cal said. "I'll load up equipment and a few more guys, then return to Sinlis Park, the town closest to here. I'll set up a temporary home base there until we have a ransom or a resolution. You two will need to sleep," he said, motioning at Declan and Zac, "but I also want two people patrolling the building at all times. At night, there will be three. We'll run eighteen on and six off, so make good use of those six off. Understood?" Both men nodded, so Cal continued. "I'd like more men to cover the property, but I can't bring an army until we know what the kidnappers want."

"If the kidnappers are watching, won't they notice the security guys anyway?" Bec asked, leaning on the table. Her head hurt, and while she could hear better now, the ringing in her ears made it hard for her to concentrate on the situation.

"There's no way around that," Cal said with a shrug. "I'm shocked you didn't always have security on the building."

"We did," she said, "just not in human form. The biometrics we use to run this lab is our security. There's no way in or out of the building without me or Dr. Hoerman."

"Wait, you mean none at all?" Declan asked, glancing at his boss.

"None," she said again. "We have to scan our thumb or retina to open any door in the building. You could only enter the loading dock door because the security system went down when the systems went offline."

"That was the only way for the kidnapper to get into the building then," Cal said, turning to her. "First, he had to make sure the systems went offline if he stood any chance of breaching the facility."

Bec's heart paused for a beat at the thought. "You're

right. I didn't even think about how they got in here. Without the biometrics, we're sitting ducks."

"We've got you," Zac said without hesitation. "Our first order is to lock down all but one exit until Iris gets the biometrics up and running again. We'll keep a close eye on that exit, but in case of a fire, head to the loading bay if you can't reach the side door. We'll extract you from there."

"Got it," Iris said with a nod. "Time is slipping away from us. I should get to work."

"Agreed, and I need to get back to Secure Inc.," Cal said. "I'll turn it around as quickly as possible, but I expect to be gone at least six hours. Bec, is there somewhere in the area where I can rent four-wheelers or UTVs?"

"There are several places in Sinlis Park. We're between hunting seasons, so they should be easy to come by."

"I'll get Mina on that so the guys can get back and forth from here to town without taking the two we have." Cal reached into his pocket and pulled out a small button. "This is a panic button." He pushed it toward her. "We all wear one. Put it somewhere that's easy to activate but won't be accidentally pressed. It's waterproof, so wear it at all times. If you ever get in a situation where you need immediate assistance, press it. It's a GPS locator, so it's silent but tells us where you are."

"Got it," she said, swiping the button off the table and tucking it in her pocket.

"Are there sleeping accommodations here in the facility?" Cal asked, addressing her again.

"Not many," she said with a shake of her head. "I have a small apartment where Iris can rest, but there isn't room for multiple people."

"What about the storage room off the loading dock?" Declan asked. "It's nearly empty, so there's room for several cots, which is all we'll need if we're running shifts."

"That would work," Bec agreed. "There's a bathroom and a decontamination shower just outside of that room as well. "There's a small break room with a microwave and fridge on that floor. There isn't much to cook with, though."

Cal chuckled. "We're all used to MREs when in the field. Food is the least of our worries." He pointed at Declan and Zac. "Head out and get those exits secured. We can't risk the kidnappers returning when we aren't prepared. Once I know who will be coming in to help you cover, I'll radio in. We'll bring the needed supplies for bedding down along with extra food."

"You got it, boss," Declan said. "Safe travels. Danger, out."

"Zulu, out." Zac saluted his boss and followed Declan, leaving just the three of them.

"Danger?" Bec asked.

Cal bit back a smile. "His call sign in the service. Let me reiterate that when I say don't call the police, I only mean if you can avoid it." He glanced between them. "If one of my men is hurt, the place goes up in flames or one of you is in trouble, then you call the police."

"Understood, boss," Iris said. "Not that it would matter. The police are so far away that by the time they arrived, we'd be dead anyway." Bec gasped, immediately noticing Iris's grimace. "Sorry. I should stop talking."

Bec shook her head as her shoulders slumped forward. "Iris, you didn't say anything that isn't true. It just took me by surprise when you pointed it out."

Bec felt terrible that she'd upset Iris and made her

feel she had to stop talking. That was the very last thing she wanted. The woman was captivating in her beauty, knowledge and matter-of-fact way of seeing life. She could appreciate someone who wasn't afraid to say it like it was, whether by choice or not. Life was short, and trying to dance around important subjects was never an effective way to communicate. However, what surprised her most about Iris was how quickly she calmed her with just one touch. A warm hand on her shoulder or brush of her fingers across hers, and Bec's heart rate slowed. While she didn't interact with anyone much, that wasn't the reason she was comforted by the woman's touch. Iris Knowles was intriguing. In any other scenario, she'd ask her out for dinner and drinks, but they were in a fight for their lives, so the last thing she could do was distract her from her job.

"We have a built-in system for fire suppression," Bec said to cover her momentary lapse into silence. "She's right about the police. Sinlis Park only has one full-time officer and one part-time, so the closest force that could help is over thirty minutes from here."

"Which is why I'll be setting up a command post in Sinlis Park," Cal said. "It keeps us within a few miles of the facility, allowing us to monitor everything closely. To do that, I need to get back to Secure Inc. Since the kidnapping occurred only a few hours ago, I'm confident that you're safe here with Declan and Zac. If you need anything, you know the protocols," he said to Iris, who nodded.

"Get after it then," he said, patting her shoulder. "Charlie, out."

He spun on his bootheel and strode from the room, leaving the two women facing each other. "That was a lot," Bec said as Iris ducked her head to stare at the table. "Do you need a breather?"

"I'm okay. I'd rather get started if that's okay with you."

"That's absolutely fine," Bec said, motioning her forward. "Where would you like to set up your machines? Let's avoid Dr. Hoerman's office for now. If we have to call the police, they'll want it untouched."

"I'd like to be wherever you are," Iris said, and Bec glanced behind her to catch Iris's eye for a second. "I get nervous in new environments and don't like to be alone until I know where everything is and—"

Bec turned and took her hands. "You're safe here with me, Iris. Please, don't feel you have to justify anything to me, okay? Just know you're safe, and I'm here to help you, whether you need coffee or have a question about the system."

Iris smiled and held her gaze momentarily, which she took as a solid win in her column. "Thank you, Bec. I appreciate that you don't think I'm weird like most people do. Well, not the people I work with, but everyone else."

"Sweetheart, it upsets me to know others make you feel that way. We're all different, but wouldn't this world be boring if we weren't? Now, we could pull one of the empty tables over to sit next to my desk. That way, as you work, you will also have easy access to my computer. Does that work for you?"

"That would be a good idea," Iris agreed, staring at the floor again. "I'll call Declan to come move the table. My foot drop makes it hard to push things around."

"I got this," Bec said with a wink. "I can do the heavy lifting with this since you'll do the heavy lifting that matters."

Forcing herself to turn away from the woman who had charmed her so quickly, she prayed Iris had the skills to fix this mess before mankind suffered unimaginable pain and loss. She was betting on the quiet, unassuming woman who thought she didn't matter to prove just the opposite was true. Bec vowed to make sure Iris understood her worth, or she'd quite literally die trying.

Chapter Five

Iris pulled her hands from the keyboard and took her glasses off to rub her eyes. She'd been working on getting the containment and ventilation systems under Bec's control again by writing a workaround code for the malware. Ace still controlled the entire lab system, so she was confused about why they hadn't received a ransom request yet. He held all the cards and could demand anything he wanted, so why hadn't he? Why had he kidnapped Dr. Hoerman if he didn't plan to leverage him for money? Her biggest fear, that he would use him to access the virus, was still a real possibility. He could demand the virus and open the lab long enough for Bec to get Ignis Cerebri before meeting him with the deadly pathogen. She had been half convinced that two things were happening until Bec mentioned biometrics was the only way to get inside the facility. Ace and the kidnapper had to be working together or were one and the same, otherwise the kidnapper would never have gotten inside. Frustrated, she blew out a breath and tried to refocus. She had to keep working regardless of what he might do.

"How about a break?" Bec asked, setting a cup of coffee down in front of her. "You've been at this for hours."

Iris greedily picked up the coffee cup and took a long gulp of the hot liquid. "Oh, that's good," she said with a sigh. "Thanks. If I don't finish this workaround soon, I'll need another gallon." She took another sip. "Is that caramel?"

"Yep," Bec said, sitting at her desk with a mug, too. "It's my guilty pleasure. I have it shipped in from a place in Wisconsin. I had it once at a hotel in Door County and have been a fan ever since."

"You don't get out much, do you?" Iris asked, and Bec chuckled. "I'm sorry. That wasn't meant sarcastically. Like, I meant, you don't get to go out much while working here, right?"

"I know what you meant," Bec promised, patting her leg and sending a tendril of heat into Iris's belly. She had known Bec less than twelve hours yet somehow, it felt like they'd been intimate partners for years. Something in Bec's touch told her she felt the same way. "And you're correct. I've been working here since May and haven't left the compound other than for a daily walk."

"Five months is a long time to be this secluded," Iris said. "Is that by choice?"

Bec's laughter filled the space, and Iris thought it was a lovely sound. It reminded her of Hannah Grace's laugh when she was on the swing on a sunny afternoon. "It's not a choice in the respect that I can come and go as I please. I could leave if I had to, but organizing that would be more effort than it was worth for an occasional outing. It was better to keep working on the vaccine since, as you know, the sooner the better when it comes to this virus."

A shudder racked Iris, but it wasn't from the cold. "The very idea of it is disconcerting. Especially knowing those systems are still under someone else's control."

The idea was too much to bear, so Iris set her mug down and started typing again. "I keep telling myself he has to know that if he lets this virus go free, he's dead, too, right?"

"I've been telling myself the same thing, but we can't know that for certain. That said, he wouldn't know what we even housed here for viruses unless he hacked our system, which is entirely possible."

Iris paused her typing to glance at the woman next to her. "That's not true."

"What now?" Bec asked, setting the mug down. "What's not true?"

"That he has no way of knowing what's here. Have you ever googled this place?"

"I haven't needed to," Bec answered defensively.

Iris motioned at her phone with her chin. "Do it."

Bec reached for the phone, and Iris noticed her fingers shaking. After a few moments, she glanced up from her phone. "There's very little here other than Walter's interview with a science journal."

"Click it," Iris ordered with her fingers still tapping on her keyboard.

Bec was silent for several minutes before she inhaled sharply. "Nightmares are real, and one resides in my lab." With a heavy sigh, Bec tossed the phone onto the desk. "What was he thinking? He knows better than that!"

"It was a science journal. Maybe he thought no one else would see it?" Iris asked, her fingers still typing even as she spoke.

"I suppose that's possible, but he knows everything ends up on the internet. When was that dated?" She grabbed the phone again and checked the date. "April. I got here in May."

"Was there a head research scientist before you?" Iris asked, and Bec nodded. "Yes, but he didn't last long. I think he started in February but was gone by April. That was when I was hired."

"Do you know why he left?"

"I don't," she said with a shrug. "It could have been the isolation of the job, inability to work closely with Walter, or fear of the viruses themselves."

"Or did he get the information he wanted regarding the deadly viruses to leverage against the center?"

"I guess anything is possible," Bec agreed.

"Do you remember his name?"

"Yes. Samuel Gill."

Iris nodded as she typed. "When I finish this line of code, I need to call Secure Watch for my midnight check-in. We can give Mina his name, and she can look into him while we keep working."

Bec reached over and put her hand on Iris's shoulder. "You have to sleep, Iris."

"I'll sleep when this is over," Iris said, not breaking pace. "Or at least once I get the most important functions under our control again."

"What if you can't?"

"Then I'll die trying." She stopped looking at the computer long enough to glance at the woman beside her. She read the terror in her eyes and held her gaze longer than anyone she ever had before. "How do you do that?"

"Do what, Iris?"

"Make it so easy for me to make eye contact."

"I can't answer that question. Only you can. It might be easier for you to answer this question. Why do you struggle to maintain eye contact with others?"

"Judgment," she said without hesitation. "I'm always worried they're going to judge me."

"Then maybe the answer to your first question is that you aren't worried I'll judge you."

"I'm not," she agreed immediately. "You already said you wouldn't."

"And you believed that without even knowing me."

"I'm good at reading people. Ever since my accident, I could always tell when someone was silently judging me. Teachers. Friends. Employers."

"My guess is you don't feel judged at Secure Watch?"

"Nope," she agreed. "But I still struggle with eye contact there. It's easier, but not like with you."

"Are you worried that your TBI might affect your employment?"

"It's always a worry. Sometimes, I feel like a burden to Mina and Cal, so I try not to make waves. That was the only reason I planned to come here when Mina asked. Until I saw you on the screen for the first time. You were so beautiful, and when you spoke, your voice calmed my racing heart and helped it beat normally again. Ugh. Why am I like this? I'm going to stop talking now."

Bec chuckled and patted her shoulder. "Never feel like you can't be honest with me, Iris. I'm grateful you're here, no matter how that decision happened. It's nice knowing Declan and Zac have my back with security, but knowing I'm not alone inside the lab is everything right now. I'm terrified and exhausted, but you're making it easier by being here."

Iris smiled but didn't say anything more as she typed. Before she replied, she wanted to think about what Bec said to decide how it made her feel. She'd learned to take time to think over interactions with new people before she said something she couldn't take back. Especially in high-stress situations like they were in tonight. They'd been working for hours, and it was late, but she couldn't rest until she had some control over the lab.

"Do you know of anyone with a grudge against you, Dr. Hoerman or the center?" Iris asked instead.

"Other than past scientists, no. I wouldn't know if they had issues with the center since I never met them."

"Other scientists had grudges against him?" Iris asked, surprise in her tone.

"It's possible," Bec said with a shoulder shrug. "None of them lasted long, but I don't know the circumstances. I was simply saying that I only know the names of the last few scientists who worked here. Anything else was information I didn't need."

"Would Dr. Hoerman have information on former employees in his office?"

"I'm sure the names of the past scientists would be in a file somewhere, sure," Bec answered. "Without him here, I wouldn't know if they had any issues with the center, though."

"If you can find their names, Mina could look into them, if nothing else," Iris said just as her tablet started to ring. "Speaking of Mina." She tore her hands from the keypad and grabbed the tablet, hitting the answer button.

"Secure Watch, India."

"Secure Watch, Whiskey," Mina replied before the camera flipped on. Mina sat at her desk in her private office. "Iris. How are you holding up?"

"Tired, but still working," she answered, glancing at Bec and motioning her closer. "Have you guys found anything regarding Ace or Dr. Hoerman?"

"Nothing so far," Mina said. "But Cal just got to a motel

at Sinlis Park to set up an outpost station for us about an hour ago."

"More likely the only motel," Bec said, and Mina laughed.

"You're not kidding, but it's the closest we could get without being obvious. Have you heard anything more from Ace?"

"I would have called you instantly if he'd contacted us," Iris said. "But Bec did think of something you might be able to help us with."

"Hit me," Mina said, grabbing her pen and notebook, so Iris motioned for Bec to fill her in.

"The last scientist to work here before me only lasted a few months. I don't know why that is, but Iris thought it might be important."

"That's absolutely worth a little investigating on my end. What was his name?"

"Samuel Gill. I don't know anything more than that about him, but he was a cell, molecular and disease biologist like me, so there can't be many of those in the country with the same name."

"That should narrow it down," Mina agreed. "Anyone else?"

"We were just talking about that," Iris said. "I suggested that she go through Dr. Hoerman's files and see if anyone else left after such a short period of working here."

"I wasn't sure it would apply," Bec jumped in. "I don't know any of them or their circumstances for leaving, so it could be a wild-goose chase."

"Could be," Mina agreed. "But Iris is correct. It's important to run a background check on everyone who used to work there just like we did on you and Walter."

"You ran a background on me?"

"Before you get onto the big screen, you're vetted," Mina answered. "We don't play at Secure Watch, but your circumstances were dire enough to bring in the team while still checking you out."

"That's fair," Bec said. "I think it would be a waste of time, though. Ignis Cerebri hasn't been in the facility for that long."

"Be that as it may, you've always had deadly viruses and pathogens there, correct?" Mina asked, and Bec nodded. "Then it stands to reason Ace could be any scientist who previously worked there. They may not know about Ignis Cerebri, but they know you don't want anything inside that lab to escape or fall into the wrong hands."

"I hadn't thought of it that way, but you're right. We can only hope and pray they don't know Ignis Cerebri is here."

"Do you have access to Walter's personnel files?"

"Sort of. He keeps them in a file cabinet in his office, but he has the key on his belt. Cal also told me not to mess with anything in his office until we can bring the police in on this."

"A key is no problem. Zac can open a file cabinet in his sleep. You have gloves there?" Bec nodded as Mina smiled. "Even though your prints are already on everything in that lab, wear gloves and touch only the cabinet. Grab any and all files for the employees who quit or were fired. Especially anyone who wasn't a scientist."

"Why?" Iris asked.

"Scientists usually aren't big tech people," Mina answered, and Bec pointed at the screen.

"True that. We can do what we need to do for our research and work, but what we're dealing with here is a level unlike anything I could ever think up, much less know how to write a program to take control of an entire system."

Mina nodded. "The faster you can get the information, the better. Iris, I would like you to record it from start to finish. We want to document anything we do in his office that requires breaking and entering to prove it was necessary during the course of the investigation."

"I still think we need to call the police," Bec said, biting her lip. "The only person who will pay for waiting will be me."

"While I would normally agree with you, I can't in this instance. If we bring in the cops, they'll take over and prevent Iris from getting her work done. Not to mention, that also puts more people in the middle of Armageddon. We can't take our eyes off the prize until the facility has been secured again and there's no risk of those pathogens finding their way out the door. After that, we'll call the police, FBI and any other three-letter organization we need to find this guy."

"What if it's too late for Walter?" Bec asked, and Iris heard the tremble in her words. Her heart hurt to know Bec was going through this, and there was nothing she could do to help other than keep mashing away on the keys and pray she could turn this around for them. Well, there was one other thing she could do, so she did it. She slid her hand over Bec's knee and gently squeezed it to let her know she was there for her.

"It could already be too late for Walter, but it's not too late for the rest of the world. I know that's a hard pill to swallow when your friend is in danger, but this is a rock and a hard place situation if I've ever seen one. Give Iris twenty-four hours to get the place locked down safely.

We'll bring in the authorities if we haven't heard from Ace by then. My gut says Walter is still alive. Ace isn't done with us, and he'll need Walter alive as a bargaining chip if he hopes to get any money out of the facility. There was no other reason to storm in and take him. He could be traveling to a different state or letting you sweat for a while, so you're more apt to do what he demands when he reaches out. Either way, we stay the course until we hear from him."

Bec nodded several times before she straightened her spine. "You're right. I called you guys in to help, so I need to trust what you're telling me to do. If I'm left holding the bag and go to prison at the end of this, it will be worth it as long as no one dies a horrible death due to one of the pathogens in this facility."

Iris squeezed Bec's knee again. "Cal and Mina won't let that happen. Neither will I."

"She's right," Mina said with a smile. "We got you. Trust the process and get me those names ASAP. I'll radio Zac to head in and open the cabinet for you now. Keep me abreast of anything that comes in from Ace or if you get the systems back online."

"Will do," Iris said without letting go of Bec's knee. "India, out."

The screen went blank, and Bec's shoulders sank the moment they were alone again. "I don't feel good about this, Iris, but I'll do it if we can save Walter."

"I'm sure he would want you to do anything you can think of to help him," Iris said, turning her chair and taking Bec's hand. "Remember that Secure Inc. won't let you get caught up in this mess. That's why you hired us to help. We wouldn't have taken the case if we didn't think we could handle it."

Bec blew out a breath and nodded. "Right. I need to remember to trust you."

"You trust me?"

"From the moment Cal introduced you," she said, her smile small as she dropped her gaze to their hands. "I just hope you trust me, too."

"I wouldn't be holding your hand if I didn't," Iris said before she grimaced. "Sorry—"

Bec put her finger to Iris's lips. "Remember that you can be yourself here without apologizing for it. I hate that people in your past made you feel like you had to, but not with me, okay?"

Iris forced herself to hold Bec's gaze for several seconds, and she found herself lost in her eyes for a beat longer than she had expected before she answered. "Okay. I'll probably forget more than I remember, though."

"Then I'll keep reminding you until it comes naturally," Bec said with a wink. "Why did you call yourself India on the call with Mina?"

"Oh, I should tell you about that. Secure Inc. uses code names when contacting another team member on assignment. Mina is Whiskey because her real name is Wilhemina. Cal is Charlie. I'm India."

"Declan is Danger," Bec said, laughing as though she finally understood the situation.

"Yes, and while he can't say what he did for the army, Danger was his call sign. Essentially, if a team member were ever to use something other than their code name, we would know they're in trouble and need help."

"That's incredibly smart. It keeps the majority of the team safe and gets help to the team member in trouble without showing your hand."

"Secure One, Zulu."

"Case in point," Iris said, spinning in her chair to see Zac standing in the lab.

They both stood, and while Bec explained to Zac what they needed and why, Iris turned to grab her tablet to record the encounter. She used that short minute to take a deep breath and remind herself that she had one job to do here. She couldn't let her desire to know more about the beautiful and engaging scientist beside her keep her from doing it. With her resolve set, she followed them to the office, but for the life of her, she couldn't convince herself there wasn't a way to do both.

Chapter Six

The file cabinet held a few employee files but nothing recent, which surprised Bec. "It isn't like Walter not to have files on previous employees."

"Maybe he put them on the computer?" Iris asked after she stopped recording. "We didn't see one for Samuel Gill, so maybe he moved everything to digital files to make space?"

"It's possible, but he's not super techy. I can barely get him to work with the programs we use for the labs."

"This wouldn't be hard, though," she said, motioning at the few files on the desk. "With a scanner, he could easily upload them. Even your basic idiot can make a folder on their computer."

Iris slapped a hand over her mouth, and Bec stopped her before she could apologize. "Don't say you're sorry. You're correct. Walter is good with scanners and does basic tasks with a computer, but we can't look at his laptop, which hampers us in knowing if that's where the files are."

"We have records for the three years before this one, right?" Iris asked, and Bec nodded. "Let's send Mina those names. She'll want to do a deep dive into each person, and we have five people for her to track down besides Samuel. That will take them a few days, and if nothing turns up, at least we tried. It seems like an especially high turnover rate, but I could be wrong for a job like this."

"It is high," Bec said, falling into her desk chair after they left Walter's office. "After working here for five months, I may know why."

"People are scared of the viruses? I know I am." Iris bit her lip as her gaze strayed to the labs.

Bec reached out and squeezed her knee. "Don't let the fear in. If you let the fear in, it makes it impossible to get anything done. Keep your eyes on me and your head in the game."

"Right," she said with a nod. "Eyes on you. That's hard for me, but you make it easier." She cleared her throat as though to gloss over that admittance. "Why do you think people keep quitting the lab?"

"Fear isn't one of them," Bec said with a shake of her head. "If they accepted a position here, they already knew what kind of work was required. I suspect the reason no one lasts long is twofold. The first is the isolation. It's lonely out here, and if you aren't dedicated to the job or took it for a reason that wasn't your own, you won't last."

"You must have a good reason if you've lasted long enough to make a vaccine."

"It's purely selfish," Bec admitted. "If I could research and implement a vaccine for something like Ignis Cerebri, it would mean I could write my own ticket to work anywhere in the world."

"That makes all of this isolation worth it?" Iris asked, the fatigue showing as each minute ticked away.

"Well, before Ace hit, the answer was yes. I hoped

to get into a university somewhere, but now I'll just be happy to get out alive."

"You and me both," Iris agreed. "What's the second reason?"

"The management."

"Dr. Hoerman isn't a good manager?"

"Not great," Bec admitted with a mirthless chuckle. "Super nice guy, but if you need direction or questions answered promptly, you won't get them from him."

"Is his job to manage?"

"Indirectly," Bec said, hoping to explain it better. "He's the project manager, meaning he finds the projects people need done, organizes, brings them in and implements them."

"That sounds like a manager to me."

Bec motioned at her. "Me, too, but he believes that if we're qualified to get the job as head scientist, we're his equal. He's not wrong—however, he knows the project parameters better than we do since he's the intake guy."

"So if he doesn't communicate the parameters well, that leaves you frustrated," Iris deduced and Bec pointed at her in agreement. "Are there other scientists working here?"

"Since Ignis is here, we only have one lab tech right now. Walter and I decided the fewer people in the lab with this virus, the better."

"Where is the lab tech now? Did he quit?"

"No, his name is Zafar. He's on vacation. He's scheduled to be out for another week. I'd try to call him, but he's at a wedding in Poland. I'd rather wait and see if we can get a handle on this first."

"Agreed. Does Mina have his information to do a background check?"

"Yes. I gave her that when we first connected."

Iris rubbed the bridge of her nose and pushed her tablet toward Bec. "Would you send Mina the information while I get back to work on the system?"

"No," Bec said, pushing the tablet back toward her. "It's 3:00 a.m., and we're both exhausted. Mina is in bed and won't get the message anyway. We need to rest before we do anything else."

"No time to rest," Iris said, shaking her head adamantly. "We don't know what Ace is going to do next. We must get control of this place."

Bec squeezed Iris's shoulder while she ducked her head until she found the woman's eyes. "I trust you, Iris, with my life, but I also know how working tired can be more dangerous than taking a few hours to rest and then coming back to it."

"Secure One, Danger." They both jumped and turned to see Declan standing in the hallway. "Sorry, I didn't mean to scare you, but she's right. I was leaving the break room to bed down for a few hours of sleep when I overheard the discussion. Per Cal's instructions, you are to get a few hours of sleep each day," he said, lowering his brow at Iris. "You've been up for twenty hours. It's time to grab a couple of hours' rest so you can return refreshed. Otherwise, you're just spinning your wheels."

Iris sighed heavily. "Fine, but two hours. That's it."

Declan nodded once. "I can deal with that. Zac and I will start rotating shifts since Cal sent Mack and Efren over to cover. If you need us, we're on the loading dock."

"Got it. Thanks, Declan," Bec said, standing and holding her hand out for Iris. She wasn't sure if the woman would take it, but she yearned for that connection again. When Iris's warm, soft skin slid across her palm, she had to take a deep breath to slow her racing heart.

"Will you show me where the loading dock is?" Iris asked as Bec led her through the cavernous workspace and into the hallway.

"You're not going to sleep on the loading dock. You'll sleep in my apartment, where it's safe and comfortable."

"But, no. I'm supposed to sleep with the team."

Bec paused and turned back to the beautiful woman just as Iris pushed her glasses up her adorable pixie nose with her free hand. Rather than argue further, she snapped the walkie-talkie off her belt and pushed the button. "Declan?"

"This is Zac," the voice said, and Iris huffed but didn't say anything.

"Iris insists she should sleep with the team on the loading dock. I think she should be squirreled away safely in my apartment. What's your opinion?" She released the button and raised a brow at the woman across from her, who now had her hand on her hip even if she was staring over her shoulder at the wall beyond them. Bec couldn't decide if it made her look sassy, sexy or angry.

"If she can sleep in your apartment, that would be ideal," Zac responded. "I'd rather she wasn't this close to the action if something goes down outside."

"You got it," Bec said, releasing the button with a satisfied smile.

"Okay," Iris said with a huff. "But I'd be fine on the loading dock."

"Maybe, but this way, I can keep an eye on you. Something tells me if I let my guard down, you'll be back at that computer typing away."

When they stepped onto the elevator, Iris's smirk told her that was her plan to a T.

IRIS GLANCED AROUND the small apartment while Bec was in the shower. Using the word *apartment* was a stretch, if she was honest. It was the size of a hotel room with a queen-size bed, a small kitchenette, a two-person table and a nightstand. The bathroom off the main space was small but functional. Iris still couldn't imagine working and living here day after day without a change of scenery. Her room at Secure Inc. was small, but she had the entire building and grounds to roam whenever she needed a break.

Bec walked into the room wearing lounge clothes that in no way showed off her physique but were still far more alluring than her white lab coat. Iris dropped her gaze rather than continue to stare. "Oh good, you got the bed turned down," Bec said, rubbing lotion into her hands. "I was hoping you'd make yourself at home."

"I made tea," Iris said, pointing at the two mugs on the table. "It's not my favorite, but coffee before bed won't work so well."

"I couldn't agree more." Bec offered her a tired smile.

Iris walked to her and pushed her hair back off her face to check the cuts that peppered her skin from the attack. "I'm so sorry you went through that this morning. Are you sure you don't need a doctor? Are you having any symptoms of a concussion?"

"I'm fine," Bec promised, taking her hand. "The glass cut my face, but I never hit my head."

Her sleeve slipped down from her wrist when she grasped Iris's hand and revealed what she'd been hiding under the lab coat. Iris's gasp was loud in the room. "You're not fine, Bec. Why didn't you show this to someone? What happened?"

Iris inspected her arm. It was red, blistered and covered in gashes of different depths.

"I don't know what happened, if I'm honest. I think I threw my arm up to protect my face and it got hit with hot shrapnel. When I wrapped it earlier while waiting for you guys to arrive, it wasn't red and blistered yet. I thought I'd let it breathe while we were sleeping."

Iris bit her lip as she stared at the wounded flesh. "That's probably not smart. You could get an infection, or what about tetanus or something? You should probably go to the hospital. I need to call Cal to take you to the hospital. This isn't good. This is really not good." Her breathing was at a fever pitch now, and her vision had gone tunnel as she stared at the damaged skin.

The next thing she knew, she was sitting on the bed, and Bec was kneeling before her. "Take some deep breaths, Iris." She coached her by breathing with her until Iris stopped shaking and sound filtered back into her ears.

"That was embarrassing," she said, staring at the floor. "I'm sorry for freaking out. It happens more than usual when I'm stressed out."

Bec tipped her chin up to face her. She didn't force her to hold her gaze and didn't say anything when Iris couldn't. "Don't apologize for caring, Iris. I don't know who made you feel like you have to stare at the floor rather than hold your head high, but here in my apartment, you can be unapologetically you without hanging your head in shame, okay?"

"That's not why," she said, staring over her shoulder at the wall. "It's easier to talk to people when I don't have to look at them. My brain works better that way."

"To a degree, I believe that," Bec said. "But I think

you started doing it when you realized that your bluntness, as you put it, can embarrass you or others, so staring at the floor means you don't have to see the judgment on others' faces."

Iris didn't want to admit she was right, so she didn't answer. "I think you should cover your arm with something before sleeping. It would be bad if you scratched it accidentally in your sleep. I know you're like a doctor and everything, so it's fine if you don't want to do that. As my mama always said, I see things very literally and with too much common sense, so I'm probably wrong."

"I am a doctor, but not a medical one. I hadn't thought of your point about scratching it in my sleep. Getting an infection wouldn't be convenient right now, so I'll wrap it in gauze."

Iris nodded just as a yawn overtook her. She covered her mouth with her hand, apologizing for being rude.

"Don't apologize. We've had one hell of a day. Go ahead and get comfortable while I wrap my arm, and then we can shut down the lights for a few hours."

"If you tell me where to find a sleeping bag or extra blankets, I'll make my bed."

"What do you want those for?"

Iris glanced down at the floor and back to her momentarily. "It's no problem. I can sleep on the floor without a bag. Do you have an extra pillow?"

"You're not sleeping on the floor," Bec said with a chuckle as she motioned her to the head of the bed. "You have the most important job in the place now. That means you're sleeping in the bed."

Bec pulled the blankets around Iris and then grasped the bows of her glasses to slide them off. There was something evocative about the sensation of the metal leaving her face when it wasn't of her own volition. She was used to doing everything for herself, and having someone care for her was a foreign sensation. "Where are you going to sleep?"

Bec turned back to her, wearing a nervous smile. "Right next to you. I'll keep you safe, Iris."

Then she disappeared into the bathroom, leaving Iris to decide if sharing a bed with the beautiful scientist was more dangerous to her health than the unchecked pathogens in the lab above their heads.

Chapter Seven

Iris's fingers flew across the keyboard the second they hit the keys. She had fallen asleep before Bec had returned from the bathroom, but when she woke, to say she was disoriented was an understatement. Her anxiety was not being kind, but she'd managed to get her braces on and get out of bed without waking Bec. They had shared a bed, and while it had been entirely innocent, a large part of her wanted it to be so much more.

Bec hadn't come out and said she was gay, but she didn't have to for Iris to know. For her, it came down to their connection when their skin touched. The moment their eyes met, she knew. That was saying a lot for someone who struggled with connecting. When Bec was in the shower, she also noticed a magnet on her fridge for Out to Innovate, an organization for LGBTQ+ scientists and technical professionals. She recognized it because she'd been a member for years.

Since Bec didn't know she was also a member, she'd keep it that way. Mostly because she was struggling with how kind and understanding Bec was about her TBI. Sure, everyone at Secure Inc. was kind and patient, but they worked together every day. This was different. She and Bec had barely met before Bec immediately reassured her she belonged. She accepted her and allowed her to take up space in a way that didn't result in judgment or sarcastic comments despite her overreaction to several situations. It usually took months or years for people to get comfortable with her and how her brain worked. Sometimes, people were never comfortable with who she was despite knowing she couldn't change it. She'd experienced that with friends and girlfriends enough times over the years that she tended to keep to herself now. That was why she enjoyed working at Secure Watch. The core team stayed the same, making it easier for her to relax and be confident there without worrying about being judged.

No one ever questioned her skills on the job, and she knew she was better at her job than many in her field, but that was because of how her brain worked. The most challenging part was proving herself to others when they couldn't see past her diagnoses. It wasn't an untold story for neurodivergent people. No matter how much people were educated about neurodiversity, there would always be a level of prejudice against them for something outside of their control. But then, that was a problem for marginalized communities as a whole. She couldn't fix that by herself, unlike the code she was writing to get the lab back under her control. She was close. She could feel it in her fingers with each new line of code she wrote.

A glance at the clock told her it had been several hours since she'd left Bec's apartment. That wasn't a big surprise. If there was one thing she could get lost in, it was her work. Truthfully, she worried Bec would be upset that she got up and left, but she also didn't want to wake her after so few hours of sleep. After the day Bec had yesterday, she needed rest, especially with the injury to her arm. As soon as Iris finished the code, she planned to text Cal to ask him if he had brought Selina from Secure Inc. with him. Selina was a nurse who usually traveled with them on assignment. Iris wasn't sure if this qualified since Cal wanted to keep as many people out of the fallout zone as possible, but she suspected Selina wouldn't give him a choice. He needed a medical professional on-site for every case, so she hoped she was right. She wanted her to look at Bec's arm and treat it if need be. The blisters would pop sooner rather than later, and the last thing she needed was an infection that required her to leave the facility. Without Bec here, they would have to turn this over to the police, which could get them all killed.

Not that Iris thought she was all that when it came to fixing this situation, but she knew this was not the kind of place that could be left unattended, or worse yet, have the police bring someone in to break into the labs. The very idea made her shudder, and she forced her fingers to move faster as her eyes tried to track the lines on the screen, but the hours she'd already put in were catching up to her.

"Come on, come on," she chanted, finishing the last line and gingerly pressing the return key as the elevator door dinged.

She momentarily lifted her gaze from the keyboard and waited for something to happen, though she had no idea what to expect.

Bec walked into the room carrying two cups of coffee just as a whirring started above their heads. Iris stood up. "What is that? It just came on!"

Bec set the mugs on the table and swiveled toward Iris. She ran to her with a whoop and threw her arms around her while jumping up and down. "You did it! That's the ventilation system!"

"You mean it's working?" Iris asked when Bec released her.

"Yes!" She motioned her toward a lab door. "Look." Iris peered into the room where papers fluttered on a table. "You did it!"

"Okay, so the ventilation system is working, but the labs don't have the lights on over the doors," Iris said, pointing above them.

"Those lights indicate lab access and the containment system, not the ventilation system. The lights won't come on until the containment system is working again—at least, I think that's what will happen. They may be working, but I have no way to know when I can't control the system from here."

"Are the viruses just floating around in there now that I put the vents back on?"

"No," Bec assured her, hands out to keep her calm. "That's not how it works. The viruses are safely locked up right now."

"If that's the case, why the big deal then?"

"Because Ace could release them if he controls the containment system. Now that you have the ventilation system back, the filters in the vents will be working again. If anything is released, it should get trapped before it gets vented out of the facility. We don't know how long Ignis Cerebri stays alive in the air. All we know is, once inhaled by the primary case, it will spread like wildfire."

"Are there other viruses here, too?"

"Many," Bec agreed, walking with Iris back to the desks. "Those are viruses and bacteria that we know more about, though. Releasing them could be dangerous, but when you have an unknown like Ignis Cerebri, that's your focus. I have seen what it can do to animals. We don't want it set loose on the population."

Iris lowered herself back to the chair. "I need to get the containment system under our control then. Right now."

"If you can do that, the world will be safe from anything behind those doors while we wait for Ace to contact us."

Forcing herself up again, Iris eyed the hallway. "I should let the team know the ventilation system is secured."

"We will," Bec said, taking her hand. "Take a deep breath first." Iris inhaled with her, and then Bec patted her back.

"What are you doing?"

"I'm giving you a pat on the back for getting that system under our control again. I know it's your job, but it wasn't easy, and you deserve recognition for it."

"It was a lot," Iris agreed. "What I learned can be applied to the next system, too, which hopefully means it won't take me as long to get the containment system back online. Whoever this Ace guy is, he's talented in a diabolical way, but he doesn't seem to be watching his code closely, which has been working in my favor. Regardless, we need to put him behind bars."

"We will," Bec assured her, squeezing her hand. "Thanks in no small part to you."

"There's a lot left to do, Bec," Iris said, wanting to pull away but transfixed by the trust in her big, beautiful brown eyes. "We can't get ahead of ourselves."

"I know, but I also know you never stop to consider how imperative your skills are in many people's lives."

Iris shrugged as though she was unbothered by the

compliment when it meant everything to hear. She didn't know how to show that or what to say, though.

"I suspect it's hard for you to accept compliments, and that's okay, but I want you to know how much I appreciate you."

"And I appreciate how kind you are to me, Bec. I'm not used to that. You look beautiful today. Not that you didn't yesterday, I just meant—"

Bec's finger came down on her lips, forcing her to resist the urge to kiss it. "You just meant that yesterday I was tired and had been through a lot."

Iris nodded until Bec dropped her finger. "That's what I meant. How is your arm?"

"Sore," she admitted. "I'll keep an eye on it."

Iris snapped her fingers. "That reminds me of something I have to ask Cal. We need to find the team, update them and then return to the code."

"Yes, Captain!" Bec said, standing straight with a wink. "Let's take our coffee to go."

They grabbed their coffee cups and headed for the elevator just as it dinged, and the doors slid open. Zac ran out but stopped when he saw them.

"You're okay."

"Of course," Iris answered. "Why wouldn't I be?"

"We heard whirring from the loading dock but couldn't raise you on the walkie-talkie."

Her heart rate picked up speed when she realized her mistake. "Oh no," she whispered, staring at the ground. "I left it in the apartment this morning. It was charging last night, and then I forgot about it. I don't usually have them. See, this is why I can't be trusted! Cal's going to be so mad. He's going to convince Mina to fire me!"

Chapter Eight

Zac held his hands out for calm, but she didn't feel that way. "Iris, no," he said. "No one is mad. We were just worried."

"But you don't know that," she whispered, walking backward until she bumped into Bec. She nearly tipped over until Bec grasped her waist and held her in place. She was trembling and embarrassed, knowing her misstep had caused confusion and concern for the team.

"Iris, take a deep breath," Bec instructed. "Focus on my words. Breathe in quickly twice and back out slowly."

Iris followed her instructions, trying to keep from spiraling into all the situations that could arise from her inability to remember things outside her regular routine. She could write code all day and never forget a character, but other tasks—things like what to get at the store or remembering she needed to carry the walkie-talkie around—were more difficult. When she started living independently, she needed notes to remind her of every task, but she no longer needed to depend on them as she used to. "I don't usually have one and forgot to put a note on my phone the way I usually do when I have to remember something important."

"Why didn't you call her phone?" Bec asked, and Zac smacked himself in the forehead.

"Never even thought of it. That's on me. I'm sorry for upsetting you, Iris. I should have texted you. We're used to using the walkies, so I didn't think about it."

Bec patted Iris's waist before she spoke. "Listen, everyone here is under a lot of stress and pressure, so let's make sure we give ourselves and each other a little bit of grace, okay?"

"Secure One, Charlie, and I couldn't agree more," a voice said from behind them, and they all jumped to see Cal standing there with several others.

"Cal. When did you get here?" Iris asked, her voice steady now that Bec had her arm around her.

"We took the stairs," he answered, motioning behind him.

"I got the ventilation system going again," she said in response, wanting him to know she may have screwed up one thing, but she was still doing her job. "Bec said that's important but not as important as the containment system, so I'll do that next."

Cal stepped forward and patted her shoulder. "I'm proud of you, Iris. Way to go! I knew you were the right woman for the job."

"But I messed up and—" Bec squeezed her waist, and she stopped speaking, taking a deep breath rather than continuing.

"You forgot the walkie, which is no big deal," Cal assured her. "If I know you, and I do, you didn't sleep much and then got up early to get back to work on the system."

"Yes, sir," Iris answered, glancing up to read his face. He didn't look upset, which was a relief. That was when she noticed Selina in the group. "Selina!" She ran and hugged her, which was not an uncommon reaction for her as they had become good friends since she started working at Secure Watch. She was worried about Bec's arm and was glad she'd come with Cal this morning.

"Hi, Iris," Selina said with a pat on her back. "Are you feeling okay?"

"Yes, but Bec got hurt more than she said yesterday. Could you look at her arm? It's burned."

"Burned?" Selina asked, glancing at Bec.

"There are some blisters. I don't know what happened. I do remember it was the arm I threw up to cover my face."

"Stun grenades can cause burns," Cal said. "The heat of the blast can heat things in its way. Like this metal table."

Bec's lips drew into a thin line. "It's possible that I touched one of these tables when disoriented."

"I'll look at it once we're finished with the update," Selina promised.

"Iris was just telling Zac that she got the ventilation system working again," Bec said, motioning toward her. "Thank God for that."

"But then Bec told me if I don't get the containment system online, Ace could release all kinds of things, so it wasn't that great of an accomplishment."

"Wrong," Cal said, his brow dipping. "Any system you can get back is an accomplishment. We can't protect the world if we don't protect this facility."

Bec nodded once. "She's had less than three hours of sleep but still got this far. I know she can get the containment online, too."

"What's left after that?" Cal asked, glancing between them.

"Nothing that could kill anyone," Bec answered simply. "But if she can get the lab door function back, at least I could lock things down further inside the main lab to protect everyone were we forced to abandon the facility."

"That's what we do then," Cal said. "Iris, how long do you think before you get the containment system online?"

"If I apply what I learned with the ventilation system, and assuming Ace isn't aware that I've messed with his code, which I don't think he is, I should be able to do it in two hours. I have to write a workaround for his code and then protect it, so he doesn't kill it again."

Cal's nod was tight. "Once you have the containment system live, I want you to rest. While Bec is correct that we want to protect everyone from what's inside those labs, it can't be at your expense."

"I'll grab a few hours and then get back at it. I'll feel better once I know Bec can protect the world from that nasty virus."

"I want to know why we haven't heard from Ace yet," Bec said, glancing between the team. "He kidnapped Walter almost twenty-four hours ago. Why do that if you aren't going to ask for ransom?"

"A question I've asked myself, but this isn't unheard of," Selina said. "Sometimes people are kidnapped, and it's days or even weeks before a ransom is demanded."

"They're letting us sweat," Iris said, her gaze on the table. "If we think he has control of everything and also the head scientist of the lab, the one person who can fix anything, then we're more likely to cooperate with him."

"That's a possible scenario," Cal agreed.

"Walter isn't the head scientist," Bec interjected. "He's a scientist, but an administrator-level scientist at this point. He's near retirement and hasn't worked in a lab for decades. He has nothing to do with the pathogens other than to write the proposals and accept the assignments. Ace should have taken me if he wanted that kind of bargaining chip."

"Would the general public know that?" Iris asked, peeking at her as Bec shook her head.

"Probably not. It would be an assumption of someone unfamiliar with the way places like this are run that he was the one to take."

"That was Ace's first mistake," Iris said with a shrug. "His second was underestimating your ability to think on your feet and bring in the firepower needed to handle this situation."

"Couldn't have said it better myself," Cal agreed with a chuckle. "While you're working on the code, we'll tighten our security plan and prepare exit strategies should we need them. Selina, join us downstairs when you're done checking Bec's arm?"

"It's fine, really," Bec said, holding up her hands. "I can manage it."

"If it's blistered, then I disagree," Selina said. "That means the burn is at least second-degree and will need special cream and care until it heals so you don't get an infection. I'll check it every day while I'm here. I'll grab my medic bag and meet you in your apartment."

Selina headed to the elevator as Bec grinned sheepishly at Iris. "I guess she told me." That got a snort from Iris. "She can do her thing with it, and then I'm going to make some breakfast and bring it up here for you to eat while you work. You'll be okay while I'm gone?"

"Yes," Iris said with a nod. "I'm not afraid to be alone. I've been alone all my life."

The look on Bec's face before she headed toward the stairs told Iris that it made her sad, and she felt terrible for doing that to her. It wasn't her intention, but she didn't know how to do anything but tell the truth. Sometimes, like right now, it would be easier if she could tell a little white lie now and again.

"Shouldn't have said that," Iris said when she was gone. "Now she's going to feel sorry for me, which I don't want."

"Bec doesn't strike me as the type to feel sorry for anyone, Iris," Cal soothed. "Let's stay on track. Do you need Mina's help with anything? She's waiting in the wings if you do."

"Is she still running down the information on the scientists we gave her last night?"

"Yes, that's her plan for this morning, but she can drop that at a moment's notice if you need help with something."

Iris nodded and blew out a breath as she rubbed her forehead. "Once I get the critical parts of the lab running again, I'll search Ace's code for a signature."

"Signature?"

"Usually, coders who spend time on the dark web or those with God complexes like Ace will have a signature. Something they do every time they code that makes them feel superior. It's usually how they write a specific tag or start the first part of a line," she explained, alternating her gaze between him and the poster on the wall. It was about pathogens and how they travel between people. "I hope to send some lines of code to Mina. If Ace is familiar to the community, we'll know quickly. It's faster for her to run that down while I keep working on protecting the system here."

"You have the support of all of Secure Inc.," Cal assured her. "I know you can do this, so I'll let you get back to it, but Iris?" he asked, and she shifted her gaze to his. "I never knew you had such beautiful eyes."

"Sir?" she asked, tipping her head in confusion.

"That was the first time you made eye contact for over three seconds. Thank you for trusting me."

She lifted her head and held it high, even if she was staring at the poster again. She nodded. "It's not that I didn't trust you."

"It's that you couldn't show me," Cal said. "I've always understood that, and I accept you no matter what. You'll see that's true of others if you give them the benefit of the doubt."

"In time, I suppose that will get easier," she agreed. "For now, I better get back to my work so we don't feel like we're watching the clock tick down on a bomb we can't disarm."

"Couldn't have said that better myself. I'll have Selina bring you the walkie-talkie when she's done helping Bec. You know where to find us if you need anything?"

When she nodded, he strolled from the room, whistling like they weren't fighting for their lives.

Chapter Nine

Bec kept her eyes glued to her arm as Selina unwrapped the gauze. She'd lied to Iris when she said it was fine and that she could handle it herself. When she got up this morning, it ached like nothing had before. She hadn't the nerve to take the bandage off it, so she was glad Selina had arrived with Cal.

"Do you see these red streaks here?" Selina asked, motioning at the spot above the gauze, and Bec nodded. "That's what we call lymphangitis. It means your arm is already infected. The streaks are infection of the channels going toward the lymph nodes in your armpit."

"When you saw that, you knew I couldn't handle it alone," Bec finished.

"I didn't want to alarm Iris, so I didn't say anything, but that's correct."

Bec hissed when she pulled the gauze off the wound. As soon as the air hit it, it told her the skin was indeed burned.

"Sorry," Selina said, glancing back at her as she tossed the gauze in the garbage. "The good news is, my bag is fully stocked with burn cream and antibiotics, so we'll have it fixed up in no time. That said, I'll still check it daily to be sure it's getting better and not worse." She rested Bec's arm on the table, grabbed a Sharpie from her bag and started drawing on her skin.

"What are you doing?" Bec asked with curiosity.

"Marking the streaks," she explained as she worked. "Your homework will be to keep an eye on them. If they grow past these lines," she said, showing her the ones about an inch above where the streaks ended, "you need to call me immediately."

"And if they don't?" she asked while Selina took supplies from the bag.

"I'll still clean, rewrap and inspect it tomorrow."

Bec chuckled with a nod. "Noted. I didn't know flash-bangs could do this kind of damage."

"A stun grenade can do so much more than this," Selina said, inspecting the blisters with a trained eye. "They can kill in the right instances. They can also cause lasting hearing loss and tinnitus. Do you have any problems with your hearing or vision?"

"No, not since yesterday," she said, yelping when Selina sprayed something across her skin. "Could you have warned me?"

"I try not to," she answered honestly. "See, I'm used to working with a bunch of guys, and when you tell them what you're going to do, they try to get up and walk out. I've learned to ask for forgiveness after the fact." She winked, which made Bec smile. "In fairness, that was numbing spray. You'll appreciate it when I start cleaning it. Let me know when it feels tingly, and then I'll do a second layer."

"I didn't know the cleaning would be this extensive."

"I didn't know the infection was already this bad or the burn this deep. If we were in any other situation, I'd send you to the ER, but that's not an option. It's not that I can't handle this—I can, so don't worry. I just meant that they could give you intravenous antibiotics there where I can't here."

"I'm not worried," Bec said with a nod. "Something tells me even in this situation, if it were life or death, you'd be shipping me out of here."

"You'd be correct," Selina said with a lip tilt. "We aren't there yet, so I'm glad Iris mentioned it. Is it numb?" Bec nodded, so she sprayed it down again.

"She saw it last night and made me wrap it back up again. She was worried about infection."

"Guess she has some psychic abilities," Selina said with a wink as she cleaned the blessedly numb skin.

"Iris has a lot of abilities, even if her confidence in them is occasionally lacking," Bec answered, closing her eyes to avoid watching what she was doing. She was getting nauseated thinking about how badly it would hurt if it weren't mostly numb. She could feel enough to tell her it would be excruciating.

"We all care about Iris. None of us want to see her get hurt," Selina said as she ran something cool and soothing across the skin.

Bec's eyes popped open to see her swiping on burn cream. "I don't want to see her get hurt, either. If I could go in there and destroy all those pathogens, I would."

"Wasn't talking about the pathogens," Selina said, resting the arm on her elbow so she could start wrapping it in gauze.

"Oh, do you mean me? Why would I hurt Iris?"

"I'm not saying you would."

Bec bit back the eye roll since the woman held her sore arm in her hands. "It sort of sounds like you are to my ears. Maybe you think something is going on here that isn't?"

"Is that it?"

"Can I ask you a question?" Bec asked, hoping to buy herself time. Selina nodded, so she plastered on a smile. "Does Cal have a training school on how to answer a question with a question?"

Selina snorted with laughter, which was the response Bec was looking for. Crisis diverted. "Before I worked for Cal, I was a Chicago cop and trained search and rescue K-9 handler."

"Which means you're saying without saying that you've seen a lot of different ways someone can die?" Her lip tilt at the end was quirky in hopes Selina would laugh.

She didn't.

"In less than fifteen seconds, I saw what I needed to see, Dr. Roth," Selina answered, taping the wrapped gauze in place.

"It's Bec, and I'm not sure I follow."

"Iris trusts you, but she doesn't trust very many people in this world. The fact that you gained her trust in less than twenty-four hours says more than words."

"Call it forced proximity and shared terror?" Bec asked, this time dead serious.

"You could. I prefer to call it understanding and acceptance."

"I know about lack of understanding and acceptance, so I extend it to everyone until they show me they don't deserve it. I doubt that will ever be the case with Iris."

Selina was silent as she packed the supplies and pulled out bottles and vials. "Iris has suffered a lot of terrible things in life, and her family was the cause of them. She has a new family, but we won't let anyone hurt her."

"I'm confused about why we're having the family exerting dominance on the new love interest discussion."

"Offering fair warning," Selina said. "Nothing more."

It was Bec's turn to snort. "You're implying that Iris is also gay, and if I had thoughts about, what? Getting involved with her or leading her on? That I shouldn't."

"So you know," Selina answered.

"It was inferred when her laptop sticker said, 'I might look straight, but lesbihonest.'"

A smile split across Selina's face. "She loves that sticker." Selina drew something from a vial into a syringe.

"You're implying that I also need one of those stickers."

"I am implying, but lesbihonest."

Bec's laughter filled the room at that answer until they were both giggling. "Well played."

Selina held up the syringe. "This is an antibiotic. Since I can't do it intravenously, I'm going to give you a heavy bolus intramuscular and then have you take oral pills. Tomorrow, I'll give you another bolus if we're still in this predicament. Once I see that the oral antibiotics are clearing the lymphangitis, we can stick with them. Make sense?"

"Yep," she said, turning in her seat so Selina could access her arm easily. "I appreciate all your help with this, Selina. The pain was getting worse by the hour."

"I'd give you an injection of pain meds as well, but we need you alert and oriented."

"Agreed. I can tough it out."

"Lucky for you, I have a heavy dose of ibuprofen that I'll also leave with you. Just make sure to eat something with it. But then you told me when I got down here that you planned to make Iris breakfast, right?"

With a heavy sigh, Bec shook her head. "Selina, I have no intention of hurting Iris. We're in a sticky situation here, but my only goal is to keep her calm while she tries to solve this."

"Mmm," Selina answered as she dropped the syringe into a small sharps container and tucked it in her bag. "I concur that's what I witnessed up there as you helped calm her for the sake of the facility."

"Selina—"

She held up her hand to stop her. "Listen, I'm not saying we have any control over consenting adults. I'm just saying we know how to get justice when someone we love is wronged. I'm sure you've been introduced to Iris's disabilities and understand them."

"To a degree," Bec agreed. "Her right eye has tracking issues, and the bilateral foot drop requires technologically advanced foot orthoses and an altered gait. She's been open about her neurological changes after the TBI. I've worked with a lot of neurodivergent people. I can understand the disabilities without needing to know the cause."

"Good," Selina said with a nod. "Because Iris doesn't talk about what happened to her. It's an unspoken rule that no one asks."

"And I never would," Bec agreed. "Are we done with the third degree? I should make her breakfast and keep her fueled and hydrated as she works."

Selina pushed two bottles toward her. "You've been a good sport, so yes, we're done. Take one of these three times a day," she said, pointing at the antibiotic bottle. "And one of the ibuprofen every six hours as needed. Call me if those streaks start creeping toward the line, or the arm suddenly becomes extremely hot, red and sore, or you develop a fever despite taking ibuprofen. Make sure to wrap your arm in plastic before showering. Understood?"

"You got it," Bec agreed. "Thanks again for your help. I needed it with my arm. Not so much for Iris, but I respect your position."

"I can't ask for more than that," Selina said, hoisting her bag over her shoulder. "I'll let you start cooking while I take the walkie-talkie up to Iris and check in with her."

"Great. Let her know I'll be up shortly."

"See you tomorrow," Selina said on her way out the door.

"God willing," Bec answered, to which she got a tip of Selina's fake hat.

Bec grabbed the bottles off the table and walked to the kitchenette. All she wanted to do was crawl back into bed and elevate her arm, but that wouldn't get the job done. Instead, she strapped on an ice pack over her shirt sleeve and got to work scrambling some eggs while the bread was in the toaster. She could picture Iris upstairs typing away in her own little world, but she didn't want her to do it hungry. A glance at the clock told her they were going on lunchtime instead of breakfast, but fuel was fuel, no matter the time of day.

Having the ventilation system working again was a big win for them. It wasn't as huge as the containment system, but at least the air exchanges and safety features worked again. Once Iris got the containment system online, Bec would insist she take another nap. She had no idea how long Iris had slept, but something told her it wasn't long. She got at least an hour because that's how long Bec had been awake watching Iris sleep.

Bec chuckled to herself as she buttered the toast. It sounded creepy, but it didn't feel that way last night. Iris intrigued her. Especially when she saw how peacefully she slept. It was the first time her face relaxed, and she sighed deeply. Maybe they weren't sighs of relief, but she was content. She just wanted to offer Iris contentment as much as possible while under this roof. It was easy to see that she found life difficult to navigate sometimes and that changing her daily routine was stressful for her, so if she could offer her a moment of pleasure in the day, she'd do it.

But not the kind of pleasure Selina was hinting at.

She scooped the eggs onto plates, added the toast, grabbed two bottles of orange juice from the fridge, and set it all on a tray.

She sighed heavily as she shut down the lights and rode the elevator to the main floor. It wasn't that she didn't want to offer Iris the kind of pleasure Selina implied— just the opposite was true. But working here meant putting aside her wants and desires for the betterment of humanity. Every time she stared into Iris's eyes if only for a split second, she understood the old saying, "wrong place, wrong time," all the way to her soul.

Chapter Ten

It turned out that Bec was a good cook. It was just bacon and eggs, but as far as Iris was concerned, it was exactly what she needed. She'd shoveled it in quickly so she could return to her work, which wasn't unusual. What was unusual was how she didn't want to. She wanted to linger over breakfast with a beautiful woman and enjoy her company. Had they been in any other situation, she may have, but lives were on the line, and she couldn't—wouldn't—put her team's lives at risk for her desires. Maybe once she got the containment system working again so Bec had control, she could take a rest, but not before then. Since they still hadn't heard from Ace, she could only hope he didn't realize that she'd broken his code and got part of the system back.

"No," Bec said from behind her. "No, no, no. Don't do that. No."

Iris spun around in the chair immediately. "What's the matter?" Bec pointed at the screen on her computer, which had gone blank.

"Did he just brick it?"

Iris walked over to her desk, unconsciously inhaling deeply when she got within range of the woman sitting there. Bec's body wash smelled of flowers and sunshine, bringing fond memories of her childhood. At least her childhood before her accident. She was seven when she'd been injured and rarely had memories of anything before that time. The scent reminded her of being at a park with her mother. They were laughing as they sat on a swing together. Whether it was a real memory or one fabricated by the injury was a question she'd have to ask herself later.

"Did you touch it?" Iris asked, leaning on the desk as she stared at the screen.

"No. The screen blinked, which caught my attention, and then went black. Did the cord get knocked—"

A cursor flashed on the screen, and a message started to scroll across as though someone was typing.

"'If you want to protect the world and see your colleague alive, you'll have fifty million dollars ready in forty-eight hours,'" Iris read. "'More instructions to follow. Try anything funny with the police, and you and half the world will be dead.'"

They waited silently, but nothing more came across the screen.

"We knew it was coming, but fifty million is a lot of money," Bec said as Iris texted the team. "Why cash? Why not cryptocurrency?"

"Cash is harder to trace," Iris answered, pulling Bec's chair back. When Bec looked at her in confusion, she pointed at the computer. "I don't want you to touch something and have it disappear." She opened her phone camera and took a picture of the screen. "Every cryptocurrency transaction is recorded. Especially one the size of fifty million."

"There must be a way to put tracers in the cash, right? Isn't that how they catch people all the time?"

Iris snorted, finding a little levity in the situation. "I'm certain that was the point of the 'try anything funny' line that he added. Besides, it's harder than you may think to trace the cash. They'll move it to a new bag, remove any wrappers and immediately convert it to gold bars or other untraceable currency."

"Secure One, Charlie!" Cal called as the stairwell door burst open, and he, Declan and Zac ran in.

Surprised, Iris jumped, juggling her phone as it flew up into the air until Bec grabbed it and put her arm around her waist to calm her. "Deep breath. You're safe."

Iris nodded as the team gathered around the computer to read the message.

"Doesn't seem like he knows you already have the vents back," Cal said after he read it. "We need to keep it that way."

"Agreed," Bec said. "My question is, how will he know that we will do it? We can't respond."

Iris glanced back at the computer and then held up her finger. "The cursor is still blinking. Let's see if we can reply."

She put her hands on the keyboard, but Bec's warm fingers wrapped around her wrist to stop her. "What if that bricks the computer?"

"That's a risk we have to take," Cal said from behind them. "Do you have a backup of your research?"

"Of course," Bec agreed. "But the cost to replace these machines will be astronomical for our investors."

"Not as astronomical as the cost of another global pandemic," Zac pointed out. "I'm sure they are well insured."

Bec tipped her head in agreement and motioned for her to type. Iris took a deep breath and hit the U key, but nothing happened. She felt everyone's hopes deflate, knowing they couldn't communicate with the kidnapper. Getting fifty million dollars together in two days would be extremely difficult.

"Fantastic," Bec moaned. "I've got to call the board. If I can find their contact information."

"You don't know how to reach them?" Cal asked, and Bec shook her head.

"That information was need to know, and I didn't need to know. Walter took care of the administration side of things. I could find the contact information easily if I could access his computer, but I can't."

"Do the investors have fifty million dollars?" Zac asked.

"I have no idea. I know some of their names, but I haven't been here long enough even to have met them. Again, I'd need Walter's computer, which I don't have access to."

"Yet," Iris said. "If I work all night, I might be able to break the code."

"You can't work all night," Cal said.

"But we only have forty-eight hours!" Iris exclaimed. "Do you think I can sleep knowing this virus could slip through our fingers?"

Bec lowered her hand onto Iris's shoulder, giving her a place to focus her mind other than on the anxiety. "We won't let that happen," she said. "All we need is access to the containment room. I can protect the world if you can get me inside there."

"But you can't save Walter if you don't pay them," Iris said. Cal sighed heavily, and she glanced at him. "What?"

"I think we all know that even if we pay them the money, they won't let Walter go, right?"

"Doubtful," Zac agreed.

Iris slid her hand up to her shoulder to squeeze Bec's hand. "We have to try."

"We haven't gotten proof of life," Bec said matter-of-factly. "Chances are, he's already dead, but on the off chance he's not, we have to try."

"Then we try," Cal said. "All I need is one name for an investor, and Mina will dive in and find the information. Once we have that, we'll get back together. In the meantime, Iris, you know what to do."

"I'm on it," she said, returning to her computer. "And I'm close."

"How close?" Cal asked on his way to the stairs.

"An hour. Two at the most," she said. "I'll keep you posted, but please don't come running in here like Rambo. You shave ten years off my life every time you do that."

Cal's laughter was loud as it bounced around the cavernous space. "I make no promises, but I'll try. While you're working on that, I'm heading to the motel to fill in Mina and the team at Secure Watch. Charlie, out."

Once the door to the stairwell closed, Iris turned and walked to Bec, who was standing in the same place. Without hesitating, she put her arms around her for a hug. When Bec slid her arms around Iris's waist, holding tightly to her as she buried her forehead in her shoulder, Iris felt a settling in her soul she hadn't felt with anyone ever before. For just a split second, she could be herself and offer comfort without being judged.

"We'll figure this out," Iris promised the woman in her arms. "You're not alone."

"I can't tell you how grateful I am that you're here, Iris. It's awful to feel so useless."

"I know it's hard to feel like you can't help, but you can." Iris leaned out of the hug and sat at her desk. "While

I'm working on this, you can make a list of the investors' names to send to Mina. Even if you have one name, she can start tracking them down." She paused and tipped her head. "Do you think he'd have that information in one of the file cabinets?"

Bec's lips jumped into a small smile. "He might! I'll check it out while you keep working on the code."

"Mina said I need to record it whenever we mess with Walter's office."

Bec tipped her head back and forth a couple of times. "Really, what's the point now? Walter is being held for ransom, which we can prove. Recording our movements in his office proves nothing. Unless we put a camera on it that runs all day, the police can say we messed with the office when we weren't recording."

"The interior of the building isn't under surveillance?"

"Not like the outside," she said. "There was no need to record the labs all day. We go long days without messing with anything besides computers and research. If I work in a lab or with a pathogen, I turn on the cameras, which are only set up in the labs. At this point, it's worth the risk to tear apart his office and not worry about what the police will think. If we don't get the name of someone on the board, we're dead in the water. No pun intended. I can't be certain I have the correct name, so if I give it to Mina, she could chase her tail trying to track it down."

Iris thought it over and finally nodded. "You're right. We're out of time now that Ace contacted us. See what you can find while I code."

Bec clapped once and squeezed Iris's shoulder before she took off for Walter's office. Iris turned her attention back to the computer and kept typing, her fingers working in tandem with her brain as she inserted bits and pieces of the code she used for the ventilation system. She was tired, and that made it difficult to convince her eye to keep tracking the code. Her diplopia was severe in her right eye, and even with the prism lens, when she got tired, the eye often refused to cooperate. As much as she hated to admit it, Bec and Cal were right. She'd need to sleep once she finished this—if she finished this.

Not finishing it wasn't a choice, though. She had to complete this code to protect everyone from certain death. Walter may well be dead already—there was no denying that. But if she could protect the rest of the world, then maybe he wouldn't die in vain. She could continue to hope and pray that everyone survived this, and that Ace held to his promise of releasing Walter once they had the money—if they got it. Her huff was loud in the quiet room. She had to stop this and concentrate on the task before her. If only it was that easy when, at the very least, she was trying to keep one man alive and, at the worst, the entire world. No pressure, right?

Iris could hear Bec in the office moving stuff around, crunching through glass, and opening and closing cabinets. She forced herself to concentrate on the computer screen and not turn to see what the bright beauty was doing. She'd rather spend a quiet Saturday evening with her, walking the grounds of Secure Inc., where they could sip wine as the sun set over the man-made pond at the back of the property.

"When this is over, do you want to watch the sunset with me at Secure Inc.?" she called out to Bec without turning.

"There's nothing I'd love more," Bec replied, her voice soft enough for Iris to know she was still in the office.

With a smile, she pictured them sitting on the bench

on the dock, the water lapping gently against the shore as the stars came alive in the dark Minnesota sky. The dark used to scare her, but when she moved to Secure Inc., she learned to appreciate those moments of solitude when the stars were so bright that you could count them one by one. Maybe she felt safe because the property borders were so heavily guarded, or maybe she felt safe because the people within those borders were kind and understanding. It could be some of both, but over the last few years, Iris had seen a downtick in her anxiety, which made it easier for her to work with others. She still liked to work at night when fewer people crowded the space, but socializing had become more manageable, and working with the team instead of beside the team was now possible.

Something flashed in her peripheral vision, and she looked up. "Bec, what does a green light over the lab door mean?"

"That means the containment system is on," she called from the office right before footsteps ran toward her. "Is there a green light?"

"That's why I asked," Iris said, trying to keep her heart rate even as she continued to type.

"You did it! My goodness, Iris, you did it!" Bec exclaimed as she tipped her head up to stare at the light.

"Not yet," Iris answered, still typing. "The light might be on, but if I don't protect my code, he could break through it again. I don't know how closely he's paying attention to what's going on here."

Bec picked up the walkie-talkie and pressed the button. "Secure Watch, Bec," she said, releasing the button as Iris smiled. She was proud of her for remembering to follow the protocol.

"Secure One, Zulu." The box squawked with Zac's voice before Bec pushed the button down.

"Iris has the containment system active again!"

When Bec released the button, Iris heard Zac let out a whoop. "That's great news!"

Bec pushed the button, but this time, Iris jumped in. "It's good news," she clarified. "It won't be great news until I protect the code. I'm working on that now."

"Keep us posted, but it's still a great job, Iris. The elephant on my chest just lumbered off into the woods."

Iris smiled, knowing he was joking but also understanding what he meant by that. Breathing was a bit easier now that Ace didn't hold the fate of the world in his hands.

Bec set the walkie-talkie down and lowered herself to the chair. "If Ace isn't working with anyone, chances are he's busy trying to keep all the balls in the air," she said. "I would guess he also thinks his code is unbreakable."

"I was thinking about that," Iris agreed, finishing her code and hitting Enter before she spun her chair to stare at the little green light above the lab door. She did a fist pump when it stayed green and spun back to Bec. "We will have to run only the necessary functions of this place through Secure Watch computers."

"Why?" Bec asked, her head tipped.

"If I break the code entirely and it removes the malware from the computers in the facility, he will know we have control again. As long as those computers remain locked, he might well think he still controls everything and won't bother messing with anything. We only need to hold out until we have the ransom. If we don't have the money by the deadline, we'll have to make a new plan."

"I hadn't thought of that, but you're right. It's unfortunate since having access to Walter's computer would be helpful, but we'll make do."

"Did you find any of the names we can give Mina?"

Bec snapped her finger and jogged back to the office. When she returned, she held up a slip of paper. "I have several names of board members. They could also be investors. There's no way to know."

"There is one way to know," Iris assured her, grabbing her tablet as she winked. "We give those names to Mina Jacobs."

Chapter Eleven

"How is your arm?" Iris asked after they'd climbed into bed. Bec had cooked them a simple meal of frozen lasagna and garlic bread, but it had hit the spot. After checking in with Secure Watch and giving Mina the names she'd gathered from Walter's office, she had promised Mina to make Iris sleep for at least three hours before she was allowed back at the computer. Now that the containment system was working, she'd like to gain access to the labs again, but if they couldn't, at least the containment system would hold Ignis safely until she could.

"It's feeling better already," she promised the woman beside her in the dark. "I'm not just saying that, either. You were right about it getting infected, so I'm glad Selina showed up today."

Iris turned on her side to take the arm and check it over. "Me, too. Are you sure it doesn't hurt?"

"Positive," Bec promised, putting her hand over hers to stop it from fussing with the gauze. "Selina's cream and medications did the trick. It's funny, though. When I lived in the Amish community, my parents raised us around fires our entire childhood, and I never once got burned."

"You're Amish?"

Bec almost laughed until she remembered that Iris wouldn't understand that she was laughing at her tone of voice and not her question. "Not anymore," she clarified. "I left when I was sixteen."

"Left? Like you can stop being Amish?"

"You can," Bec said as Iris twined her fingers into hers. She suspected Iris didn't realize she had done it, so she made sure not to move. "It's frowned upon, of course, but when you turn sixteen, you're allowed to experience the outside world without conforming to the religion or principles."

"Rumsprouta. That's not right," she said, shaking her head.

"Close, though," Bec said. "*Rumspringa*. I had been preparing for it since I was twelve and realized that I was gay."

"I noticed the magnet," Iris said. "I'm a member, too."

"I saw the sticker on your laptop."

"Lesbihonest, I didn't need the magnet on your fridge, and you probably didn't need the sticker on my laptop," Iris said, snickering.

"Nope," she agreed.

"I assume you can't be gay and Amish?"

"Well, you can be, but you can't be out of the closet, which means you're miserable your entire life and then you die."

"Jeez, that's depressing. I may apologize for being a lot of things, but gay isn't one of them. I'm sorry they made you feel that way."

Bec smiled, squeezing her hand in agreement. "Thank you. It wasn't easy, but I knew I couldn't live that way. On the first day of my *Rumspringa*, I went to the public library and read about science and how it affects our world. We weren't taught much science in school, but what little they did teach us intrigued me, and I wanted to know more. We were taught that being gay was a sin and something that only happened in other cultures, but science taught me that being gay is part of human nature and not just certain cultures. I could never go back after learning the truth and feeling so deceived by my parents. At that same library the next day, I saw a poster on their announcement board. It was an open-door support group for gays and lesbians, and as I'm naturally curious, I decided to go. Truthfully, I didn't know what I was looking for when I walked through the doors, but by the time I left, I knew what I'd found. An entire community of people who lived full lives in loving relationships who promised they would help me survive outside my family."

"That's how you became a scientist?"

"To make a long story short, yes. Several couples let me live with them so I could go to high school and then college. They helped me get everything I didn't have to survive in the world, like a social security number, vaccines and a job. I was lucky. There are a lot of kids who can't escape their religion or family to be their authentic selves. I try to help as much as possible with Out to Innovate. They do so much for LGBTQ+ youth."

"I knew you were smart, strong and brave, but I didn't know how much until you shared that with me. Thank you."

Bec turned on her side and slipped her hand up Iris's cheek, stroking her temple with her thumb. Connecting with her when she wasn't wearing her glasses was nice. She felt like she could see her beautiful soul for the first time. "I hope you understand I didn't want to leave my family."

"Of course, you didn't. You wanted them to accept you for who you are, which wasn't too much to ask. When they didn't, you made the only choice you could. Look what you've done with your life since making that excruciating decision. I'm proud of you, Bec. I know it wasn't easy."

"I really want to kiss you right now," she whispered, her thumb straying to Iris's lips to rub across them.

"I wouldn't object."

Before Iris could finish the thought, Bec took her lips. They were soft, warm and tasted of the sweet wine they'd had with dinner. Just a little, she'd said as Bec poured, insisting they had to be clearheaded for work. She was the furthest thing from clearheaded with Iris's lips on hers, but she didn't care. She'd been dreaming about kissing Iris since she'd walked into her lab no more than a day ago. Bec had never believed people when they said, "When you know, you know," but how wrong she'd been. The sweet way Iris sighed when Bec slipped her tongue along the edge of her lips told her she sensed it, too.

"You are the most unexpected part of this whole situation, Iris Knowles," she said, kissing her way to the woman's neck to rest her lips against her pulse. It was fast from their kiss, but it slowed the longer she caressed Iris's collarbone with her thumb and tenderly kissed her skin.

"When I saw you on the screen, my heart slowed, and my anxiety disappeared for the first time in as long as I can remember. I didn't know why, but I knew I'd do anything to help you. I wondered if you were who I'd been looking for in life, but I struggled to believe that was possible—until we met. The way you understood, accepted and didn't judge me made you the first in my life ever to do that."

"That makes me sad, Iris," Bec whispered, stroking her chest as she spoke. "We're all different, but in the end, we're all the same. We want to give love and be loved. That's all any human wants."

Iris slipped her hand under Bec's shirt, cupping her rib cage with a silent question in her eyes. When Bec nodded, their lips connected, and so did their hearts.

IRIS FORCED HER concentration back on the screen as she tried to write a malware patch for the lab doors. It wasn't as imperative to have access to the labs now that they had the containment system working, but she would do what she could while the rest of the team tried to track down the money to use for ransom. The last update she'd gotten from Cal was Mina had found one board member, Allen McCarthy of California. He was currently out of the country, but they were conferring with him to explain why it was so important that the police weren't called until after Walter was returned safely. She still expected Bec to hear about this debacle from him or one of the other board members he was likely to contact.

Bec.

Her fingers strayed to her lips briefly before she forced them back to the keyboard. After knowing her barely twenty-four hours, she'd made love to the gorgeous scientist. That was so not her MO. Intimacy was usually tricky for her, but it wasn't with Bec. Natural. Unhurried. Romantic. Intimate. Those were all words she could use to describe making love to Bec. She was gentle, understanding, patient and loving. They had passed out in a tangle of limbs afterward, and when Iris woke about an hour ago, she hated to leave her. Unfortunately, duty called, so she slipped from the bed without disturbing her.

The story Bec had told her about leaving her community and depending on others in an entirely new one kept running through her mind. She had to have so much bravery and strength at such a young age to do something so drastic, yet she'd come out the other side a successful scientist. Everyone told Iris she was brave for what she'd gone through in life, but she didn't have a choice. Bec did, which made her so much braver for taking the step to go it alone.

Something caught her eye, and she stopped long enough to write it down. Then she started again, surprised when she saw the same thing a few lines later. Her heart rate picked up as she grabbed her tablet, took a shot of the computer screen and typed out a message to Mina before sending it. If what she was seeing in the code was a signature, Mina would know faster than anyone. In the meantime, she'd keep going, channeling the feel under her fingers of the labs clicking open as they unlocked, allowing them entrance. She vowed to stop short of unlocking them, though. She wanted Bec to be awake and ready to enter the lab to ensure all pathogens were safely tucked away. The last thing she wanted was to have those doors slide open and something to spill out.

A shudder went through her, so she dropped her hands from the keyboard and walked to the restroom at the end of the hall. Once done, she stopped in the break room for a coffee from the Keurig and a pastry that Cal had sent over from home base. She was grateful he kept the room stocked for them since the Secure One team had set up their break room in the basement, so they didn't have to announce themselves whenever they wanted coffee. She had to admit it was easier on her nerves.

When she returned to her desk, her phone rang, so she grabbed it and swiped it open. "Secure Watch, India."

"Secure Watch, Whiskey. I got your code."

"Oh, good," Iris said, spinning in her chair to stare at the screen again. "I'm hoping that's Ace's signature."

"It could be, but I need more than this. I'm going to remote access your laptop, so save your work. I didn't want to screw anything up."

"You're good to go," she promised after hitting several keys. "Did you sort out the situation with the board?"

"We're in the process. I'm convinced he understands the importance of the situation now, so once he contacts the rest of the board, we'll work with them to get the money. It will be tight to get that much money so quickly."

"You don't think Walter is still alive, do you?" Iris asked, noting the tone of her voice. She was resigned, a surefire bet that Mina felt it was all in vain.

"I don't know what to think," she admitted, and Iris could hear her keyboard clicking on the line. "This was planned in a way that says whoever is behind it has a serious grudge against the facility or someone in it, but all of the previous scientists and employees check out."

"At least the ones you can look into," Iris pointed out. "We can't access all of the files, making it harder to get the full picture."

"That's true, but I've been fortunate to reach out to some of the past scientists who gave me names of other employees they worked with at the time. I know it's not a comprehensive list, but with our limitations, it's better than nothing."

"Did you talk to any of those new names?" Iris asked.

"I spoke with two of the scientists. When I asked why they left, they reiterated the same thing Bec had. Walter was difficult to work with as a colleague. He disliked working long hours and spent more time at home than in the facility. They didn't want to say more, but the overall vibe was that management was a problem."

"I wonder why the board kept Walter on as their administrator when people were in and out like a revolving door."

"I can't say for certain, but I would bet none of them reported Walter's inability to manage to be their reason for leaving. That would only reflect poorly on them in the industry, and let's face it, everyone knows everyone in that community. Not to mention, I can't imagine it would be easy to find well-qualified individuals who want to live isolated for years on end. If the—"

Mina paused and fell silent, but Iris knew her boss well enough not to hang up until she told her to. Either she was hot on the trail, or she would have more questions for her. Her mind returned to the woman downstairs, wondering if things would be awkward in the light of day. Something told her it wouldn't be. What they had shared was pure, open and honest, and when you share open communication, there's nothing left to feel awkward about.

"What?" Mina asked, and Iris snapped to attention.

"I didn't say anything."

"I know. I'm asking what because the source code control system tells me this malware was written on a computer connected to the service inside the facility."

"That's not possible, Mina. There has to be a mistake," Iris said, leaning forward to peer at her screen as though it held all the answers.

"There has to be. Give me ten, and I'll call you back."

The line went dead. Iris held the phone as the back of her neck prickled. Unless it wasn't impossible. Maybe the person who wrote the code was sleeping off their love-making just below her feet.

Chapter Twelve

Bec woke slowly, confused and disoriented by the bright light that had her squinting against it. She was on her stomach, her arms behind her back as someone tried to tie her wrists together.

"Help!" she screamed, unsure if the Secure One team could hear her from where they were. "Somebody help me!" She kicked and fought, finally getting the better of the person so she could flip over. Her lips froze on the next call for help when Iris was the person holding a computer cord in her hands with her eyes wild. "Iris, what are you doing?"

"I'm stopping you from hurting anyone!" she exclaimed, her eyes darting around the room. "I trusted you!"

Bec raised her hands in front of her and tried to speak calmly. "Iris, I don't know what you're talking about. Why would I hurt someone?"

Iris reeled off a bunch of numbers and letters that only confused her more. "Does that ring a bell?"

"No, Iris. I don't know what you're talking about. What is going on?"

"We know, Dr. Roth," she said, and Bec's gut sank when she used her full name.

"Know what, Iris?"

"That the malware was written on a computer attached to the mainframe within the facility."

Bec stood but kept her hands out in front of her to show she wasn't being aggressive. She wanted to calm Iris down but not scare her. "I don't know what a mainframe is. Is that a computer?"

"Everyone knows what a mainframe is!" Iris exclaimed and Bec shook her head slowly.

"I've heard the term, but I don't do computers for a living. What was that other thing you said? All the numbers and letters."

"That was a line of code from the malware I'm trying to patch. Mina said it originated here."

"If that's true," Bec said softly in hopes she'd listen to her, "It didn't come from me. I don't know how to write code. I can perform the tasks I need to, but they don't include that. If that were required for the job, I'd have to attend code-writing school."

Iris snorted as she rolled her eyes. "Code-writing school. It's called computer science. You must have taken that in college."

"I took computer classes, sure, but never for coding," Bec promised. "There are specific programs we use here for different aspects of the research, but none of them were written here. They're available nationwide to any lab who purchases a license."

Iris dropped the cord to her side and took a step toward her. "What's Python?"

"A snake?"

"Java? PHP?" Iris asked and Bec grasped the other woman's elbows.

"Coffee and a drug? No, that's PCP. What's PHP?"

"Python, Java and PHP are all types of coding languages. Java has been around forever, Bec."

"I grew up isolated from electricity, much less computers," Bec reminded her. "By the time I started public school, I was so far behind that the only way to graduate was to concentrate on the core classes. It wasn't me, Iris. Why would I call you in to help me secure the labs if I was the one who wrote the malware? That doesn't make sense."

"But you said Walter doesn't know anything about computers, either."

"He always acted like he didn't," Bec confirmed.

"Who takes care of your technology needs then?" Iris asked as Bec pulled on clothes.

"An IT firm, as far as I know. That information should be in Walter's files. Let's go look."

Iris waited while Bec used the bathroom and brushed her teeth, which gave her a few minutes to calm her breathing and try not to be hurt that Iris thought she was capable of this kind of deception. Once she got Iris to calm down, she could see in her eyes that she was scared and confused, but Iris didn't really believe she had anything to do with writing the code.

"How did you figure out the code was written in the facility?" she called from where she put her socks and shoes on.

"I found a suspicious line of code and sent it to Mina."

She grabbed her phone, slipping it into her pocket just in case one of the investors called her. "You said you were going to look for a signature. Is that what you meant?"

she asked as they hurried upstairs. Bec would have preferred to start the day with a kiss and a cup of coffee instead of accusations and attempted confinement, but this was not a normal day.

"I'm sorry for trying to tie you up and making accusations that weren't true," Iris said as they stood in the elevator. "I shouldn't have let the anxiety take over the way it did. You've been here the whole time helping me, so I should have known you weren't behind it because that doesn't even make sense, but—"

Bec put her finger to Iris's lips before she hit the stop button on the elevator panel. "But you are under a lot of stress, and fighting the anxiety is hard minute to minute in a situation like this. Suddenly discovering that the code was written in the facility made it easy to jump to conclusions."

"Yes, but I shouldn't have. Not after last night. I know you on a level that…"

She paused and Bec waited, but she didn't finish the thought. She slipped her arms around Iris's waist and snugged them belly to belly. "You know me on a soul-deep level that strips away everything but the truth, even if we've only known each other for a few days?"

"Yes," Iris whispered, lowering her forehead to touch hers. "You said I can't say I'm sorry, but I truly am."

"I'm not upset, sweetheart," she promised, lifting her face to kiss her lips. "I understand that you're stressed and tired, not to mention scared. We can get through this if we trust each other, okay?"

Iris didn't answer with words. She lowered her head and kissed Bec deeply, reminding Bec of the passion and desire they had shared last night when they bared their souls to each other. Bec smiled at the woman when the kiss ended, gazing deeply into her eyes. Her heart melted, knowing she trusted her enough to do that without fear.

"What do you say we get to the bottom of this nightmare so we can get on with living?" When Iris nodded, Bec hit the start button for the elevator.

"I find it difficult to believe that an IT firm would be behind this," Iris said as they left the elevator and walked toward Walter's office.

"Unless it's one bad apple that they don't know is in their midst," Bec answered, skirting the glass still on the floor as they walked into the office. "I sure wish we had access to the security videos."

Iris leaned on the desk and crossed her arms over her chest. "Why? There's no way to know when the code was written, so it's a needle in a haystack situation."

"No, not for the coder," Bec said, pulling out the drawer marked operations and rifling through the files. "For the kidnapper. Something is bugging me about the person, but I can't put my finger on it. The flash-bang disoriented me and blurred my vision, but I feel like they were familiar."

Iris pushed herself up and grabbed the walkie-talkie off her belt. "Secure Watch, India."

"Secure One, Charlie."

"Cal? Are you here?"

"Just arrived with Selina," he answered when she released the button.

"Would you come to the lab? We have a question."

"Ten-four."

"Oh great, he brought the torture nurse with him," Bec muttered with a grimace.

Iris immediately pulled her into her arms. "She means

well and is trying to keep you from getting worse. I'll hold your hand if that will help."

Bec patted her back before ending the hug. "That was a joke, Iris. I very much appreciate Selina. I was teasing."

"Oh. Sorry, I'm not good at picking out sarcasm or teasing. I take things quite literally."

"No need to apologize. I should have thought of that. I'll tell you the next time I'm teasing, okay?" Iris nodded as Bec returned to the cabinet to pull out the file she'd been looking for, holding it up in victory. "Got it!"

"Let's go to the lab and wait for Cal," Iris said, motioning for Bec to go first. They were barely out of the office when Iris's tablet started ringing. She grabbed it from the desk and hit the answer button. "Secure Watch, Whiskey."

"Secure Watch, India," Iris said, and Mina joined them on the screen.

"Is Bec there?" Mina asked, and Iris nodded. She walked over to a high lab table and propped the tablet so she could see them both.

"Good morning, Mina."

"Hey, Bec. I know Cal and Selina are on the way, but I discovered some information about one of the employees I wanted to run past you."

"Sure, whatever I can do to help. I haven't personally worked with many of them, though."

"This one you have," Mina said. "Zafar Zimmer."

"Yes, our lab tech. He's been here as long as Dr. Hoerman, so close to six years. I've only been here five months. What about him?"

"I don't think he exists."

"What now?" Bec asked, glancing at Iris before turning back to Mina. "I work with him every day."

"What I mean is, I don't think his real name is Zafar Zimmer. The few people in the world with that name don't live in the United States, nor have they bought plane tickets to Poland from the United States."

"Maybe he used a different last name, or someone else bought the ticket for him?" Bec suggested, but Mina shook her head.

"Even if someone else bought it, the ticket must be in his name. There were no passengers on any flight to Poland over the last year with the name Zafar. There were only ten males in the age range you gave me for your lab tech who flew to Poland on or around the dates you gave me. None of them were named Zafar, and none of them were your lab tech."

"I don't understand what's going on," Bec admitted. "Should I try calling him?"

"We already did," Mina said. "We got the message the number was disconnected, changed or no longer in service."

"What is going on?" Bec asked just as the door to the stairs opened.

"Secure One, Charlie," Cal said as he walked in with Selina.

"Hi," Iris said, turning to them. "We're talking to Mina."

Mina took a moment to catch Cal and Selina up on their discussion.

"Right before she called, we were in Walter's office," Iris said. "We were looking for the file with the information for the IT company the research center uses to see if they would know who had written the code."

"Did you find it?" Cal asked. Bec nodded, tapping the file on the table.

"But in the process, Bec said she wished she could see the security footage from the day of the kidnapping."

"Why?" Selina asked. "You said the person was dressed head to toe in black."

"They were," Bec agreed. "But they seemed familiar to me. I can't explain it more than that. I caught a glimpse of them after my vision cleared from the flash-bang, but not enough to put my finger on it."

"I'm afraid there's no way to look at the camera footage," Cal said.

"We know," Iris agreed. "The footage can only be watched on Walter's computer."

"Not what I meant. The malware virus also disabled the security cameras. None of them were active when we arrived."

"That doesn't make sense," Bec said. "Those cameras don't even go down when the power goes out. They stream on Walter's computer, but he can transfer them to my computer or tablet when he leaves for the night since we're always running double duty out here."

"When I checked them on arrival, they were turned off," Cal explained. "I didn't turn them back on since there was no way to watch them with the computers not working, and it didn't matter since we were providing security. You didn't turn them off?"

"Absolutely not," Bec answered. "We don't get much traffic out here, but they alert us if someone arrives at the loading dock or approaches any of the doors."

"What about at night?" Cal asked. "Who watches them at night?"

"My apartment has a computer that I run them on there as well, and it emits an alarm if anything is amiss and wakes me."

"Why doesn't the facility have a security company to handle the cameras?" Mina asked, her head tipped to the side. "Someone that could call for outside help if anything happened to the few of you inside."

"I asked the same question," Bec said, facing Mina again. "Walter told me the company was always messing up, so the board agreed to move them in-house. I don't know when, but it's been this way since I started working here."

Mina raised a brow. "Sounds fishy to me."

"Fishier than a Friday night smelt fry at the VFW," Cal agreed. "Especially since the cameras were manually turned off."

"I meant to ask how you secured the side door again after the kidnapper broke in?" Bec asked, spinning toward Cal.

He stood there staring at her, his head tipped in confusion. "Secured the side door? It wasn't broken. You buzzed me in, which I assumed was how you always did it. The biometrics system was down, but the door was locked. Since then, we've used the loading dock to go in and out."

Bec closed her eyes and tried to fight the rising panic as her heart pounded. "Cal, if that's true, then—"

"The kidnapper had a key," Selina finished.

"Does Zafar have a key, Bec?" Mina asked.

Bec stumbled backward, caught by the warm chest of the woman she'd spent the night with. "We—we all do," she said, fear and anger making her body and voice shake.

"Sit," Selina ordered, pressing a chair under her and helping her down before she took her pulse. "Take some deep breaths."

Bec did what she said, and the spots in front of her

eyes slowly disappeared. "I'm sorry, but it struck me that only three of us have keys to this place."

"You, Zafar and Walter?" Mina asked, and Bec nodded.

"With the caveat that my vision was wonky after the flash-bang, it's entirely possible the kidnapper was Zafar."

Chapter Thirteen

Iris put her arm around Bec's shoulders, hoping it would stop her quaking. "It's okay," she whispered. "Tell us why you think that?"

"He was the same height and build," Bec said, her words shaky. "I know that doesn't mean anything since there are plenty of six-foot-tall skinny guys in the world, but not as many who know how to navigate this facility in silence or where Walter's office is."

"Did the kidnapper have to walk past you to get to Walter's office?" Cal asked, and Bec nodded immediately. Iris held her tighter, hoping to offer her strength and warmth.

"Yes, yes," Bec said, turning in the chair and pointing to the spot by the lab door. "I was there when the flash-bang went off."

"That's close to the hallway," Cal said, walking over there. "But you didn't see anyone down here?"

"No, but I had just half turned back toward Walter's office to answer a question he'd asked me. Then the bang and the light disoriented me until I caught a glimpse of the kidnapper in the office with Walter."

"Which means the kidnapping was targeted because it would have been easier to take you and run," Mina said.

"Unless it was opportunity driven," Cal said to her point. "He may have realized that she was stunned, so better to take the guy who could still move quickly and call for help."

Someone handed Mina a piece of paper off camera, and everyone was silent while she read it. When she glanced up, Iris knew the game had changed.

"Unless the good doctor was in on it." Mina waved the paper in the air.

"In on what?" Bec looked around, confused, until Mina clarified.

"A fifty-million-dollar payday."

"No." Bec shook her head. "Absolutely not. Walter wasn't hurting for money and was close to retirement."

"You're correct. He wasn't hurting for money now." Mina shook the paper in her hand. "But Walter Hoerman was deep in debt until a few years ago."

"Does it say to who?" Cal asked.

"According to this, just about everyone, including the taxman."

"What on earth?" Bec asked. "Where was all his money going?"

"Gambling?" Selina suggested.

"That's possible, though I can only see his verifiable debts."

Cal shook his head as he leaned on the lab table. "Regardless, I smell a rat or two, but they aren't in Poland."

"Same," Mina, Iris and Selina said in unison, giving them a moment of levity in a situation that was anything but funny.

"I think that Walter got in over his head with something, then took a payoff to clear his debt. Chances are, that payoff came with stipulations, and he devised a way to get out from under the thumb of his creditors. He befriends a young, impressionable kid and convinces him he'll get half of the big payday for writing some malware and fake kidnapping him."

Mina shrugged as she leaned on her desk, fatigue written on her face. "Anything is possible, but what concerns me is that Zafar is untraceable, which feels like a—"

"Setup," Selina finished. Since she'd been set up not too long ago by her thought-to-be-dead sister, she would smell a similar ploy from a mile away.

"Zafar was playing ball for two bad guys?" Iris asked, glancing at Selina. "But who?"

"That's the fifty-million-dollar question," Mina said.

"You mean the sixty-four-dollar question," Iris corrected, then she noticed Mina's raised brow. "Oh, right. Fifty-million-dollar ransom."

"The problem is, there's no way to confirm this," Bec pointed out. "We conveniently cannot access Walter's computer, and the cameras were off during the kidnapping."

"I tried tracing Zafar's phone, but the last time it pinged was a week ago. That lines up with the dates you said he'd be gone to Poland," Mina said to Bec, who nodded. "But it also says it's no longer in service, so I believe he ditched the phone rather than flying off to Poland."

Cal nodded. "Agreed."

"Did you track Walter's phone?" Iris asked.

"Walter has his phone?" Mina asked, but Bec answered.

"I believe he does. He was holding it when the kidnapper broke in, and it's nowhere to be found here."

Mina grinned, which told Iris she was pleased with this information. "I have the number. Do you know if he has the find-my-phone feature on it?"

"It was the latest model, so I'm sure it's there. I don't know if it's on. Don't you think he'd shut it off, though? Everyone knows cell phones can't be traced if they're off."

"Everyone should know that," Selina said with a snicker. "But not everyone has a Mina Jacobs on their team who can get around pesky things like powered down phones."

Mina winked. "Whiskey, out."

"That was a strange turn of events." Bec turned to look up at Iris. "I'm concerned."

"We're all concerned," Cal agreed. "But until Mina gets back to us, there isn't much we can do. Selina will take you to the apartment to check your arm while we're waiting. Then we can get together once Mina calls back."

Bec pushed herself up from the chair and patted Iris's shoulder as she walked by with Selina.

Once they were gone, Cal sighed. "I was afraid this could be an inside job."

"You were? Why?" Iris asked, surprised to hear him say that.

"Nothing quite added up. If it had been one thing, I could have written it off, but not all of this."

"What can we do in the meantime?" She stared at the floor, wishing to be with Bec, but she didn't want to look clingy or needy.

"How close are you to regaining access to the labs?"

"I don't know," she admitted. "Less than an hour is my hope. But I don't want to unlock the labs until Bec is ready to go in and be sure everything is locked down."

"And once that's done, where are we with the systems?"

"Once we can get into the labs, we'd control all the important systems, including the biometrics. I don't want to take full control back and unlock the computers in case he's paying attention to his code. If he thinks we've got control of the facility again, thereby rendering his hostage useless, then he has no reason to keep him alive."

"Unless his hostage is in on it." Cal used air quotes around *hostage*, to which she nodded. "I agree with you, though. Let's work on access to the labs while we wait for Mina. We can make a better plan once she gets back to us."

Iris checked her watch. "We have twenty-seven hours until the ransom is due, and we haven't heard from the board, either. That doesn't give us much time."

"It sure doesn't, but you do your job, and I'll do mine. Hopefully, the two will align so we can get to the bottom of this before anyone else gets hurt."

Cal patted her on the shoulder and left the room, allowing her to ponder if that was true. Leaving here—leaving Bec—was going to hurt.

"ARE YOU SURE this is okay?" Iris asked as she was nearly finished with the code to unlock the labs.

Bec knelt before her and grasped her chin, forcing eye contact with her for a second before Iris looked over her shoulder. "I'm positive, Iris. The lab is a level three lab, which means there's an airlock between the door you're going to open and the one that holds the bad guys. Only I can open the one that holds the bad guys. I'll go in, get dressed, put on my ventilator and then use my biometrics to enter the lab."

"But what about anything that escapes when you open the second door? Something bad could happen to you. That's what I'm worried about."

"Nothing can escape because of air pressure. I'll wear my safety equipment, so I'm protected even if something is floating around the lab that didn't get trapped in the filters, but I don't believe that's the case. It's a lot to explain right now, but trust me, there's no risk to me or you if you open that door."

"Can I talk to you when you're in the lab?" Iris asked, still unsure how she felt about letting her go in there alone. Not that she had any choice in the matter, but she didn't have to like it.

"Unfortunately, no. Normally, we have a comms system that allows for that, but you don't have time to get that working, so we'll use sign language. I'll give you a thumbs-up once I'm in the lab and know everything is good, okay?"

"And if it's not good?"

"I'll give you a thumbs-down, but we'll have bigger problems on our hands at that point," she said with a wink. "Do you trust me?"

"Yes, but I'm also concerned about you getting hurt."

Bec took her hands and leaned up, passionately kissing her but without lingering. "That's one thing you don't have to be concerned about. I plan to kiss you ten thousand more times, so I will follow every safety protocol and take zero risks. Okay?"

"For the first time in my life, I want to hold someone to a promise like that, Bec."

"And I want to be the first one who doesn't break one to you." Bec caressed her face before she dropped her hand and walked to the lab door. "Ready when you are, sweetheart."

With butterflies in her belly, Iris put her hands on the keyboard and finished the code before she hit Enter. The light over the door switched to red, and Bec used her credentials to open the door. She gave her a thumbs-up and blew her a kiss before the door slid closed again and locked the woman she cared about inside a room with dangerous pathogens. The thought struck her, and she stilled. She cared about Bec, and not just as a friend or colleague. She cared about her as a love interest.

The surprise was less from the idea that she could care about Bec as a love interest and more from the fact that she could care about her as a lifelong partner. Her past relationships had all ended for the same reason, at least according to what they told Iris as they broke up with her. They were convinced she couldn't care about another person deeply in a lasting relationship. They tried to break it to her in an "it's not your fault" kind of way, but over time, it ate at her until she believed that she could never love someone deeply enough for them to stay.

Now, gazing at Bec as she worked inside the lab protected by the bubbled hazmat suit, she could see she was waiting for the right woman to love deeply. Too bad the right woman was one she could never have even if she would always care about her. They were too different in both experiences and distance. Bec lived here, and even if she left the facility after this situation, she would work somewhere else at a college or university far from Secure Inc. While Iris could work remotely and remain employed by Secure Watch, she worried the stress would be too much for her, and she'd fail at the relationship and her job.

After protecting her patch for the doors, she pushed

herself to standing and blew out a breath. It was time to quarantine those thoughts to the background, as they had too much to do to worry about what would happen after this case was over. If they didn't get a bead on Walter or Zafar before the end of today, she couldn't predict what would happen. They didn't have fifty million dollars, and convincing the investors to give that up for one man, when they already knew they had control of the facility again, would take more time than they had.

With one last glance at Bec, still working inside the lab, Iris walked to Walter's office. It was time to get to the bottom of this so everyone could safely move on with their lives. Well, everyone but Walter.

Chapter Fourteen

Iris stood staring at the giant cherrywood desk that occupied most of the office. The wood gleamed, clearly polished regularly by someone who cared. The top was neat and orderly, with only a blotter, pencil holder and computer monitor. There had to be information somewhere in the behemoth to tell them if Walter and Zafar were in this together. If Walter wanted out from under someone's control, this plot could be driven by desperation rather than greed. If that was the case, and Walter was behind this, why was Secure Watch on the job? She couldn't figure out why Walter had allowed Bec to call Secure Watch if he was the mastermind behind this scheme.

Her gaze drifted to the shattered glass next to Walter's office door, and Iris couldn't help but wonder if they hadn't intended to keep Bec alive long enough for it to matter. Walter wouldn't have a choice but to let Bec attempt to get help to reboot their system, but if they planned to kill her before Secure Watch arrived, then he wouldn't need to argue with her about it. He could let her make the call, knowing it wouldn't matter anyway. A shudder racked her at the thought of losing that beautiful woman who was valiantly fighting to save them all from being killed by putting herself between them and some deadly bugs.

But if that was his plan, why was she still alive? Had the gunman thought he'd hit her? According to Bec, that was possible since when the glass broke, she fell backward. Maybe they hadn't stuck around long enough to double-check, which was a mistake on their part, but one Iris was so glad they had made. She walked to his desk and faced off with it, knowing the computer was useless but wondering if he had anything in the drawers to give them a place to start. A name. A phone number. Anything that could give them a lead about where they might be.

She sat in his desk chair and started pulling open desk drawers, which, unfortunately, were ridiculously tidy. Other than office supplies, there weren't random slips of paper or business cards that didn't belong. She lifted the blotter, hoping something might be taped to the desk, but again, she was disappointed. There was no point in searching for a hidden drawer in the desk. That was a little too mystery-novelish even for her.

The thought that something might be taped to the desk ran through her mind, and she got down on her hands and knees, searching under the desk drawers for any scrap of paper taped anywhere. Nothing. Undeterred, she searched behind the filing cabinet and inside each drawer before starting on the files. She glanced over her shoulder to check on Bec, who was still working inside the lab.

Iris was determined to search every file, but ten minutes later, she was still empty-handed. He must have kept anything he didn't want found at home. That was the only answer. She would have to send Cal or one of the other team members over to his place to search. The information had to be somewhere unless he was innocent.

If he was, that made this a wild-goose chase that ended in Walter dying when the ransom wasn't paid.

Iris sat on the edge of the desk to rub her face from exhaustion, fear and sadness. One way or the other, the events at the Research Center of the Advancement of Biogenics would be over soon and she would have to return to Secure Inc. with the team, leaving behind the only woman she'd ever cared about in life. That was a tough pill to swallow, made more so by the fact that regardless of how she felt about Bec, there was no way someone like her would ever want to be in a long-term relationship with a woman riddled with anxiety, fear and compulsions.

The thought stood Iris up straight. The anxiety and fear were there, but her compulsions had faded since she arrived. For the first time since the incident, she was functioning without everything being exactly how she thought she needed it. Maybe it was just the situation she was in and nothing more. Her therapist had told her years ago that a change in her routine was necessary if she was going to heal from the past and find any enjoyment in life. Iris hadn't believed her for a hot second. Her brain was wired differently now, meaning she would always deal with the consequences of that day, right?

As the anxiety medication lessened her fear about facing each day, the intensity of her compulsions slowly lessened, too. She still liked things orderly, but she could handle slightly more chaos in her routine short-term. What she was dealing with here was more than chaos, though. Her anxiety should be through the roof despite her medication, but she had found a way to remain relatively calm through it. Bec was the reason. She was sure of it. Iris searched her memory for the last time she had done her mental repeating to soothe herself. It was something she'd done since the incident to keep her anxiety lower or at bay. As a child, she was convinced that nothing bad would happen as long as she did it once every hour.

New places aren't safe. You can't trust anyone. No one can love you now.

Iris paused at the thought. *No one can love you now.* She'd been telling herself that for twenty-six years! No wonder it had become a self-fulfilling prophecy. When she glanced over her shoulder and laid eyes on Bec, she forced herself to change those inner thoughts.

Some new places aren't safe. Stay guarded. You can trust the people who have proven themselves to you. You deserve love, and your past doesn't make you unlovable.

After lowering herself to Walter's desk chair, she waited. Waited for the feelings of fear to spike and the trembling to begin. While she waited, she focused on Bec in the lab, walking back and forth between the sink and a giant hood that covered half the room. She repeated the phrase aloud this time. "Some new places aren't safe. Stay guarded. You can trust the people who have proven themselves to you. You deserve love, and your past doesn't make you unlovable."

Again, she waited. Her heart rate didn't rise beyond unacceptable levels, she didn't start to sweat, and her hands didn't tremble. She glanced down at them to see they had a slight tremor, but nothing like she was used to.

Iris said the phrases again and then again until the words came to her as easily as the old ones used to. Was she healed? No. She was still clammy, and her heart raced, but underneath it was a peace she hadn't felt in twenty-six years. Her gaze strayed to the woman dressed like an astronaut still walking around the lab. Maybe surrounding yourself with the right people was the answer. The only way to know was to keep doing it, but that would be impossible if they didn't figure out what Walter knew. She pulled the walkie-talkie off her belt and pressed the button. "Secure Watch, India."

"Secure One, Charlie," Cal answered.

"I've been searching Walter's office for anything that might tell us what he knows or if he's behind this," she said, releasing the button.

"Did you find anything?"

"Nothing, which is also suspicious if you ask me. He has to be keeping it at home or in his car."

"We've checked his car. There was nothing."

"I think it's time we check his house. The information we need to save him might be there."

She released the button and waited for Cal to respond while keeping an eye on Bec. It looked like she was finishing up and decontaminating her suit.

"We were just talking about that," Cal agreed. "I'll put together a team and head over there. I don't have permission to enter the property, but I'll find a way in."

"That sounds good. Can you keep me posted?" she asked, releasing the button and waiting for him to respond.

"Will do. We'll gear up and head over there. Charlie, out."

Iris set the walkie-talkie down on the desk and sighed as she pulled open a drawer. If she was sending Cal to Walter's house to look for information, she'd check the desk one more time for completeness as well. Then, if Cal also found nothing, they could say with certainty it was nowhere that they could easily access it.

If she wanted to hide something, she would put it in

the biggest drawer, so she pulled it out of the desk and dumped it out, disappointed when the bottom of the drawer was solid. After cleaning up the mess, she slid it back into the desk and pulled out the middle drawer, doing the same thing and earning the same result. There was only one more drawer, so she pulled it out, but when she dumped it, something thunked. Her heart started racing as she realized despite the drawer being empty, it was far heavier than it should be. She set it on its edge on the desk and inspected the bottom panel, surprised when the bottom of the drawer was a different color than the inside top layer. There was no way to know that unless you pulled it out, which told her it was on purpose.

The question was, how did it open? She wiggled the top piece of wood, but it didn't give. There wasn't a hole to hook her finger or an indication that it should open. "Because it shouldn't," she said, flipping it over so the bottom faced up. There was a hinge halfway down the drawer and a cloth tab. She pulled the tab, and the drawer came open, revealing a laptop nestled between the two pieces of wood. It wasn't easy, but she wiggled it free of the drawer. Had she found what they were looking for?

"Iris? What is that?" Bec asked as she stepped into the room.

Iris swung toward her with the computer in her hand and grinned. "Walter's only chance."

Chapter Fifteen

"Is that Walter's computer?" Bec asked in shock as Iris joined her in the doorway.

"I found it in his desk, so I sure hope so. We're about to find out, but first, tell me everything was alright in the lab?"

"Yes," Bec said with a head nod. "Nothing escaped, and all the safety protocols worked. I've secured all the viruses, so they can't hurt anyone."

"That's a relief," Iris said as they walked to the workspace. She'd searched the drawer but couldn't find a charger, so if the computer had no juice, they'd have to wait for Cal to tear apart Walter's house before learning what secrets it held.

"I still can't believe you found a computer," Bec said, squeezing Iris's shoulder. "You may have single-handedly saved Walter's life if he's not behind this."

"Once I had the lab doors working again, it made sense to try and figure out where to look for information on how to save Walter before the deadline was up. I was hoping to find a phone number or name to give Mina so she could run a trace, but I found nothing. I wasn't even going to check the drawers. It felt too…"

"On the nose?"

Iris nodded, her lips tilting up a bit. "Exactly that, so I didn't check them the first time through. Once I convinced Cal to go to Walter's house, I decided to do my due diligence, too. It was in the top drawer, but I started at the bottom. Nearly gave up, if I'm honest."

"So glad you didn't," Bec said, leaning down and kissing her lips. She'd intended to keep the kiss light and easy, but it quickly heated and morphed into a kiss filled with unspoken emotion. She wanted to weep, knowing that when this was over, Iris would return to Secure Watch, and she'd have to go on with her life without the woman she loved. The idea of loving Iris after only a few days left her off-kilter, but that didn't change the truth. She had never felt this way about anyone in her life, and not just sexually. The emotions that filled her were startling, but every single one felt right. "Thank you for trusting me," she whispered, caressing her cheek before dropping her hand. Iris smiled with a nod. "Before starting on the computer, we need to eat something. I want to wash up, so let's go to my apartment."

"You go ahead," Iris said, trying to sit. "I should get started on this while Cal is at Walter's."

"No." Bec set the computer on the desk. "It will be there when we're fueled and rested. Besides, if Cal doesn't find a charger at Walter's, we may need to rethink how we do it so we don't waste too much battery power."

She could tell Iris didn't want to, but she finally agreed and followed her downstairs once she promised they wouldn't take too long to eat. After letting Declan know where they would be, Iris set her tablet on the table and turned to her.

"You clean up while I cook. We have a lot to do yet."

"Other than the computer, which may not tell us anything, we're waiting for everyone else to give us information. Let's use that time to shower and eat." Bec walked backward while holding Iris's hand, even as she tried to pull her to a stop.

"But what if Cal calls?"

"He'll call back," she answered, turning the shower on to warm once they were in the bathroom. Then she walked to Iris and kissed her, stopping the stream of excuses falling from her lips until the only thing she heard were moans of pleasure. In a flurry of arms, they stripped each other of their shirts and bras before Iris sat. Bec pulled her shoes, braces and pants off before she helped her into the shower.

Walking without the braces was dangerous as she noticed Iris often tripped on her toes, so Bec had her sit on the plastic chair she'd taken from the break room for Iris to use. Once settled under the warm spray, Bec stripped off the rest of her clothes, wrapped her arm in the plastic wrap and joined her, pulling the curtain before she leaned down to resume their teasing kisses. Water warmed them as they explored each other's bodies, almost allowing her to forget the reason why they were together to begin with. Almost.

Standing behind Iris, Bec massaged shampoo through her short blond hair until she tipped her head back and her mouth fell open from pleasure. Taking advantage, Bec walked back to the front of the chair and straddled her, kissing those open lips as the water rinsed their hair. Iris found the soap and lathered it, running her hands over Bec's body, teasing and taunting her until she came apart in her arms. Iris's lips absorbed her shuddering gasps as she floated back to earth.

"Anyone ever tell you that you have magic hands?" Bec asked, treating Iris to the same torture once she could move again.

"It's never been my hands that were the issue," Iris answered, moaning as Bec caressed her breasts, moving aside so the water could rinse them before she suckled a nipple.

All talking ceased as Bec showed Iris all the ways she cared about her without caring about any of her issues until the water cooled and she accepted that they had to rejoin reality. Once the water was off, she dried Iris head to toe before helping her out of the shower to sit on her bed. She wrapped her in a blanket and then carried her braces back to her.

"Could you please check the tablet and see if we missed any calls?" Iris asked, so she hurried to it and pressed the power button.

"Nothing yet," she answered.

They dressed in silence, and then she pulled a chair out from the table and motioned for Iris to sit before she pulled out cold cuts, cheese, bread and chips and set them all out on the table. She returned for water before sitting across from the woman she had just made love to in a way she'd never done with anyone else. There was something intoxicating yet soothing about their time together. Like the outside world, and all the fear that came with it, disappeared and they could find peace with each other.

"Thank you," she said, squeezing Iris's hand as she reached for a piece of bread. "For indulging me when your brain told you to do anything but."

"Before I met you, I doubt that would have been possible. It's not easy for me to stop in the middle of a task and not obsess over getting back to it. My neurologist says that's typical after my kind of brain injury. My therapist says it's typical of someone who's afraid or fears change."

"Who do you think is correct?" Bec asked, taking a bite of the ham sandwich she'd made while they talked.

"They both are, to a degree. My brain was injured, but I found comfort in the routine. Soon, I came to depend on it to feel safe."

"I'm glad you feel safe with me," Bec said with a smile, but Iris wasn't looking at her to see it.

"Never said I did," she answered instead, taking a bite of her sandwich.

"You didn't have to. The fact that you're sitting at my table talking to me about it shows me you do."

"Don't you want to know what happened to me?"

"Yes, but I promised Selina I wouldn't ask. That said, I don't need to know what happened to you to know that I like you for who you are now."

Iris kept her eyes pinned to the table as she chewed. Bec could tell she was uncomfortable, but she didn't say anything. It was okay to be uncomfortable in a safe environment. That was the only way to grow and find healthy ways to process trauma.

"It was my uncle. He kidnapped me when I was seven."

"Iris, you don't have to tell me," she said, reaching for her hand. "We're under enough stress as it is. Don't stress yourself out more."

"What if I want to?" She glanced up so quickly that Bec almost missed it, so she was glad she was smiling when she did. "There's no one alive but my therapist who knows the truth now. Sometimes, I think I could help people if I discussed it more."

"What does your therapist think about that?"

"She agrees but also knows how hard I've worked to be able to function at the level I do. She would never advise me to do something that could set me back."

"That's fair. As a clinician, she wants you to keep progressing in your recovery, not regress."

"The thing is," Iris said, catching her eye for longer before she stared at her sandwich. "I've been stuck in the same place of my recovery for years. Remember when I said my therapist says I'm afraid of being afraid? She's right. Whenever I think about telling someone the truth about what happened or try to think about what using my story to help others might look like, the fear gets too strong to overcome."

"Iris, look at me," Bec said firmly, waiting several minutes in silence until she lifted her head to look into her eyes for a quick moment. "You're stronger than your fear."

"No, you don't understand—"

Bec held up her finger. "Were you scared to come here?"

"Terrified, but I had to do it. You needed help, and so did Cal."

"Which is why I say you're stronger than your fear. The right motivation makes the fear worth it sometimes."

"Never thought of it that way. I've always thought that talking about it would hurt me again, and I feared that."

"How would it hurt you again? The emotions would cause too much anxiety?"

"You're going to laugh and think I'm dumb if I answer that."

Bec stood and knelt beside her chair. "I would never do either of those two things, Iris. You are the strongest and smartest woman I've ever met, and I've met a lot of strong, smart women. Whether you tell me anything more about your past or you never say another word, that won't change how I feel or think about you."

"I believe that," she agreed, staring at her hand on her thigh. "The truth is, for the longest time, I worried if I talked about what happened, he would come back and hurt me."

"Since you were seven when it happened, that's understandable, Iris."

She sat there, nodding and staring at her lap, until Bec stood, kissed the top of her head and sat back down at the table. "He's been dead since the second month of his prison sentence, though. The obvious answer is that I'm afraid of what happens after I tell someone the truth. Will you hate me? Will you think it was my fault? Will you not want to be friends with me anymore?"

"I wouldn't do any of those things, Iris, which I know is easy to say but hard for you to believe and trust. You were a child, so none of it was your fault."

"That's true. Everything I know about what happened before I was taken came from my mother. She had put me to bed and showered while waiting for my dad to come home. She worked the late shift at the hospital, and he was normally home for dinner but had to work late. She finished getting ready for work, and when he came home, he stopped to kiss me on the way to the shower, but I wasn't there. My window was open, and they found footprints below it."

"You don't remember that part?"

"Thankfully, I don't. The doctor said the damage to

my brain was the cause and not repression. There isn't a single day that goes by where I'm not thankful for that after hearing the truth about what happened. See, my anxiety and OCD are because of the physical injury, not the memories of it since I don't have many."

"I understand," Bec assured her.

"They suspected my uncle was the one who took me. He was my uncle by marriage, and my aunt was divorcing him. He hated our family and knew how much my aunt doted on me, so he took me to make them suffer. For two days, he beat and molested me until he heard sirens one night. Thinking he'd been found, he slammed my head into the concrete floor and took off, leaving me for dead."

"But you didn't die," Bec said, taking her hands across the table and holding them tightly. "You're a survivor."

"I'm lucky to be this functional, according to the doctors. I spent over six months in the hospital learning how to do just the basic things like sit up, walk and eat. Once I was released, we tried to get back to the business of living, but it was hard on my parents, both emotionally and financially. My dad took a new job working on an oil rig where he made a lot of money but was gone more than he was home. He died in a work-related accident that set us up for life, but it broke my mother. She was never the same, and when she was diagnosed with cancer when I was fourteen, she refused treatment. Said there was no point in fighting it."

"Oh, Iris," Bec said with a sigh, but she just shrugged her shoulder.

"I didn't know how to convince her that I was worth fighting for when I was the reason her entire life had fallen apart."

"No," Bec said firmly. "Your uncle was the reason her

life fell apart. You were an innocent victim, just the same as her and your father."

"That's what my aunt tried to help me understand, too, once I went to live with her at fifteen. Different aunt, not the one he was married to." Bec nodded her understanding. "Anyway, she took care of me and made sure I got through a technical program for coding, then set me up with my first apartment and job. It wasn't long after that when she passed away. That was when the struggles kicked in, and I learned just how much people judged those who were different. I was so lucky the day I met Mina."

"How did you meet her?" Bec asked, taking another bite of her sandwich. She was glad the heaviness of her childhood story was behind them. Iris had told someone she trusted about what happened, and now Bec had to ensure she understood that her opinion of her hadn't changed.

"Mina was at the doctor with Hannah Grace one day when I walked in looking for a job. I was desperate to find something. I got a small stipend from the money left from my dad's settlement, but it wasn't enough to live on, and I'd been evicted from my apartment. The brain injury made it difficult to work somewhere if there were too many people in the same room or where I had to face the public. It limited what I could do and made finding work that paid a living wage extremely difficult."

"That's understandable. You probably would have qualified for disability?"

"Maybe, but my skills were second to none in the right situation."

"I can't argue with you there," Bec agreed with a wink.

"Mina overheard me asking the receptionist about a

job, and when she said they didn't have anything, I got sort of upset. Not like yelling or anything, but I started crying and tried to run out. And, well, we both know I shouldn't run."

Bec chuckled and nodded, her heart breaking for this woman who had overcome so much in life only to suffer even more injustices.

"Mina helped me up, sat me in a chair and then handed me her card. She asked me if I had any experience in cybersecurity work." She paused and looked around the room before she leaned in and whispered, "I lied to her."

Bec gasped in feigned horror. "Iris Knowles lied about something? That was teasing, by the way."

Iris smiled. "I figured that out because your voice has a different lilt when you tease."

"Really?" she asked, and Iris nodded. "I never knew that. I learned something new about myself today. Thank you."

She squeezed Iris's hands as she started speaking again. "It wasn't an outright lie. I knew how to do the job but had no experience besides my initial training."

"Ah, that's what we call inflating the résumé. Everyone does it," Bec said with a wink. "Go on."

"That's pretty much the whole story. Mina found out I'd been evicted and was living in a hotel with all my belongings in my car. She told me to follow her back to Secure Inc. and gave me a room for the night. The next day, she hired me as one of their digital private investigators. Once she learned my skillset, I transitioned into doing more and more coding and hacking as we set up websites for clients. I still do some digital PI work when the need arises."

"The first time I met you, I knew you were a spectacular woman, and everything you told me solidified that opinion. Thank you for sharing your story with me, Iris. It means everything to me that you trust me with it. I won't let you down."

She lifted her head to hold her gaze. "You're not like, I don't know, disappointed or put off by any of it?"

Bec shook her head immediately, standing and walking to her, straddling her legs as she lowered herself to her lap. "Why would I be disappointed or put off? What you went through was horrific and the result of the kidnapping has changed your life, but it also shaped you into the woman you are today."

"Not everyone thinks that's so great," she whispered, not making eye contact until Bec tipped her chin back to face her.

"Look around you, Iris. Everyone you work with thinks you're great. They love you. So much that when Selina was treating my arm, she gave me the third degree and then threatened bodily harm if I hurt you."

"Your voice didn't change there, which means you weren't teasing about her threatening you, right?"

Bec shook her head. "I wasn't. She was dead serious when she said it. My point is that the only person who hasn't embraced your greatness is you. Do I understand why? Yes. Do I understand that accepting yourself will be difficult or even impossible? Yes. Do I hope you'll one day believe that you matter to so many people and deserve happiness? Also, yes. You deserve to be happy, Iris. When you can grab even a moment of it, do it. I promise it's worth the little bit of fear you'll feel in doing it."

"For the first time in my life, I want to try," she admitted, smiling as she stared at their joined hands. "You've shown me that happiness comes in places you least expect." Then Iris lifted her head and held her gaze long enough to tuck a piece of hair behind her ear that had fallen from her braid in the shower.

"I couldn't agree more," Bec whispered before kissing her sweet, plump lips. Hopefully, it told her how happy she was to hold her in her arms. They were just getting to the good part when the tablet started to ring.

Chapter Sixteen

Breaking the kiss, Iris grabbed the tablet and hit the red button. "Secure One, Charlie."

"Secure Watch, India," she responded, and Bec could tell her attention was now solely on the tablet. Cal's muffled voice probably startled Iris, as it did her.

When Cal appeared on the screen, he wore a hazmat suit and a respirator. "We found something in the basement. I'll turn the camera so Bec can tell us what it is."

Bec gasped when the camera revealed a lab space in Walter's basement. "That's a class three biological safety cabinet," she said without hesitation. "What is it doing in his basement?"

"I was hoping you could tell us," Cal said from behind the camera.

"Those are well over twenty grand, Cal. I don't know why he'd have one in his home. They're used when working with biohazards or dangerous pathogens that can't become airborne."

"Like viruses?" Cal asked.

"Yes. Usually, when working on gain-of-function research," Bec agreed.

"What's that?" Iris asked.

"Gain-of-function research helps us understand how pathogens adapt to environmental pressures. That allows us to plan better disease control measures and explore vaccines and therapies."

"That sounds dangerous were it to fall into the wrong hands," Cal mused.

"It is," Bec couldn't help but admit. "If gain-of-function research fell into the wrong hands, it could be used for biological warfare without question. That's why this facility is secretive. Having security around us would make us an obvious target, but we also need to protect ourselves from bad players."

"Which is why Walter saying in the interview that you have the deadliest virus in your lab was risky," Iris deduced.

"It was, but now I wonder if he did it intentionally. Maybe he was looking for an investor or to set up a bidding war once he had a working vaccine for Ignis Cerebri. Cal, can you pan the camera around the room?" Cal did as she asked until she said, "Stop. That cabinet. Walk to it, but don't open it. Does it say ultra-low freezer?"

"Yes," Cal answered. "Should he not have that, either?"

"Since they start at ten grand, it's not there to hold his beer," she muttered, and Iris snorted.

"I see a lot of lab equipment, too," Cal said, pointing out a centrifuge and other pieces they use in the lab at the facility. "Does Walter work from home sometimes?"

"Yes, but not with viruses. That's taking your life into your own hands. Not to mention your neighbors. The biosafety hood helps, but it's seriously lacking when you don't have the benefit of the rest of the lab's safety features."

"You're saying it's like driving in NASCAR without a helmet? You can do it, but you shouldn't."

"Essentially," Bec agreed, still laser focused on the freezer. "The only reason he should have any of that equipment there is if he's working with live viruses, which doesn't make sense. That's what this facility is for, and in the length of time I've been here, he's never once entered a lab."

"What's in the freezer if it's not drinks?" Iris asked in confusion.

"Viruses." Saying it aloud sent a shiver down Bec's spine.

The camera flipped, and Cal filled the screen again. "Are we in danger by being down here?"

"Not from what I can see. The hood is clean, and there weren't any open vials inside it."

"There's a layer of dust on everything," Cal interjected. "It doesn't look like it's been touched in at least a year."

"Is the freezer plugged in?" she asked, and Cal nodded. "Is it running?"

"Let me check." Cal walked back to the freezer and knelt, leaning behind the small dorm-sized refrigerator for a moment. "I can hear it humming, and the side is cool."

"That would make sense. Those freezers go as low as minus 112 degrees Fahrenheit."

"Why does something need to be that cold?" Iris asked, and Bec couldn't stop the nervous laughter from bubbling up.

"To protect humankind from some very nasty pathogens. Cold storage allows labs to keep viruses and bacteria safe and alive until they need it for experimentation.

Then they thaw whatever portion they need to conduct whatever test they're doing."

"That still doesn't explain what Walter is doing with it in his house," Cal said. "What if I open the freezer?"

"I want you to, but you must follow my directions closely, okay?" Bec asked, and Cal nodded. "Turn the camera around to face forward and have someone else open the door. Once the initial cold escapes, hold the camera down so I can see any printing on the vials. Do not get your hands anywhere near the inside of the freezer. When I say close it, whoever opened it should close it with their foot."

"Is it safe for Lucas to open it with an ungloved hand?"

"Yes, but once it's been opened, that plastic will get cold, so I don't want him to close it that way. With any luck, it's empty."

"And if we aren't lucky?" Cal asked. "Well, I guess I can puzzle that one out for myself. Ready when you are."

She said okay once the camera was forward facing, and Lucas, a Secure One operative, opened the door. Inside was one vial rack with four vials standing upright. "Can you get closer?" she asked, and Cal zoomed in on the vials. As soon as the recording stabilized, she gasped. "Close it."

Lucas's black-booted foot struck out to close the door as Cal flipped the camera around. Iris put her arm around her shoulders to help quell her shaking.

"What did you see?" Cal asked.

"Four vials and one said IC."

"Ignis Cerebri," Iris deduced, and she nodded.

"There's no reason for him to have a vial at his house. His *house*," she said, emphasizing the word in a way that said it didn't belong there.

"Is it fair to say Walter's behind whatever is happening?" Lucas asked from where he stood next to Cal, both still wearing respirators.

"More than fair to say," she agreed. "Did you find anything else?"

"The place is wiped clean," Cal said. "When he left here last, he didn't plan to return. At least not for some time to come."

"But he left viruses there unsecured," she said, vibrating with anger.

"I'm hoping he returns for them," Lucas said. "Something tells me if he saved a vial of it, he plans to backstab whoever paid him to make the vaccine by turning around and selling more of the virus to someone else. Total warfare tactics."

"We've got the place covered in cameras. We installed a system that will lock him in if he shows up. I want to have a word with the good doctor."

"I want to do more than talk to him," Iris growled.

"Easy now," Lucas said with a wink. "You put all your anger into sorting out the computer. We did find a charging cord. Did you get past the password?"

Bec cut her gaze to Iris, who, thankfully, was nonreactive other than shaking her head. "Not yet. I was hungry, so we're grabbing a sandwich, and then I'll get back to it."

"You do that while we secure the house. We'll head back to the facility in under an hour," Cal said.

"I think you need to get out now." Bec took the tablet from Iris. "He may know you're inside or have left that vial there for someone else to pick up. Someone else, like a terrorist organization, and they won't care that you're the good guys. Unplug that freezer, get out and get back here, please."

Cal glanced at Lucas before answering. "Unplug the freezer? Won't that damage the samples inside?"

"Absolutely." Bec laughed, and even she thought her laughter sounded deranged. "It will kill the samples and render them useless to anyone. They're trapped in the vials and won't escape, and the viruses will be dead by the time anyone finds them. You can thaw viruses, but it must be done by slowly returning them to room temperature. Anything else means the pathogens will die a fast death. Unplug it." She paused and then tipped her head side to side. "Actually, don't unplug it. Just turn the dial on the freezer to off. If he does show up and notices it's unplugged, he might plug it back in. He'd have to check the dial to see that it isn't working, which he won't do. He'll just assume it is. Once you do that, get back here. I know you're security guys, but you're no match for terrorists."

"Fair point," Cal conceded. "It would be great if you have something for us to run down when we arrive."

"You got it," Iris said. "Come on up once you've sorted things there. I'll hopefully have the rest of the answers we need to find Zafar and Walter before this goes any further."

"Ten-four, Charlie, out."

The screen went black again, and Iris lowered it to the table. "You're a bad influence on me, Rebecca Roth. I just lied to my boss."

"Technically, you lied to Lucas, but I accept the title of bad influence if I get another shot at you in the shower."

"Now you're trying to get me fired!" Iris exclaimed.

Bec laughed loudly and hugged her, loving how her curves wrapped around her own. Everything that happened over the last few days had been unexpected, but Iris

Knowles was the most unexpected. Her chest squeezed when she remembered they had so far to go yet, and when it was over, a life with Iris was not guaranteed.

She pulled back and traced Iris's lips. "What's the smile for?"

"I realized that since I got here, I've been able to let my guard down and make some jokes. That's never happened before," Iris admitted.

"Maybe you feel comfortable enough here to be yourself."

"Because of you, I'm sure," Iris agreed.

She didn't care that they were racing against time to find her boss when she leaned in and took her lips. The kiss turned heated the moment their lips collided. Bec took the lead, twining and cuddling their tongues until they were panting and had to break for air. Iris leaned her forehead against hers, something she noticed she did to maintain intimacy without forcing eye contact. Bec didn't care. It was a connection she craved, and she would take every last second of it until this was over and they could find a path to help them stay together.

"We should go upstairs and face Walter's computer," Iris whispered. "I don't want to drop the ball for Cal."

"I agree," she said, kissing her nose before unhappily extricating herself from the embrace to put the food away.

Bec desperately wanted the computer to be empty and just as desperately wanted it to answer all their questions. One meant Walter was innocent and in danger, and the other meant he was guilty but safe. On second thought, neither was a great option. Oh, Walter. What did you get yourself into?

They'd made their way upstairs by the time she finished her internal debate. Iris turned the computer on, and the screen waited for a password. She tried 1234 and got nothing. Then she tried 0000. Still nothing. "Any idea what it might be? There are ways around it, but they suck a lot of power and time."

Bec pondered the question. "Try Ace." Iris typed it in, but again, it returned to the screen, this time also displaying a password reminder: *Sagacity.*

"Doesn't that mean understanding?" Iris asked, and Bec nodded.

"Yes, but it also means wisdom or knowledge."

"Could it be the college he attended or a professor's name?" Iris asked, but Bec stared at the screen with her head tipped to the side for a few more seconds before she pointed at it.

"Try cerebri."

Iris typed it in, and this time, the home screen loaded. "You're amazing!" she said, her fingers clicking on the trackpad as she opened the utilities.

"It made sense. Ignis Cerebri is a virus that burns the brain. What are you doing?"

"I'm turning on the battery saver. By doing that, our battery power will be extended. As long as we don't need the internet, we should have—" Iris glanced down at the corner of the computer "—about an hour before it goes dead. By then, Cal should be back."

"Okay, but where do we start? Files?"

"That would make the most sense, but see this?" She hovered the cursor over a cloud icon. "That's OneDrive." She clicked it, and when the app opened, she ran the cursor down to something called Personal Vault. "I'm betting the information we need is here, so let's begin. It requires a password. We only get ten tries before we're locked out. I would guess he doesn't know that the same password that opens his computer also opens this." She typed it in and sure enough, the vault opened.

"How did you know that?" Bec asked, pulling a chair next to Iris so they could see the screen.

Iris glanced at her for a second. "It's my job to know these things, but also, doesn't everyone know that?"

Bec held her hands by her chest as a silly grin lifted her lips. "I'll admit that I didn't know that either."

Iris shook her head in disappointment. "I'm going to let this one go because you'd be surprised how many people don't know how to utilize their OneDrive folders properly. Though, I'm sure you have programs you use for the lab with their own cloud."

"Yes, that," Bec agreed, feeling less out of touch now. "We only save to the cloud. I'm surprised Walter saves to his OneDrive. Maybe this is just for his home computing?"

"I would say it could be, but why did he have it in a secret compartment if it were? That doesn't make sense." She clicked open the files, but they all seemed innocuous to Bec.

"Those are all files for running the facility itself," Bec said, pointing at the spreadsheet Iris had just opened. "Maybe he kept the computer hidden so it didn't fall into the wrong hands should the facility be overrun. We don't want our operations information to be used against us."

Iris didn't answer as she continued to click files open and read them as though Bec didn't exist. Usually, she'd feel slighted by being ignored, but she knew Iris wasn't doing it to dismiss her purposefully. She was lost in her own world of computer language.

"You're concerned by what Cal found in Walter's house," Iris finally said, still searching the computer.

"There's no reason for him to have a biosafety hood and vials of the virus, Iris. That's how things go bad very quickly."

"I got that impression when you insisted Cal get out of the house."

"We don't know where Walter is, but if he was kidnapped by someone trying to get the virus, he could tell them he had a vial at his house. I don't want Secure One there if they show up. I can't believe how wrong I was about Walter. I've even had dinner at his house, and he was hiding that in the basement the entire time."

"Wait. When you started working here, where did Walter tell you he got the virus from?" Iris asked, taking her hands off the keyboard.

"He never actually said," Bec said, rubbing her temples. "I assumed this was one of the government projects we were working on. According to the literature I was sent, the lab has worked on government contracts in the past, and I didn't think it could be anyone else. Now, I'm not so sure, but it's not like I can call to ask."

"You're not sure because of the vial in the basement?" Iris asked to clarify.

"That, and looking back at all the times I asked him who was backing the research so I could note it in my paperwork, he just kept saying use dot gov until the bureaucracy decides what they want."

"You're right. That is a strange answer. You weren't suspicious?"

"It felt weird, but I had bigger fish to fry with this vaccine. I told him we had to decide on it soon because I'd need to publish the first paper if we would continue to be funded. I thought the government was funding us at the time, so I followed their guidelines. Why didn't I ask more questions?" The sentence sounded more like an exclamation than a question, but Iris squeezed her hands until she felt calmer.

"You had no reason to believe you were being deceived," Iris pointed out. "We don't know that it's not the government fronting this research, so keep that in mind. We do know that Walter kept some of the virus for himself, so we need to find out why."

Shaking her head, Bec glanced up at the ceiling before she told the woman she'd come to care so much for what she knew for sure. "Baby, the only reason Walter would have a biosafety cabinet like that is if he worked with the viruses himself. Those other three vials in the freezer were the base mutation viruses for Ignis Cerebri."

Chapter Seventeen

Iris tipped her head in confusion for a moment. "Wait, you're saying Walter created Ignis Cerebri?"

Bec nodded slowly, her lips drawing into a thin line. "I want to know why. Why was I deceived? Am I that gullible? What is wrong with me? I should have done more research, but my research and the people I talked to said this center was cutting-edge. It might look like a sleeper facility, but it was doing big things."

"Were they wrong?" she asked as she returned to the computer to keep working. She didn't have time to waste in case the battery died.

"Not about it being a sleeper facility and cutting-edge. I can't say the part about doing big things. I've only worked on a project steeped in controversy and deceit. I should have seen this as a too-good-to-be-true situation," Bec chastised herself. "Why would anyone hire me to create a vaccine for a yet unknown virus? Why wouldn't they hire an entire team to do that?"

Iris turned to her again. "Did you know you'd work alone when you took the job?"

"No, not exactly. I knew I would be the head scientist in charge of gathering the data and directing workflow.

I expected there to be others who would contribute, like medical, clinical and public health microbiologists, all working together to look at it from every angle. Once I arrived, Walter told me only one lab tech would be available to help me."

"And you believe you should have suspected that whatever was happening here was nefarious and walked away?"

"At the very least, I should have demanded more answers. Instead, I dove in headfirst, spurred by the very real threat of what another pandemic would do to the world."

"Fearmongering is real in any form, Bec. If you were led to believe that a vaccine was necessary sooner rather than later, it makes sense you would buckle down and get to work to solve the problem. Don't beat yourself up because you tried to do good and help millions of people from possible demise. Hindsight is always twenty-twenty, which is why it's called hindsight."

Bec's laughter was soft when she leaned in and rested her forehead against Iris's. "You're right. It's easy to see now that I was afraid of not being good enough or not measuring up because of what happened when I was a kid."

"Let me tell you what Mina told me when I started working for Secure Watch and felt the same way. She said they tell us as kids we can be whoever we want to be but show us the exact opposite is true by dictating what we can be and when. We can't change our past, but we can shape our future by being who we wanted to be as kids. Who did you want to be then, Bec?"

"Myself," she whispered. "I just wanted to be myself.

Someone who helped others, was kind, made a difference and was happy in my skin."

"You help others, are kind and make a difference. The question is, are you happy in your skin?"

"Yes. Since I met you, I've never been happier, Iris."

"Me, too," she whispered, leaning in to kiss Bec's lips. "So let's work the problem together. No more blame game, okay? Cold, hard facts, just like if this was a science problem you had to solve."

Bec sat up with a smile. "You're good at tough love, Iris. I'll give you that. Okay, no more pity party. Let's solve this problem so we can get on with our lives."

Iris turned to the computer, but the screen before her swam as she blinked back the tears that filled her eyes. She couldn't let them fall and risk Bec noticing that she was upset. It wasn't as though she didn't know they'd go their separate ways when this was over, but having her confirm it broke her heart. She tried to tell herself how important it was that she learned she could love someone, but her heart didn't want to hear it.

Clearing her throat, she focused on the files, running her finger down the screen without looking at the wonderful, intelligent, gorgeous woman beside her who could never be hers. "Do any of these names sound familiar?"

"No," Bec answered immediately, as though she'd already been reading through them.

"They aren't abbreviations for diseases or anything?"

"I guess they could be, but I wouldn't know what without opening them all. If I saw H1N1 or HEV, I would know they were viruses, but that's not what these are."

"Then we open them," she said, clicking the first one. However, the file was empty, as were the next six.

"How can they all be empty?" Bec asked, leaning in

close enough that her floral scent tickled Iris's senses, adding to the sadness already engulfing her.

"Red herrings?" Iris asked, clicking out of the file and hitting the start button before clicking all apps.

"What are you looking for?"

"An app that fronts as something else but is a vault for files and photos. Something tells me Walter wasn't as bad at technology as he led you all to believe."

"That's becoming apparent," she agreed while shaking her head. "He had me fooled, though."

"No, he kept you busy. There's a difference. He could say whatever he wanted, but you were too busy to see what he was doing." She paused for a moment and then grinned. "There you are."

"What?"

Iris clicked on an app, which brought up a password box. "Folder Hider. A classic app for hiding and encrypting files."

"Do you think the password is the same?"

"The hint for this one is Ignis plus Cerebri," Iris said, pointing at the words under the empty password box. "I doubt he'd make it the same."

"Brain burning," Bec said instantly.

With a tip of her head, Iris typed in the two words but was told it was the wrong password.

"Add a hyphen. He always added a hyphen to the two words when he wrote it out."

Iris added the hyphen. This time, the box opened, revealing files and pictures that weren't encrypted. She opened the first file and clicked through pictures taken of Walter and his setup in the basement.

"It looks new in these pictures," Iris pointed out, and Bec nodded.

"Maybe he took them to prove he had a system set up?" Bec asked as Iris kept scanning through them. At the end, there was a video, and Iris clicked Play.

"As you can see, I'm more than prepared to meet your organization's needs. The lab is complete, and I'll await your specifications and go ahead." Walter spoke to the camera as though he was addressing a specific person or place.

"It's dated one year ago," Iris said, pointing to the date of the video.

"This explains why the other scientist didn't know what Mina was talking about when she mentioned Ignis. He hadn't made it yet. I was the sucker he brought in to make the vaccine for it."

"Why would they need a vaccine for it if they're terrorists?" Iris asked. "That part confuses me."

"Simple. They don't want to die. They'll take the vaccine and protect themselves and those they love while sentencing everyone else to death."

A shudder racked Iris at the thought. "We know that Walter set the lab up at someone else's request, so now we need to find out who that was. If I were Walter, I'd want a contract, right? Let's see if we can find one."

She clicked open several more files, but Bec shook her head each time, telling her they were information about the base viruses she had seen in the freezer at Walter's house. None of it told them why he was mutating a new virus or for whom. After ten minutes of searching, Bec blew out a frustrated breath.

"Maybe he didn't have a contract or never uploaded it."

"There had to be a contract, but maybe it's smarter to follow the money trail. Mina said he went from being deeply in debt to being debt-free almost overnight. Unless she discovers a rich dead relative, it's a bit suspicious."

Bec snorted, but it wasn't out of amusement. "Walter doesn't have a rich relative."

"My gut says the same unless his rich relative is very much alive and very much a bad player. So far, we have proof that he set the lab up at someone's request. There has to be another file here to tell us who—"

A loud bang made them both jump. "What was that?" Bec asked.

Iris grabbed the walkie-talkie. "Secure Watch, India." She released the button and waited but got no response. "Secure Watch, India!" She waited but still didn't get a response. "Something's wrong, Bec."

"Let's give them a minute in case they can't stop doing what they're doing to respond."

Her heart pounding, she closed the laptop and set it aside, grabbing the tablet to call Cal when the stairwell door slammed open.

"Thank God," Iris said, but the rest of the thought died on her lips.

Four men, dressed head to toe in black with only their eyes showing, marched into the lab, assault rifles aimed at them as they approached.

"Who are you?" Bec asked, putting herself between the men and Iris. "You have no right to be here."

"Walter sent us," one of the men sneered. "We're here for Ignis."

"You can't take a dangerous pathogen out of the lab. That's suicide."

"He said you completed the vaccine," another one said from the left.

"Completed, yes—proved its effectiveness, no. That will take years."

"We'll take our chances," the first guy said. "Open the door to the lab."

Iris shook with fear as the men aimed their rifles at them, making it almost impossible to think about what to do next. Were Declan and Zac alive? Had they been hurt? Had Cal arrived yet? Cal! The thought penetrated her terror, and she leaned over to cough, hoping it didn't sound fake. While bent over, she hit the panic button under her shirt, alerting everyone at Secure Watch that she was in trouble. If Cal was still at Walter's or headed back, he'd know they needed help.

"Where's Walter?" Bec asked. "I won't do anything until I talk to him."

"We'd like to know the same thing," the ringleader said. "We've been trying to reach him since he missed our scheduled call. We're not waiting any longer."

Was Walter planning to double-cross them by taking off and leaving Bec holding the bag? It was starting to look that way to her.

Slowly, Iris stood up, enraged at the thought that her friends could be hurt or worse. "What did you do to my friends?"

"Relax. They're fine. Or they will be once they wake up from their little nap and find a way to untie themselves. We aren't here to hurt anyone. That includes you. As long as you do what we say."

Iris could hear the hint of an accent but couldn't pinpoint where it was from. Bec reached behind her and took her hand, squeezing it.

"What do you want us to do?" Bec asked, and the guy motioned to the lab with his gun.

"Open the lab door, but don't make any sudden moves."

Bec nodded. "I'm going to turn around and explain to my friend what she needs to do on the computer so I can use my metrics to open the door. I'm not trying anything. We've had some computer difficulties. Not everything is working properly."

"Hands where we can see them," he responded, and Bec raised her hands before she turned to face Iris.

"You're okay?" she asked, and Iris nodded, her eyes wide. She wasn't okay, but she didn't want to freak Bec out and make her worry when she had four guns aimed at her back. "I'm going to need you to go through the sequence just like last time so I can enter my biometrics at the door."

"But Bec, that's dangerous."

Trust me, she mouthed, and Iris snapped her lips shut, even if they continued to tremble as she faced off with the woman who had taught her so much about herself in such a short time.

"Just sit down slowly and wait for me to get to the lab door, then type everything in exactly as you did last time."

Bec turned around, and the guys walked her to the door, where she waited. Iris was confused because she didn't need her to open the door. Since she didn't know what she had planned, she sat down and typed away on the laptop as though she was doing something important. She occasionally glanced at Bec, who had moved to the side while the guys lined up in front of the lab door. She kept typing, hoping to buy time in case Cal got her SOS alert and was on his way.

"Come on already, we don't have all day," the ring-leader growled.

Bec gave her a nod, so with shaking hands, she hit the enter key dramatically. The woman Iris realized she had big feelings for entered her biometrics and waited for the door to slide open. From there, everything happened at once. The door opened, and Bec pushed the men into the room, sidestepping the ringleader as he yelled, but she didn't get him into the room before he looped an arm around her neck and dragged her backward, training his gun on Iris.

Chapter Eighteen

"Don't hurt her!" Bec yelled, but her words were strangled from the chokehold she was in.

"You should have thought about that before you decided to play games!" The ringleader yelled, red-hot anger tightening his arm around her neck.

She put her arms up in the "don't shoot" position. "I'm sorry," she croaked. "I'm scared."

Iris sat in the computer chair, her arms up in the air, but they trembled so much they fell limply to her lap. She shook violently, and tears fell down her cheeks as she locked eyes with Bec for a brief moment. Bec could read the terror in them. She had to defuse the situation, but she had no idea how.

"Boss," another guy said as he walked out of the lab. "There's nothing in there."

"Where's the virus?" he asked, tightening his hold on Bec's neck.

She couldn't answer because black dots filled her vision and she struggled to breathe. She clawed at his arm until he finally released her enough for her to suck in air. "I destroyed it!"

Iris gasped from across the room and brought her trembling fingers to her lips, the fear in her eyes telling Bec she understood the pickle they were in.

"You did what?" he growled, dragging her backward toward the lab. "What about the vaccine?"

"I told you the vaccine isn't finished! It's in pieces and parts that need to be tested." That wasn't true, but he didn't appear to be the kind of guy to understand how vaccine research worked. She had a vaccine, but it wasn't proven yet. The dose she had wasn't enough to use, even if it was safe to use.

"Then you'll get the pieces and parts," he grunted. "You're coming with us."

"No!" Iris said, jumping to her feet.

A shot rang out, and Bec screamed as Iris went stock-still for a moment before dropping to the floor.

"You shot her!" Bec screamed, trying to run to Iris, the fear in her gut telling her in that moment that she was in love with her, but the animal kept hold of her.

"The shot went wide," he said, laughter filling the room. "She's being dramatic."

"She has anxiety and PTSD from a kidnapping when she was a child," Bec spat. "I need to check on her."

"You'll do no such thing," he said, walking her toward the lab. "You'll tell my men where to find the vaccine, and then you'll come with us."

Bec's entire body froze at his words. "What do you want me for?" she asked with fake bravado. "I don't know anything about what's going on here. The government hired me to work on a vaccine and nothing else."

"You were hired to work on a vaccine, but no one said anything about the government. My employer bought and paid for that virus and sent us to collect it."

"It's not here!" she exclaimed again as he tightened his arm around her neck.

"That's okay. We have the next best thing—someone who can recreate it. If we can't find Walter, at least we have you."

A glance at Iris, still unmoving on the floor, told Bec what she had to do. "The vaccine is in the small freezer on the left of the hood. They're marked V1 and V2. Put them in the small red cooler next to the freezer."

It was a lie. There was no vaccine since she had turned off the freezer and let it thaw after she destroyed the viruses kept in a separate part of the lab. Thankfully, she had left the vials in the freezer until they had thawed. It would have been hard to keep this ruse up if she hadn't done that.

The ringleader motioned for one of the men to do as she said, and once he returned with the cooler, they pulled her down the long hallway.

"Iris!" she screamed, clawing at the guy's arm as she tried to free herself to run to her. "Iris! You have to wake up! Iris!"

As the door to the stairwell closed, the beautiful, vibrant woman remained crumbled in a ball, and Bec was afraid it was the last memory she'd ever have of her.

IRIS BLINKED SEVERAL times as she awoke, a fuzzy snout licking her cheek. Lucas's PTSD dog, Haven, was nuzzling her with his nose when her eyes came open.

"Iris," Cal said softly from where he knelt beside her. "We got your SOS."

SOS? Had she activated her panic button? Why did she feel wrung out as though she'd run a marathon? That only happened after an intense panic attack. She sat up and glanced around, the lab coming into focus until the memory of Bec in that guy's arms and the gun going off ran through her mind.

"No, no," she cried, frantically searching the room as her heart rate went from normal to off the charts, and her limbs once again felt like lead.

Someone lifted her arms and wrapped them around Haven's neck. "Haven is safe," Lucas said in a calm, even voice. "No one can hurt you now. Take some deep breaths so you don't pass out again," he coached, and she tried to do what he said, but her chest was paralyzed by the thought that those men had taken Bec.

"Be-be," she stuttered, trying to form the words and tell them what happened, but her panic made that impossible. She couldn't speak. Her heart felt like it was going to explode, and the dots in her vision were getting worse by the second. Burying her face in Haven's fur, she tried to breathe with him, but nothing was helping. All she could hear was the gun going off and then the way Bec's face filled with terror.

"I need to get to her." Iris heard Selina's voice, and she lifted her head to see Haven posturing to keep her safe.

"Haven, friend," Lucas said, and the dog lowered himself back to the floor and looked up at her under his bushy eyebrows.

"Iris, open your mouth. I'm going to put this under your tongue. It's an extra dose of anxiety medication." Selina held a tablet, so Iris opened her mouth without thinking or questioning. The tab went under her tongue, and she prayed it worked quickly. She had to help Bec. "Are you hurt?" Selina asked, but Iris just shook her head. "Let's get her into a chair."

Cal and Lucas helped her into the desk chair, where

Selina checked her blood pressure and pulse before handing her an ice pack to hold to the goose egg on her head. She must have hit it on the floor when she fainted.

"Did B-Bec activate her panic button?" Iris finally managed to ask.

"Not yet," Cal said, squeezing her knee.

"Zac and Declan!" she exclaimed, trying to fight her way up, but Selina and Cal held her in the chair. "They're tied up downstairs!"

"They're fine," Lucas said, moving Haven next to her and resting his head on her lap. Then he put her hand on his head and encouraged her to pet him. She did because his head was soft and warm, soothing her jangled nerves. "They're both nursing headaches from being knocked out but are otherwise okay. They said they were jumped and never saw the guys coming."

"We didn't, either," Iris admitted. "We heard a loud bang, and those guys were here before I could get anyone to answer on the walkie-talkie."

"Who are they?" Cal asked. She could tell he was trying to be patient with her, but it was hard for him.

She inhaled a deep breath as the antianxiety med started to lessen the adrenaline in her system and allowed her to think. "We don't know who they were. There were four of them, and they wore all black and had assault rifles. They wanted us to let them into the lab to get the virus because they couldn't reach Walter, and he missed their phone call or something like that." She waved her hand in the air in confusion before blowing out another breath.

"They were looking for Walter but couldn't reach him, so they came here?" Cal asked, and she nodded.

"Yes. I think Bec was going to try and trap them in the

lab, but the one guy who was mean grabbed her around the neck and wouldn't let her go. He got meaner when the other guys couldn't find the virus."

"Where did it go?" Lucas asked in total confusion.

"Bec said she destroyed all the viruses. She must have done it while I searched Walter's office for the computer."

"What happened to make you pass out?" Selina asked, squeezing her shoulder.

"He shot her!" Iris exclaimed, tears running down her face as Haven whined and put his paw on her lap. "He shot her."

Selina grasped her chin in her hand and shook it gently. "Iris. There's no blood anywhere in the lab. Are you sure you saw him shoot her?"

With great difficulty, she met Selina's gaze. Her eyes said she wasn't lying. She paused, trying to sift through the fear to find the truth.

"The gun went off," she insisted. "But I'm not sure where the bullet went, truthfully. I thought he shot her, and I passed out from a panic attack."

Lucas stood and walked around the work area while they continued to talk to her.

"Without blood, it's safe to say Bec wasn't shot," Cal said. "The question is, where is she?"

"They took her!" Iris moaned the words more than she said them. "Right before I passed out, they told her to get the parts of the vaccine that she had left because she was going with them."

"Did they say why they wanted her to go with them?" Cal asked.

She shook her head. "No, but I can only assume it's because they think she can either recreate the virus or get Walter to cooperate with them."

"Boss," Lucas called from behind her. "Found the bullet, but I don't think this printer will print another day."

"Oh, thank God," Iris said, her shoulders slumping in relief. "We have to find her!"

"We will," Cal assured her. "I'm holding out hope that she activates that panic button sooner rather than later. If only we knew how long she's been gone."

"Does it tell you what time I activated the panic button? I was probably conscious another five minutes before he fired off the shot."

"Great thinking!" Cal said, grabbing his tablet and calling it up. "She's probably been gone thirty minutes, which seems like a lot of time, but in this part of the country, you can't get far in thirty minutes. That said, we don't know what they're driving, so until she hits that panic button, we have no choice but to wait."

"What? No!" Iris exclaimed, trying to stand but being forced back into her seat. "We can't wait! We have to call the police. They can find her!"

"And what am I supposed to tell them?" Cal asked gently. "That a woman has been kidnapped, but we don't know by who, what they look like, or what they're driving? I'm confident that Bec will activate that SOS button as soon as possible. Do you know where she kept it?"

Iris's cheeks heated before she answered. "I showed her how to hide it in her bra."

"Good," Selina said, patting her shoulder. "Less chance of anyone taking that when doing a body search."

"I tried to remember what Cal taught us," Iris agreed.

"If they tied her hands behind her back, then she might need to wait until she can convince them she needs the bathroom before she can activate it. Let's be patient. If they took her and the vaccine, they want something from her, so they're not going to hurt her."

"I hope you're righ—"

Cal's tablet rang, and he glanced up at them. "Mina," he said before he answered with their traditional greeting.

"I've got a bead on Walter," she said without preamble. "His phone pinged at a cabin about thirty minutes from your location yesterday."

"Yesterday? Had it been off before then?" Cal asked, and Mina nodded. "I wonder why he turned it back on."

"For the call," Iris said without hesitation. "Maybe the coverage isn't good, and the call didn't go through, but he had to know those guys were going to call."

"I was thinking he was checking to see if the ransom had been paid early," Mina said. "What call by what guys?"

Cal filled Mina in on what had happened and that Bec was taken. "Send me the coordinates for the cabin. They're likely gone, but on the off chance they're still there, I need to check it out. Keep an eye on Bec's SOS button. If it goes off, notify me immediately, and I'll change course. Did you find a deed for the cabin? Do you know who owns it?"

"Walter," Mina answered without hesitating. "It appears he bought it last year around the same time he paid off all his other debts."

"That's not a coincidence," Lucas said, to which Cal agreed. "What direction is the cabin? His house is only about thirty minutes from here, too."

"It's south of you instead of north like his house."

"I predict we find Walter's belongings there, but he'll be long gone. Regardless, we're on our way."

"Ten-four," Mina said. "But wait, Iris, do you know if Bec has her phone on her?"

"I don't know," Iris said, leaning forward. "Let me call it."

"No!" Mina exclaimed, holding out her hand for calm. "If she has it and you call, that could alert them." She held up her finger and typed on her computer before she spoke. "I'm running a check on it. It last pinged off a tower about ten miles from your facility. Hasn't pinged since."

"Coverage out here is extremely hit and miss," Cal said.

"Or they took it from her and tossed it," Iris said, her lips in a thin line. "Come on, baby, you gotta activate that panic button."

"She will," Selina promised, squeezing her shoulder while Cal and Mina finished their conversation.

"Selina, would you stay with Iris? I'll let Zac and Declan know we're heading to the cabin. Efren and Mack are doing patrol, so I'll leave them here. Lucas will come with us."

"I'm going, too," Iris said, standing from the chair.

"That's unnecessary," Cal said, holding his hand out to her. "This is just a quick check to see if Walter is there. It's probably a waste of time, but we can't assume they're already gone."

"If he is there, I have a few words for him," Iris said between gritted teeth. "He's put Bec in danger and needs to answer for that!"

Cal held his hands out to her as though that would calm her.

Think again!

"Iris, it's better for your health if you stay here with Selina."

"I can't sit here and do nothing!" she exclaimed. "I'll stay in the car, but I want to go."

Cal's gaze darted to Selina, who shrugged her shoulder. "There's little she can do here, and it might help her anxiety if she has something else to focus on."

Cal sighed and put his hand on his hip. "Fine, but you stay in the SUV and do whatever I say without questioning me."

Iris saluted him, which lifted his lips in a half smile before he turned on his heel and headed to the stairs. She offered Selina a grateful smile before she followed, praying that they would find Walter at that cabin and the woman she couldn't wait to hold in her arms again.

Chapter Nineteen

The engine roared as the driver gunned it across the highway onto a dirt road. Bec wasn't sure how long they'd been in the car, but she was disoriented from the blindfold they'd strapped over her eyes as soon as they were out of the facility. The only part about the blindfold she liked was that it meant they didn't want her to see where they were going. That meant they didn't plan to kill her immediately. She took some comfort in that while she tried to figure out her next move.

When they pulled her out of the center, she hoped they wouldn't check her for a phone, but she should have known that was too good to be true. They chucked it out the window onto the side of the road, never to be seen again. Unfortunately, all she could think about was Iris crumpled on the ground. She hadn't seen any blood, so she didn't think she'd been shot. Sure, the megalomaniac who took her said he shot wide, but she couldn't be sure of that. Her heart had stopped beating for that moment when Iris gazed at her with so much fear and then collapsed. Was it likely she'd had a panic-induced fainting spell? Yes, but there would be that little niggle of doubt in her mind until she saw her again. If she saw her again.

No. When *I see her again.*

It wasn't easy to stay positive, but she had to for Iris's sake. There was no way she'd put her through the trauma of losing someone else in her life, not after she had been so open and honest with her. What Iris went through since she was seven was cruel and brutal. All she wanted to do was be her resting place and carry some of the burdens for her. Without a doubt, her employment at the research facility was over, so whatever she did after this, she would make sure it worked for both her and Iris. She didn't intend to give her up if they ever got a chance to be together again.

First, she had to get out of this alive. The only way to do that was to give these guys what they wanted—a deadly virus and a working vaccine. She wasn't doing the first, and there was no way she had time to do the second, which meant she had to convince them she could do both without doing either. She bit back the anxious laughter bubbling up from within as the car slowed to a stop. One of them opened the hatch of the SUV where she'd sat for the entire ride. With her hands and feet tied, it made staying upright difficult, but she'd managed by leaning against the back seat after she wedged herself into the corner. The blindfold was ripped from her eyes, which shocked her until she realized they were still wearing their masks, so she couldn't identify them. Now that they'd reached their destination, it didn't matter if she saw where they were. A quick glance out the window told her it was a small cabin in the woods.

Dragged from the vehicle, she immediately fell to the gravel driveway. "My legs are asleep," she muttered when they ordered her to get up. "I can't feel my arms or my legs. You need to untie me."

"So you can run? Not a chance in hell." The guy she had started to call RL, short for Ringleader, was the one who spoke.

"Then someone better carry me inside." Her bluster got her fireman carried into the cabin before they tossed her onto a couch, where she landed with an *oof*, shooting pains filling her body as her arms twisted painfully behind her. "Hey!" she yelled, nearly falling onto the floor. "If you want me to be able to use my arms to help you with your little problem, they're going to need to work. Can't you at least untie my wrists? If my feet are still tied, I can't go anywhere. If I don't get blood flowing in them soon, there will be permanent damage."

RL cut his gaze to her. "Fine, but don't try anything."

"Again, where am I going to go?" she asked as one of the guys closest to her snapped the flex-cuffs apart. Her shoulders screamed in pain as her arms fell to her sides, but she didn't let them see it. She just rubbed at her wrists as she leaned back against the couch to rest her tired back.

"What now, boss?" one of the guys asked.

"We bring a virus and working vaccine back to the client. I don't care how long it takes."

"How? We're missing the scientist who can make the virus." One of the guys hooked a thumb at her. "She can make the vaccine, but that's useless if we don't have the bug."

Bec cleared her throat and followed it up with an eye roll. "You realize I can create an even deadlier virus than Ignis Cerebri, right? All Walter did to get it was basic gain-of-function research. He mutated other viruses and changed their DNA profile to create something deadlier than any could be alone." She was throwing out every term and idea she could think of to confuse them in hopes they'd decide she knew what she was talking about. In truth, she did know what she was talking about and could recreate Ignis Cerebri, but they didn't know that. To them, she was a vaccine creator only.

"Wait," the ringleader said, turning to face her. "You can create the viruses, too?"

"I hold a PhD in cell, molecular, health and disease biology. Of course, I can create a virus."

"My boss wants Ignis Cerebri yesterday and is running out of patience."

She remained quiet, wondering how she would pull this off. Only Walter had the information for making the virus, and she had no idea how he did it or how long it took.

Walter!

"What if I told you I knew where to find another sample of Ignis Cerebri?"

"I'd say I'm listening," RL said, walking over to her.

Internally, she smiled. She had him right where she wanted him.

IRIS WAS MORE than pleased when she realized that Cal had an SUV rather than a UTV to ride in. She had climbed in the back and prayed that Bec would be at the cabin when they arrived. Logically, she knew that wasn't likely, but a little piece of her heart wanted to hold on to it, so she allowed it. Maybe Walter had turned his phone back on to call the guys who took Bec and they were having a rendezvous. She didn't want anyone to get hurt, but she desperately wanted to find Bec.

Cal slowed as his navigation system told him they were approaching the road where the cabin was located. He'd pushed the speedometer over eighty miles per hour to cut their trip time, but now it was time to proceed with caution and not show their hand to anyone who had Bec. Iris was hanging on to the idea that they'd taken Bec because she had the knowledge and experience to recreate Ignis Cerebri and give them the weapon of mass destruction that they'd paid for. She would never do it, but they didn't know that. Iris suspected Bec would let them think she would for as long as she had to so they could find her. Why hadn't she activated that SOS button yet?

Iris's phone started to ring, which surprised her, considering how spotty the coverage was. She saw Mina's number and answered immediately. "Secure Watch, India."

"Secure Watch, Whiskey," Mina said. "Bec hasn't activated the panic button yet, and her phone hasn't pinged again. Where are you?"

"Nearing the turnoff to the cabin," she answered, her heart sinking to know Bec was still off the grid. But then she reminded herself that those guys needed her alive if they wanted a working virus. "Would you do me a favor while we're checking out the cabin?" she asked, and Mina agreed. "See if there's a lab facility within a reasonable driving distance of where we are. Maybe a private lab or hospital?"

"To what end?"

Iris hesitated momentarily until she remembered the fear in Bec's eyes when the gun went off. "The guys said their employer had paid for Ignis Cerebri, and they'd come to collect it. We know they took her to recreate the virus, so to do that, she'd need a place to work. It would have to be somewhere with access to virus samples because she would need that to make the new one."

"I'm not sure it's possible to waltz into a lab and demand access to deadly viruses, Iris," Mina gently said. "That's not legal."

"That didn't seem to bother these guys when they broke into Bec's lab and kidnapped her at gunpoint!" Haven nudged her with his nose, reminding her that he was there and she was safe. Lucas sat beside her and squeezed her shoulder as Cal glanced in the rearview mirror. "Sorry, Mina," Iris said. "Please don't fire me."

"I'm not going to fire you," Mina assured her. "You do make an excellent point. If they want her to recreate that virus, and that's the only reason to take her, they're going to need a lab and samples to do it. Assuming they don't have their own set up somewhere."

"I hadn't thought of that," she agreed, chewing on her lower lip. "Why hasn't she activated the panic button?"

"Could be a lot of reasons," Mina said to calm her. "Give her time. Maybe she forgot about it or hasn't been able to do it discreetly yet. It can't hurt to look for labs within driving distance of the research center. I'll do that while I await your assessment of the cabin."

"Thanks, Mina," she whispered before she hung up. When she glanced up, she noticed the car was silent. "I'm sorry for yelling. I'm so worried about Bec."

"Completely understandable," Selina promised from the front seat. "It's not easy when someone you care about is in danger."

"I know it feels like we won't find her, but we will. I believe she will activate that button as soon as she can. Once that happens, we'll call the police and get her rescued," Cal assured her.

"But you said the police will just muck everything up and put people's lives in danger. We can't risk that," Iris said, grabbing the front seat.

"I did say that," Cal agreed calmly. "But when I said it, we were in a different situation. When you're talking about a hostage situation, we'll have to involve the police. There aren't enough of us here to get her out safely. We'll need SWAT, at the very least, depending on where they take her. One thing at a time," he said, turning left onto a dirt road. "Let's see if Walter is at the cabin."

"What's the plan, boss?" Mack asked from the back seat. He'd insisted on coming along for extra backup. Iris appreciated that.

It was beyond pitch-black now that they were off the highway. With clouds obscuring the moon, even the headlights barely made a dent in the darkness that surrounded them. All too soon, Cal switched those off, too. They would have to approach on foot on the off chance Walter and Zafar were at the cabin.

"From what I can see, we're about as far as we dare go with the car," he answered, pulling to the side of the road. "We all go in on foot, but Selina and Iris hang back with Haven once the cabin is in view."

"We could wait in the car," Selina suggested, but Iris objected.

"No. I want to be there if Bec is inside."

Cal shook his head. "Selina, I know your shooting skills are superior, but I don't think it's a good idea to leave you here with Iris unprotected. If it was just you, I'd say you can hold your own, but not if you're worried about her. We all go. I expect this to be a wild-goose chase, but regardless, I want you to cover the road approach while we check the cabin. If something moves, shoot it. Clear?"

"Ten-four," Selina said, opening her door.

They left the SUV, and Haven jumped down to follow

Lucas out before she and Mack followed. She took deep breaths, concentrating on the image of Bec's face in her mind after she'd made love to her. Happy. Sated. Maybe there was a touch of disbelief that they could feel that way about each other when they had just met. The truth was that Iris knew everything she needed to know. Bec was her due north, and if—no, when—they found her, she vowed to find a way to be with her. She didn't know if she could leave Secure Inc. and follow Bec somewhere else, but for the first time, she wanted to try. The thought of being without her was harder than risking everything to be with her. There was nothing she wouldn't do to hold her again. Kiss her. Touch her. Spend her life with her. Her anxiety felt manageable when she was in Bec's arms. It would never be gone, but it was as though Bec agreed to carry a little bit of it for her so she could rest for the first time in twenty-six years.

As she picked her way down the road behind Mack, with Lucas and Selina bringing up the rear, she realized the changes she'd seen in herself in the last few days were astounding. She would always be neurodivergent and have multiple disabilities because of her brain injury— love couldn't cure that, but honestly, she didn't want it to. Those disabilities made her who she was and taking them away would have put her on a different path where she may not have met Bec. Would her life have been easier? The short answer was yes, but she couldn't say that definitively. There are no guarantees in life, and anything could have happened at any time to make her life just as difficult. She thought about Bec, and the strength and fortitude required to leave her home at such a young age and trust people she had never met to keep her safe. The idea slowed her heart rate, and she inhaled deeply for the first time since leaving the car. Bec was going to be okay. She was smart and savvy, and she could think on her feet. All Iris had to do was trust her, just like she'd asked her to do before she opened that lab door.

Cal held up a closed fist when the cabin came into view, and they all stopped. Cal, Lucas and Selina dropped into a crouch, but she and Mack both had foot drop and couldn't do that. He lowered himself to the ground and sat, so she followed his lead. One light was burning from within the structure, which was clearly someone's old hunting cabin. She doubted there were more than two rooms inside, but that didn't matter if it was just a place to hide out until their gigantic payday sent them off to the tropics, never to be seen again. A car was parked to her right, and Cal motioned for Lucas to check it out.

He approached it silently, popping his head up to peer into the windows several times before he ran his hand across his neck as though to say, *no go.* It was empty.

Cal whispered. "Let's approach as though whoever is behind those doors is alive and well."

The three men walked toward the structure while Selina pulled her and Haven behind the car, her gun aimed at the dirt road they'd crept up. She planned to take Cal literally when he said to shoot anything that moves.

She heard the squeak of a doorknob and then silence. The longer there were no voices, the more her heart sank. If Bec was in there, she would have said something by now, right? But then it hit her that there were no voices, not even those of the Secure One guys.

"Secure One, Charlie," Cal said as he came around the car and picked Iris up by her waist. He ran up the road, everyone falling into place behind them.

"Put me down, I can walk," she said, confused about what was happening.

"We have four minutes to get the hell out of here before that cabin blows," he said tightly. "This is a run, not walk, kind of situation."

Before she could reply, she was shoved in the back of the SUV as everyone piled in behind her. She tried to right herself as Cal whipped the SUV and slammed the accelerator. She had no sooner buckled her seat belt than a loud blast blew her back in her seat.

Chapter Twenty

"What the hell happened back there?" Selina asked, turning to take Iris's hand. "How are you doing?"

"I'm worried about Bec," she admitted. "I have to assume she wasn't in the cabin."

"She wasn't," Cal said tightly.

Selina dug into the bag at her feet and sat up with a bottle of water and a pill.

"What's that?" Iris asked, her head cocked in confusion.

"Another dose of your anti-anxiety medication."

"I don't need it but thank you." She did take the bottle and cracked the lid, gulping some of the water. "Thanks. I haven't had anything since lunch."

"You're handling this very well. I'm proud of you."

She held her head high and made eye contact with her friend. "Thank you," she said.

"Was anyone in the cabin?" Selina asked, turning back in her seat.

"Walter," Cal said with a nod. "Another person I can only assume was Zafar. Both died relatively recently, but there were no guns, so they weren't self-inflicted or murder-suicide. It looked like they'd been surprised and dropped where they were standing. The door was still unlocked, which was how we got in."

"Anything else of interest?" Selina asked.

"You mean other than enough C-4 to blow three cabins that size?" Mack asked, to which she snorted.

"Yeah, other than that."

"There was a computer on the desk," Cal said. "It had the message up that Ace sent to the computers at the research facility. That confused me because how was there internet way out there?"

"There was coverage, though," Iris said. "Mina called me as we turned down the road."

"Maybe that's why Walter bought that cabin," Selina mused. "He knew they'd need to use a hotspot to send the message through."

"The bomb is confusing," Lucas said. "It was attached to the door, so if it was opened again, it would blow, but five minutes on a timer gives someone plenty of time to leave. Case in point, us."

"It does," Cal agreed, "but if the cabin and the bodies get blown sky-high, there's no evidence to collect even if someone does report it."

"But wait," Iris said, her mind trying to link together everything she knew so far. "The guys who took Bec said that Walter missed their call. If he's been dead this whole time, that means they didn't kill him."

"Nope," Cal agreed.

"That means there's a third player in the game, right?"

"Most likely," Lucas said. "Our guess is Walter decided to double-dip."

"Like he took the money from the employer of the guys who took Bec and then set up the ransom? But why?"

"It's possible the employer of the guys who broke into

the facility figured out he planned to double-cross him and had him killed, then sent the guys to get what he was owed," Cal explained. "We need to get back to the research facility and secure it. With Walter dead and Bec missing, it's time to call someone in to take control of it."

"Not until we find Bec!" Iris exclaimed. Haven raised his head, and she took a deep breath before speaking again. "We need to find her, and we need to find the evidence on Walter's computer that says she's not behind this. We need proof of her innocence once we find her."

Cal nodded as they neared the research center. "I've had Delilah tearing apart the computer while we were here. I'm hoping she has a report when we get back. If she doesn't, it will be your job to help her while we wait to get a bead on Bec."

Cal's phone rang, and he hit the phone button to answer it. "Secure One, Charlie."

"Secure Watch, Whiskey," Mina said. "Did you find Walter?"

"We sure did," Cal said, filling her in on their discovery. "I didn't want to call you until we were clear of there."

"I guess you can let the board president know the money won't be needed when he arrives later tonight."

"Wait, the president of the board is arriving tonight?" Iris asked from the back seat.

"Considering they currently have no one in charge of the facility under their employment, they thought it prudent to secure the viruses safely."

"There aren't any viruses," Iris said. "Bec destroyed them all once she could get back into the lab."

"Well, that's something," Mina said with a sigh. "All the same, it's their right to take control of their business."

"Did they give you an ETA?" Cal asked, checking his watch.

"His flight lands in Grand Forks at 2100 hours. It's another hour and change to the research center."

"That doesn't give us much time to find Bec, but if they kick us off the property, we'll set up a base at the motel in Sinlis Park."

"He's coming alone, so I doubt he'll kick you out unless he picks up an entire security team along the way. That said, I wouldn't talk about anything around him that you don't want him to know. I sent Delilah his name and information. It will be waiting for you to read through when you arrive. I'm also keeping an eye on Bec's panic button. So far, it's still quiet."

"Ten-four. Charlie, out."

He hung up the phone and sighed. "Just what we need. More people to muddle the mess we already have."

Lucas was on his phone and finally hung up as the lights of the research center came into view. "That was Zac. It's been quiet since we left. They're expecting us."

Iris let out a breath to hear that news. She didn't want her friends to get hurt again, and the last thing they needed was another round of unnamed goons to surprise them. Once the car was in Park, they all climbed out to stretch. Lucas and Mack stayed to fill Zac, Declan and Efren in on what happened at the cabin while Cal and Selina ushered her into the facility and up to the lab. With any luck, Delilah had found something on Walter's computer that would help them sort out who might have Bec.

That low buzzing of anxiety sat in Iris's belly as they stood in the elevator. She didn't know if it was because she was afraid Delilah hadn't found anything or that she had. Maybe her worry for Bec was catching up to her.

Once the doors opened and everyone stepped out, she held Selina back while Cal went ahead.

"I was maybe wrong to turn down that extra dose of meds."

Selina dug in her pocket and pulled out the tablet, popping it out of the packaging into her hand. "Right under your tongue. It's not a big dose. Just enough to take the edge off." She rubbed her back several times while she waited for it to dissolve. "It's only been three days since you left Secure Inc., but I can see a fundamental shift within you."

"Bec has taught me a lot about myself in a short time," Iris agreed. "Like the fact that my therapist was right all these years."

"About what?"

"That a lot of my anxiety is based on the fear of talking about what happened to me and being judged for it. When I told Bec, and she didn't judge me, it hit home that I'd had control all along."

"Wait. Bec promised me she wouldn't ask you about it."

"She didn't. It was my choice to tell her. She told me I didn't have to, but I wanted to help her understand what happened to me."

"That's impressive, considering you've never told any of us," Selina said with a head tilt.

"Let's be honest, Selina. Mina knew what happened to me thirty seconds after running a background check. You all know."

"Fair, but you've worked for Secure Watch for years and have never uttered a word to any of us about it. You've known Bec for three days. That's my point."

"When Bec trusted me with her story about leaving

the Amish community so young and how difficult that was for her, it made me want to be equally honest with her about my past. My therapist told me years ago that not talking about it allowed me to stay caught up in the fear where it felt safe."

"The fear felt safe?"

"To me, yes," Iris admitted. "At least everything I kept around me because of the fear. Some of my compulsions and intrusive thoughts were tied to keeping everything a secret."

"Do you know why?" she asked, and Iris nodded immediately.

"Fear of being judged. I think you can probably understand that, right?"

Selina's chuckle filled the hallway as she nodded. "I spent years being someone else to avoid being who I was. Granted, there was a mobster who wanted me dead, but even if that hadn't been the case, like you, I found safety in keeping my secret safe inside. Being honest meant running the risk of losing someone else in life when they learned the truth."

"Until you meet the one person who doesn't make you feel like that would happen."

Selina flashed her ring finger. "I married that one person."

"If I can find her, I just might do the same," Iris said with a grin. "I don't know how it will work, but if I ever get to hold her in my arms again, for the first time, I want to try."

"That's so wonderful to hear, Iris," Selina said. "We all deserve someone in our life who makes us feel like we can slay dragons, and if we can't, they'll do it for us."

"There's that," Iris admitted. "Since love doesn't cure my disabilities."

"No, but when it's real and true love, it doesn't care about your disabilities."

"And that's what Bec has taught me," Iris agreed. "We both know I'll always have anxiety and OCD. That's part of my brain's pathology now, amongst other things, but what she's shown me over the last few days is that my therapist was right. If I work hard, I can find a way to live my life without being on edge every second of the day. Once I put the effort in of confronting what happened to me and how it shaped me, a lot of the anxiety I carry about that event will fall away, and what I'm left with is easier to treat since my fight-or-flight response is not constantly assailing it."

"That's incredibly self-aware, Iris. Everyone at Secure Inc. will be proud of you. Bec will be, too. For putting yourself in the back of an SUV just in case you'd find her in a cabin where the risk to yourself was great. She'll be proud that you didn't give up on her."

"Never," Iris said. "But I should have realized it would get the better of me eventually. It always does."

"No," Selina said, holding her out by her shoulders. "The fact that you get up and fight every day to work and be part of our family says something else entirely. Baby steps, Iris. You're stressed in a new environment and worried about someone you care about. You're upright and fighting through it, which is impressive. I'm here for you, and I'll be here for Bec when we bring her home. We will bring her home."

Iris nodded once, the tension in her belly releasing from Selina's encouragement. She didn't have to be

afraid of being afraid. That was compounding the problem. Don't try to block the fear. Feel it and then put it to
use. She remembered the hundreds of times her therapist
told her that and suddenly understood what she meant.
Blocking out half of the fear let her focus on the part she
could do something about.

"Now, lift that chin, and let's go find your girl," Selina said with a wink as they walked into the workspace.

Chapter Twenty-One

When Iris and Selina entered the workspace, Delilah had Walter's computer open on one of the high tables with a writing pad next to it. She and Cal were conferring but turned to them when they walked in.

"Hi, Delilah. Thanks for helping with this," Iris said, hugging her friend.

"Not a problem, sweetie," Delilah promised, patting her back. "I've found some interesting tidbits I was just telling Cal about, and we both think Walter had some big plans."

"What did you find?" she asked, walking behind the table to look at the computer.

"From what I can tell, Walter had no intention of giving the virus to only the group who commissioned it."

"Do you know who that is?" she asked, and Delilah held up her finger.

"We'll get to that. I want you to read this and tell me if I understand it correctly."

"Delilah, you worked for the US Government as a cybersecurity expert. You have far more experience than I do."

"All the same," she said, motioning for her to read through a document on the screen.

"It looks like a standard contract of goods to me, with Mr. A as the buyer and Mr. W as the seller."

"Okay, that was my thought, too. Now—" she held up a finger and brought up another document "—read this one."

Iris read it several times before she flipped back to the other contract. "It's the same contract, but it just says Mr. X as the buyer."

Delilah held up her finger and pulled up yet another one on the screen. This one had Mr. L as the buyer.

"Are you telling me that Walter planned to sell Ignis Cerebri to three different people?"

"Or countries," Cal said.

"It could even be different viruses," Delilah said. "According to Cal, he had four samples in his basement freezer, correct?"

"Yes, but according to Bec, some of them were the base for Ignis."

Selina shrugged. "All that means is he had one massive bioweapon and three smaller ones."

A word fell from Cal's lips that described exactly how she felt. "That means we have three potential bad guys all looking for a virus promised to them by someone driven by greed."

"And one of them has the woman I love, so we need to tear this place apart until we find their names and where they call home," Iris said, her hands in fists at her side.

"I'd argue, but she's not wrong," Cal said. "Are there dollar values on these contracts?"

"No," Delilah said with a frown. "They read that the agreed upon fee will be paid at delivery."

"Shouldn't that be on a contract?" Selina asked as she leaned on the desk. Iris could tell the long days were catching up to them, but they couldn't stop until they found Bec.

"Oh, I'm sure it's on the final contract. This is probably an early one before all the specifics were worked out. As you see, they aren't signed."

Iris turned to Cal. "You guys went through his house, and there was nothing there?"

"Nothing," Cal said. "The place had been wiped clean other than the vials in that freezer. According to Bec, they had to remain in a deep freeze, which meant he couldn't take them with him. He probably planned to get the ransom and then return to his house long enough to get the viruses to fulfill the contracts. Chances are, the final contracts are in a safety deposit box somewhere."

"How much money did this guy need?" Selina muttered.

"But wait," Iris said, waving her hand. "There's something here that doesn't make sense, or should I say someone."

"Someone?" Cal asked, and Iris nodded.

"Bec. Why bring her in to make a vaccine when Walter knew the virus would have to go to the buyer long before she could make a working one?"

The room fell silent other than Cal tapping his fingers on the table. "Hadn't thought of that, but you're right. It doesn't make much sense to promise a virus and working vaccine to someone and then not give the scientist time to make said vaccine."

"Unless there's another player," Selina said. "A legitimate one."

"You mean one who wanted Ignis Cerebri for evil and one who wanted it for research like Bec thought?"

Selina pointed at her with a nod. "Bec doesn't know what happened before she arrived, only after. So if the original requestor of the research was dealing with Walter, it would be easy for him to see an opportunity to capitalize multiple different ways on it."

Iris considered that until she remembered something. "But Walter had that video on this computer." She held up her finger and then found it again, pressing Play for them to watch.

"Okay, but he just says to fulfill their needs," Cal said. "That doesn't mean he was referring to Ignis Cerebri. For all we know, he could have made other viruses. The video was uploaded a year ago, but we don't have the actual date it was recorded. It could have been long before he uploaded it."

"True, and if that's the case, it's safe to say they aren't the ones who stormed in here and took—" Her tablet started ringing, and she jogged to her desk to grab it.

"Secure Watch, India," she said when she saw Mina's name on the screen.

"Secure Watch, Whiskey," Mina answered. "Bec just activated her panic button. She's headed toward Sinlis Park!"

BEC LEANED AGAINST the back of the couch while she waited out her captors. They were hard at work looking for a lab to overtake so she could "do her work" with the virus. Maybe she didn't know who their boss was, but she knew they were afraid of him. They'd been clear that they'd better return with the virus and vaccine, or they would be pushing up daisies.

She couldn't figure out why Walter would promise them a virus *and* a vaccine when he knew that vaccine research takes years, not months. Sure, she'd developed one over the last five months, but it was an early attempt, and the final version wouldn't even resemble the current one by the time it was finished because that's how it worked. Trial and error. Tweaks and changes. Not that it mattered now. Ignis Cerebri was dead, and it would stay six feet under if she had anything to say about it. Thankfully, these boneheads didn't know that, so she had the element of surprise on her side. Maybe it was the element of deceit on her side, but either way, she would use it to get out of this jam. First, she had to let them get good and frustrated with finding a place for her to work.

No matter how she looked at it, she couldn't make any of it make sense. Walter was a scientist and knew how virology worked. Since none of the other scientists Mina spoke to knew about Ignis Cerebri, she could say with certainty that he didn't roll it out until she took the position five months ago. Was that on purpose? Did he want as few people as possible to know about it? Then why mention it in that interview? She thought about the date of the interview, and it hit her. That interview was long before Ignis existed. Why would he say that if he hadn't even created Ignis yet?

Her breath caught in her chest. This wasn't the first time he'd made and sold deadly weapons to people! That would explain why he went from deep debt to debt-free almost overnight. He hadn't used a prepayment—he'd used payment from selling a different virus to a different organization. Most likely, one who planned to use it for warfare. Fury rose in her chest at the man who had duped her, and at herself for being so gullible. Iris had said Bec couldn't look at it that way because she acted in good faith. That was true. She had interviewed with Walter, and the board had accepted her application and credentials, though she had never met anyone on the board. She didn't think that was unusual since they were spread around the country on each coast. That was why they had Walter in charge of the facility.

Bec realized it didn't take him long to figure out how that benefited him. He could do just about anything he wanted as long as he made it look to the board like everything was on the up and up. When no one was checking on the facility regularly, it was easy to alter paperwork and make it say one thing while you did something else entirely. That was how he had pulled all of this off. She had to give him credit if that was true. It wasn't easy to fool people in their community, but he'd done it many times over to multiple scientists. That also made her feel slightly less bad about her part in it.

What buoyed her spirit was knowing that she could do something about it now to end his reign of terror and prevent deadly viruses from falling into the hands of the wrong people. It was frightening that she even had to think that, but in the day and age of cyberwarfare and bioweapons, it was a realized fear. She shuddered to think what would have happened if she hadn't called in Secure Watch.

The thought gave her pause. Why had he let her call in Secure Watch if he was behind what was happening? Why would he demand ransom from the board when he was making millions or even billions selling viruses to terrorists? She replayed the scene that morning where Walter was "kidnapped," and it hit her. The bullet that had broken the glass in Walter's office wasn't meant to scare her off. It was meant to kill her. Calling Secure Watch didn't matter because he planned for her to be dead by the time they arrived. Secure Watch would walk in and find her on the ground, dead from a bullet, while Walter escaped scot-free. Red-hot fury filled her, and she leaned forward, ready to make her move.

"I know of a lab where I can do this work," she said, breaking into the conversation the guys were having.

RL turned to her. "Why didn't you say something before?" His tone was accusatory, but she simply smiled and shrugged.

"You'll have to forgive me, but being forcibly kidnapped and held hostage has slowed my thought processes. Listening to you just now, I remembered that the place where the viruses are also has a functional lab. It's rudimentary but more than suitable for my purposes." She leaned back smugly, though she kept her expression neutral for their benefit.

"You're bluffing," RL said. "How could you possibly know that?"

"I worked with the guy who owns the lab, that's how. I've been there. Call your boss. He knows."

All four guys glanced at each other until RL shook his head slightly. "We can't call our boss. If he finds out we don't have the virus, we'll be dead by morning, and so will you."

"Well, I, for one, want to get out of this situation alive, so I guess you're going to have to trust me with yours."

Another round of stares happened before the ringleader responded. "How far away is this lab?"

"Since I have no idea where we are, all I can say is in relation to the research center, it's about ten miles. It's in Sinlis Park."

"There ain't nothing in Sinlis Park, boss, much less another lab," one of the other guys said.

"Sometimes, sleepy little towns hide bigger secrets than you know, gentleman," she said.

"Will it hurt anything to check it out?" one of the black-clad ninja wannabes asked his leader.

"Only if it's a trap," RL answered.

"It's not," she answered immediately. "Only one other guy knows about it, and he's been kidnapped, so I assure you he's not there."

The guy turned to her slowly. "Walter Hoerman?"

"You guessed it. He has a full lab in the basement of his house. If you can get me in there, I can have your virus in a matter of hours." Man, she was rolling out the lies left and right. "I can have a tentative vaccine in twenty-four hours." Bec struggled to keep a straight face saying that bald-faced lie, but she did it. In her opinion, she deserved an Oscar.

"I know you're lying," RL said as he stalked toward her, striking fear through her. Was this it? Had she gone too far? "We searched Dr. Hoerman's house days ago."

"There was that one room we couldn't get into, boss." The goon's words made RL turn back to him. "Remember, no matter what we tried, we couldn't open that door?"

"A lead-lined door," she explained. "They're used to protect other areas of the lab, or in this case, the home, from radiation and viral escape. Very common." If she didn't stop all this lying, she would surely go to hell. It did make her wonder how Cal got into the room, but knowing Secure One, they had their ways.

"How are you going to get in, then?" he asked as if it was a "gotcha" question she wouldn't have an answer for.

"I know where the key is." At least, she suspected she

did. "Listen, we can sit here all night and debate this, but the clock is ticking, according to you, and your boss wants his virus. So, what's it going to be?"

The ringleader turned back to the other three, who were all nodding, shaking their heads and shrugging as though they didn't know the correct answer, but doing nothing meant certain death. When he turned back to her, he smiled, the whites of his teeth jarring against the blackness of his mask.

"We'll do it your way, but one trick, and you're dead. Understood?"

"Completely," she agreed, saving her smile until he turned away.

She had them right where she wanted them. She patted her chest to check on her panic button. It was ready and waiting. She'd click it as soon as they were ready to leave, leading Secure Inc. right to Walter's door. Of the five in the room, only she knew that once inside, they weren't getting back out.

Chapter Twenty-Two

Her heart pounding, Iris gripped the tablet tightly. "Where is she? Can we intercept them?"

Mina shook her head. "Not unless you know what they're driving, which we don't."

"How far out are they from Sinlis Park?" Cal asked, grabbing his phone and texting someone while he waited for her answer.

"Twenty minutes, give or take," she answered. "I don't know that they're going to Sinlis Park, but that's the direction they're heading in. Intercepting them there is easier since they have to drive through the city to continue on the highway. It's almost 11:00 p.m., so it shouldn't be hard to pinpoint them once they're going slow enough that I can give you landmarks their vehicle is passing."

"That's assuming they aren't coming here," Cal said, and Mina tipped her head in agreement.

"That seems less likely as they have to know that by now, the research center has been locked down and the cops have been called."

"Walter's," Iris said, slowly turning to address Cal. "She's taking them to Walter's."

"Why would she do that?" Mina asked as Cal pointed at the tablet in agreement.

"Think about it, Cal. You found a lab in Walter's basement. They took her so she could create a virus, but the samples here at the lab were already dead. Now she needs more samples."

"But the ones at Walter's are dead, too," he pointed out. "She had me turn off the freezer."

"But they don't know that," Iris said with a grin. "Bec knows if anyone walks into Walter's, they're not getting back out until Secure One arrives."

"You could be right," he said, grabbing the tablet from her. "Mina, don't lock that house down once they're inside."

"I thought that was the point," she said in confusion.

"It was the point when the plan was to trap terrorists, not scientists. If they think for any reason that she set them up, they could kill her. I won't risk that."

"You'd better leave now then if you're going to beat them there. I'll patch you into her GPS so you can monitor their progress or in case they're just passing through."

Cal checked his watch. "We have a few hours until the board member arrives?"

Mina nodded. "I just checked, and his flight was delayed. Why?"

"I don't have enough people here to save Bec and keep the research center covered. I'll have to pull everyone over to Sinlis Park and hope it's not a trick."

"A trick?" Iris asked, more confused than ever. "What's a trick?"

"You mean that they aren't planning to return to the research center?" Mina asked, and he nodded.

"No," Iris said adamantly. "She's taking them to Walter's."

"You can't know that for certain, Iris," Mina gently said.

"I do know that because I know her!" she exclaimed, tears pricking the back of her lids. "Bec knows I'm here, and she would never endanger me by bringing those guys back here."

Selina grasped her shoulders in comfort. "We believe you, Iris. Just take a deep breath."

"Honestly, I'm with Iris on this one," Delilah said. "She was in the room when Cal told them anyone going in wouldn't get back out. She's counting on it."

Cal nodded once. "It's decided. We're headed to Walter's," he said, pointing at the camera. "Get that GPS patched in and shut down that security system. Call the cops and fill them in, then link them to my phone."

"On it. Whiskey, out," she said, and the screen went blank.

Everyone started talking at once until Cal whistled, and the room went silent.

"I'm coming with you," Iris said.

"Yes, you are, but only because we're abandoning the center. However, you'll be waiting at the motel with Delilah while the rest of the team heads to Walter's."

"Cal, no," she started to say, but he slashed his hand through the air.

"Listen to me, Iris. You are not qualified in any way to be part of this operation, and I can't be worried about keeping you safe while trying to save the woman you so obviously care about."

"You can say it. I love her, and that's okay."

Cal held up his hand. "It's wonderful, but that doesn't

change the fact that your only experience with criminals is from behind a keyboard. When I have Bec safely in hand, Delilah will bring you over. Okay?"

She could see no point in arguing, so she nodded once. After grabbing her tablet, she followed the rest of the team to the elevator, which they rode in silence other than Cal barking orders into his phone as they descended. There was no doubt in her mind that Bec was leading those guys back to Walter's. She had every intention of being there to take her in her arms when she was freed and then never let her go.

BEC WATCHED AS the lights of Sinlis Park came into view. She was one step closer to making her way back to Iris. She just had to hold on a little bit longer. The car slowed as they pulled into town, and she took slow, deep breaths so she wouldn't overplay her hand. She had to get them into that house and get downstairs to the lab before they realized they couldn't get back out.

"You better not even think about double-crossing me," RL said from the driver's seat as he turned right and drove down the block where Walter's house sat. He drove around the block several times as all four craned their necks, looking for anything unusual.

"I have no reason to," she promised. "The sooner I make the virus, the sooner we can part ways. No one wants that more than I do." Bec said it like she believed they were going to let her go once she finished the virus. She wasn't naive. She knew they wouldn't, so she needed to lead these guys to Secure One's doorstep. She could have hit the panic button much sooner, but she had no idea how long the battery lasted on them. She needed to wait until Secure One had the best chance of finding her.

It still surprised her how well Secure One and Secure Watch worked together to protect their clients. Whether you needed cybersecurity, personal security or both, they were up for the job. Thank God for that, or this whole thing could have ended differently.

Still could, Bec. Don't get ahead of yourself.

With the reminder fresh in her mind, she took a deep breath. *Play it cool, Bec.* "If you drive around this block one more time, it's going to be you who looks suspicious," she said, hoping not to rile him up but to make him stop and think.

"She's right," the guy in the passenger seat said. "We either commit or get out of here. I haven't seen anything out of place."

The ringleader slowed the car and parked at the end of the block with Walter's house in the middle. He turned to the back seat and pointed at one of the guys. "You stay with her." Then he looked at the other two guys. "We do a sweep on foot. There's too much light here for the night vision goggles, so stay alert."

They exited the vehicle quietly with the dome light disabled so no one could see inside. When they disappeared, Bec worried her lip between her teeth as she waited. What made her the most nervous were the deadly assault weapons they still carried. If Secure One was waiting for them, someone could get hurt, and it would be on her conscience since she had led them here. At least they were familiar with Walter's house. There was less chance of an ambush when you knew the property than when you didn't, right?

"Bring her in," the radio on her guard's shirt squawked, making her jump. "Remind her if she tries anything, we know where her friend lives."

Iris.

Bec swallowed around the lump in her throat. "I'm not going to try anything. I'm not in the mood to die tonight. I just want to make your virus and get out. I didn't sign up for this when I took the job."

The guard climbed out, making a show of slinging his rifle around as he walked to the back of the SUV and opened the hatch, motioning her out. He kept his gun pointed at her as she climbed out, and then he prodded her along with it. They stayed in the shadows, but she still couldn't help but think they better hope no one was looking out a window.

Once they were around the back of the house, the ringleader let them in the back door while everyone filed in, guns pointed as they cleared the house. It was empty, which relieved and distressed her at the same time. Then again, maybe Secure One wouldn't move in until they were locked inside the house, assuring them no one could get the jump on them.

"You," RL said, pointing at her guard. "Outside on patrol. If you see any cars, report back immediately." He reached for the door, and Bec held her breath. What happened next? Did an alarm go off when they tried to leave but couldn't? Did the door refuse to unlock?

It took her more than a second to register that he'd not only opened the door and let the guy out, but no alarm had sounded when he opened or closed it. What the hell? Something wasn't right, so she had to hope and pray that her panic button had transmitted her location.

"You. Downstairs," RL said, motioning her down the stairs as soon as he flicked on his flashlight. It was treacherous, but she managed to get down the stairs.

"I'll need light if you want me to create a virus."

"Then you better hope that room doesn't have windows, or it's going to be by candlelight," he growled.

Bec grabbed the lab coat next to the door and slipped it on. It was miles too long for her, but she had to play the part. She stuck her hand in the pocket and pulled out a key.

"You mean the key was in the coat the whole time?"

"I assume so," she said, walking to the closed door at the end of the room.

He blocked her way with his gun, holding her back from the door as she put her hands up. "How did you know it was there?"

"I didn't," she said, her words wobbling slightly. "But it made sense. The first thing a scientist does is put on his lab coat, so I knew he'd have one here. Logic told me putting the key in the pocket meant he'd never lose it."

Still somewhat skeptical, he motioned at the door with his gun, so she stuck the key in and turned it, pushing the heavy door open to reveal the lab Cal had shown them. She was relieved when there were no windows in the lab. Instead, the vent of the biosafety cabinet went out the side of the house in what used to be the window. Walter really had her snowed. He cared so little about people that he endangered his neighbors with this setup. Sure, the cabinet had a filter, but filters fail, and then what? Obviously, Walter didn't care.

A small desk lamp sat on a table, and she snapped it on, taking in the room. She didn't need PPE since the viruses she'd be working with were already dead, but the meathead behind her didn't know that, so she had to make an effort.

There was a loud crash above their heads, and he turned to the door. Bec saw her chance.

"What was that?" she asked, feigning fear as she came up behind him.

"I don't know, but don't move," he said.

Too bad he didn't know she already had. There was one shot at this and one shot only, so she sent up a prayer and then grabbed the door and threw her body weight behind it, shoving him out of the room and locking herself in. She stumbled backward with a sigh and awaited rescue.

Chapter Twenty-Three

"Bec!" Iris screamed as Cal brought her out of the house. She was wearing a lab coat that made her look like she was wearing her daddy's clothes, but she'd never been more beautiful.

"Iris!" she cried, grabbing her in a hug the moment she was within reach. "Thank God you're okay. They wouldn't let me check on you after you fell. I wasn't sure if you were hit by the bullet or had just passed out from fear."

"Definitely the latter," Iris promised without releasing her. "I've been so worried but knew you could handle yourself. I'm so proud of you for playing these guys!"

Bec's laughter filtered into the ragged edges of Iris's heart and smoothed them out. They were both okay, and once they got this sorted out, they could be together. "Who are these guys? Did you find anything on Walter's computer?"

"You won't believe this," Iris said, leaning back to peck her lips with a kiss. She had to keep it short as there were too many cops around for PDA. "According to what we found on Walter's computer, there are at least three different—"

"Rebecca Roth?" someone behind her asked. Iris turned and came face-to-face with another cop.

"I'm Rebecca Roth," Bec said, stepping forward. "I suppose you have questions for me."

"You could say that," the cop said. "Turn around and put your hands behind your back." He took out handcuffs and opened them. "You're under arrest."

"For what?" Bec asked, following orders as she put her hands behind her back.

"Suspicion of murder and being an accomplice to a terrorist."

"What?" Iris asked, her voice an octave higher than normal. "You can't arrest her! She didn't do anything! This is all Walter's fault!" Strong arms grabbed hers as she was about to wade in and grab Bec away from the cop. "Let me go!" She tried to free her arms, but Cal's grip was too strong.

"Relax, Iris," he whispered in her ear. "You can't stop this from happening by assaulting a cop. That's going to land you in the cell next to Bec."

"But we can't let them arrest her! She didn't do anything, Cal!"

"We know that, but the cops know nothing right now. We need to get back to the research center and find all the information we can to prove Walter's guilt and her innocence. Without proof, they can hold her for as long as they want."

"No!" Her cry was plaintive as the cop led Bec away, sticking her into the back of a cop car. Bec pressed her forehead to the window and met Iris's gaze, fear filling her eyes. "You can't let them take her."

Cal flipped her around to face him. "Iris, listen to me. I have no control over what the police do. I'm lucky we aren't the ones in the back of the cop car. Until we have evidence to show the police that Bec had nothing to do with this, she's at their mercy. That said, if she's in a jail cell, she's safer than at the center. We still don't know who all the players are in this game, and until we do, it's better if she's tucked away under the watchful eye of an entire police precinct. Let's stop wasting time here and return to the center. We have less than an hour before the board president shows up. That's not much time to find something to prove her innocence."

"If anyone can do it, you can, Iris," Delilah said, approaching them. "But is it safe to go back there, Cal?"

"I can't answer that," he admitted. "We still don't know who their employer is, nor do we know if there's anyone else out there looking for a virus they were promised. I want you to get that laptop and our equipment out of there before Mr. McCarthy shows up. I'm sending Lucas, Selina, Zac and Declan with you two. I have to stay here until this mess is cleaned up. Mack and Efren will stay with me. The guys who took Bec are long gone, but thankfully, we have them on our surveillance to prove to the cops Bec wasn't here willingly."

"Meeting up at the motel?" Delilah asked, and Cal nodded.

"The moment you have everything cleared out, get out of there. I don't want to be there when Mr. McCarthy shows up. He's worried because no one under his employ is in charge of the center, but I'm worried he will accuse us of something far worse. Mina will keep you posted on when he's expected to arrive. You should be long gone before that time."

"Ten-four. It won't take us long to pack up the computers and get out. She didn't bring much in," Delilah said.

Cal turned to Iris. "While she's packing the equipment, I want you to grab everything from Bec's apartment. Once we get her released, there's no telling when she'll be able to return to the center for her things. I'd prefer it if she didn't have to at all. Can you do that for her?"

Iris nodded quickly, her gaze darting to the street again, where Bec was still in the car. She'd turned away and stared out the windshield, tears on her cheeks. "She doesn't have much there other than her clothes. She told me most of her personal belongings were in storage. I won't let you down, Cal."

"More importantly, you won't let her down. Now go. Time isn't on our side."

Iris darted after Delilah, her drop foot braces barely allowing her to walk fast, but thankfully, Delilah was used to it and didn't push her to move faster than she could. Zac pulled up in Cal's SUV, and they piled in before he did a U-turn and headed back toward the highway. Iris couldn't get past the tears on Bec's cheeks, and one fell down her own, which she quickly swiped away. Now was not the time to fall apart. She had to keep it together for Bec. Cal was right. She was safe, and at least in jail, no one who had a grudge against Walter could get to her.

"There has to be another vault app," she muttered, staring out the window.

"What now?" Delilah asked, waiting for her to respond. "Another vault app?"

Iris turned to her. "Walter had to have used a cloud vault. One that he could access from any of his devices. A hidden computer isn't always convenient."

"That's true," Delilah agreed. "I didn't look for cloud-based vault apps on the laptop because I was so busy with the one already on the computer."

"A red herring?" Declan asked from the front seat.

"Could be," Iris said. "Either way, that's the first thing we look for once we have the computer again."

"I have the computer," Delilah said, a cheeky grin on her face. "I stuck it in my bag when we headed to Walter's. I didn't want to risk someone else coming in and taking it when the place wasn't under our protection."

"I should have thought of that." Iris grimaced. "Thank God you did."

Delilah patted her back. "Don't beat yourself up about it. You had other things on your mind. As soon as the guys clear the space, I'll pack up your equipment while you pack Bec's stuff. We can be in and out in under fifteen."

Zac nodded from the front seat as he put the car into Park next to the loading dock. "We'll send you two in the SUV with Lucas as soon as you're ready to go. Declan and I will load up the UTVs and be right behind you. Lucas, stay with them while we go clear the place?" Lucas nodded, and the two men in the front piled out and headed toward the building, which looked completely innocuous. However, as she had learned the hard way, it was anything but.

IRIS SAT DOWN at the computer and stared at the screen, the words swimming before her eyes as they filled with tears. She couldn't do this today. She couldn't spend another shift pretending she could help people solve their cyber problems when she couldn't even help the woman she loved. Despite spending more than twenty-four hours searching Walter's computer and finding proof that he was the mastermind behind the plot, it hadn't been enough to get the woman she loved out of jail. The simple reason was that she had no evidence to prove that Bec hadn't been part of the plot. Guilty by association, Cal called it, and while no one had given up, Iris was out of ideas.

Since Bec was remanded to the FBI, Iris couldn't see her or even get a message to her. She hadn't seen her in over two weeks, and it weighed more and more on her as each day passed. She walked out onto the Secure Inc. grounds as dusk settled over them. Now that autumn had arrived in full swing, it got dark early, so as the hour approached 4:00 p.m., the sun was low in the sky as she sat on the bench that overlooked the manmade pond on the back of Cal's property. It was one of her favorite places to sit before or after a shift when she wanted to find a little Zen in a world that was often overwhelming. It was more like always overwhelming, but some days were worse than others.

That was one thing that had changed over the last few weeks. Since returning from North Dakota, she had been better able to manage her anxiety. She wanted to stay strong for Bec and dedicate herself to finding the evidence they needed to prove her innocence. When she couldn't do that, she allowed herself to fall apart but found it easier to pick herself up and start again. She kept telling herself that she would see Bec again, but each day that passed, it got harder and harder to believe. Innocent people had spent life in prison for less than what they accused Bec of doing.

Her phone rang, and she saw Mina's number on the display. With a sigh, she answered, "I'll be right in. I just needed a minute."

"I'm not rushing you," Mina said. "I was just warning you that people will be on the grounds out there, so you don't get scared if you hear someone. Why don't you take the night off? You can try again tomorrow."

"I can't keep doing that, Mina. You need me to work."

"No, I need you to feel ready to work. Until you do, we'd have to double-check your findings, and there isn't much point in that."

"You sent me out there to do a job, and I've let you down. There aren't enough ways for me to apologize for that."

"Stop, Iris," Mina said. She had the patience of a saint, in her opinion. "You don't need to apologize. You did the job we asked you to do, and you went through a lot to do it. The very least we can do is support you for a few weeks until your feet are under you again. Okay? Now, stop worrying. Enjoy the sunset and then come in and enjoy a nice dinner."

"I will. Thanks, Mina."

It was nice to work with people who understood her. Iris couldn't deny how wonderful they'd been to her since returning to Secure Inc. Somehow, she had to find a way to get her life back on track and return to work. She wasn't sure how to do that when the woman she loved wasn't by her side. In a way, she felt like she was abandoning both Bec and Secure Watch.

"You were right. This is a beautiful place for a sunset."

Iris jumped up and spun around to face the very woman who hadn't left her mind for one second of the last two weeks. "Bec!"

"Hi," she said, walking into her outstretched arms. "I've missed you, Iris." Iris wanted to speak, but the torrent of tears kept her words at bay. Knowing she needed to sit, Bec helped her to the bench and lowered her down before she knelt before her. "You're okay, sweetheart," she promised, producing a tissue from her coat pocket and wiping the tears until Iris could speak.

"You're here. How?"

"They released me this morning. I had a message to deliver to you, so I contacted Mina, who sent Zac to pick me up in Fargo."

"A message?"

"A very important one," she promised, lifting her glasses off her face to dry her eyes. Bec cleaned the lenses before she slipped them back on her face.

"You're free? Like, for good?"

"Yes," Bec promised, kissing her lips despite the salty tears covering them. "It took a while, but eventually, they cleared me."

"You don't know how hard I tried to find evidence that you didn't know what Walter was doing," Iris said, taking Bec's hands.

"Maybe I do since I know you, Iris. Also, the FBI agents told me that if it weren't for the information you found and turned over to them, innocent people would have died. You led them to the terrorists who bought the first virus from Walter. From there, Homeland Security found the boss of the four guys who kidnapped me and took him into custody."

"But there was a third," Iris said, leaning forward and squeezing Bec's hands. "There were three contracts."

Bec nodded as she stood and sat down beside her. "That's correct. Mr. A was none other than Allen Mc-Carthy."

Iris gasped. "The board president?"

"The one and only," Bec agreed.

"No wonder he was so anxious to get to the research center once he returned to the States and learned about what was happening. I never met him since Cal didn't want us in the building when he arrived."

"That was to protect Secure Inc., but in hindsight, it probably saved all your lives. They caught up with Allen this morning trying to make a run for it but were able to apprehend him on a plane headed to a country without extradition treaties with us."

"I honestly didn't see that coming. It should have been the first thing I thought of. There was no way that Walter didn't have someone on the board helping him slip all of this past the rest of the members."

Bec shrugged. "I didn't think of it, either, until after I had time to sit in jail for a few days," she admitted. "Suddenly, it made sense that there was no way for Walter to convince every person on that board to stay hands-off unless someone else was working behind the scenes on his behalf. To be clear, Allen wasn't buying viruses from Walter. The contract was for services rendered, which included manipulating the rest of the board and finding the clients who wanted to buy the viruses."

"Which is just as bad as buying them, in my opinion," Iris whispered, wiping her face again. "I still can't believe you're here."

Bec kissed her again as though she somehow understood it would help her believe this wasn't a dream. She buried her hands in her hair and let the soft locks run through her fingers. Her whimpers of happiness were only overpowered by Bec's moans of happiness. Too soon, they had to come up for air but couldn't find the strength to untangle themselves from each other.

"I've missed you so much, sweetheart," Bec said, wiping a tear from her eye. "I wanted to call you, but they refused to let me talk to anyone but my lawyer."

"I know," she said, smiling now that reality was setting in. "We talked to your lawyer, and he promised that you were okay and hanging in there. That kept me going as I searched for the answers we needed to free you. I still can't figure out who Zafar was and why they sent the ransomware to the center computers?"

Bec laughed as though that was the funniest question anyone had ever asked. "It turns out that Zafar's real name was Zafar Bolat, and he was Walter's illegitimate son. When he worked in Turkey, Walter had a fling with Zafar's mother, who never told him she was pregnant. Zafar tracked Walter down using one of those familial DNA websites. It wasn't long before Walter pulled his son into the family business of extorting money."

"Was the ransomware their escape route, or were they just greedy?"

"No way to know that for sure. My opinion is it was both. It made Walter's kidnapping appear legitimate to the board, and they'd be less likely to ask too many questions while under stress. The FBI found communication between Walter and Allen indicating they knew things were getting hot and it was time to 'get out.' That was according to the message Allen sent, which was uncovered on his phone. He was also leaving the country and would get a cut, so it behooved him to convince the board and their insurance company to pay the ransom demand. As soon as the FBI realized Allen had been in the Emirates right before he'd returned at the urgent request of Secure Watch, they started looking more closely at him as a player."

"That makes sense, but who killed Walter and Zafar? They were dead when we got there, but Cal said it hadn't been for long."

"That's a mystery I thought would never get solved until Cal told the FBI about the markings he saw on the C-4. They traced it to none other than Allen McCarthy."

"Wait. It was like a double double-cross?" Iris asked, her mouth falling open.

"It appears so, though Allen isn't talking, of course. His original flight to North Dakota was delayed, or should I say the flight he told Mina he'd be on. However, the FBI knows he flew in on a private jet, drove to Walter's cabin, and then headed to Grand Forks to make it look like he landed there from his flight. They can't prove he killed Walter and Zafar, but they don't need to. He's going to prison for a very long time, with or without the murder charges."

"Diabolical," Iris said, shaking her head. "It's over then?"

"It's over," Bec promised, leaning in for a kiss that told Iris how much she missed her. "The facility won't reopen as a private research center. There isn't an investor alive who wants to touch it now. Maybe the government will take it over, but it will remain closed until the case is cleared up."

"What will you do for work if you don't have a job?" Iris took her hands, needing the connection so her anxiety didn't spike. The thought of losing her again was just too much.

"That brings me back to the message I came to deliver," Bec said with a lip tilt.

"Oh, right! What was the message you had to deliver?"

"I love you, Iris Knowles. I don't want to spend another day apart."

"You love me, too?" she asked, lifting her head to gaze into Bec's brown eyes. She would learn to hold her gaze forever if it meant she didn't have to go another day without her.

"Too? If you're saying you love me, then, yes, I love you, too."

"I do love you," Iris said, laughing at the word salad she'd found herself making. "I never want to spend another day apart, but Bec, there's no work for you here."

The woman she loved paused long enough to bring her knuckles to her lips for a kiss. "I would work anywhere if it meant we didn't have to be apart, Iris."

"But you can't work just anywhere. You're a doctor. Your job is to help people by researching diseases and stuff, right?"

"Ultimately, yes," she agreed.

"My job here at Secure Watch can be done remotely. Did you know that? A lot of our agents work from all over the Midwest."

"Zac may have mentioned that once or twice on the ride back today, but I would never ask you to leave somewhere you're comfortable, Iris. I love you too much to ask you to be outside your comfort zone."

"Three weeks ago, I would have agreed with that, but then I met you and learned that my comfort zone is wherever you are. As long as we're together, I'll be happy and okay."

"Me, too," Bec whispered as she leaned in and kissed her passionately, making up for the two weeks they'd been separated. When they broke apart, she ran her thumb under her eye. "But, as it turns out, they need someone in the public health department in the county seat. I'd be doing important things that would impact the lives of everyone in the county, which is why I became a scientist. Maybe someday, we'll decide to move on, but right now,

I could get used to coming home to you every night to enjoy these sunsets. How does that sound to you?"

"Yes," Iris said, nodding while a giant smile lifted her lips.

"Yes?"

"Yes to sunsets, to anything, to everything, Rebecca Roth. Yes, to you and me sharing our lives together."

"I wish there was a minister here right now. That was the start of the perfect vows, Iris Knowles."

"Give me time, and I can come up with something even better," she promised with a wink.

Bec lowered her head and stopped millimeters from her lips. "Sweetheart, you can have the rest of my life."

When their lips met, the sun dipped below the horizon, and a moonbeam lit up the night to christen the first kiss of the rest of their lives.

* * * * *

COLTON'S FINAL SHOWDOWN

JENNIFER D. BOKAL

To John.
Thanks for being by my side through all our adventures.

Chapter One

Kansas Colton opened the front door of her parents' home to welcome the guests. She was happy to see the newest arrivals—her cousin Mitchell and his girlfriend, Dove. "Hey," she said, smiling brightly. "I'm so glad to see you."

It was the first Saturday in December, which meant it was her parents' annual holiday open house. For as long as she could remember, the Coltons had invited people over to celebrate all the winter holidays. As a child, Kansas had been given the job of answering the door. It didn't matter that she was now an adult and part of the Search and Rescue team for the Alaska Department of Public Safety, she was still the official greeter.

Her brother, Spence, stood at her shoulder. "Can I take your coats?"

Since the first party, it had been his job to collect the jackets and deposit them on the bed in the guest room. Even as a kid, Spence claimed that he'd been pressed into service—he was going through a pirate phase at the time—and he always wore an ugly Christmas sweater as a joke and a protest. This year, his sweater had a smiling face of Bigfoot in a Santa hat.

A gust of cold air blew past; the chill was welcome.

Beyond the dozens of guests at the holiday party, there was a roaring fire in the hearth and the room was already stuffy.

Dove slipped out of her shearling and gave it to Spence. "Thanks."

Mitchell handed over his wool peacoat. "Nice sweater. That one might be my favorite."

Pulling Kansas in for a quick hug, Dove said, "We missed you at class this afternoon."

Since Dove had reopened her yoga studio Kansas had been a regular at the Saturday afternoon practice. Namaste had been a staple in town for years and bounced back after being closed due to some recent vandalism. Tilting her head toward the living room, she said, "I was here. Helping my mom."

Dove leaned in closer and lowered her voice, "How is she?"

Kansas scanned the room. Her mother and father were chatting with Kansas's cousin Parker and his live-in girlfriend, Genna.

Genna wore a long dress with Christmas lights printed on the fabric and a Santa hat headband. She smiled at Kansas's mom, appearing to be as happy as she was festive. What's more, Kansas was happy that Genna had become a part of the Colton Clan. After Kansas's cousin Lakin left the family business, Rough Terrain Adventures, Genna had been a lifesaver. She stepped in when there was nobody available to run the front desk. She also took over all the bookings and customer service. Without Genna, who knows what would have happened to the business.

Kansas turned her gaze back to her own mother. Holding a glass of wine in a plastic cup, she laughed at something Parker had just said. "She's fine now. But earlier, Mom was stressed about getting everything done on time."

"I don't know why Abby worries. Her parties are always great."

It was true that Dove had attended several of the Colton holiday parties. The two women had been best friends in middle school, even though Dove was a year older than Kansas. "Speaking of great," said Kansas, reaching for the other woman's hands. "Look at you. You look fabulous."

And she did. Dove wore a sparkly green dress that matched her eyes perfectly. From hours of teaching yoga, she was toned. The wrap-style dress accentuated her trim waist and long legs.

"What about you?" said Dove. "You look amazing, too."

Rolling her eyes, Kansas said, "You know how much I hate getting dressed up. But this outfit is okay." For this party, she'd donned a pair of black velvet pants and short black boots. She also wore a red silk top with a neckline that was low enough to show off a little cleavage. Her hair, usually worn in a ponytail, was loose and skimmed the tops of her shoulders.

"I'm more comfortable wearing all my gear for Search and Rescue missions." Hiking boots. Gor-Tex coat. Wool socks. "But for tonight, I figured I could look a little chic."

"And sexy," Dove added with a wink.

"Yeah, well." Kansas liked the way she looked. But what had been the point? After all, there was nobody here she wanted to impress.

"Well, you look happier than the year your mom made you wear that pink dress."

Kansas laughed. "I'd forgotten about that bubblegumcolored monstrosity." She gave a fake shiver. "Just thinking about all that lace still makes me itchy."

"I'll let you two catch up," said Mitchell. "I'm getting a drink."

Her brother stood nearby. The coats were draped over his forearm. "Help yourself to whatever you want," he said before adding, "There are coolers in the kitchen."

"Can I grab either of you something?" Mitchell asked.

Kansas had been standing at the door for the better part of an hour to greet guests. She was ready for a little bit of holiday cheer herself. "I could go for a beer."

Mitchell lifted his thumb in the air, a sure sign he'd heard her over the din of voices and Christmas music.

"Well, I better go say hi to your mom," said Dove. She gave Kansas another hug and then she was gone.

Before Kansas had a chance to close the door, another couple approached. It was her cousin Eli and his new girlfriend, Noelle.

Kansas stiffened. It wasn't as if there was something wrong with Noelle. But she'd come to the town of Shelby to collect the body of her sister. Allison had been murdered by the Fiancée Killer. As if that wasn't bad enough, Kansas had been the serial killer's obsession all along. In a weird way, she felt responsible for the death.

"Hey, you two," she said. "Welcome."

Noelle's dark bangs skimmed the tops of her glasses. She gave a small smile. "Thanks for inviting us."

"How are you?" Kansas asked, not wanting to ignore everything that Noelle was going through. And at the same time, she didn't want to press for information.

"You know." Noelle gave a shrug. "Some days are better than others."

The thing was, Kansas knew about good days and

bad. Since it was discovered that Scott Montgomery—a former coworker at the ADPS—had killed six women to get her attention, Kansas had been on edge. "I get it."

Spence was back. "Can I take your coats?"

They both wore parkas in different shades of blue—deep navy for Eli and a brilliant turquoise for Noelle.

"How's Asher?" Kansas asked.

Asher Rafferty was Eli's partner in the Major Crimes Division at Alaska Bureau of Investigations—another section of ADPS. The Fiancée Killer, as Montgomery had been dubbed, detonated a bomb, and Asher had been caught in the blast. The injuries left him recovering in the hospital with a severe concussion. If she were being honest, Kansas was never completely sure how she felt about Asher. He was handsome and good at his job. But he also teased her about everything. She found that part of his personality exasperating.

Then again, he'd gotten injured working the Fiancée Killer case. So, just like what happened to Noelle's sister, Kansas felt responsible for Asher getting hurt.

"He was released from the hospital," Eli said, shrugging out of his coat. "He's been home for more than a week."

"I'm glad that he's doing well enough to leave the hospital," said Kansas. "How's he handling being cooped up at home?"

"He's pissed that he's been placed on medical leave until the beginning of the year." Eli paused and gave a wry smile. "I guess it's a good sign that he has enough energy to get mad."

"I guess," she echoed. Then again, Kansas had spent hours at the hospital sitting at Asher's bedside. While she watched him sleep, she couldn't help but wonder *What if?*

What if Asher wasn't her cousin's partner? What if they weren't colleagues? What if he didn't make her want to cuss every time he opened his mouth? "Tell him I said hello."

"You can tell him yourself," said Eli. "Your mom invited him, too. When I talked to him earlier today, he said that he's stopping by tonight."

As if they'd summoned him from the night with their conversation, Asher Rafferty appeared out of the darkness. He was six one and muscular in a lean way. His light brown hair brushed the collar of his coat. His beard and mustache looked as if they could use a trim. Then again, Asher's hair always needed a cut. His hazel eyes were bright.

"Hey, guys," he said.

"Well, speak of the devil," said Eli. "We were just talking about you."

"Oh yeah? What were you saying? I hope something good." Then he looked at Kansas and grinned. "Then again, with this one, I know it never is."

Her cheeks burned as if she'd been slapped. His offhanded comment left her throat tight and her eyes burning with anger and frustration. She wanted to yell at him, but she couldn't. Or rather, she wouldn't tell him off and ruin her mother's party.

What was the matter with Asher? It didn't matter what she said or did, he always came back with some smart-assed comment. Taking in a deep breath, she cooled the white-hot anger that filled her chest. "Spence can take your coat."

Her brother still stood nearby, with Eli and Noelle's jackets draped over his forearm.

Asher slid out of his bright red ski jacket before handing it to Spence. "Here you go, man. Do you need any help?"

"I got it," said Spence. With all three jackets in his arms, he walked through the crowd toward the back bedroom.

She watched her brother work through the crowd as Asher's comments still rang in her ears.

To her brother, he'd offered to help.

She knew Asher wasn't a misogynist.

He treated everyone with respect. Everyone except for her, that is.

What was his deal?

She drew in another long breath. Exhaling, she let go of her frustration. After all, it was a holiday party. It was the time of year to be merry. "So," she said, trying again, "how are you feeling? You look good."

"Oh yeah?" He waggled his eyebrows up and down. "I heard you visited me when I was in the hospital. I hope you didn't try to peak under my robe while I was sleeping."

Really? That's what he had to say? She'd spent hours at his bedside praying that his injuries weren't permanent. It's more than she'd do for most of her other coworkers. But he didn't care. Instead, he had to give her crap. This time, she didn't bother to tamp down her ire. "What's your problem, Rafferty?"

His jaw went slack, and his cheeks turned pale. "What? I was just joking."

"Yeah, well. I don't think you're funny." She still held the door handle. Her grip tightened until her palm bit the metal edges. She shoved the door closed. It hit the jamb with a *crack*. The room went silent. Kansas felt the eyes of each and every guest on her. Her face flamed with embarrassment, until she was sure that her cheeks matched her crimson blouse. "Sorry," she mumbled. "The wind sucked the door out of my hand."

The din of conversation grew slowly.

Asher leaned in close. His breath smelled of minty toothpaste. "I really am sorry. I didn't mean to make you mad."

She waved away his words. "Forget about it."

"I know you came to the hospital," he said as if she hadn't even spoken. "I appreciate that you were concerned."

Kansas wasn't in the mood to accept his apology. "Forget it," she snapped. "In fact, just forget about everything. Okay?"

Asher held up his hands in surrender. "Consider it forgotten."

Eli and Noelle stood nearby. The pair watched them, their eyes wide.

Great. Now they both thought Kansas was unreasonable.

"Hey, man." Eli clapped Asher on the back. "Let's go see what there is to eat. My Aunt Abby makes the best seafood chowder in the state."

Kansas could feel Asher's gaze on her face. Yet she refused to glance in his direction.

"Seafood chowder sounds great," said Noelle. Her voice was too bright and happy to be anything other than forced. "Come with us."

"Yeah," said Asher. "Sure. Whatever."

From her periphery, she watched them go. Then Kansas leaned on the door. Suddenly, the room was too hot. The air was too thick.

Mitchell returned with a bottle of beer clasped in both

hands. "I wasn't sure which one you wanted, so I grabbed two kinds."

Without a word, she accepted the seasonal ale. Lifting the bottle to her lips, she took a long drink. "Thanks, I needed that."

"I hope you don't mind me saying, but you don't look so good."

Leave it up to Mitchell—the lawyer in the family—to be brutally honest.

"The room's getting too warm," she said. "Can you watch the door for me? I'm gonna step outside for a minute."

"Are you sure that's the best idea?" Mitchell took a sip of his own beer. "Nobody's seen Scott Montgomery for a while. Who knows where he is now?"

"I don't need a babysitter," she said, her tone sharp. The thing was, she wasn't upset with her cousin. The encounter with Asher had put her on edge. She said, "I know that you're concerned about Scott. But he was almost captured once. Trust me, he's smart enough to know that everyone in town is looking for him. I doubt he's around here anymore." She took another long drink of her beer. For years, she'd worked with Scott Montgomery and never suspected that he was anything other than sweet and maybe a tad goofy. After opening the door, she placed her hand on her cousin's arm and gave it a squeeze. "I'll be careful. I promise."

Stepping into the brisk air, she let out a long breath. Maybe it was the beer. Or maybe it was the cold air. But some of her animosity for Asher slipped away. Kansas folded her arms across her chest and breathed deeply. The cold burned the inside of her nose. She exhaled in a single gust and her breath formed a frozen cloud.

Cars were parked on either side of the driveway, allowing for a narrow path up the middle. Beyond the blacktop was an expanse of trees and brush. Carefully, she walked down the drive. At the road, she paused and tilted her face to the sky.

Fat clouds floated overhead, pregnant with snow. She'd been too busy with the party preparations to pay attention to the weather forecast. Still, she could tell that there'd be a fresh layer of powder by morning.

In the tree line, a twig snapped.

Kansas turned and peered into the darkness. Trees stood sentinel around the property, grown so close together that their branches touched. She watched and waited. Nothing moved. There was nothing amiss.

Still, she called out, "Hello? Anyone there?"

Nobody answered.

Yet she had heard something.

What had it been?

ASHER LEANED AGAINST the kitchen counter, holding a paper bowl in one hand and a plastic spoon in the other. The creamy scent of seafood chowder wafted upward in a cloud of steam. He ate a spoonful. It tasted as good as it smelled.

Eli and Noelle leaned against the opposite counter and ate their own soups. "Are you sure I can't get you something to drink?" Eli nodded to a set of coolers on the floor. "Looks like there's beer, hard seltzer and wine."

Asher ate another spoonful and shook his head. "I'm not allowed to have any alcohol until I see the doctor next."

"Oh?" said Noelle. "When's that?"

"I have an appointment after Christmas." Asher didn't want to talk about his injury or his recovery. Something else was on his mind. "Do you think Kansas was really mad at me?"

Noelle bit her bottom lip and glanced at Eli. His work partner shrugged. An unspoken conversation was happening between the couple.

He asked, "What is it that you two don't want to say?"

"You know," Noelle began, "we saw her at the hospital while you were still unconscious. She seemed really worried. Teasing her like that might've hurt her feelings."

"But it was just teasing." He wasn't ready to admit that Noelle was right. "I rib her all the time, and she gives me grief in return. It's our little dance." Without warning, an image flooded his brain. Kansas was in his arms as they swayed to music that only they could hear. He shoveled another spoonful of soup into his mouth. It burned. But he didn't mind the pain. It gave him something else to think about other than Kansas.

"I know you try to joke around with her," said Eli, "but she hates it."

Crap. How had Asher never known? He liked their playful banter. Hell, he thought that she enjoyed it, too. What's more, Kansas gave as good as she got—so, it was never like she lost an argument or anything.

Then again, maybe he should've guessed that Kansas didn't think he was funny. She'd never laughed at his jokes...

Realization, a punch to the chin, hit him. Had he really been acting like an ass for years?

"I never meant to hurt her feelings," he began. Even in his own ears, his excuse was lame. The soup sat in his gut like a rock. The last thing he wanted to do was upset Kansas. He set the bowl on the counter behind him. "I should probably say something to her. Clear the air, you know."

"Good idea," said Eli.

A doorway from the kitchen led directly to the living room. From where he stood, Asher couldn't see Kansas— her dark hair, so shiny it reflected the overhead light. Or her eyes that were the same icy shade of blue as Shoup Glacier. Or that red silk top that dipped so low he could see the top of her breasts.

After working his way through the crowd, he stopped at the door. Mitchell Colton leaned against the wall, drinking a beer. "Hey." Mitchell lifted his chin in greeting. "How are you feeling?"

Asher ignored the question. "Where's Kansas?"

"She went outside. Said she needed some fresh air."

"Outside?" His pulse spiked with anxiety at the thought of her being alone. Scott Montgomery could be anywhere. Asher's head started the throb—a symptom of his concussion, no doubt. Although, he knew different. He was worried about Kansas. She shouldn't be alone. Scott was a dangerous man, and Asher had the injuries to prove it.

Without another thought, he opened the door and stepped into the night. He recalled how easily the door slammed earlier and took care to close it slowly. On the stoop, the cold slapped him in the face. He sucked in a deep breath. But he saw Kansas standing at the end of the drive. Even in the dim light, she was unmistakable. The fantasy of dancing with her came to him again.

Maybe that's why he didn't notice the other figure right away. Tucked between two SUVs was the shadow of a person. Maybe it was another guest arriving for the party. But then, why were they only watching Kansas?

Asher stepped off the porch and began to walk down the side of the driveway. The person didn't move. They didn't hear his approach. As he got closer, he could see more details. The person was tall and lean. He was pretty sure they were male. The height and build were both right for it to be Scott Montgomery. Had the killer come back?

Asher swallowed. He was on medical leave. Protocol dictated that he should call for backup. But hesitating could be the difference between catching the killer and letting him go free. Stepping into the shadows of other cars, he approached the man.

That's when the figure stepped out from behind the SUV. They glanced over their shoulder and froze. Asher still couldn't see any facial features. But he could tell that the guy was staring straight at him.

There was no point in being sneaky now.

"Hey, you," he called out. "I want a word."

From where she stood at the end of her driveway, Kansas turned to look.

The man tensed before sprinting into the tree line at the side of the drive. Asher decided to run after the guy even before he started moving. Weeks of bedrest had left his legs heavy and his joints sore. His lungs burned and there was a pull at his side. Yet he kept moving.

"Stop." Kansas's single word rang out like a shot. "Alaska Department of Public Safety."

He could hear her breath coming in ragged gusts as she closed the distance between them. Then she was at his shoulder. He wanted to turn and look at her, but he dared not take his eyes off the stalker. The guy was faster than them both. He extended his lead and seemed to melt into the trees. For a moment, Asher could see a darker shadow against the dark night.

Then there was nothing.

As if the woods had swallowed him whole, the stalker was gone.

Chapter Two

Asher kept running, even though it felt like his chest was filled with broken glass. Kansas, sprinting at his side, matched him stride for stride.

"Where in the hell did he go?" he wheezed. "Do you see him?"

She slowed her sprint to a jog. He kept his pace with hers. Using a bottle of beer to point, she said, "There's a trail leading to the street that way."

He knew what she was thinking. Whoever had been watching Kansas had parked a vehicle on the roadway. Not for the first time, he wished that he had a sidearm. But he'd had to give that up until the symptoms of his head injury subsided. Nobody wanted a trooper with double vision to fire a weapon—least of all Asher.

He doubted that Kansas had a gun on her either. After all, she was at her parent's holiday party and wouldn't need to be armed. "Let's check it out."

They moved through the forest. Soon, Asher spotted the narrow track that wound through the undergrowth. For several minutes, they walked without speaking. It was prudent to be quiet and Asher was fine with the silence. His pulse had yet to slow, and his chest was still tight.

"We aren't far from the road." Using her bottle, she pointed again.

Asher could see an opening in the trees and a strip of pavement just beyond the gap. He knew that the stalker was close. "You wait here," he said, his voice not much louder than a whisper. "It might be dangerous."

"Dangerous." She huffed out a breath. "I'm not the one of medical leave."

Kansas stepped around him. Without making a sound, she walked toward the trailhead. Asher wanted to argue. But what was he going to say? Instead, he followed.

As they came to the roadway, a dark sedan roared past. It was gone as quickly as it had arrived. Asher didn't get a chance to see the make, model or even figure out an exact color. Where the manufacturer's emblem should be, there was nothing. The license plate had also been removed. The driver wore a black hoodie, pulled in around his face, and dark gloves.

Kansas ran after the car. As the vehicle sped away, she threw her empty bottle. It hit the road and shattered. "Bastard," she grumbled.

Asher waited as she walked slowly back to where he stood.

"Did you see who it was?"

Kansas shook her head. "No. Did you?"

He hadn't seen anything other than a shadowy figure on a dark night. And yet, he had his suspicions. "It was Scott Montgomery."

She turned to look at him. "You know that. Or are you speculating?"

"It's more than a guess. The height. The build. The way he moved. The fact that he was fixated on you."

"That's not conclusive." She began walking down the road, heading back toward her parents' house.

Jogging to catch up, Asher said, "It's enough. If dispatch got a call with what we saw, they'd send out investigators."

Kansas shrugged. "You might be right."

Patting his front pockets, Asher searched for his phone. Then he remembered. Damn. It was in his coat, which was back at the party.

"Do you have your cell?"

Kansas opened her arms. The fabric of her shirt stretched across her breasts. He wanted to stare but knew he shouldn't. As he dropped his gaze, she said, "No phone on me."

"We have to call this in when we get back to the house." He paused, knowing a better way to handle the stalker. "Or just tell Eli when we get back."

"I'd hate to ruin the night for him. It'll ruin Noelle's night, too. She needs a little cheering up."

"Ruin the night?" Even Asher could hear the incredulity in his own voice. "Scott Montgomery is back. That kinda ruins a lot of things for a lot of people."

"We're still guessing that Montgomery is back," said Kansas, her words coming out as a frozen cloud.

Asher's fingers were numb. He shoved them into the front pockets of his jeans, trying to collect as much heat as he could. It didn't do much good. Instead of warming his hands, his thighs ended up cold. He continued to walk, thinking through what he wanted to say next. "Even if that guy wasn't Scott, it was some creep who was watching you from the woods. If I hadn't shown up when I did, who knows what would've happened?"

"I would've coldcocked the bastard with my beer bottle."

"I imagine you would have." Asher smirked at the irony. While running after a stalker, she hadn't even dropped her drink. He wasn't sure if she'd purposely brought it with her—a single weapon. Or if, in the moment, she never thought about throwing it aside. "And to think, I came out here to apologize for hurting your feelings."

Cupping a hand around her ear, she said, "My hearing must be going. I thought you said you wanted to apologize."

"Har-har." He faked a laughed. "I'm trying to be nice and you're being a smart-ass."

"You're being nice to me?" Kansas gripped her chest, in mock cardiac arrest.

That's when it happened. Her hands were on her heart one minute and the next, they were whirling through the air as she tried to keep her balance. Asher didn't think, he just reacted. Reaching out, he grabbed her waist. He pulled her to him and kept her steady.

Kansas was pressed against his chest. Her breath was hot on his shoulder. He could smell the floral scent of her shampoo. He inhaled her scent, and his pulse took off like a rocket. It felt nice to hold her—too nice, in fact. She was long and lean, but somehow soft. In short, she was everything he wanted in a woman. More than her looks or how amazing she smelled; Kansas was smart and competent. But she was also Eli's youngest cousin and that meant that she should be off-limits.

He still felt bad that he'd hurt her feelings. But he knew why he teased her so often. The animosity created a little distance, but also friction. It was the kind of back and forth that lit a fire inside Asher.

The thing was, after being caught in the blast of the

house bomb, he knew that life was short. It meant that he had to live each moment to the fullest. While lying in his hospital bed, Kansas came to mind more than once. As he recovered, he decided to take his shot and see if they could be more than coworkers.

Was now his moment?

"Thanks for saving me from busting my butt," she said, her voice soft. "I think I stepped on some ice."

Let her go, Asher. Just let her go. But his arms wouldn't loosen. His body craved her touch. Instead of doing what was right, he said, "It is cold. Nice night to snuggle up by a fire."

Not his best line, but it was a place to start.

She ran her teeth over her bottom lip and gazed straight into his eyes. She really was beautiful. "It's the perfect night for that kind of thing," she said.

Did she want to snuggle up with him? Well, if she did, he didn't mind.

As they stood in the middle of the road. Fat snowflakes began drifting lazily from the clouds. His hands were on her waist. Her fingers were laced behind his neck. Kissing her would be the most natural thing in the world.

But the glow of headlights cut through the gloom.

Had the stalker come back?

KANSAS STOOD ON the road. Her arms were wrapped around Asher's neck. His hands were on her waist and his fingertips dangerously close to touching her butt. She wanted him to kiss her. Hell, her lips already tingled with the feeling of his mouth on hers. But as the glow of headlights cut through the night, she knew that pursuing anything romantic with a fellow trooper would be a mistake.

She stepped out of the embrace and onto the gravel shoulder.

"Be ready." Asher situated himself between her and the road. She placed her hands on his shoulders. His muscles were tense and ready for a fight. "If he's back, you need to run. Go through the woods and back to your parents' house. Don't wait for me."

The thing was, Kansas was capable of taking care of herself. Yet she found Asher's fierce protection to be endearing. She looked at the lights. "I don't think it's the stalker. He drove a sedan. These beams are too high."

Asher's shoulders relaxed. "You're right. I think it's a white SUV."

She could see the color of the vehicle and the profile of the driver now. "That's Hetty," she said, mentioning her brother's fiancée.

"Still, we have to be prepared for anything."

The vehicle slowed as it approached. The passenger window lowered with a whir and the SUV came to a stop. Hetty sat behind the steering wheel. Her curly hair was pulled into a bun at the back of her neck. She wore a suit of blue velvet that gleamed in the lights of the dashboard. Leaning on the center console, she asked, "Hey, you two. Everything okay? Need a ride?"

Without Asher's arms around her, Kansas was cold. The interior of the SUV was warm and inviting. She gave an involuntary shiver. "A ride would be great."

Asher reached around her and opened the passenger door. Honestly, she wasn't sure what to make of this new chivalry. Still, she gave him a smile before sliding into the seat. "Thanks."

"Not a problem," he said before closing the door.

Using a toggle on the armrest, she raised the window.

Asher got into the back seat, settling into a second-row captain's chair.

"Thanks for stopping and offering us a ride," said Asher. "It's only a mile back to the party. In weather like this, it'd be a long walk."

"Obviously, I was going to stop," said Hetty.

For a moment, nobody spoke. Kansas assumed that Hetty was waiting for the story as to why she and Asher were standing on the side of the road and in the freezing cold, no less. The thing was, Kansas wasn't sure what to say. Certainly, there'd been someone in her parent's driveway who ran off when confronted. But who was it and what did they want?

After a moment, Hetty tried again, "I'm glad I found you, Kansas. I wanted to talk to you about something before we got to the party."

"Oh?" That was unexpected. "What is it?"

Hetty's eyes flicked to the rearview mirror. She didn't want an audience for whatever she wanted to say. As Kansas gazed out the window, a million different problems came to her at once. Had Hetty changed her mind about the wedding? If she had, Spence would be crushed. Hell, everyone in her family would be devastated. They all loved Hetty.

"Is everything okay?" she asked without looking at her future sister-in-law.

"Yeah. Of course." She shook her head. "It's just a silly girl thing."

Then she glanced in the rearview again.

"Don't worry about Asher," said Kansas. True, she wanted to know what Hetty wanted to discuss. But she also knew that once they got back to her parents' house and told everyone about the stalker, all hell was going to break loose. Even if the trespasser wasn't Scott, there had been someone on the property. After that, who knew when she and Hetty would have a chance to talk again? "Just pretend he's not here. I do it all the time."

Sure, Asher had apologized for teasing her. But it was also true that old habits died hard.

From the back seat, Asher chuckled. "Yeah, I forget where I am sometimes and that was even before the explosion."

The sound of his laughter landed in her middle, warming her on the inside. She could still feel where he'd placed his hands on her waist. Feel his breath as it washed over her cheek. Her face flushed with desire. Thank goodness the inside of the car was dim and nobody could see her blush.

Maybe she'd been too hard on him all these years. He was a good-humored guy and got along with everyone— well, everyone except her, that is.

With most people at work, she was able to give a joke and take one, too. But Asher had always been different. She'd wanted him to like her. The fact that he teased her relentlessly left her off-balance, irritated, and feeling as if she could never be good enough.

Maybe Asher wasn't the whole problem.

Maybe the real reason she was always upset by his teasing is that from him, she wanted more...

"Well," said Hetty slowly, drawing Kansas out of her thoughts. "Spence and I are getting married soon."

The couple planned to hold the wedding on New Year's Eve at RTA. Since they both worked at Rough Terrain Adventures, it was the perfect place for the happy couple to hold their ceremony. "I'm excited—but not as excited as my mom. She already planned the menu for the reception." Kansas wasn't much of a cook. And yet, she asked, "Is there something else I can do?"

"Actually, there is." Hetty looked at Kansas. "Would you be my maid of honor?"

Love for her brother and his future wife filled her, leaving her lightheaded. "Of course I'll be your maid of honor. I'd be, well, honored."

"Okay, then, it's settled. I'm so happy you said yes."

From the back seat, Asher faked a sob. "I'm just so excited, I'm emotional."

Kansas turned in her seat and glared at him. "You can stop being a jerk anytime, you know."

"The fact that I'm a jerk is one of the things you love about me," he said. "Admit it."

Again, she could feel the whisper of his breath on her skin. The pressure of his hands around her waist. She had to ignore more than his comments, but the spark of desire had been ignited in her chest.

"So, what should I wear?" she asked Hetty. "I know your colors are green and silver. Oh, and if I'm the maid of honor, we have to have a bridal shower. Saturday afternoons are usually best. What day works for you?"

Hetty smiled as she turned up the driveway to the Colton family home. "As far as what you wear—anything is fine with me. I just want you by my side when I marry your brother. And a bridal shower sounds nice. I don't really have anything planned for the next couple of weeks, so pick a Saturday and I'll be there."

That was one of the things Kansas appreciated about Hetty. She was a no-nonsense kind of person.

A long line of cars lined the driveway leading to the house, forcing Hetty to park near the road. She eased off the pavement and turned the ignition key, stilling the engine.

"Thanks for the ride," said Asher. "If it weren't for you, we'd still be freezing our butts off."

Hetty unfastened her seat belt and turned to face him in the back seat. "I never asked. What were you two doing outside, anyway?"

"It was Scott Montgomery," said Asher. "He was stalking Kansas."

"Oh my gosh." Even in the dark, she could see that Hetty's eyes were wide. "Are you okay? What happened? Where's Scott now?"

"We don't know that it was Scott." Annoyance ran like a river of lava through Kansas's veins. Despite the cold, she started to sweat. "And I don't want to get people all upset over nothing."

"Nothing?" Even she could hear the disbelief in Hetty's tone. She opened her door. A gust of wind blew through the cabin. Kansas shivered with the chill. Hetty continued: "Knowing that Scott Montgomery came here isn't nothing."

Asher opened the rear door and stepped onto the driveway. "I agree with Hetty."

Hetty slid from the driver's seat. "Is Eli here already? You need to tell him what you saw."

They both closed their doors, leaving Kansas sitting in the dark and cold interior. It left her with nothing to do other than exit the vehicle herself. She stood on the pavement and folded her arms over her chest. It was more than the cold. Her annoyance with Asher was still fresh. "You go up to the house, Hetty. I need a word with Asher before we go inside."

Hetty paused a moment before saying, "Yeah. Sure."

As her future sister-in-law began trudging up the drive, Kansas called out, "Thanks for asking me to be your maid of honor. I really am flattered."

Hetty stopped and turned to face Kansas. "I was think-ing. Maybe we should hold off on the wedding. If Scott Montgomery has come back, a big party might not be the top priority."

"Oh, no. I'm not letting you cancel your celebration because of me."

"Not cancel. Just postpone."

"I don't want you to do that, either," said Kansas. She smiled, despite her rising anger at Asher. "We'll talk as soon as I get inside."

She waited a moment for Hetty to climb higher up the driveway. Then she turned to face Asher. She asked, "What the hell, man?"

"What the hell *what*?"

"Don't play dumb with me, Asher Rafferty. I happen to know that you are a smart man."

"I'm not playing at anything. I just don't know what's gotten you all upset."

"You can't keep telling people that we saw Scott Mont-gomery. Especially since we don't know if it's true."

He held up his hands and took a step back. For a mo-ment, she thought he was about to surrender. "I don't get you. Montgomery killed six people already. I would've been victim number seven, except I got lucky. So did Eli."

She knew what he was getting at and struggled for a reply. Nothing came to her.

He continued: "I've known you long enough to know that you feel responsible for everything Scott's done. But all that carnage is on him. It's got nothing to do with you."

"It has everything to do with me," said Kansas without thinking through what she was saying. "If it weren't for his obsession with me, all of those people would be alive."

Asher shook his head. "There's something inside him

that's broken beyond repair. If it wasn't you, he'd find something else for a fixation. But in dismissing his threat, you don't make other people safer. I know you know that."

Everything Asher said was true. "I hate being the victim."

"C'mon." Wrapping his arm around her shoulder, he led her up the drive. "Let's get inside and talk to Eli. He'll come up with a plan as to what we do next."

She found herself leaning into Asher's side for warmth and support. "Just do me one favor. Let me tell everyone what happened. I promise not to leave out anything important."

They stopped on the stoop. "I won't say a word, so long as you tell Eli now."

To do anything less would be a public disservice. She reached for the handle. "I'll talk to Eli as soon as I find him."

Kansas opened the door. A wave of warm air crashed over her as she stepped inside. She expected the room to be filled with voices and music and laughter. But it was eerily silent. She crossed the threshold as everyone watched her walk inside.

Hetty stood with Spence and Eli. Her brother's brow was drawn together in concern.

Kansas didn't need to work for the Alaska Bureau of Investigation to figure out what had happened. Hetty had shared the possible Scott Montgomery sighting with Spence. Then Spence immediately told Eli. After that, word had spread. It was the proverbial spark to dry grass, and now the party had gone up in flames.

Kansas's mother, Abby, was the first to speak. "There you are." She crossed the room. Her red plaid skirt swayed with each step. She pulled Kansas into a hug.

Her mother's arms were warm and reassuring. "I heard what happened…" With a shake of her head, she let her words trail off.

"I'm here, Mom. I'm okay." But what if Scott Montgomery had come to her parents' home? What if he had been watching her from the woods? What if Asher hadn't come out when he did? She pulled away from the embrace. "It's all thanks to Asher, though."

Abby rubbed Asher's shoulder. "You two are freezing. Let's get you something warm to eat and drink."

Kansas's father grabbed her hand and gave it a squeeze. It was obvious that her mom had chosen his outfit for the party. He wore tan slacks and a shirt with the same plaid as her skirt. "I'm glad you're back. There's mulled wine and more chowder."

Eli spoke. "I'd like to speak to Kansas and Asher first."

"Well—" Abby herded the trio toward the kitchen "—talk in there. Get something to eat at the same time."

Kansas reached for her mom's hand. "I'm sorry about the party." Certainly, all the guests would be gone once she was done talking to Eli. "I hate that everything got ruined."

Her mother rubbed a circle on her back, just like she did when Kansas had been a little girl. "Everyone understands and we all just want you to be safe."

She didn't recall walking the rest of the way into the kitchen. Nor did she remember who handed her a bowl of soup or a steaming cup of mulled wine. Kansas leaned against the counter, and she took a sip of the spicy wine. But she knew that everything was about to change.

"What happened?" Eli asked.

Asher stood at her side. Like her, he had a bowl of seafood chowder. Instead of wine, he had a cup of coffee. Lifting a spoonful of soup to his lips, he blew on the steam. "You tell him."

Of course it was what she'd asked him to do. But now, she couldn't find the right words. "I'm not sure where to start," she said.

"My suggestion is the beginning," said Eli. "You were on greeter duty, like always. Why'd you decide to go outside?"

She glanced at Asher. "I was upset. Overtired. Over-heated. I just needed a little break from everything." Once she started telling the story, she couldn't stop. She filled in Eli how she'd been drinking her beer and watching the sky. How Asher had yelled, and that's when she turned around. She told him about the man clad in a black hoodie with the hood pulled up, watching her. How the man had run into the woods once he knew he'd been spotted. The fact that Asher had run after him. And that Kansas had gone after the guy, as well. She also mentioned the dark sedan without a license plate that sped by.

By the time she was done, Eli was pale. "Christ. Why didn't you call it in? Or call me directly?"

It was Asher who answered. "Neither one of us had our phones." He shoveled a spoonful of soup into his mouth and swallowed. "There is one important detail she missed."

"Oh?" Eli looked back at Kansas. "What'd you forget to mention?"

She let out a long breath before taking a sip of wine. "We never saw the guy's face. But his build—height and weight—are consistent with Scott Montgomery."

Dragging his hand down his face, Eli cursed. "There's no question in my mind. Scott Montgomery is back. And, Kansas, he's coming for you."

Chapter Three

For Kansas, the next ninety minutes passed in a blur of activity. All the party guests had gone home. The only people still at the house were Spence and Hetty, Eli and Noelle, her mom and dad, Asher, and of course, Kansas.

Using her parents' living room as a makeshift headquarters, Eli had called in a team of investigators to look for Scott Montgomery or the dark sedan. A public service announcement had been released with a warning that the killer had been seen. There was also information about his vehicle. People were urged to stay inside.

Sitting on the sofa, Kansas watched them work. She wasn't convinced that Scott was back, but she understood the alarm. Still, she said nothing.

"Now," said Eli, "the last thing we need to do is find a place for you to stay. You also shouldn't go back and forth to work."

Kansas looked at her cousin. "Me?"

"You can't go home," he said. "It's not safe to be by yourself."

"She can stay here," said her dad. "I'm retired. I can hang out at the house with her."

The last thing Kansas wanted was to be back in her

parents' home and be treated like a kid. But there were other reasons she didn't want to be at her parents' home, as well. "If it was Scott who was watching me, then this place isn't safe, either. He obviously knows where you live and could easily suspect that I'd be here. He might come back." The possibility that Scott Montgomery had actually returned to Shelby hit her like a punch to the chest. It stole her breath. Her eyes stung with tears she refused to shed. Kansas rubbed her breastbone. "I'm not putting you or mom in any more danger."

"That's sweet of you." Her mom dropped onto the cushion beside where Kansas sat. Abby pulled her into a hug. "But we're the parents. It's our job to protect you."

"We don't have any outings scheduled until after the New Year," said Spence. "I can stay here, too."

The offer to be with her family was tempting. But she wasn't ready to give in just yet. "What are my other options?"

"We can get you on a plane to Anchorage," Eli suggested.

"What would I do in Anchorage?"

Rubbing the back of his neck, Eli said, "I'd suggest that the ABI put you in protective custody. You can stay at a hotel. Binge-watch holiday movies. Order all the room service you want."

"Protective custody is still custody," said Kansas. "It doesn't matter how nice the jail is, I'm still going to be locked up."

"It's a hotel room," Eli corrected. "Not a cell."

For her, it amounted to the same thing. Neither choice was palatable, which meant she really didn't have any options.

"I have a thought." Asher sat in a recliner. During the

last chaotic hour and a half, he hadn't said anything to Kansas. But he had been consulting with Eli. Despite being on medical leave, he'd made several phone calls to surrounding communities and warned their local law enforcement about the Scott Montgomery sighting. "What if Kansas returned to her home."

"No way," said Eli, interrupting whatever Asher was going to say.

Holding up his hands, Asher continued, "You didn't let me finish, man. She can go home and have someone with her for protection. They can also set up a security system."

Eli let out a long breath. "Anyone you have in mind?"

Asher shrugged. "I can do it."

"You? You're on medical leave."

"Precisely. That's why I'm perfect for this assignment," Asher said. "I don't have any other duties. In keeping an eye on Kansas, I'll get to stay involved in the case."

"Having someone from ADPS stay with her is a good idea." Eli shook his head. "But I don't know if you're the best choice."

Asher asked, "Why not?"

Kansas couldn't tell if the indignation in his voice was faked or real.

"Well—" Eli paused a beat "—you two never seem to get along."

"What do you think?" Asher asked. "Can we get along, at least for a little while?"

A big part of Kansas wanted him to stay with her—and it had nothing to do with being safe. It was all about the fact that she was a woman, and he was a handsome man. Then again, if she put all of that aside, Asher's plan made complete sense.

"I know you," she said, speaking to her cousin, Eli. "You'll get every trooper hunting for Scott."

"I will," he agreed.

"Which really doesn't leave anyone else to provide me with security, other than Asher." Even as she spoke and knew what she was going to say next, she had to wonder if it was a mistake. She remembered the strength of his chest as he held her close. The memory of his breath, hot on her neck, was as real as the room in which she now stood. "I think we'll be fine. Our bickering notwithstanding, I know that he's a true professional and I'll be in good hands."

But was this really the best solution?

Being distracted by Asher wasn't something she could afford—not when the stakes were so dangerous and deadly.

ASHER STOOD IN the backyard of Kansas's home. She lived in a two-bedroom ranch-style house in one of the more established neighborhoods of Shelby. Holding a flashlight, he shone the beam on a window. The screen was intact. The frame wasn't damaged. He continued to walk the perimeter. A steady snow fell, blowing flakes down the collar of his jacket. He ignored the cold and checked two more windows. At the back of the house, he met up with Eli.

"Nothing out of ordinary here," he said.

"I didn't see anything suspicious, either," said Eli.

Together, they walked to the front of the house. The snow was falling faster now and had already filled in the footprints he left only moments before.

Kansas had left her vehicle at her parents' house. Eli planned to have it towed to the crime lab. Scott might've tampered with her car, and it wouldn't be safe to drive until it was checked. She now sat in the passenger seat of Hetty's SUV. Kansas's brother was behind the steering wheel. A cloud of exhaust billowed behind the vehicle. The dashboard lights glowed, bathing Kansas in a silvery light. It made her look ethereal. Asher's hands itched with the need to hold her again.

He'd always liked Kansas.

She was dedicated to her job and passionate about her work. Kansas was smart, spunky, and beautiful. So, even though they butted heads from time to time, there was a lot about her to like.

No, his feelings were more complicated than liking her.

He found her both endearing and infuriating. Now he was about to stay with her for several days. He was responsible for her safety. But with such convoluted emotions, he had to ask himself a simple question. Was he really suited for the task at all?

He now knew how it felt it hold her—and damn, it felt good.

Great, really.

Would he be able to compartmentalize his attraction to Kansas to keep her safe? If it was any other person on the planet, he'd talk with Eli about his problem. But admitting that he was attracted to Kansas would cause a whole different set of issues.

Shoving his hands deeper into the pockets of his coat, he shuffled through the snow. Spence rolled down his window as he and Eli approached. "How does it look around back?"

Eli held out a hand. Within seconds, snow covered his gloved fingertips. "With all this," he said, "it's hard to tell if anyone had been prowling around the house. But nobody tampered with any of the windows, so I don't think Scott tried to get in. We'll do a sweep inside and come back to get you."

Asher said nothing. After all, he was on medical leave and Eli was the one running the show. But he didn't like Kansas sitting in a car with only her brother as protection. Then again, he figured it'd be pretty damn hard for anyone to force her from a locked vehicle—especially since both the driver and passenger had brought firearms with them from Ryan's gun safe.

"Hey, Asher." Kansas rolled down her own window. A key ring dangled from one finger. "You probably need these. The house key is the silver one."

He walked to her side of the SUV and held out his hand. Her fingers pressed into his open palm. A current of electricity shot up his arm. His pulse spiked and his mouth went dry. He shouldn't be surprised by his reaction. Yet, he was. How long would it take for him to get over the thrill of simply touching Kansas? "Thanks," he mumbled.

Dual sconces were attached to a brick wall on either side of the door. Eli was already waiting for Asher on the stoop. The first thing he did was examine the lock. She had a typical setup—a lever handle with a cylinder lock—and something that could easily be picked. She also had a dead bolt, which was better for security.

He pushed down on the handle to make sure it was still locked.

It was.

After inserting the key into the keyhole, he pushed down the handle. The door swung open.

"I don't like that the dead bolt isn't engaged," said Eli.

He wore a holster on his belt and removed his Sig Saur. "You wait here."

Asher wasn't the type to stay outside and let his partner take all the risks. "I'm coming with you."

"You're on medical leave. Plus, you aren't armed."

For a moment, Asher thought about getting a gun from Spence or Kansas. But they were wasting time by standing outside and arguing. "I'm not letting you go in alone. If Scott is in there, he knows we're coming. But he'll have a harder time with the two of us."

Eli must've seen some wisdom in Asher's words. "Come on," he said, before adding. "But stay close."

They crossed the threshold and entered a small living room. A standing lamp was illuminated, casting a golden pool of light on the floor and making it bright enough to see the whole room. A Christmas tree, yet to be decorated, sat in a corner. Three cardboard boxes sat next to the tree. Written on the side of all three were the words: *X-Mas Decorations.*

There was a wingback chair and a sofa. Both were upholstered in blue fabric. A TV sat on a narrow table. There was a coffee table and a rug in the middle of the floor. In the corner was another table and a coordinating lamp. It was obvious that Scott Montgomery was not in the room. Still, Asher picked up the lamp on the table. He weighed it in his hand. The base was heavy.

Eli glanced at him and lifted a single eyebrow. "What the hell are you doing?"

"Just because I don't have a gun doesn't mean I shouldn't be armed."

"Whatever, man. Just don't get shot."

From the living room, they moved to the kitchen. Eli flipped a wall switch, flooding the room with light. A cereal bowl and coffee cup sat in the sink. A knife block sat on the counter. Each slot was filled. At least if the killer were in the house, he hadn't stolen a kitchen knife.

"He's not here," said Eli.

They returned to the living room. There was a hallway to the left. Eli flipped another switch, turning on a ceiling light. The short corridor was ringed with doors—one left, one right, one at the end. Pointing as he spoke, Eli said, "That's the guest room. That's the bathroom. The one in the back is Kansas's bedroom."

"I'll open the doors," said Asher. "You do a sweep."

They stopped at the first room on the right. Asher pressed his back against the wall and set the lamp next to his feet. Lifting his fingers as he mouthed the words. "One. Two." On three, he turned the knob and opened the door. Then he pressed his back into the wall again. Dropping to a knee, Eli pointed the barrel of his gun into the room.

Light from the hallway stretched across the floor. The room was, as Eli had described, a spare bedroom. A desk, covered in papers and a laptop computer, sat under the window. There was a metal filing cabinet, a wooden bookcase and several framed commendations on the wall. There was also a narrow bed, unmade, with a folded quilt hanging over the footboard. Other than that, the room was empty.

"It's clear," said Eli, although that much was obvious.

Asher nodded to the other side of the hallway. "Should we check there next?"

Eli nodded.

Moving to the other door, Asher gripped the knob. He held up his fist and, like before, counted. "One. Two."

On three, he pushed the door open. It hit the wall with a crack.

The bathroom was small. A toilet. Sink. Vanity. Tub-shower combo. The shower curtain was pulled back. Scott Montgomery wasn't hiding there, either.

That meant there was only one more room to check.

Asher picked up his lamp, where he'd left it on the floor next to the guest room. The bedroom door was ajar. The gap was narrow and dark. If Scott were in the house, he was undoubtedly watching them now.

For a moment, he remembered being outside of the house where Scott was hiding moments before the bomb detonated. He'd been confident that they'd cornered Montgomery. Then there was the blast. The noise. The heat. The shockwave that knocked him off his feet. Then there was nothing.

Had the killer planted another explosive device?

For a moment, Asher considered returning to his car. But the thought was gone as quickly as it had come. "Ready?" he whispered.

Eli nodded.

"One. Two. Three." Asher pushed the door open.

The master bedroom was larger than the office. Two of the corners were lost in the gloom, making it impossible to tell if the room was empty—or not.

The headboard of a large bed was pushed up against one wall. A rumpled comforter covered the mattress. There was a chest of drawers with a TV on top. A standing mirror with an ornate frame stood next to the window. A silky robe hung from one of the corners. For some reason that grabbed his attention. Maybe it was because it seemed inconsistent with the Kansas he knew. Or maybe it was because he could picture her in that robe, the pale silk falling over her figure like water.

Eli turned on the overhead light, pulling Asher from the fantasy. With the room completely illuminated, it was obvious that Scott was not in the house. "I'll tell Kansas and Spence that it's safe to come inside now."

Asher followed him down the hall. As Eli went outside, he set the lamp back on the table. The front door opened.

"What are you doing?" Kansas's question tickled the back of his neck.

Asher glanced over his shoulder. She wore a large gray parka over her outfit and held a handgun with the barrel pointed down. She shoved the firearm into the back waistband of her pants. But all he could see was her in that silk robe. He shook away the image and stared at his hand, where he was holding the lamp's electrical cord. "I'm plugging this in."

"I see that." Kansas kicked off her boots by the front door. Eli and Spence came into the living room, closing the door once they were inside. "Why was it unplugged in the first place?"

Immediately, he knew that using a lamp as a weapon was a ridiculous idea. "I had it with me." Kneeling on the rug, he reached behind the table to find the outlet. "You know, just in case."

"What were you going to do?" Kansas asked. "Hit Scott on the head with the lamp."

The plug slid home, and he rose to his feet. "If I needed to, yeah."

Kansas shook her head. "Unbelievable."

"You were the one who said they'd hit Scott with a beer bottle. Hell, you threw a bottle at his car."

"Are you two going to be okay together?" Spence asked. "If not, I can stay."

Asher wasn't about to give up his piece of the investigation. "I'm good staying with Kansas. That is, if she wants me."

"If I have to have security," said Kansas, "then Asher makes the most sense. He's a trained law enforcement officer and he already knows the case."

He was glad that she saw things his way.

"All right, then," said Eli. "I'm going to get back to work. Call if you see or hear anything out of the ordinary."

"Got it," said Asher at the same moment Kansas said, "Got it," as well.

She smirked and pinched his arm. "You owe me a coke."

He hadn't played Jinx since he was a kid. Still, he loved that she was always willing to be genuine and vulnerable. Emotional. Angry. Playful. It didn't matter. Kansas was always one hundred percent herself. "I think we'll be fine."

Spence opened his arms. Kansas stepped into an embrace. "You take care of yourself, Sis."

"I promise to be careful and to be smart."

He chuckled. "I think I've heard that before, and I don't know if I should believe it now."

"You aren't thinking of the time she went sledding?" Eli asked.

"Actually," said Spence, "I was."

All three Coltons began to laugh.

There was obviously something Asher was missing. "Dare I ask?"

Eli opened the door. A gust of cold air swirled through

the room. Fat snowflakes blew in from outside, settling on the carpet before they melted. "I'll let Kansas tell you all about that."

"You mean the time we went down the biggest hill behind your house?"

"That's exactly what I was thinking of," said Eli as he said as he stepped outside. "You take care of her, man."

"I will," Asher promised.

"Thanks for stepping up," said Spence while giving a quick wave.

Then the two men stepped into the night and closed the door.

Asher and Kansas were alone. An image of her wearing that silky robe and nothing else flooded his brain. His pulse thrummed at the base of his skull. Now, how was he supposed to remain professional?

Chapter Four

It was surreal for Kansas to think that Asher would be staying at her house. Truly, she didn't mind the company, even though she thought that being watched was overkill. After all, she was a law enforcement officer, as well. But she knew enough not to argue with Eli. He had enough to do with the investigation, and he didn't need to get grief from her.

Asher stood in the middle of the living room, still wearing his big red coat.

"Can I take your jacket for you?" she asked, holding out her hand.

"Yeah. Sure." He slipped out of the parka. "Here you go."

For the party, Asher had donned a black sweater that zipped at the neck. Underneath was a gray T-shirt. The weave of the sweater was tight and fit him like a second skin. Long before tonight, she'd noticed his toned biceps and his well-developed pecs. But since he'd always had a snarky comment or two, she never saw him as anything other than a pest.

Well, that wasn't exactly true, either.

She always wanted his respect—something she never

got. That was what rankled most of all. But what if he was trying to create some kind of bond with her? What if she'd always misunderstood his motives?

Well?

That would change everything.

Now, he was in her house and too close.

His male scent, pine and snow and sweat, filled the room and left her dizzy.

"Do you want me to put that somewhere?" he asked.

"What?"

"The coat. Do you want me to put it somewhere for you?"

God. How embarrassing. She'd been standing in the middle of the room, holding his jacket for too long. "No," she said. "I've got it. I'm just distracted, is all."

"It's been a lot to take in," he said.

She hummed in agreement. A small coatrack stood next to the door. She hung his jacket on the peg before removing her own coat and hanging it up, as well. Her firearm was still tucked into the small of her back. She really should put it in the gun safe that was tucked into a drawer on her bedside table. Although, if Scott Montgomery had really returned, she wanted her sidearm nearby.

Now what were they supposed to do?

It wasn't much past 9:00 p.m.

Sure, it was dark outside. But Kansas hadn't been to bed that early since she was in fifth grade. Then, she got an idea. Two remotes sat on her coffee table. She lifted them both. Using one for the power and the other for the cable, she turned on the TV.

Holding up both remotes, she said, "This one has the volume. This one controls the channels. Make yourself comfortable," she said, setting both remotes back on the coffee table. "I'm going to pick up my room and put clean sheets on the bed for you."

"I'm not stealing your bedroom," said Asher. "I'll be fine in the guest room."

"You're still recovering from a concussion. There's no way I'm making you sleep on that narrow bed."

"I'll be fine."

"I'm trying to be a good hostess."

"I'll be fine," he repeated, emphasizing each word.

She inhaled deeply, filling her lungs until it hurt. Then she exhaled. "Why do you have to argue with everything I say?"

"I'm not arguing."

For a moment, they both glared at each other.

Then Asher's lip twitched. "I guess I was fighting with you a little."

God, he was cute. Kansas tried to look stern, but a laugh bubbled up from her middle and burst free. "I guess I was being argumentative, too." She paused. "Can I get you something to drink? A beer? A whiskey?"

"I'm not supposed to have any alcohol because of the concussion."

Oh yes. With all the excitement, she'd forgotten. "A hot chocolate, then?"

He nodded. "That'd be great. Thanks."

Leaving Asher in the living room, she went into the kitchen. There, she heated milk and found a bag of chocolate chips. Oh sure, she could make hot chocolate with just water and a packet of brown powder. But for some reason, she wanted to be hospitable. Kansas tried to tell herself that it was her way of thanking Asher for staying at her house. Or maybe it was her way of calling a truce from their constant bickering.

Deep in her soul, she knew the truth.

She wanted to do something special for him because he was a special person. He was always professional—well, except when he thought it would be fun to give her a hard time. As she watched the pot, Kansas remembered one of the first times she'd gone out on a search and rescue. It was a hunter who'd gone missing. The man, who'd come to Alaska from Iowa, had gotten separated from his friends.

He been lost for almost two days and all available personnel were looking for the missing hunter. Asher was one of those people. He was there when they found the man.

Thankfully, he'd gotten lost in August, and the temps never dipped below 40 degrees. What's more, there'd been plenty of rain, so the man had been able to collect water. Still, the guy was tired, wet, and hungry.

It was Asher who sat with the man and listened to his story. As the medical team prepared to transfer the patient, Asher had given him a candy bar. Later, she learned that he'd stopped by the hospital, just to check in.

The milk began to steam. She stirred in the chocolate chips and wondered if Asher carried a candy bar with him still. The bits began to melt and soon, she had a creamy and fragrant drink.

After turning off the stove and removing the pot from the burner, she pulled two mugs from the cabinet. Kansas filled them both. Holding a handle in each hand, she returned to the living room.

Asher had opened the tops of each box that held her Christmas decorations. He'd found the tree lights, all tangled into a ball. Sitting on the sofa, he was unwinding the wires. A Christmas movie—the one where Santa starts out as an ad exec—was on the TV.

"Here you go." She set the mug on the coffee table in front of him. "Enjoy."

He looked up from the ball of lights. "I hope you don't mind me working on these for you."

She took a sip of her hot chocolate. It was like a warm hug on a cold night. "Knock yourself out," she said. Then she realized that might not be the best phrase for someone who had just gotten a concussion. "Actually, don't knock yourself out. But I appreciate your help." She took another sip. "My dad always gets on my case about not properly storing the decorations."

The thing was, when Christmas was over, Kansas was always ready for the dark season to end. Really, she couldn't put everything away quick enough.

"Well, I agree with your dad."

Kansas peered into one of the boxes. Several clumps of old newspapers were bunched inside. Setting her mug next to Asher's, she pulled out some crinkled papers. She started unwrapping the ornaments. The first one she found was a miniature Russian Orthodox church—a souvenir from Sitka, Alaska. The town used to be the capitol of Russia's North American empire before the territory became part of the U.S. Even though the land broke with Russia decades earlier, the town still had a decidedly Eastern European feel.

"I went to school there, you know," said Asher as she set the ornament on the table.

"Oh yeah?" The University of Alaska had campuses all over the state. Sitka was just one of many. "It's a nice town." Aside from all the shops on Church Street, there were several museums. Her favorite had been the Russian dancers who performed at the visitor's center.

He nodded. "When I wasn't in class, I took tourists sea kayaking. Well, when it was warm enough, that is."

"What'd you study?" she asked.

He shrugged. "Law enforcement."

"Outdoor and adventure studies," she said, mentioning her major. "Juneau campus."

"Oh, the big city," he said, making a joke.

Alaska really didn't have any big cities. But as far as the coastal communities were concerned, Juneau was by far the largest. "It seems like I was in college forever ago."

"Forever?" He set the lights on the cushion and leaned forward, reaching for his mug. "You're what? Twenty-six? That's not too long." Lifting the cup to his lips, he took a sip. "Wow. That's good."

She ignored his comment about her age and just focused on the fact that he liked her hot chocolate. "Thanks."

"No, really. You are a rare woman, Kansas. Smart. Funny. Pretty. And now I find out you make excellent hot chocolate. That's quite a combo." He took another sip. "That really is delicious."

"Did I just hear you give me a whole list of compliments?" she asked. Too late, Kansas realized that every word was filled with snark. How could she expect Asher to be kinder if she wasn't willing to do the same? Holding up her hand in surrender, she continued. "That came out wrong. But I have to ask you something. If you think all these great and wonderful things about me, what gives? Every time we talk, you're giving me crap."

"Honestly," he said, "I don't know. I do think you are great and wonderful. It's just…"

"It's just what?" she urged.

"It's just that I need to create distance from you."

"I don't get it," she said. Although she thought that she knew exactly what he meant. The thing was, she wanted to hear him say it.

"I like you. As in, I *like you*." He emphasized the last two words. "But I shouldn't have any feelings for you other than camaraderie. You're a fellow trooper. Hell, you're my partner's cousin. You're off-limits on all levels."

Despite the TV, the room was too quiet. Snow tapped on the windows. Kansas could hear Asher's breathing and her own heart beating wildly against her chest. In all these years, she never imagined that he saw her as anything other than a pest. It was like the first rays of sun after months of a dark winter. The light was blinding, disorienting, but finally everything was clear.

Asher watched her from where he sat on the sofa. "Would you say something? Can you tell me what you want?"

"I want…" she began "…you to kiss me."

THE ONLY LIGHT came from the computer screen. Scott Montgomery sat at a table in the remote cabin. It was deep in the woods outside of Shelby. He'd inherited the property from his paternal grandparents. And so far, the cops didn't know it existed. He'd pulled the shades over the windows so no light could escape. Instead of starting a fire in the hearth, he had a small electric heater sitting by his feet. The red coils did little to chase away the chill. Tucking his hands into his armpits, he waited for his laptop to connect to Wi-Fi.

It wasn't the computer's fault. The internet this far into

the wilderness was crap. But he didn't dare complain to the cable company—not unless he wanted to get caught for something stupid.

A narrow bar on the bottom of the screen slowly filled with white.

He exhaled, his breath collecting in a faint cloud. Rising from the seat, he crossed the floor and went to the adjoining kitchenette. There was a small refrigerator—the kind he'd had in his dorm room at college. A sink. A two-burner stove. A toaster oven. A microwave.

It wasn't much, but it was all he needed.

Filling a kettle with water from the tap, he placed it on one of the burners and turned the dial to ten. Crossing back to the computer, he dropped into the seat and stared at the screen. His home page appeared. On it were copies of two photographs. One was of Caroline Colton—the young model who was murdered in her prime. The other picture was of Kansas Colton. It was a snapshot he'd taken with his phone at work one day when she wasn't watching. Her eyes were bright, and sunlight reflected off her hair. Someone must've told her a joke, because she was laughing.

He touched Kansas's image. "To think," he said, "we'd be together now if it wasn't for that oaf, Rafferty."

God, he'd always hated that guy. Too much confidence. Too much swagger.

The only consolation was that Asher annoyed Kansas as much as he bothered Scott.

Sitting back in his seat, his fingers danced across the keyboard. The program loaded slowly. He stared at the reflection. The room behind him was clear. Yellow recliner. Sofa covered with a quilt. Brown curtains. His own image was caught in the screen as well, yet slightly distorted. Big forehead. Little chin. His hair needed a trim, and his eyes were lost in the shadows on his face. It was all because he was on the run. But once he and Kansas were together, it would all be over.

A shrill whistle came from the kettle.

Taking the teapot from the stove, he cursed again. Out here, where the air was thin with the cold, noises traveled far. As a forensic expert with the ABI, he'd learned important lessons. It was the small mistakes that that got people caught.

A chink of light in a dark forest followed by the shrieking whistle was enough to get anyone nearby interested. It meant visitors he didn't want to see. Or worse yet, calls to the police. He poured steaming water into a cup and added a tea bag. The tea swirled through the water, stretching out brown tendrils.

He added half a spoonful of sugar. Usually, he liked his tea sweeter. But he didn't know how long his provisions needed to last. Scott carried the cup back to the computer and sipped his tea.

Tonight had been a disaster.

He'd only gone to the Coltons' home to see if he could catch a glimpse of Kansas. But when she stood outside, it was as if she'd been waiting for him. He'd been so caught up in the moment that he hadn't noticed Asher Rafferty, the oaf, coming down the driveway.

Now the police were definitely involved. And what's more, they knew he was back.

It was one of those stupid mistakes.

Scott wouldn't let it happen again.

He should lie low for a few days and let the cops chase down all the bogus sightings. Once they'd gotten tired and lazy, he could reemerge.

He took another sip as the program finished loading. The screen was broken into four smaller images. Each picture was connected to a camera that broadcast live videos from Kansas Colton's house. With his crappy internet connection, none of the cameras were displaying in real time. But he could get them to open one at a time.

He double-clicked on the first screen. The image of Kansas's bedroom filled the screen. Even though the lights were off, he could tell that she wasn't in the room. Next, he tried the bathroom. He'd situated the camera so he could see when she got into and out of the shower. But the room was dark, so she wasn't there, either.

He moved the mouse to hover over the living room camera. *Click-Click.*

Kansas stood next to the coffee table. A movie was on the TV. Outside, he could hear snow and sleet pelting against the window. But there was more. Asher Rafferty sat on the sofa. In the little cabin, Scott's blood turned cold.

Asher's voice came through the computer's small speaker. "Would you say something? Can you tell me what you want?"

"I want..." Kansas began "...you to kiss me."

Red-hot fury erupted from Scott. He slammed down the lid of his laptop. Tea splashed out of the mug and onto his wrist, burning his skin. "Goddamn it."

He threw the cup across the room. It hit the wall with a satisfying crack before falling to the floor. Staying in his cabin was the smart move, but he couldn't let Kansas fall for the likes of Asher Rafferty.

Had her disdain for the man been a stunt all along? The thought made him want to retch.

Kansas belonged to him.

That meant Scott Montgomery needed to do something. And he needed to do it now.

KANSAS'S WORDS STILL filled the room.

"I want you to kiss me," she had said.

Asher didn't need a second invitation to touch her. He was on his feet and at her side before realizing that he'd moved. He wrapped his arms around her back and pulled her to him. He placed his lips on hers, claiming her with his mouth. She tasted of chocolate, milk, and mint. The combination was intoxicating.

She wound her fingers through his hair, pulling him closer. Her breasts were soft. Her muscles were lean. She fit into him perfectly, as if they were made for each other. He pulled her closer, kissed her deeper. His hands moved from her waist to her hips.

She gave a mew of surprise and rocked her hips into his pelvis.

The motion went straight to his dick. His balls tightened. His shaft lengthened. He wanted her so bad he could taste the desire.

Moving his mouth from her lips, he trailed kisses from her cheek to her neck to the front of her blouse. He unfastened the top button and kissed her again.

She raked her fingers through his hair, pulling him closer. "Oh, Asher," she moaned.

Honestly, he didn't know how it was possible, but his cock got harder.

He pulled another button free.

The top of her bra—a black lacy number—was visible at the gap of her shirt.

He trailed his tongue down her chest. "God, that's so

sexy," he said, breathing the words into her skin. His hands traveled from her rear up, to her waist. He stopped when his fingers touched something cold and metal at her back.

She pulled away, abruptly ending the kiss. "Damn it," she cursed. "My gun." She took another step back from Asher. "I need to put this away."

Blood coursed through his veins, but he had no choice other than to let her go. Standing in the middle of the room, he watched as she walked down the hallway. She paused at her bedroom door. For an instant, he was sure that she was going to invite him to come with her.

Then she pushed the door open and stepped inside. Without a backward glance, she closed the door. Even where he stood, he could hear the unmistakable *click* of the lock being engaged.

Asher ran his hands through his hair. His hot chocolate still sat on the coffee table. He picked it up and took a sip. The liquid was tepid now but still sweet. He drained the mug in a single swallow. The sugar buzzed through his system, but it did nothing to ease his lust. With the mug in hand, Asher placed his cup in the kitchen sink. Then he returned to the living room and sat on the sofa.

The ball of Christmas lights sat on the cushion. He picked up the tangled wires and started to create a long strand. He hoped that the mindless task would be enough to distract him from thinking about Kansas or the kiss.

But he doubted that it would be enough.

Her scent was on his skin. His mouth still held the memory of her lips. He could still feel her soft skin on the palm of his hand.

In short, after a single kiss, Kansas Colton had rocked his world.

Chapter Five

Kansas sat on the bed in her room. Her pulse raced and her hands shook. She wanted Asher with her now and on this bed. His mouth on hers. She wanted to touch him. To taste him.

But that would be a bad idea.

He was only here to keep her safe. Eventually, they'd go back to simply being coworkers. She made it a point to never date anyone who worked for ABI, because the aftermath would be hella awkward.

And still, she wanted more.

With an exhale, Kansas flopped onto her back. The gun bit into her flesh. She sat up and pulled the firearm from the back of her waistband. Holding the Heckler & Koch LP .22 handgun on her lap, she stared at it and snorted. "I don't know if I should thank you or not. Because of you, I'm not rolling around on these sheets with Asher."

Rising from the bed, she walked to her bedside table and opened the single drawer. At the back of the box was a metal case. She removed the container and placed her thumb on a raised pad. A green light blinked twice, and the latch opened with a click. Her own Sig Saur was already stored in the safe. She placed her father's firearm with her work-issued gun and shut the lid. Then, she replaced the safe and closed the drawer.

Concentrating on putting away her LP .22 gave her room to think.

Sure, she had kissed Asher. But it couldn't go beyond the single embrace. If she was going to avoid the danger that was Scott Montgomery, she could not be distracted by a man—even someone as handsome as Asher.

She unbuttoned her blouse. A tingling lingered at each spot Asher had kissed. After slipping off her shirt, she removed her slacks, as well. Kansas rehung all her clothing, before placing them in the closet. After slipping out of her bra, she tossed it into a corner. From a drawer, she removed a pair of fleece pajama bottoms and a tank top. The fabric was soft and warm, perfect for this time of the year and the duo was what she wore most nights to sleep.

Honestly, she wanted to just crawl into bed and forget all about this evening.

But she couldn't. Even though Asher wasn't exactly a houseguest, he was still her responsibility. She caught a glimpse of herself in the standing mirror. The outlines of her nipples were visible through the thin fabric of her shirt. She couldn't go into the living room like this. Not unless she wanted to send signals to Asher that she was up for another kiss. If he kissed her again, there'd be no way she'd be able to stop.

A silk robe hung on one of the corners of the mirror. She never wore the thing but pulled it loose. Dust billowed up from the fabric, tickling her nose and eyes. Working her arms into the sleeves, she walked toward the door. After pulling it open, she strode down the hallway.

Asher was still in the living room. He had untangled

her lights and then strung them on the tree. Now each bough was ablaze with color.

His back was to her as he knelt next to a box and removed wads of crumpled papers. His shoulders were broad. Even under the fabric of his sweater, she could see the outline of his trapezius muscles.

"That's beautiful," she said.

He glanced over his shoulder and smiled. "I could say the same thing about you."

"The tree." Her face warmed. "I mean the tree is beautiful."

"I like your robe." He rose to his feet. "It's very elegant. The color suits you."

She pulled out on the hem. The fabric was cool and slid through her fingers. "I never wear it."

"You should," he said. "It's flattering."

"I'm not sure what to do with this kind and charming Asher Rafferty."

"Well, you can start by putting some of these ornaments on the tree." He picked up the miniature Russian church made of resin. "Here you go."

She stepped forward and took it from him. Her fingertips brushed the back of his hand. A delicious warmth filled her palm. "Thanks," she said.

Kansas placed the ornament on a branch. Then, she returned to the table for another. This one was a clear ball with the seal from the Alaska Department of Public Safety etched into the glass. It had been a gift from Eli, given to her the first year she was on the job. She hung it near the church.

For the next thirty minutes, she and Asher fell into a rhythm. He unwrapped the ornaments and made sure they had hooks. She placed them on the tree. She told him the story of how she'd come by each decoration. It seemed like every branch told a tale of Christmases past. When they were done, she turned off all the lights.

A warm glow from the tree reached every corner.

"It really is beautiful," she said, admiring their work.

Asher stood at her side. She could feel his gaze on her face. "Beautiful doesn't begin to describe it."

"So," she said, "what are we going to do now?"

He checked his watch for the time. "It's almost eleven. I don't know about you, but I'm beat."

A kernel of guilt caught in her throat. Asher was still recovering from his concussion. He shouldn't have been chasing after Scott Montgomery—or whoever it had been—in the woods. And he definitely shouldn't be awake this late. "You can take the guest room," she said. "Unless I can convince you to swap with me and take my room."

"I'll be fine in the spare bed."

She kept her extra bedding in the closet of her office. Kansas selected a bed pillow, set of sheets and two quilts—enough to keep Asher warm and comfortable. She returned with the bedding.

He was already sitting on the mattress.

"I can get everything set up for you, if you'd like."

"No, just put it all right here." He nodded toward a chair that sat next to the desk. "I'll get myself settled."

"If you don't need anything else," she said, "I'm going to turn in."

"Thanks for everything," he said. "G'night."

She wandered to the end of the hallway and caught sight of herself in the standing mirror. The robe fell over her body, hugging her curves in all the right places. The ivory color matched her complexion, making her cheeks rosier and her lips a darker shade of red. Asher had been right. She did look good. Maybe she should wear the robe more often.

After slipping under the covers and turning off the light, she closed her eyes and tried to force herself to sleep. Yet, she was painfully aware that Asher Rafferty was in her guest room. She'd recognized that he was a handsome man. But his snotty comments always dimmed some of the shine off his good looks.

Flipping from her back to her side, she plumped her pillow and closed her eyes. Just like Dove encouraged during Savasana, the last pose of a yoga class, she breathed deeply and cleared her mind.

Only a second passed before Asher entered her thoughts again.

True, his reasoning for why he liked to torment her felt like something a third grader might say. Now that she was an adult, if she liked someone, she told them.

Still, he had been honest. To her, that counted for something.

The phone on her nightstand began to glow the moment before she heard the ping of an incoming text. She reached for the cell and opened her message app.

The text read:

Attention SAR leader
ADPS has received a report of a missing five-year-old boy.
Last seen by his parents at their home North of Shelby.
Contact your team and report to the following location.

An address was included.

Kansas was on her feet before she ever recalled standing. At twenty-six years old, she was the youngest SAR leader in ADPS history. She inherited the position when the former team lead Aquwik Peterson's wife had their first child. He wanted to stay home more and passed on the job to Kansas. Using the lighted screen, she pulled up her contact list and placed a call to her second-in-command and former boss. Aquwik was a member of the Sugpiaq tribe that were the first men in Prince William Sound. The phone rang four times before it was answered by his sleepy voice. "Kansas?"

"Hey." Adrenaline filled her veins and left her breathless. "I'm sorry to call so late. But I wouldn't reach out at this hour unless it was important."

"Give me a second," he said, whispering. She could imagine him slipping from bed, trying not to wake his wife. While waiting, she turned on the overhead light. After a moment, he spoke again, his voice louder. "What's up?"

"There's a boy missing from just north of town." She gave him the address while crossing her room to the window. Pulling back the curtain, she watched thick flakes falling from the sky. The snow was the enemy during any search and rescue operation. "In weather like this, we can't call in air support." She paused a moment to think. Any trail the little boy left would be covered by drifts. It left her with only a few options. "I need you to contact the K-9 units." She paused for an instant and made a plan. "The area around that house gets mountainous quickly. I'll reach out to Alaska Mountain Rescue." The nonprofit group specialized in finding people lost in the rocky terrain.

Her go bag, with everything she needed, was stowed on the top shelf. She pulled it down and set it on the bed. Aside from dressing in all the gear needed to keep her safe and warm in the elements, she still had to get to the rendezvous point. The storm would make travel dangerous. She wanted to be looking for the missing child already, but in reality, it would take time to get everything, and everyone, organized. Add to the fact that she'd left her car at the party.

"I'll need a ride," she said, knowing that each second was the difference between life and death. "Can you pick me up?"

"Hey, Kansas," said Aquwik, ignoring her, "can I ask you a question?"

Her thumb hovered over the phone icon, ready to end the call. She turned on the speaker function before tossing the phone onto the bed. "Sure."

"Are you the best person to run this search?" Before she could get angry at his question, he continued, "I know you're a capable leader, but I heard about the party at your parents' house this evening." He paused a beat. "I mean, what happened with Scott Montgomery? Will you be safe?"

Kansas tamped down her anger. It would do no good to lash out at someone who cared. "I'll be fine," she said. "Neither Asher nor I got a good look at the person. It might not have been Montgomery at all." She continued: "But the little boy who's lost is in our area. Bringing in a team from somewhere else will use up time that we don't have."

"Wellll," said Aquwik, drawing out the word, "you make some good points. Forget I said anything."

"You're watching out for me. I appreciate that. But honestly, I'm not worried."

"All right," he said. "I'll see you in fifteen minutes."

"Be here in fourteen minutes and twelve seconds," she said, kind of joking—kind of not.

She stripped out of her pajamas and redressed in a base layer of wool. A medium layer of fleece. She put on her official red SAR Gor-Tex snow pants as her top waterproof layer.

She made sure she had her hat, gloves, headlamp, GPS tracker, first aid kit, waterproof matches, and a dry pair of socks. All of that, and more, was stowed in her bag.

While lacing up her boots, she wondered what to do about Asher. After all, he was staying with her to keep her safe. Should she wake him? Leave without saying a word? Kansas couldn't decide and grabbed her official SAR parka from the closet. After turning off the light, she opened the door.

As it turned out, she didn't have to decide what to do about Asher. He stood in the doorway of the guest room. A table lamp had been turned on. The light shone on him from behind, and she could only see his silhouette. His broad shoulders. Powerful arms. Long legs. The sight of him left her palms damp and her mouth dry.

"Hey." The word came out as a croak. "I hope I didn't wake you."

"I wasn't asleep," he said, before adding, "I heard your call. Aquwik is right. You can't go out."

Anger churned in her chest. Who was Asher Rafferty to tell her how to do her job? "You shouldn't be listening in on private calls."

"I wasn't exactly eavesdropping," he said, pointing to the guest room door. "You started talking and I couldn't keep from hearing what was said."

He was most likely right. But it did nothing to quell her ire. "I'm going."

"Eli put me in charge of your safety and security. I can't let you."

"Eli knows that my job is important."

Asher shook his head.

"Are you really standing in my house telling me *no*?"

"I can't force you to stay here," he said. "But think about this—Scott Montgomery is out there, somewhere."

"We don't know that Scott was outside my parents' house tonight." She was exhausted by the argument. "But here's what I do know. There's a little boy who's lost. It's my job to find him. If we have to wait for another SAR team, it could be hours." Her pulse was racing, using up all her oxygen. She inhaled deeply before continuing, "I'm not leaving that little boy all alone and in the woods."

"Fine," said Asher, holding up his hands in surrender. "You win."

"Thank you," she said, although she wasn't completely sure what he had done to deserve her gratitude. "I'll be back as soon as I can. But it might be a few hours. Don't wait up for me."

"I'm not going to fight with you about going on this search and rescue," he said.

"I know, because I won."

"Because," said Asher, stepping farther into the hallway, "I'm coming with you."

KANSAS LET AQUWIK know that she had a ride to the rendezvous site. As Asher drove, she placed several more calls. In that regard, having him tag along was useful. The snow was falling heavily, making driving treacherous. Talking on the phone while navigating through the storm would have been reckless at best and disastrous at worst. By the time they turned onto the road where the missing child was last seen, she had contacted the ADPS office in Shelby. Four troopers had already been dispatched to the location. More were being called in from their patrol routes and expected soon. Since Asher was still dressed in his party attire, she had requested that an extra set of cold-weather gear be brought for him, as well. She also contacted Alaska Mountain Rescue for help. They promised another five people who could be on sight within the hour.

Kansas and Asher arrived at the home of the missing child—a boy named Glen Anderson. The Anderson family had rented a one-story house that was located five miles past the Shelby town line. The lot was wooded, like most of the land in the hills. Two cruisers were already parked in front of the house. There were two lamp-posts on either side of a snow-covered walkway and twin sconces on the door. The glow from the lights illuminated the yard and caught the continual snowfall. A pair of troopers, their blue uniform parkas zipped up to their chins, stood in front of the door. A man and woman, both in pajama pants, boots and winter coats, stood with the troopers. Kansas guessed they were the parents of the missing child.

Asher pulled in behind the second cruiser in the line, his bumper almost touching the fender. As soon as the car stopped, Kansas opened the door and trudged through the snow. Lifting a hand in greeting as she walked, she introduced herself, "I'm Kansas Colton, head of the Search and Rescue team for the Alaska Bureau of Investigation."

The woman gave her a tight-lipped smile. "I'm Beverly Anderson and this is my husband, Mike."

Kansas drew closer, getting a clear view of the parents. Beverly's eyes were red and puffy, probably from crying. She didn't blame the woman; losing a child was terrifying without having to deal with the perpetual darkness and the storm. "Beverly, Mike," she said, nodding at the parents, "I'd like to ask a few questions about your son." It was a sad reality that many calls about a missing person were to cover up other crimes. She knew that the troopers had already talked to the parents and determined that the kid really had wandered off on his own. But she wanted to hear what the parents had to say, something in their words might give her a clue as to the where the boy had gone. "Tell me about tonight. I heard that you rented this house. Is that correct?"

"I teach college in Phoenix," said Mike, "and we're on a semester break right now. We rented this place for the month because Glen hadn't seen snow before. He was so excited when the storm started and wanted to go out and play."

Mike choked on emotion and Beverly picked up on the story. "We came outside for a little bit, but it was frigid. We aren't used to this weather. We coaxed Glen back inside. Boy, was he mad. But I made dinner. After we ate, he wanted to go out again, but at that time, it really was snowing too hard. We promised him that he could go out in the morning. We all watched a movie. When it was done, I put him to bed." Her eyes filled with tears. She blinked them back, and Kansas was struck by the parents' bravery. "We thought he was asleep. We never imagined…" She began to sob. Mike hugged Beverly to his chest.

Kansas stood next to the couple and waited quietly. She knew that the parents needed time to deal with their emotions. But she could feel the seconds pass with each snowflake that swirled by. After a moment, she asked, "When did you discover that your son was missing?"

Mike seemed to have found his words by comforting his wife. He said, "We last saw Glen about thirty minutes ago. We were in bed when we heard the front door open and then slam shut. Of course we were worried about an intruder. But we looked around and saw that Glen was gone. His coat and boots and gloves were gone, too. I could see his footprints across the yard but lost them in the tree line." Mike pointed to Kansas's right. "I kept yelling for him. He didn't call out, and pretty soon, I was worried that I'd get lost, too. I came back to the house. Beverly had already called 911."

She was aware that Asher stood behind her, dressed now in a cold-weather uniform provided by one of the troopers. In the past several minutes, six other troopers had arrived. Her second-in-command, Aquwik, was also on the scene. Kansas knew what to do. It started with re-assuring the parents.

"You both have done the right thing in looking for your son and also calling us. Tell me, do you have a special code word in your family?" One of the many problems when the missing person is young, is that they're taught to be wary of strangers. He might actually hide when hearing his name called out by people he didn't know. If the Anderson family had a special word or phrase that only they knew, then Glen would be more likely to make his presence known.

Mike shook his head. "We don't."

"What about a nickname?"

Beverly wiped her eyes with the back of her hand. "Glenny Bug."

"Glenny Bug," Kansas repeated. "Here's what I want

you two to do. Mike, do you have a coat, boots, snow pants, hat, gloves? Gear good enough to keep you warm if you're outside for several hours."

"I think everything I have is good enough." He gave a wry smile. "But I am from Phoenix, so what do I know?"

She appreciated his sense of humor. It'd help him get through the next several hours. "Go and get dressed. You're coming with us. Beverly, I want you to stay here. I'll have a trooper remain with you. Glen might find his way back to the house, and the last thing I want is for him to find this place empty." She glanced around at the gathering team. The K-9 units had yet to arrive. "We're going to use dogs to track your son, as well. When they get here, I need you to have some of Glen's clothing available for them. The dirtier, the better. It'll help the dogs to catch a scent."

"I can do that." Beverly gave a single nod. Then the parents returned to the house.

As soon as the door closed, Kansas turned to face her fellow troopers. "Thank you all for coming out tonight. We have a missing eight-year-old boy from Arizona. His name is Glen Anderson, but his parents call him Glenny Bug. He left his house about thirty minutes ago to play in the snow. Aquwik, I want you to stay and wait for the AMR and K-9 units. Everyone else, you're coming with me as soon as the father is dressed. So grab your gear. Get hydrated. In just a minute, we roll out."

Chapter Six

Kansas waited as the troopers returned to their vehicles for hats, gloves and water. She never knew how long they might be out on an operation, and she wanted everyone on her team to be safe. Asher was the only one who remained. She could feel his gaze resting on her face.

She glanced in his direction. He was smiling.

"What?"

"You," he said. "You really are amazing."

She faked a groan, even though his compliment warmed her to the core. "You can't start getting all mushy on me," she said, before adding, "I need to get into your car."

Asher used a key fob he had tucked into his pocket to unlock the doors. The lights flashed as they walked, side by side, through the snow. Her go bag was stored in the back seat. She unfastened the top zipper and checked her equipment. It was all there. Then she had another thought. Turning to Asher, she said, "I need a favor. Go to the house and ask the parents for a blanket or toy of Glen's. Once we find the kid, having something special will help him stay calm."

"Do you really think you'll find him?" Asher asked.

She didn't fault his pessimism. He worked in the Violent Crimes unit. Most of those victims found justice. But it was during a trial and always after a tragedy. It was Kansas's job to prevent a disaster from happening. She had to stay optimistic, despite the fact that the little boy had been lost in a storm for too long. "I believe that we'll find Glen."

Believe. It was her family's motto.

He gave her a quick nod before pulling the fob from his pocket. "Lock it up when you're done," he said. "I'll be right back."

She held out her palm and he placed the keys in her hand. She could feel his fingertips through the fabric of her glove. Kansas's heart skipped a beat. She had to get over her reaction to Asher. She'd never find the missing child if she didn't. Closing a fist around the fob, she said, "Alrighty, I'll make sure it's locked up tight."

He nodded his thanks and walked away.

Inside, she cringed. Had she really said, *Alrighty, I'll make sure it's locked up tight*?

Good God, was she turning into her father?

Well, he'd been a hell of an outdoor guide and tracker when he was younger. So maybe channeling a little bit of him would be a good thing. She slipped on her backpack and tightened the shoulder straps. Then she walked toward the house where the other troopers were gathered. It was time to find a little boy and bring him back home safe.

ASHER HAD TO ADMIT—even if it was just to himself—he was impressed with Kansas Colton. Sure, she had a reputation for being good at her job—a reputation he didn't doubt because of her stats. But he'd never seen this side of her. She was professional. Determined. Focused.

The first thing she'd done was organize everyone into a line. She wanted less than two feet separating the shoulder of one trooper from the shoulder of the next person in line. With minimal space between people, it was almost impossible to miss the body of a child, even if he was covered with snow. Everyone had a flashlight, and they were ordered to shine the beam on the ground in front of them.

Mike Anderson was placed in the center. Kansas was at his left. For three paces, Mike would call out to his son. Ten paces would be taken in silence, listening for a response. For the next three paces, everyone yelled for Glen. Then they took twenty silent paces, listening for any signs of life. After that, the cycle started over.

Beyond managing the physical search, Kansas was in contact with Aquwik. He was still waiting for the K-9 units to show up. Kansas's group had been in the woods for seventeen minutes and had traveled less than half a mile. Only a few stray flakes fell from the sky. Soon, an aerial search might be possible.

As a new cycle began, Mike started yelling, "Glen! Hey, Glenny Bug. Can you hear me? Call out to Daddy if you can."

Step one. Two. Three.

Then he stopped yelling. The only sound was the wail of wind in the trees.

A single snowflake was caught in the beam of Asher's flashlight. It fell lazily to the ground—not carried by a gust. That's when he realized that there wasn't even a breeze. So, what had he heard?

"Everyone," said Kansas, ready to start the chorus of voices again.

Asher held up his hand. "Wait. I think I hear something."

The line froze. Asher held his breath and listened. The only thing he could hear was his racing pulse. He inhaled, ready to admit defeat. But he heard it again. It was a thin cry. Without a word, he sprinted toward the noise. He still held his flashlight. The beam shone in an arc across the sky. Asher was aware of several people following him, but he couldn't lose the sound.

At the bottom of the hill, he stopped. His breath came in short and ragged gasps. Using the sleeve of his jacket, he wiped his damp forehead.

"You heard something?" Kansas stood at his side. She was barely breathing hard.

"I thought," he said, wheezing as he spoke, "I heard someone crying."

Kansas stood at his side. "Glen!" she yelled. "Glenny Bug!"

Asher glanced over his shoulder. Four troopers stood a few feet back. Nobody said a word. Nobody made a sound. There was nothing beyond the silence.

Had Asher been mistaken?

Kansas was thankful for her wool base layer. In running down the hill, she started to perspire. If it weren't for the wool to absorb the sweat, she would've caught a chill. Being cold was a sure way to lose focus and eventually become sloppy in the search.

Asher had heard something. She was sure of that.

But what had it been?

"Maybe I was wrong," he began.

She held up a hand for silence. She's heard something, too. A whimper maybe.

It could be a wild animal. It could also be a child.

"Glen!" she yelled. "My name is Kansas Colton. I work for the Alaska Department of Public Safety. Your parents called 911 when they realized you left the house. I know you like the snow, but it's time to get you home."

She waited and listened.

There was the noise again.

Maybe the child was injured and couldn't call out for help. Maybe he was still frightened of either getting into trouble or the fact that Kansas was a stranger. She looked at the group of troopers who'd followed her to the bottom of the ravine. Aside from her and Asher, there were four other troopers. One of the troopers, a middle-aged woman named Wanda, was friends with Kansas's mom.

To Wanda, Kansas said, "Get the rest of the search party. I want Mike down here. Also, call Aquwik." Each trooper had their own radio, so Wanda would be able to get in touch with anyone on the team. Sure, Kansas could reach out personally, but she didn't want to break the flow of her concentration. Now was the moment she needed all her faculties. After pausing a beat, she added, "We need the dogs to search this area."

"I'm on it," said Wanda. Then she began to hike back up the hill.

Kansas's pulse started to race. This was the moment in every search where her body and mind were at odds. Sure, she was excited that they were close to finding the missing boy. But if she didn't focus, she might miss something important. It was the small details that were the difference between success and failure.

And Kansas never failed.

So she had to slow her racing pulse and take in everything.

Drawing in a deep breath, she scanned her surroundings. She stood in a gully. A stream would run down the middle of the narrow gap between the hills for much of the year. Now the water was frozen solid. Because of the water source, the trees were taller. The trunks were thicker. They grew closer together. During the dark time of the year, it was damn near impossible to see more than a few feet in front of her.

"Does anyone have a portable light?" she asked before adding, "and hopefully a collapsible pole."

One of the troopers, a new guy named Ray—or maybe it was Roy—stepped forward. A large bag was slung over his shoulder. "I've got it here."

"Help me get this set up," she said. "The rest of you, sweep the area with your flashlights. Keep calling out to Glen. He's around here somewhere. I can feel it in my bones."

Asher took the bag. "Thanks, Roy. I can help Kansas."

The young trooper nodded before pulling out his flashlight and heading into the trees.

Within a minute, it was only Asher and Kansas. She removed a battery-powered light from a hard case that was in the backpack. Along with it was a tripod that could extend up to ten feet. Of course, it was hard to imagine that it would telescope so much. Folded up, it was only two feet long. Kansas handed Asher the pole. "Help me with this."

She turned off her flashlight before stowing it in a side pocket on her backpack. She removed the headlamp and secured it over her beanie. Kansas flipped on the light.

The beam showed exactly where she was looking. It only took her a moment to attach the lamp to the base.

"Here it comes," she said while turning on the light. Twelve thousand lumens shone like a spotlight into the sky.

"Jesus." Asher's eyes watered. "That's bright."

"I did warn you," she said, opening the tripod feet.

"I know," he said, wiping his eyes with his shoulder. "And I wasn't even looking at the damn thing."

She loosened the pole and let it open to its full height. "You can set it down now."

Asher let the tripod's feet sink into the snow and guided the light up to its full height. The snow sparkled and the woods were brighter than noon in July. "The sound came from over there," he said directing the beam at a cluster of trees.

With the searchlight, Kansas didn't need her headlamp anymore. She pressed the power button, and the bulb went dark. "Let's check it out."

The snow wasn't as thick at the bottom of the ravine. And still, some of the drifts came up to her shins. Asher was at her side. At first, she missed it—thinking it was only a shadow. Then Kansas realized that there was a hole at the base of a tree.

"Are you thinking what I'm thinking?" asked Asher.

"That is the perfect place for a little boy to hide and get stuck."

"Yep." She could feel more than see his smile. "We are thinking alike."

"That's a terrifying thought." To show she was joking she nudged him in the side. God, the muscles in his obliques were like iron.

She got down on her hands and knees. Snow worked

into the cuff of her gloves. Cold bit her wrists. She didn't care. From the side pocket on her bag, she removed the flashlight. She turned on the power and shone the beam into the dark. There was nothing to see beyond roots and dirt and snow. "Damn it," she cursed.

Asher had removed his flashlight, as well. He did a second sweep of the hole, and that's when she saw it. A face looked up. The color was so pale she'd mistaken it for the snow.

"Hey, Glen." Kansas did a pretty good job at sounding upbeat. But the panic that she might've missed the child had settled into her bones, leaving her brittle. Sure, he was almost a dozen feet down. There were several broken roots that cast shadows on the child's face. But neither of those were a very good excuse. "My name is Kansas Colton. I work with the Alaska Department of Public Safety as part of a Search and Rescue team. Your dad is out here with us, and he's going to be happy to see you."

Asher looked at her and smiled. "You did it."

The thing was, she hadn't. "It was you."

"No need for false modesty."

"It's not false," she said, "and it's not the time for this conversation. We have to get that boy out of the hole." Raising her voice so Glen could hear her clearly, she said, "I'm coming down to get you. Is that all right?"

"Okay," he said, his voice was little more than a whisper. Had he been yelling for help so long that he'd lost his voice?

Kansas dropped the backpack on the ground. She unfastened the zipper for the main compartment and removed a rope and harness. Within seconds, she had the harness around her hips and waist. It was tied to the rope.

Asher had the rope's other end. He was using a nearby tree as the anchor of a pulley.

"Take this with you." From a pocket on his coat, he removed a blue bear. "Glen's mom gave this to me."

She'd almost forgotten that she'd asked Asher to get the child's favorite toy. "Thanks." She shoved the bear into the front of the harness, like the toy was rappelling, too.

"Be safe down there," said Asher.

"Just don't let me go."

"Never."

For a moment, she thought about kissing him. But now wasn't the time.

Dropping over the lip, Kansas lowered herself into the hole. It was a tight fit. The sides pressed in on her shoulders, her back, her chest. She wiggled down farther. Her foot caught in a root. She pulled her leg up. It wouldn't budge. The metallic taste of panic filled her mouth. She couldn't give into the fear. "How are you doing down there, Glen?"

She heard a wheeze. Had he said, "Good"?

Kansas swallowed her anxiety. She moved her foot left and right, digging the toe of her boot into the dirt wall. It gave her enough room to pull her foot free.

Bracing her feet against the wall, she freed one hand long enough to flip on the light. Kansas looked down. Glen was at the bottom of the hole looking up. His face was dirty. His lips were colorless. Aside from his eyes, he blended in perfectly to his surroundings.

She had seven feet to go. Luckily, there weren't as many roots blocking her way. Hand over hand, using the wall to support her feet, Kansas lowered herself to the bottom of the hole. Glen stood against one wall. It was a good thing, too. It was a tight fit for her alone.

"Hey, Glen," she said. "Are you hurt? Bleeding?"

He shook his head. "Just cold," he whispered.

She pulled the bear out of her harness. "I have someone who you might know."

He hugged the toy to his chest. "Blueberry Bear."

"Blueberry Bear. That's a cute name."

Glen hugged the stuffed animal.

"How about we get you out of here," she said. "Does that sound like a good idea?"

The boy nodded his head.

There was no way she could ascend with Glen in her arms. He was going to have to wear her harness and get pulled up. She tugged twice on the rope and watched the opening.

Asher's face appeared. He was smiling down at her. "You made it."

She couldn't help but smile back. "I did. You're going to have to pull Glen up."

"I can do that," he said. "Once you get him secured, pull twice on the rope again."

Kansas spent a few minutes getting Glen into the harness and giving him a quick safety lesson. "Your dad will be here in just a few minutes. Then you can go home to your mom. How's that sound?"

"Sounds great," he croaked, smiling for the first time.

"All right," she said, placing the rope in his small hands. "Hold tight and in one minute, you'll be out of here."

She gave two hard tugs. The rope went taut, and Glen slowly started to rise from the ground, Kansas kept a hand on his shoulder, then back, legs and finally feet— all the while keeping him steady. Once he slipped out her reach, she could hear the rest of the search party arrive. Since the boy started moving quicker, she had to guess that some of the other troopers were helping Asher with the rope.

Glen looked down at her and waved. Then, he was pulled over the rim and disappeared from view. Even twelve feet belowground, she could hear the cheer as the little boy was reunited with his father.

The air in the hole was significantly warmer than that at the surface. It was probably one of the reasons Glen wasn't suffering from hypothermia. But it was far from warm underground. She stood on the dirt floor and started to shiver. Sure, she was dressed for the weather, but adrenaline filled her veins, and she couldn't stop trembling. On top of it all was the question she couldn't stop asking herself. What would have happened if Asher hadn't seen the missing boy?

She knew the answer. He'd still be stuck in the hole. And there was no guarantee that he'd ever be found.

Asher appeared at the opening once again. His smile was wider than before. "I'm going to throw the harness to you. Yank twice when you're ready and we'll pull you up."

He dropped the harness into the hole. It was trailed by the rope. She caught the gear before it hit the ground.

Kansas stepped into the harness and tightened the straps. She pulled on the rope twice. The line went taut as she began to rise from the ground. Pressing her feet against one wall and her back against another, she climbed as the rope pulled her higher. Soon, she could feel cold seeping in through the opening. The searchlight had been moved and shone into the hole. After being at the bottom, the beam was blinding. Holding on to the rope with one hand, she shielded her eyes with the other.

Then she broke the surface. A cheer rose up in the silent woods.

Glen was snuggled into his father's arms. Mike rested his cheek on his son's head.

Kansas scrambled the final few feet and stood. She waved. "Thanks to everyone who came out, this is story has a happy ending." She ruffled the hair on the boy's head before adding, "Glen fell into a hole at the base of that tree. The air down there was warmer than the ground temp. That's why you were able to stay safe, bud. We also have a happy ending because Mike and Glen's mom thought to call us quickly. On top of everything, everyone responded right away. I know this is a job for all of us with the ADPS. We get a paycheck to be out here. But I also know that for many of you this is more than work—it's a calling."

"Thank you so much," said Mike, his voice hoarse with emotion.

"Thank you," said Glen with a whisper. He waved his stuffed animal. "Blueberry Bear says thank you, too."

"You are so welcome. But we have to thank everyone for all their hard work."

Her words were followed by another round of cheers and applause. Even Glen lifted his head from his father's shoulder long enough to clap.

"Everyone on this team is important. But I have to give a special shout-out to Asher Rafferty. Somehow, miraculously, Asher heard Glen calling out all the way at the bottom of the hole. He was the one who spotted him through the tangle of roots." She shook her head, trying not to think what would've happened if Asher hadn't been on the scene. "And to think, I almost didn't bring him with me."

Laughter followed.

Now there was nothing else to do besides pack up their gear. Only this time, it would be different. She'd be going home with Asher. He's kissed her once. Would he kiss her again?

Chapter Seven

Kansas was folding up her rope when Mike Anderson approached. Glen was in his father's arms. "I have to thank you again for everything you've done for Glen. For our family. I know you said that this was a job for you, but really, you are a hero." Mike's eyes were moist.

Kansas loved her job. But it was moments like this that it went beyond being a vocation to being a calling. Still, she couldn't accept the praise.

"I organized the search party." She pointed to Asher. "The real star is that guy."

He was helping two other troopers disassemble the searchlight. He laughed as he worked. To think, earlier this evening, she'd been so mad at him that she'd left her parents' party. It seemed like seeing the stalker in the driveway happened days earlier and not just hours ago. Without the powerful spotlight, the woods were once again dark.

"Well," said Mike, "you're a hero in my book."

"Blueberry Bear says you're a hero, too," said Glen. His voice was still soft, but she assumed that his speech would return with time and a few cups of hot chocolate.

"I need to call my second-in-command. We'll get an

ambulance to your house. They can examine Glen and Blueberry Bear." She pinched the bear's stitched nose. "If he needs any medical treatment, there's a regional hospital in town."

Mike thanked her again and Kansas took a few steps away from the group. She opened the phone app. Thankfully, there were two bars of coverage on her phone. This far into the wilderness, she never knew if she'd have a signal. She placed a call. Aquwik answered in the middle of the first ring. "The dogs just arrived," he said. In the background, she could hear happy barking. "Once they get a scent, we'll see where they lead."

"You don't need to worry about coming out. We found the child, he's safe and in his father's arms." Kansas gave a succinct rundown of the search for Glen Anderson. She included the fact that Asher had heard his weak cries and spotted him when her visual search had been too hasty. As she talked, she removed the harness and shoved all her gear into her backpack. After turning off her headlamp, she stowed that in her bag, as well. "Call an ambulance. Glen seems fine, but he'll need to be checked out."

"You lead a good team," said Aquwik.

His praise landed on her shoulders like a boulder.

"Maybe we should recruit Asher for SAR." But as she spoke, something in the woods moved. Kansas watched the darkness. What had she seen? A shadow? A tree? To her, it had looked human. There had been the outline of shoulders, a torso, a head. A chill ran down her spine. Still staring at the space, she removed her flashlight and cast the beam into the never-ending night. A small pine tree stood where she'd seen the figure. It was the right height for her phantom.

She tried to shake off her unease. But fear gripped her throat, making it hard to swallow.

"Kansas. Kansas? Are you there?"

What had Aquwik said? She hadn't heard a word.

"Sorry. What did you say?"

"Glen's mom is asking when you'll get to the house."

Kansas glanced over her shoulder. Everyone was standing in the snow, waiting for her to lead them back up the hill. "Tell her that we're on our way." Then she ended the call. Shoving the phone into one of the pockets on her coat, she plodded toward the team. "We got what we came for. Let's get Glen and Mike back home."

A trail of flashlights wound up the hill and through the woods. But she couldn't help but look over her shoulder and glance at the place where she'd seen...something. Maybe it was the lack of sleep. Or maybe it was the encounter with a stalker earlier in the evening. But even as she walked up the hill surrounded by her fellow ADPS troopers, Kansas could feel a set of eyes on her back.

ASHER SAT IN the driver's seat of his SUV and gripped the steering wheel with both hands. Energy still buzzed through his system. Sure, going out on the SAR and not getting sleep went against everything the doctor recommended for his recovery, but he didn't care.

Being with Kansas when they found the missing child made him feel invincible.

Add to the fact that snow caught in the headlight beams made it look like they were flying through space, and Asher felt like he was a deity.

In the seat beside him, Kansas rested her head against the side window.

She'd been quiet since the team was dismissed. So

far, he'd respected her need for silence. But now it was too much.

"Big night, huh?" he said.

She glanced at him and snorted. "Yeah. Big night."

"What's the matter?" he asked. "I thought you'd be ecstatic. We found the kid." Once he started talking, the words tumbled out of him like water over a broken dam. "Man, what a rush. I might just leave the Violent Crimes unit and join Search and Rescue."

"You should," she said, her voice lacking any emotion. "You're a natural."

He tried to ignore her missing affect, but he couldn't. "Are you okay?"

"Yeah. Sure. I'm dandy." She cast her gaze toward the window and stared into the darkness.

Okay, now he knew something was wrong.

"What's going on?" he asked.

She shook her head. "I guess I'm just tired."

If Asher was a wise man, he would let it go. Obviously, something was bothering Kansas. It was also clear that she didn't want to talk. For several minutes, he drove in silence. As they turned onto the road leading to her house, he couldn't hold back any longer.

"It seems like something's really bothering you."

She sighed. Her breath collected into fog on the glass. "I was just thinking that you really are a natural at search and rescue."

Usually, he would have welcomed her compliment. But this time, he didn't. Her tone wasn't hostile per se, but there was something more in the timbre of her voice.

"You say that like it's a bad thing." Was she upset because they'd been rivals for so long, and now they'd worked together as a team? Jesus, how big of a jerk had he been? "I know we haven't always agreed on everything." Or really anything. "But I hoped we could start to put that behind us. And that we could always put our differences aside if a child's life was at stake."

"I'm not worried about you." Kansas watched him as he slowed before pulling into the driveway. "You did great."

Asher put the gearshift into Park and turned to watch her. They should go inside. Being parked in her driveway left them exposed. He checked all the mirrors to make sure nobody was approaching the car. They were all alone. "What's wrong?"

"Me," she said. "I'm the problem."

"Now I'm confused."

"Just forget about it," she said while unfastening her seat belt.

Asher did the same. As soon as Kansas was out of the car, he followed. He waited as she slipped the key into the lock. As she opened the front door, he reminded himself to find a better security system for her house. He closed the door behind him and engaged the dead bolt.

The room looked the same as it had when they'd gone to bed. The TV remote was still on the coffee table. Empty boxes sat in a corner. The tree was filled with ornaments. Even though the lights hadn't been turned on, they still twinkled.

Kansas flipped a wall switch, turning on a lamp. She set her bag next to the sofa. With a sigh, she dropped onto the cushions and removed her boots. Bits of snow fell off her laces, leaving wet spots on the carpet.

As he hung his borrowed parka onto a wooden peg, he finally spoke again. "I know you told me to forget about it, but I'd like to help you if I can."

Her SAR coat and pants lay in a pile at her feet. She'd stripped down to her base layer—wool leggings and a long-sleeved wool shirt. It covered every inch of skin from her wrists to her neck. But the fabric hugged her curves, showing off her very womanly figure. He dropped his gaze to the floor before she noticed him taking notice of her. A lump of snow was slowly melting into the carpet fibers. He mopped the slush with his sock. The cold and damp gnawed uncomfortably at the instep of his foot.

"You were the one who found Glen," she said.

"I did," he said, still not sure why it was important. He didn't think that Kansas was a glory hog, but maybe he'd been wrong. "But why does that matter?"

"Because," she said, "I looked down in that hole first. I should've seen him, but I didn't."

"And you think you failed?"

She let out a long breath. "Think, hell. I know that I screwed up."

Asher's chest ached with her pain. He sat next to her on the sofa and placed his hand on top of hers. Being this close to her was a dangerous move. She still only wore her wool thermals. He could see the swell of her breasts. The curve of her hips. The strength of her thighs. She laced her fingers through his and his mouth went dry.

"You didn't screw up," he said. "It was hard to see Glen. He was at the bottom of a hole. His parents had given him forest camo snow pants and a tan jacket." He paused. "Who does that?"

"Someone from Arizona, I guess," she said.

"I'm not blaming the parents. I'm not blaming the kid. And I'm definitely not blaming you." He flipped his hand so they were palm to palm. "The only reason I saw him was because he waved at me. I saw the movement, not the child."

"Are you just saying that to make me feel better?"

He gripped her hand tighter. "I'm telling you because it's true. Besides, you would've looked down into that hole again."

She shrugged and leaned her head onto his shoulder. The heat from her body warmed him, heart and soul. "I guess."

"You guess?" He nudged her side.

"I know that you're right." She swallowed. "I just hate to fail."

"You didn't fail. You led the team that found Glen. You didn't need to bring out dogs. Or mountain rescue. Because of your leadership, that little boy is safe and at home instead of at the bottom of that hole and freezing to death."

"I feel like there's a punch line coming," she said, teasing him for all the grief he'd given her over the years.

"Would you believe me if I told you that I changed?"

She looked at him. Her eyes were the same color as the waters in the marina in summertime. Her lips were the color of a rich red wine. He wanted to kiss her, but he knew that he shouldn't. She was still his work partner's baby cousin. Still a fellow trooper. Still his protectee. Asher bit the inside of his lip hard. The pain was clarifying. It helped him to focus.

"What changed you?" she asked.

You did. The answer came to him without thought.

He couldn't share that with her. Not now and maybe not ever.

"I guess getting blown up changes a man's perspective. It changed mine."

She nodded and settled in at his side. He had to admit, sitting together on the couch, with the Christmas tree in the corner, was nice. It was cozy. It was the kind of domesticity that Asher tended to avoid. Over the years, he'd had his share of girlfriends. A few of them had even been serious. And then, there came a moment, when Asher knew he wasn't able to stay with them for the long haul. When the end came, he always told the women that his leaving had nothing to do with them. He assured them that it was all about him. He knew that people used the trite line all the time. But in Asher's case, he meant it.

He never could decide why he eventually got restless. It's not like he had a traumatic childhood or a horrible life that made him feel like he could never be loved.

He just always knew that eventually, the relationship would end.

But with Kansas, it was different.

Was this what he'd been looking for all along?

KANSAS WAS TIRED. Vulnerable. She wanted to feel alive. She wanted to kiss Asher again. Sitting up taller, she faced him. For a moment, their gazes met and held. Without another thought, she pressed her mouth to his, licking at the seam of his lips.

He pulled back from the kiss and studied her face, as if she were a map that he could read. What part of her had he discovered?

"Kansas?" He said her name as if it were a question.

"Kiss me," she said, her words mingling with his breath.

Without speaking, Asher placed his mouth on hers. His lips were somehow both strong and soft. He smelled sharp, like snow, and the woods. She sighed and he slipped his tongue into her mouth. She pressed her hands onto the broad planes of his chest. His pecs were hard and well defined. She explored him—his chest, his abs, his shoulders, his back—with her hands. He was solid muscle, lean sinew and everything a man should be.

"Oh, Asher," she said, sharing his breath.

He moved his kisses from her mouth to her cheek to her neck. His hand traveled from her back to her stomach and up to her breast. The fabric of her top was thin, and his touch was hot on her flesh. She arched her back, pressing her breasts into his hand. His touch sent her pulse racing.

She kissed him again. Harder. Hungrier. Over the past several hours, she'd been resentful, afraid, felt as if she were a failure. Now she wanted to replace all those feelings with something new. Asher's kisses and his touch were just what she needed.

His fingers traveled down to the hem of her shirt. His touch blazed a trail upward. He slipped a finger inside the cup of her bra and stroked her nipple. She sucked in a breath as pleasure filled her veins.

"You like that?" he asked, kissing her neck.

"Yes," she said, claiming his mouth with hers again. "Oh, yes."

He moved his hand to her other breast. Reaching under her bra, he pinched her nipple. This time, the pleasure mixed with pain and left her dizzy.

"Do you like that?" he asked.

"Oh God, yes," she mewed.

"Good." He lifted her shirt up to her shoulders and dipped his head to her stomach. He licked a trail across her abs, up her chest, and to her bra. He lowered the cups, freeing her breasts. He ran his tongue over one nipple and then the other. Suddenly, her clothes were too tight. She shimmied out of her thin wool sweater and tossed it to the side. Kansas then removed her bra, letting it drop to her lap.

"God," he said, "you're so damned perfect."

She never expected a compliment like that to come from Asher Rafferty. They'd squabbled too many times. But before she could think—much less say—anything else. He placed his mouth on hers. His tongue slipped between her lips. She was consumed by want. No, she felt more than desire for Asher. It was a need. A hunger. A thirst. And propriety be damned, she was going to have him.

Kansas raked her fingers through his hair and down the back of his neck. He growled, and the sound landed in her middle.

He reached for her, pulling her closer. She let herself be drawn onto his lap. She straddled him, dropping her knees on either side of his thighs. Beneath her, Asher was already hard. Kansas didn't mind, she was already wet. She held the sides of his face and kissed him deeper.

"It's not fair," she said, "that I don't have a shirt on, and you do."

She felt his smile. "I can take care of that," he said while slipping out of his sweater.

It ended up on the floor with her bra. Next, he removed his undershirt. They were skin to skin. Like she had felt under his shirt, his pecs were well defined. He had a sprinkling of dark hair that covered his chest before narrowing into a line that dove down the front of his jeans. His areolas were dark against his pale flesh. She ran her thumbs over both nipples, and he kissed her harder.

She moved her pelvis, riding him through his jeans. He gripped her ass, holding her still.

"God, Kansas. You are so freaking sexy. I'm about to explode right here and now. But is this what you really want?"

Of course she wanted him. To feel his body next to hers. To lay with him. To move with him. To have him inside of her.

But…

She leaned back, sitting on his thighs.

He was right to slow things down. As much as she wanted to take him as her lover, he was hardly a one-night stand. She'd known him for years. He was the guy who teased her whenever she got mad at work. After he'd been injured by the blast, she'd sat at his bedside and prayed he'd heal completely. He was the one who volunteered to stay with her so she would be safe in her own home.

So her feelings weren't exactly straightforward. But she also knew that after this night was over, he'd still be Asher. She'd still be Kansas. They'd still have a shared history and lives that were intertwined.

Of course she wanted him. But how would they move past a single night of passion?

"I'm sorry," she said. "I shouldn't have let things get out of hand."

"Don't apologize," he said. "It was both of us…and trust me, I didn't mind. But it'd kill me if I became a mistake to you."

She slid off his lap and stood on the carpeted floor. Without her top, she was too vulnerable. Folding her arms over her boobs was ridiculous and childish, but she needed to get dressed. She bent down to pick up her top. A lock of hair had come loose from her ponytail, and it fell over the side of her face, a curtain hiding her from his gaze. She slipped back into the thin sweater. It covered her skin, but her nipples were still hard and showed through the fabric.

"Well," she said, "I guess we should try and get some rest."

She wasn't sure what her duties would be—especially if everyone still thought that Scott Montgomery had come back to town. If nothing else, in the morning, she would have paperwork from tonight's SAR.

He slid into his undershirt. A blanket was draped over the back of the sofa. He pulled it down and set it on the cushion beside him. "I think I'll just hang out here. Maybe watch a little TV, if it's okay with you."

The bed in the guest room was more comfortable. Then again, if he was in the room next door, would she really stay in her own bed? "You're welcome to sleep wherever you want." Then she quickly added, "Out here. In the guest room. It's up to you." She paused. "What time is it anyway? I can never tell when it's always dark."

Asher pulled a phone from his pocket. "It's almost three in the morning."

"I'm beat," she lied. She'd never be able to sleep while the feeling of his lips was so fresh. She picked up her discarded bra. "I'll see you in the morning."

As Kansas walked down the hallway, her legs were stiff and almost too heavy to lift. Without turning on the light, she slipped under the covers. Staring at the ceiling, she had to be honest with herself. Sure, over the years she'd wondered what it would be like to kiss Asher. So she wasn't surprised by the passion that erupted between them.

But there was something more. Kansas had always

been independent—able to rely on her own capabilities. Maybe it was because she was the youngest member of the Colton clan and always had to keep up with the older kids. Or perhaps it was because she'd grown up in a small town and had a tight-knit family so she never needed anyone beyond her tribe. But, in his arms, she'd felt safe and cherished and protected. In all honesty, she hadn't expected for his embrace to feel like coming home.

Chapter Eight

Asher woke and stared into the darkness. He'd lain down on the couch and fallen asleep within minutes. Yet something had pulled him from his slumber, and he didn't know what it had been. His heart raced.

Then he heard it.

It was the unmistakable sound of a dead bolt being unlocked.

Someone was at the door.

A million different possibilities came to Asher at once. Certainly, Kansas's parents had a key to her home. Probably her brother, as well. Maybe even Eli or one of the other numerous Colton cousins.

Surely, they wouldn't stop by before 5:00 a.m.

If they did, wouldn't they call first?

And why hadn't the person unlatched the second lock yet?

He couldn't answer any of his questions.

Another thought came to him, and Asher went cold. The person outside might not be a family member at all. It could be Scott Montgomery.

Asher couldn't lay on the sofa and wait for the killer to let himself in.

Then another thought came to him. He still didn't have a gun.

But what he said earlier was still true. He didn't need a firearm—just a weapon.

Asher rose from the sofa. He didn't have time to run to the kitchen for a knife. Once again, he unplugged the lamp. He moved across the room, pressing his back into the wall as the second lock was unlatched. The door opened slowly. A gust of wind blew snowflakes onto the carpeting. The first thing that crossed the threshold was the black barrel of a handgun.

Asher's heart skipped a beat. He shoved his fear aside. No matter what, he wasn't going to let Scott get a hold of Kansas.

Immediately, he knew what to do. Holding the lamp's neck, he watched as more of the gun came into the house. As the grip of the firearm appeared, so did a hand. Wait. Wait. Wait. Once Asher saw the wrist, he swung the lamp, coming down on the intruder's arm.

There was a curse of pain as the gun tumbled to the ground and skittered outside. But Asher wasn't finished. He swung the lamp like a major league baseball slugger sending a ball over the fence. The ceramic soared through the air before smashing against the door jamb.

Damn it. He hadn't hit the intruder.

The guy, dressed in all black, had ducked. The lamp had missed his head by inches.

Asher still held the guts of the light—a brass pole and the cord.

From his crouch, the intruder grabbed Asher around the middle. Air left his lungs in a gust as the guy grabbed his torso and threw him to the ground. The guy's face was visible. Dark eyes, pale skin. Without question, the intruder was Scott Montgomery.

"You," Montgomery snarled. "How could she want you? She hates you, Rafferty. How could she have wanted you to kiss her?"

How the hell did Scott know about the kiss and Kansas's exact words? Sure, Asher had only been distracted for a second, but it was all the time Scott needed. He reached into his pocket and withdrew a needle. The sharp point glinted in the dim light.

The killer was back. Asher was the only thing standing between a murderer and Kansas.

KANSAS LAY IN her bed and stared at the ceiling. A minute ago, she'd been asleep, dreaming of Asher's touch. Now, she was awake. Her pulse galloped and it wasn't from the eroticism of her dream. She'd heard something.

But what had it been?

Flipping back the covers, she rose from bed. Standing in the middle of her darkened room she listened.

There was a grunt. A thud.

It almost sounded as if someone were struggling.

Hell, there was no *almost* about it.

Someone else was in the house.

Her heart started to pound against her ribs. She knew just what to do. Pulling open the drawer on her side table, she removed the metal gun safe and set it on her bed. Her hands shook, but she pressed her thumb onto the biometric lock. The light flashed red.

"What the…" She drew in a deep breath and rubbed her thumb on the leg of her pajama pants. With a long exhale she touched the lock pad. The light switched from red to green. The latch clicked and the lid opened. Kansas pulled her father's H&K from the safe.

Gun in hand, she opened her bedroom door.

The air in the hallway was cold.

Without the closed door, she could hear sounds that she hadn't before. There was shifting. Crunching. Something was definitely happening in her living room. She rushed down the corridor. She found the wall switch and light filled the room.

For a moment, it was impossible to take in all the chaos.

The door was open. Snow blew across the threshold.

Scott Montgomery had pinned Asher to the floor. Asher held a brass pole in both hands. He pressed the metal into Scott's arm, pushing him away. Scott held a syringe. A bead of clear liquid dripped out of the end.

"Drop the needle, Scott," she said, her voice as cold as the air outside.

The struggle on the floor stopped, but the killer didn't move.

"I said, drop the effing needle."

He opened his palm. The syringe fell to the floor.

"Now, stand up. Keep your hands where I can see them."

The killer rocked back onto his heels and lifted his palms.

Without the weight on his chest, Asher was able to stand. He came to her side. She wanted to look at him, to try and read his thoughts. But she couldn't take her eyes off Scott.

"Why him?" Scott asked, still kneeling on the floor. "Why'd you ask him to kiss you?"

His words made no sense. "What?"

"You asked him to kiss you," said Scott, his teeth gritting. "I thought you hated him."

It was true, Kansas had asked Asher to kiss her. But how did Scott know? She glanced at Asher. The instant she looked away she knew that she'd made a mistake.

Scott reached behind him. When he came forward, he held a gun.

"Don't move," he ordered, rising to his feet. The barrel of the gun was pointed straight at her heart.

Her face was numb. Her hands shook. She tightened all her muscles, stopping the shaking before it began. "What are you going to do with that thing, Scott? Shoot me?"

"No," he said. "I'm going to shoot him."

Fire exploded from the muzzle. A boom of thunder echoed in the small room. The stench of gunpowder hung in the chilly air. Without thought, Kansas pulled the trigger. Once. Twice. Once again.

Smoke rose from the barrel of her gun. She looked around her living room. Asher lay on the floor. A smear of blood had turned his cheek crimson. And Scott Montgomery was gone.

FOR A SPLIT SECOND, indecision glued Kansas to the floor. Did she chase after Scott Montgomery or did she provide first aid to Asher? Well, when she thought about it that way, it really wasn't a decision at all.

Holding her gun with the muzzle aimed at the ground, she knelt next to where Asher lay. Even from where she sat, she could see his chest rise and fall. He was alive and breathing. Both were good signs. She touched his cheek, and he groaned. Blinked.

Asher pushed up onto his elbows.

"What in the hell?"

Placing her palm on his chest, she pressed him back into the carpet. "You've been shot," she said. "I'm not sure where or how bad you've been hit, but you're bleeding. What's injured?"

He lifted his hand to the side of his head. "It feels like I got burned by a poker."

She examined his scalp. A neat furrow had been cut through his hair. It had broken the skin but hadn't damaged any bones—or so she assumed. Her shoulders sagged, releasing tension she'd been holding for too long. "I think you'll be okay." Standing, she continued, "Just lay here. I'm going to call emergency services."

Kansas walked through the snow that had blown into her house. Her feet burned with the cold. She pushed the door closed and engaged both locks.

"The dead bolt won't stop Scott," said Asher. "He has a key. He let himself in."

"A key?" she echoed, not completely believing his words. "I never gave him a key."

"Remember." Asher pushed up to sitting and leaned his back against the wall. A trickle of blood ran down the side of his face. "Until a few weeks ago, you thought he was your friend."

Asher was right. How many times had she left her bag—including her house keys inside—unattended around Scott? It was too many to count. He was smart enough to make a wax impression of her keys and then get his own set made.

He could've been coming and going from her home for months. Years, even. Suddenly, Kansas felt dirty. But even the hottest shower wouldn't wash away the traces that Scott had left behind. She shook off the feeling of being violated and said, "My phone is in my room. Wait here while I get it." He'd already ignored her order to remain prone. The last thing she wanted was for him to stand up and pass out while she was gone. Emphasizing each word, she said, "Do not get up."

Already, she knew that her directive was for naught. Asher used the wall to steady himself as he rose to his feet.

"What are you doing?" She reached for his hand.

"I think there's something." Holding on to her fingertips, Asher pulled her forward. "Underneath your TV."

Her flatscreen TV was mounted to the wall. But she saw what he'd seen immediately. There was a small glass dome, no bigger than a dime, tucked under the edge and partially hidden by the cords.

Asher bent to look at it. "Son of a bitch," he said before adding something she'd already guessed. "It's a camera."

Kansas's throat tightened, making it impossible to breath. The floor seemed to heave, making it hard to stand. Using the coffee table as a seat, she dropped down. "He has a key to my house," she whispered. "And he planted a camera in my living room."

Who knew how long Scott had had full access to her life?

It was just a miracle that she was still alive.

"I'm going to report this." Asher picked up his phone and placed a call. "Eli," he said, "you've got to get over to Kansas's house."

Even with the cell pressed to Asher's ear, she could hear her cousin's sleepy voice. "Come to Kansas's house. What time is it?"

Asher ignored Eli's question. Instead, he said, "Montgomery was here. He has a key to the front door. I've found one camera in her living room. I'm going to assume that there are more in the house."

More cameras? Kansas would've retched, but her stomach was empty.

"The bastard," Eli growled on the other end of the call.

Asher said, "I gotta be honest, I'm surprised nobody checked the house for bugs before now."

On the other end of the line, Eli cursed again. "After you were injured in the explosion, we had a meeting for the unit. I assigned the task to the new guy but never bothered to check up. We had a chaotic few days. Not that it's a great excuse, but that's what happened. I'll talk to the new guy later."

"Right now, we're safe. So that's all that matters. Just get here when we can."

"I'm walking out the door," said Eli.

"I'll see you in a minute," said Asher before ending the call. He knelt in front of her and placed his hand on her knee. "Hey," he said softly. The one word was soothing. "We have to get you packed up. It's not safe for you to stay here—even with protection."

Kansas might be the youngest one in the family, but she was hardly a baby. Still, she knew that Asher was right. "Okay," she said as she stood. "First, let me get you cleaned up."

Without another word, Kansas walked into the kitchen. She found a clean dish towel and turned on the taps. After wetting a corner, she returned to the living room. Asher now sat on the edge of the table. She knelt between his knees, gently rubbing his cheeks with the wet towel, then she said, "At least the bleeding has stopped." Carefully, she pressed the cloth to the side of his head.

"You'll need to see a doctor. This might've made the concussion worse."

"I'm not going anywhere," he said. "It's my job to take care of you."

His gaze was on her. She couldn't look anywhere other than at his eyes. They were a deep and rich shade of brown. She wanted to tell him that she could take care of herself. But Scott Montgomery was more dangerous than she'd given him credit for.

"I appreciate your help," she said. "But I want to help you, too."

He placed his palm on the back of her hand. Then he took the cloth and set it aside. She rested her fingertips on his cheek, felt his beard with her palm. She traced the line of his jaw, letting the soft hairs tickle her flesh. His breath washed over her. And his pulse thrummed at the base of his neck. She wanted to kiss him again. But this time, she wouldn't stop until she'd had her fill of Asher.

But what would happen if he became her lover?

Could she walk away and pretend that nothing had changed?

Before she could answer the question, there was a loud knock at her door. It was followed by a familiar voice. "Kansas. Asher. It's me. Eli. Open up."

Rising to her feet, she walked to the door. Even though she recognized her cousin's voice, she pressed her eye to the peephole. Eli stood on the stoop. He wore his dark blue parka and a pair of jeans. His hair stood in every different direction. If the reason for his visit wasn't deadly serious, she would've teased him for looking like a bristly hedgehog. She pulled the door open. "Thanks for coming so quickly."

He stepped into the room as a drift of snow blew around his feet. She closed the door.

"I've called several units," said Eli. "Even though the weather sucks—the snow's still coming down and the wind has picked up—we might find some evidence. Do you know where Scott was shot?"

That was news to her. "I fired at him, but I didn't realize that I'd hit him."

Eli hitched his thumb toward the door. "There's a blood trail in the snow."

"Where does it lead?" Asher asked.

"It stops at the road. He must've had a car waiting."

She knew exactly what would've happened if Asher hadn't heard him sneaking into her house. Her hands started to shake again. She folded her arms across her chest, to keep them steady. Instead of worrying about what might've been, she had to focus on the investigation.

"He had a syringe with him," she said, pointing to where Scott had tossed the needle aside. "He also had his own gun. We need to get an APB out that he's armed and dangerous."

"He left something else here, too," said Asher. He walked over to the TV and pointed to the small lens. "It's the camera."

Eli placed his hands on his thighs to get a better look. He inhaled sharply, making his nostrils flare. "It's hard to be professional knowing what lengths this sick twist has gone to get to you." He stood and drew in another breath. "To know why he's so obsessed with you. God, it takes me back to that morning."

Years before Kansas was born, tragedy had struck the Colton family. When Eli was just a kid, he'd gone with his dad to visit his grandparents. There, they'd discovered a grisly crime. Both grandparents had been murdered in their sleep. The younger sister, Caroline, was dead on the sofa—killed by the same stalker who'd murdered the parents. What's worse is that the stalker had committed suicide—but not before placing an engagement ring on Caroline's finger and posing them in each other's arms.

Scott Montgomery had discovered that crime and began to kill random women after placing a fake diamond on their finger. As it turns out, Kansas was his intended target all along. She hated to think of the connection between her and her deceased aunt. But even Kansas knew that she looked just like Caroline.

"So, what do we do now?" she asked.

"The first thing we have to do is get you somewhere safe. Obviously, you can't stay here. You need to go to your parents' house."

It was like history repeating itself. Would her parents die because they stood between her and Scott? "I can't do that," she said. "And you know why."

Eli nodded. She knew that he understood her fully. "I can send you to the mainland, but not until the storm clears."

"I have an idea," said Asher. "She can stay with me."

"You?"

"First, I have better security than those locks of yours." He counted off the reasons on his fingers as he spoke. "Scott doesn't know where I live. And even if he did figure it out, he doesn't have a key to my house."

"I like your logic," said Eli. "But it's up to Kansas. Are you willing to stay with Asher, at least until the weather improves?"

Well, if it was going to be temporary, there was only one answer she could give. "I'm fine staying at his place."

"Good," said Eli. "Get everything you need for a day or two. Once the crime scene techs arrive, we'll start looking for any other cameras."

"Cameras," she repeated, choking on the word. She had momentarily forgotten. "Christ, this really is a nightmare."

"Pack your things," Eli ordered. "It's best if you're gone before the rest of the team shows up." He paused and rubbed his jaw. "And another thing. I think it's best if you don't go out on anymore SARs, at least for now."

"You're kidding, right? You want me to stop working?"

"It's not just for your protection," said Eli. "But you need to think of your team's safety, too."

It wasn't in her nature to give up. She wanted to keep working. To help. To fight. But her cousin was right. "I'll call Aquwik."

"Don't worry about it," said Eli. "I'll reach out to your boss in Juneau and let her know what's going on."

Sure, her cousin was trying to be helpful. It's just that she hated to be dismissed from her own life. Kansas gave a single nod. "Give me a minute and I'll be ready to go."

In her room, Kansas removed a large duffle from under her bed. She set it on the comforter and began packing. She shoved in a few socks. Underwear. Two bras. She also pulled out sweatpants, a pair of jeans, sweaters and a Christmas sweatshirt. As she zipped her bag closed, she realized an important truth. She'd underestimated Scott Montgomery. But all of that was at an end. He was deadly, dangerous, and it was obvious that she was his intended prey.

The thing was, Kansas had no intention of becoming his next victim.

Chapter Nine

Before leaving Kansas's house, a pair of EMTs checked out the wound to Asher's head. They determined the wound was superficial but still offered to take him to the hospital. Asher wasn't going to let a little scratch keep him down. Instead, he got Kansas into his SUV and started driving to his condo, which was twenty miles away.

Because of the storm, it took him an hour to get home. By the time he pulled into his designated parking spot, it was almost 6:30 a.m. Honestly, he hated that he was sitting on the sideline of the Scott Montgomery case when he should be helping Eli with the investigation. At the same time, he knew that keeping Kansas safe was crucial.

"So," he said, putting the gearshift into Park, "this is my place."

His two-story condo was in the middle of several identical homes. There were eight buildings in the complex—the only one like it in the area.

"It's nice," Kansas said.

He glanced in her direction. She sat in the passenger seat with a red duffle bag on her lap. Her hair was pulled back into a ponytail. Her skin was pale and there were dark circles around her eyes.

"Let's get you inside," said Asher, turning off the ignition. "Then I can either make you some breakfast or you can try to get some sleep."

"I'm exhausted but too keyed up to get any rest," she said, unfastening her seat belt. "Breakfast would be nice."

Asher unfastened his own seat belt and opened the door. "You're in luck. Once I was able to drive, I went to the mainland and stocked up on food. I know I have bacon. Oatmeal. Three kinds of cereal. Bread. Eggs. Coffee. Tea."

"Bacon, eggs, and toast sounds perfect." A gust of wind blew, carrying her words away.

His walkway had yet to be cleared. He wanted to put his hand on Kansas's back. But were they at the point where he could touch her without asking? At the front door, he entered a six-digit code into the pad attached to the handle. A light changed from red to green as the lock unlatched with a *click*.

He held the door open as Kansas crossed the threshold. The front room was dark. He flipped a wall switch, turning on a floor lamp. It cast a warm glow in the corner of the room and provided enough light for both of them to see.

With Kansas at his side, it was like seeing his home for the first time. His single thought was, *Jesus, what a mess*.

A blanket was thrown across his sofa. A bag of chips—half full—sat on the coffee table. There was an empty cereal bowl next to the bag. Several mugs and drinking glasses were scattered around the room. "I wasn't expecting company," he said, picking up two glasses.

"Don't worry about it," she said, sitting on the edge of his sofa before dropping her bag on the floor next to her feet.

"I really don't live like this—not normally," he continued, although that was a lie. "Recovering from a concussion means a lot of laying around and boredom. Hell, for the first week, I couldn't even watch TV or read."

"That does sound boring." She shook her head sympathetically. "What did you do?"

"I listened to a lot of audiobooks." He tucked the glasses into the crook of his arm and stacked several bowls before picking those up, as well. "Make yourself comfortable. I'll be right back."

The kitchen was attached to the living room by a narrow hallway. Asher deposited the used dishes onto the counter. The sink was already full of other dirty dishes. He opened the dishwasher. Thankfully, it was empty. As he loaded the racks, he wondered how he'd let this happen. He was thirty-two years old, after all. He shouldn't be living like he did when he was in college.

"I brought you these," said Kansas.

He turned. She stood behind him, her arms filled with the rest of his used cups, bowls, and cutlery.

"Thanks." He nodded toward the counter. "You can put them all right there."

"I really don't live like this," he said again. At the same moment, he wondered when he'd last cleaned his bathroom.

"It's not a problem," she said. "I'm just thankful that you're letting me stay here until Scott is caught. *If* Scott is caught," she said, correcting herself.

They both knew the statistics. As heinous as it was to be a serial killer, it was one crime where the perp wasn't always caught. Hell, the FBI didn't even know how many active serial killers there were in the country. If the stats held, there was a decent chance that Scott Montgomery would get away with all his crimes.

Sure, Kansas was a professional and she knew the risks. But right now, she was a woman who needed to be comforted—the truth be damned.

"You know that you're safe with me. Besides, a lot of people working to find him. Eventually, he'll get caught." Asher put the final bowl into the dishwasher. He tossed in a detergent tab and closed the door. As he started the wash cycle, he added, "Scott will make a mistake, and we'll find him."

"But will that be before or after he gets to me?" Her voice hitched with emotion on the final word.

Asher's heart squeezed into a tight fist. "Hey." He opened his arms. "It'll be okay. I promise."

She stepped into his embrace and leaned her head onto his shoulder. He lifted his hand, ready to caress her hair. He stopped. Mere inches separated his palm from her head. Sure, he'd known Kansas for years, but he had to stop touching her in such an intimate way.

Her curves fit into the muscular planes of his body. Her heart raced, beating against his own chest. He wanted to place his lips on hers again. But she was emotional and exhausted. He wouldn't take advantage of her at a time like this.

"C'mon," he said, ending the embrace. "Let me show you to the guest room. You get settled. I'll start us some breakfast."

Kansas gave him a tight smile. "Sure. Lead the way."

His condo took up two levels. The ground floor had the living room, a small dining area, a half bath, and the kitchen. A set of stairs led off the living room to the second floor. Before following him up the stairs, she grabbed her bag from where it sat on the floor. It ended at a hallway. The master bedroom was at the front of the unit. The guest room, along with the bathroom, was at the back.

Thankfully, Asher never went into the guest room. It meant that the bed had been made months earlier, and then the room had been forgotten. He pushed the door open and flipped the switch for the overhead light. A thin layer of dust covered the bedside table and TV that sat on a four-drawer chest. He picked up the remote. "I don't have cable," he said. "But this is hooked up to most of the streaming services." He placed it on the bedspread. "The drawers are empty. Feel free to use them for your stuff. There's a bathroom across the hall. There's soap and shampoo in the shower, if you didn't bring your own."

She dropped her bag on the bed. "Thanks for everything."

He felt drawn to her, like a magnet to steel. He wanted to go to her, to take her in his arms once more. But he shouldn't. "Well," he said, taking a backward step into the hallway, "I better start breakfast."

"Asher. Wait." She swallowed. "Downstairs, you said that Scott will get caught. Do you really believe that? Or were you just saying that to make me feel better?"

The honest answer was, he'd done a little of both. It would do no good to admit as much to Kansas. Instead, he said, "He'll get caught. You're part of the ADPS. You're more than a colleague. You're family."

It would be smart of Asher to remember the truth of his words. It was going to be hell ignoring his desire for Kansas, especially since she was staying under his roof. But her safety—both physically and emotionally—were what mattered. Not his runaway libido.

SCOTT MONTGOMERY LIMPED into the cabin. Pain, like a white-hot poker, stabbed his thigh with each step. After turning on the light, he collapsed onto the sofa. For several minutes, he lay without moving. The agony in his leg dulled to an ache.

Sitting up, he started to remove his pants. A wave of nausea crashed over him as the garment peeled off the wound. He got them down to his feet first. Then he kicked his uninjured leg free. Using his foot, he worked his injured leg out of the pants. He picked them up off the floor. There was a rip in the leg at front and in the back. In the middle of his thigh was a blackened hole where the bullet had gone through his leg. Blood still wept from the wound.

How could Kansas have shot him? *Him.* He was so devoted to her. She had to see that he loved her so much he was willing to take another life. Scott wasn't like most killers—mindless beasts who murdered people for no reason other than their own twisted pleasure. His murders served a purpose. They were a declaration of his love for Kansas. By now, she had to understand his motives.

But there was more to worry about than Kansas. He had to examine his gunshot wound. Scott drew in a shaking breath. He exhaled. He breathed again. And again. Standing straight, he hobbled to the sink. There, he wet a towel with water from the tap. Gingerly, he dabbed at the bullet hole, cleaning away the blood. It didn't matter how gently he cleaned; every touch was torture. He wanted to scream, but he didn't dare.

Instead, he focused on his breath. In through the nose. Out through the mouth.

He kept a first aid kit in one of the cabinets. From there, he removed a tube of antibiotic ointment and large bandage. He applied both. Then he took four OTC pain-killers. He didn't care that he'd doubled the dosage. All he needed was to get rid of the pain.

Leaning on the counter, he used the breathing technique again. Maybe it was the change of focus. Maybe it was the meds. Maybe it was the bandage and the antibiotic ointment. But his leg didn't hurt as much.

With some extra emotional and mental space, Scott realized something that he hadn't before. He'd fired his gun—a fact he knew. But he'd also hit Asher Rafferty.

He could clearly see the other guy going down, a hand to his head.

Had he finally gotten rid of Asher?

The thought lifted his spirits.

Thankfully, he could find out. Scott shuffled as quickly as he could to the computer. By the time he dropped into the seat, he was sweating. He clicked the mouse, bringing his screen to life. He opened the program for the cameras in Kansas's home and waited for the images to appear.

The program opened, but the screens were black. He clicked on one camera link and then another. A message appeared.

Your equipment is no longer connected.

"No," he said, clicking the link again and again. "No. No. No."

It could be the storm that had cut the connection. But a sick feeling settled in his gut. The ABI would have scoured Kansas's house by now. Had they found the cameras?

If they had, it was bad. No, it was worse than bad. It was awful.

Could they use the cameras to find his IP address and then his physical location?

He should get off the internet. But he needed to know the truth about Asher first.

Hours of footage had been recorded to the cloud. He accessed the database and found the footage from his arrival. He watched the scene unfold as an audience member of his own life. The fight. Kansas's arrival with her gun. Scott, who reached back, until his fingertips found his own firearm.

There was an explosion of light and sound as he pulled the trigger. Asher went down.

Kansas shot at the same moment Scott raced out of the room.

Smoke hung in the air, and for an instant, Kansas stared out of the door. Indecision creased her forehead with lines. Then her jaw hardened with resolve. She knelt down next to the body on the floor. Asher sat up and touched his head.

In the cabin, Scott cursed.

The video continued to play. It took only a moment for all his nightmares to come true.

Asher noticed the camera. He stared at the lens hidden in the cords behind the TV.

Scott didn't need to see anymore to know that he'd been found out. He signed out of his internet account and turned off his computer. But was it enough?

His router sat on the corner of his desk. He jerked the power cord out of the port. The line of green lights slowly faded to black. His chest heaved. Despite the cold, sweat dampened his upper lip.

He'd screwed up.

He never should have placed those cameras in Kansas's home.

He never should have gone there in the first place.

Sure, there were a lot of things he'd done wrong. But he was done messing up. From now on, Scott would be patient. He would wait until the right moment. Then, once Kansas was lulled into a sense of security, he would strike.

KANSAS DIDN'T THINK she'd ever feel secure again. She placed the last shirt she'd packed into a drawer and slid it closed. She looked around Asher's guest room. There was a blue comforter on a double bed. A lamp on a nightstand. The TV sat on the dresser. And there was nothing else. It was a comfortable place to crash for a few nights, not a place to live or thrive.

Still, she should be thankful with her Spartan surroundings. Especially since Asher's condo, several miles out of town and unknown to Scott, was the perfect place to stay hidden.

"Knock, knock." She recognized Asher's voice and still her heart skipped a beat. "I forgot to ask how you like your eggs."

Shaking her head at her own nervousness, she tried to smile. Her skin was too tight, and the expression pained her. Raking her fingers through her hair, she stood taller and tried to fill her spine with steel. She wouldn't live in fear and worry.

Asher wrapped his knuckles on the door. "Kansas, are you there? Everything okay?"

"I'm fine," she called out. "Just unpacking." She was still wearing her wool thermal underwear. It was hardly an outfit to keep on for the rest of the day. "I'm going to change, then I'll come down."

"Eggs," he said, his voice coming through the jamb. "How do you like your eggs?"

In all honesty, she didn't expect Asher to be such a gracious host. She crossed the room and opened the door. While she'd been putting her belongings away, Asher had changed his clothes. He now wore a green sweatshirt and jeans. On his feet were a pair of suede slippers. He looked cozy and handsome and strong.

Kansas wanted to fall into his arms. She wanted him to hold her and to kiss her and tell her that everything would turn out all right in the end. She folded her arms across her chest to keep from reaching out.

Yet, his simple question still hung in the air between them. How did Kansas like her eggs to be prepared? "You're nice to let me stay here, so I won't be picky about breakfast."

"My specialty is scrambled. I hope that works."

"Scrambled eggs are perfect," she said. "They're my favorite, actually."

It seemed unbelievable that they were discussing something as mundane as food. Scott Montgomery had broken into her house hours earlier. Asher had been shot. And Kansas didn't know when she'd be able to go home. But here they were talking as if nothing had happened.

"Well," he said, "I'll let you get changed. Breakfast will be ready in a few minutes."

The salty scent of bacon and the earthy aroma of coffee filled the air. Her stomach contracted with hunger. "I'll be down in a second."

She closed the door and let her fingertips rest on the handle. If she was going to outwit Scott—and that was the only way to survive—she couldn't allow herself to become morose or weak. She needed to eat to keep up her strength—both emotionally and physically.

Maybe Asher was a genius by tempting her with a hearty breakfast. She took off her sleepwear and pulled on a pair of fleece-lined leggings along with a sweatshirt. On the front of the shirt was a set of lights and the words All Is Merry and Bright. She was neither of those things, but maybe the shirt would help. After slipping on a pair of thick socks, she opened the door. Kansas walked down the short hallway and took the stairs to the main level. Asher's phone was connected by Bluetooth to a speaker. The words to the song "Santa Baby" filled the living room.

Going into the galley kitchen, she watched Asher at the stove. He whipped eggs in a skillet as his hips shot side to side in time with the music. Leaning her shoulder on the wall, she watched. Sure, he was being silly and charming. But his jeans hugged his butt perfectly. His hips kept swaying, but it wasn't a fluid motion. There was a little hitch at the end.

So help her God, her thoughts went right into the gutter. Or make that the bedroom.

What kind of lover would Asher be? Somehow both graceful and powerful, she decided. The thought left her lightheaded. Yet she was sucked into the fantasy of him naked and between her thighs. Sheets damp with sweat were tangled around their bodies.

The image was so clear she never noticed when the song ended or when he started watching her.

"You okay?" he asked. "You look like you're a million miles away."

"Not that far," she said. Just to the bedroom upstairs. "I guess I was just thinking."

"I don't blame you for being concerned about Scott." Asher scooped fluffy eggs onto two plates. Two strips of bacon, along with a slice of wheat toast with butter, already sat on each plate. He lifted them both from the counter. "But remember, at the ABI, we're good at what we do."

For a moment, she'd been so consumed by carnal thoughts of Asher, she'd forgotten about Scott. Her appetite disappeared. "I know that we're good. It's just..."

He held out one plate to her. "Then trust that he'll get caught before he does anything else."

She took the food even though she wasn't hungry anymore. "But he's done so much already. It's all because of me." Her eyes stung again. So much for the Merry and Bright shirt doing any magic.

Asher wrapped his arm around her shoulder. He led her from the kitchen to the small table at the edge of the living room. When she'd arrived, the table had been filled with old newspapers, mail, and several jackets. In place of all the debris was a setting for two, including silverware atop of paper napkins, mugs filled with steaming coffee, and glasses of orange juice.

"Wow. Orange juice." Getting juices this far north and in the winter was quite the feat. "I'm impressed."

"It's frozen concentrate," he said, setting his plate on the table. Taking his seat, he continued, "But it's better than nothing."

After dropping into her own chair, she picked up her fork and stabbed a bite of eggs, shoving it into her mouth. They were mellow and cheesy—her favorite combination.

And yet her gut was twisted into a knot. She dropped her fork and pushed the plate away.

Asher had finished one slice of bacon and was loading eggs onto his toast. "You don't like the food?"

"Everything is great," she said, leaning back in her seat. "I'm just not as hungry as I thought." Her eyes stung again. When would the damn tears stop trying to break through? She blinked hard, refusing to cry in front of Asher.

"You've been through a lot in a short time. It's okay to be emotional."

"I'm tough," she said, though the words came out as a croak. "I help find people who are lost. I don't get lost myself."

"This isn't a matter of being tough or weak."

She thought back to all the people she'd found over the years. They'd been dazed. Confused. And just like Asher said, emotional. In those moments, she knew they were suffering from the trauma and shock. Was she in shock, too? "I just need to shake this feeling. Get back to myself."

Asher reached for her, placing his palm over the back of her hand. "This isn't something you can take off, like a dirty pair of boots. The anxiety might be with you for a while. But you have a lot of support from your family. Your friends." He studied her with his deep brown eyes. "Me."

She laced her fingers through his. "Thank you for everything."

"You want to thank me?" he asked, echoing her words with a question. "Eat your breakfast. The only way to get more bacon is to go back to the mainland."

Chapter Ten

Once Kansas started eating breakfast, she realized she had been hungry. With a fork in one hand and a piece of bacon in the other, she took alternating bites. Asher sat on the other side of the table, and for several minutes, neither spoke. Soon, her plate was clear. The juice glass was empty, and the coffee cup was only halfway full. With a contented sigh, she leaned back in her chair. "You're a really good cook. Everything was delicious."

"For the record, I love to cook. It's just that I don't have a lot of time. It seems like a waste to just cook for myself. Which means I do eat my fair share of frozen meals."

For a moment, neither spoke. She hated the idea of Asher being alone after work. Kansas was always busy with her large family. Squeezing his hand, she said, "Once this is over, you're welcome to come to my house anytime."

He smiled and her pulse raced. "I'd like that."

His words danced along her skin. She couldn't help but wonder what else Asher liked. She leaned forward, closing the distance between them. She could kiss him if she wanted. And the thing was, she wanted to kiss Asher again.

The smartwatch on her wrist began to vibrate. With a killer at large, now was not the time to ignore any calls. She pulled her hand free and checked the screen. Caller ID read, Mom.

Of course her mother had heard about the break-in. It was hard to keep a secret in Shelby. But since Abby Colton was also a reporter, keeping any news from her was impossible.

"I gotta take this," she said, while rising from the table. As Kansas walked into the living room, she tapped on the phone icon on her smartwatch, answering the call. "Hey, Mom."

"I heard all about what happened at your house," her mother said. "How are you?"

That question was easier asked than answered. She exhaled, trying to corral all her emotions. "Actually," she said, "I'm not sure. I have a lot of feelings right now."

"I understand," said her mother. "Tell me about it."

Kansas paced as she told her mother about Scott showing up at her house. How he let himself in. How Asher had been shot, but the wound hadn't needed any medical care. She told her mother about the blood trail and the cameras. By the time she was done, Kansas was exhausted.

"That's a rough morning," said her mother with a sympathetic *tut*. "How are you doing now?"

"Asher is taking good care of me. He made scrambled eggs and bacon for breakfast." She dropped onto the sofa and sank into the cushions. It would be easy to close her eyes and take a nap. In the kitchen, she could her the water running and the clink of silverware on crockery. She should be helping Asher clean the kitchen, especially since he'd made breakfast.

"I know you two have had your differences," said her mom. "But he's a good man. I'm glad he's with you."

"We've worked through a few of our disagreements." As she thought about it, she realized that they'd wasted good years being adversarial. "I'm going to get off the phone now," she said. "He's cleaning the kitchen. I should go and help."

"All right, honey. I love you. Call me soon and let me know what's going on with the investigation."

"I will." Her finger hovered above her watch, ready to end the call. "And I love you, too."

"Oh, Kansas, wait. I forgot to tell you. Lakin and Troy are having an open house at their new inn on Tuesday night. I'm not sure if you can make it, but I wanted to let you know."

The thought of seeing everyone she loved both gave her joy and misery. Of course it would be nice to be with her friends and family. But what if Scott followed her? Could she really put them all in danger by attending an event?

"I'll see where things are," she said, "and let you know."

As she ended the call, she rose from the sofa. Her legs were heavy, and her joints were sore. Yet she couldn't leave Asher with all the work. Walking slowly toward the kitchen, she peeked inside.

He was lacing a tea towel through the handle of the refrigerator. The dishes had been washed and put away. The counter was clean and free of crumbs. She hated to admit it, even if it was just to herself, but Asher looked pretty cute being domestic.

"How's your mother?"

She leaned against the wall and folded her arms across

her chest. "Good. Worried. Thankful that you're taking care of me. She called you a good man." Kansas cringed. She needed to stop sharing too much.

"And what about you?" Asher looked at Kansas, pinning her with his gaze. "Do you think I'm a good man?"

"Actually," she said, knowing that she might regret being too honest. "I think that you're the best."

SINCE GETTING A CONCUSSION, Asher had needed a nap in the afternoon just to get through the day. It made him feel like a little kid to have to have a naptime. But he got a headache whenever he ignored the need to rest.

Lying on his bed, he stared at the ceiling. It was 2:00 p.m., his typical time to rest. He could hear Kansas downstairs, picking up all the things that were scattered around. He couldn't decide what to do. Did he get up and help or keep to his schedule and stay pain-free?

His phone began to ring on the bedside table.

He glanced at the screen before swiping the call open.

"Eli," he said. "What's up? Any news on Scott?"

"We don't have anything yet," said his partner at ABI. "But APBs have been issued. Hospitals have been contacted. Someone will see something, and then we'll have him." He paused a beat. "How are you?"

"The cut stings a little, but I'm not complaining. It's better than actually being shot."

"How are you and Kansas getting along?"

Did Eli suspect that Asher had kissed Kansas? He wasn't ready to tell his partner about the embrace right now. Hell, he might never tell Eli what happened. He decided to be diplomatic rather than fully honest. "We're doing better than I thought," he said.

"I hope that's true, because I just got off the phone

with the big bosses in Juneau," Eli said. "I requested that Kansas be placed in protective custody and got a lot of balking. I won't bore you with all the details, but it turns out that a lot of people are on leave right now. People are out for both the holidays and because of illness."

"'Tis the season," said Asher jokingly.

"There's not enough troopers to follow up on the leads for the case and give Kansas round-the-clock protection."

So, the hotshots in Juneau were going to leave Kansas without any guards because of a scheduling problem? The headache he was hoping to avoid hit him with the power of a locomotive. "You're kidding me, right?"

"Wish I was."

Asher pinched the bridge of his nose. It did nothing to lessen the throbbing in his forehead. "There has to be something we can do."

"There is," said Eli, "so long as you're agreeable."

Letting his hand fall away, he asked, "Agreeable to what?"

"They'd like for her to stay with you, at least until you go back to work." Eli added, "They've agreed to pay for better security at your condo. I have Noelle with me. She's willing to give her recommendations."

Eli had dated Noelle Harris while in college. The two broke up before graduating, but for Eli, she was the one who got away. It was no surprise that the two reconnected after her sister became one of Scott Montgomery's victims. More than being his partner's friend, Noelle owned a private security firm and would know all the best tech for his condo.

And all of that didn't answer the most important question. Was Asher willing to let Kansas stay with him for the next month? Well, he wasn't going to send her back home. After all, Scott had stolen a key and then planted cameras throughout the house. Even with the locks changed, she wouldn't be safe.

When Asher thought about it that way, there wasn't anything for him to consider.

Asher said, "Put Noelle on the phone."

"Does that mean Kansas can stay with you?"

"Yeah," he said. "I'm fine with her staying here as long as it takes to catch the killer." The truth was, Asher liked the idea of having Kansas around more than he should. But he didn't want Eli to get suspicious. "I mean, Scott might get arrested in the next few days."

"That's the hope." Then Eli said, "I'm giving the phone to Noelle."

"Hey, Asher," she said, "I hope it's okay if I give you some thoughts on security for your condo."

"You're the expert." He sat up and turned on a lamp.

Outside the wind howled. Downstairs, he could hear Christmas songs and Kansas's voice as she sang the chorus.

"Since I've been to your house, I know you have an electronic lock on your front door," she said. "That's great. You should change the code in case anyone knows it and has somehow passed it on to Scott." In the drawer of his bedside table, Asher found a pen and small notebook. He took notes as Noelle spoke. "I suggest that you get alarms for all the window and doors, as well as cameras for the front and back door and the living room."

Asher wrote the final items on the list. "Got it."

Noelle concluded with, "You need to talk to your bosses about getting the equipment. But once it arrives, I'll come over and help you set up."

He knew a little bit about home security, but not as

much as Noelle. "I'd appreciate that and will let you know once I have the tech in my hands."

"Until then," she said, "just be smart. Be aware of your surroundings. Lock your doors, even if you're home, and keep a low profile. Although I'm sure you know all that already."

"It's always good to have a reminder," he said before ending the call.

Asher turned off the lamp and lay back in bed even though he knew he'd never be able to rest. Kansas would be staying with him for days. Hell, she might even be at his home for weeks. He didn't mind the intrusion. Honestly, he was happy to be part of the investigation again.

His feelings for Kansas were complicated. They squabbled at times—although to his chagrin, he thought it was funny, and she was furious. He respected the hell out of her. She was beautiful. Smart. Funny.

While in the hospital, and recovering from his injuries, he spent hours thinking about getting together with Kansas. At the time, he worried that it would cause problems with Eli. Honestly, he still wasn't sure how Eli would feel about Asher dating his cousin. But it was a risk he was willing to take.

But Scott Montgomery showing up at her house changed everything. The killer was after Kansas and to keep her safe, he was going to have to ignore any temptation.

OVER THE NEXT three days, Kansas settled into a routine at Asher's condo. In the morning, he made breakfast. Then she cleaned the kitchen. After breakfast, they watched Christmas movies. It was the only holiday cheer in his condo. She knew it was silly, but she missed her

Christmas tree with all the ornaments. At noon, they fixed lunch together. Then they played a board game or cards afterward. Asher was still recovering from his concussion and was exhausted by midafternoon. While he napped, she tidied up and then read. In the evenings, they watched TV and continued whatever game they had begun after lunch. Then they went upstairs together but parted ways in the hall.

The passionate kisses from the day that Scott had broken into her house hadn't happened again. She paid attention to Asher, watching for signs that he wanted a repeat of their embrace. But she never saw any signals that he wanted more.

Honestly, Kansas wasn't sure if she should be thankful or disappointed.

She enjoyed the respite from her regular and hectic life. But by Tuesday at noon, she was ready to go somewhere. Her cousin Lakin and her long-term boyfriend, Troy, had scheduled a party to celebrate the opening of their new hotel, Suite Inn. It seemed like the perfect reason to leave the condo.

Standing at the stove, she watched steam rise from the soup in the pot and gave it a quick stir. "Nobody has seen or heard from Scott Montgomery in days," she said.

Standing at the adjacent counter, Asher placed two slices of deli turkey onto rye bread. He glanced at her before setting sliced cheddar cheese on the meat. "That's true, but we can't really assume anything." He opened the refrigerator door. "Do you want mayo or mustard?"

"Both," she said, stirring the soup again. The first bubble broke the surface. Lunch would be ready in a few minutes. "Did you know that Lakin and Troy are having an open house tonight?"

"They sent an invitation," he said, dragging a knife through the middle of the sandwiches. "It looks like they put in a lot of hard work on the place. I think it will be nice."

"Well, I was thinking about going to support Lakin." In a family filled with brothers and boy cousins, Kansas and Lakin had stuck together as kids. They'd remained close as adults. "But I wanted to see if you thought it was okay."

"You aren't a prisoner, you know. I'm not your jailer. You are here voluntarily. Although, I'll be honest, it's best if you just hang out here and not see anyone."

"I know." She kept stirring. Kansas could feel Asher's gaze resting on the back of her neck. "I'm just curious about your thoughts."

"Well…" He let out a sigh. The sound landed in her middle, sending an army of butterflies loose in her stomach. "Like I said, from a protection perspective, you're safer staying here. Not to be too blunt, but Scott can't kill you if he can't find you."

Asher was right, and what's more, Kansas knew better. Before she could tell him to forget about it, he spoke again. "I also think it's not healthy to be cooped up. It's bad enough that it's cold and dark outside." He nodded toward the window. Even though it was noon, the sky was still the inky black of midnight. Sunday's storm had left a foot of snow on the ground and temperatures hovered in the thirties.

Pushing off the counter, Asher removed two bowls from the cabinet. He set them on plates, along with the sandwiches. As he found spoons in the silverware drawer, he said, "I think if you want to go, you should. There will be a lot of people around, and that makes it harder for Scott to do anything. You need your family—their love and support—now more than anything. One word of advice, make sure that you're never alone. Stay with the group. I won't be there to annoy you, so you won't need to take a break outside."

It had been foolish of her to not see Scott as an ever-present threat. Was she being foolish in wanting to attend the opening of Suite Inn? "You know," she said, turning off the burner. "We Coltons are always having get-togethers for one reason or another. I can skip tonight." Even she heard the disappointment in her own voice.

"Hey." Asher stood behind her and placed a hand on her shoulder. It was the first time he'd touched her since the morning of the break-in. His palm was warm. His fingers were strong. His scent, pine and snow and the wind, surrounded her. He was so close that she could feel the heat from his body through the fabric of her sweater. She wanted to lean into his chest and let him support her. "I think you'll be fine if you go to the party."

She turned to face Asher. After just a few days, she'd memorized his face. His dark eyes. His dark hair. His beard and mustache, along with the dimple in his right cheek. God, he was handsome. "Do you really think it'll be okay?" she asked. "Or are you just saying that to make me feel better."

"I'm telling you that it'll be okay because I won't let Scott get close to you ever again. I swear to you, Kansas, I will keep you safe."

Sure, she still wanted to see her cousin and his new inn. But she shouldn't make things harder on her family or Asher. She looked up at him and smiled even though disappointment filled her veins like sludge. "I can see the inn anytime. I'm good with staying home tonight."

He shook his head. "I don't believe you. But what if we make a deal?"

A deal? "You've got my attention."

"We'll go to the party together and only stay for an hour. Neither of us will drink anything stronger than coffee. I won't tease you, and you stick by my side. That way, you have your own security guard and can still go to the party."

She didn't even need to think about his offer. It made perfect sense. Holding out her hand for him to shake, she said, "Deal."

He pressed his palm into hers. An electric current ran up her arm and left her lightheaded.

"It's a date," he said.

Calling it a date was just a figure of speech. Even though she knew that Asher hadn't meant anything by it, the possibility left her pulse racing.

Chapter Eleven

At 6:45 p.m. Asher stood in his bedroom and checked his reflection in a mirror that was attached to his chest of drawers. He'd slicked some gel into his wet hair, and his usually unruly waves were under control. He wore a gray sweater with a blue collared shirt underneath. He taken time to trim his mustache and beard. He also made sure that his teeth were thoroughly brushed and his breath was fresh.

It wasn't like him to worry this much about his grooming.

For the most part, he was just a wash-and-go kind of guy.

But he didn't have to wonder why he'd taken extra time with his appearance. It was all because of Kansas.

Spending days pretending like he didn't want to hold her and her kiss her and take her to his bed and ravish her was a special kind of hell. Now they were going out. And sure, he knew that they were together for her safety. But he was still filled with the same excited energy he had before every first date.

No. Kansas wasn't like all the women he'd gone out with before.

She was, well, Kansas.

Beautiful. Smart. Kind. Stubborn. The thing he liked about her best was that she didn't put up with his crap. And Lord knew, he had a history of giving her crap every chance he got.

Glancing at his reflection once more, Asher was pleased with what he saw. He opened the bedroom door and walked down the hallway before descending the stairs. Kansas stood in the middle of his living room. She wore a dark green blouse and a pair of tight jeans that accentuated the curves in her hips and rear. She'd also donned a pair of tall black boots that made her legs go on forever.

In short, she was sexy as hell and Asher was ready to burn for his sins.

She glanced over her shoulder, her gaze meeting his. Smiling she said, "There you are." And then, "You look great."

He swallowed. "You look pretty great yourself."

Asher wanted to hold her again. To touch her. To kiss her. But he wouldn't—he couldn't—not unless he wanted to ruin their relationship—personal and professional, both. Instead, he kept himself busy with taking his coat out of the closet and putting it on. When he turned around, Kansas was already wearing her parka. "You ready?"

"I am," he said, then he opened the door.

Fat snowflakes fell from the sky, swirling on their way to the ground. The maintenance company had shoveled the walk, but a dusting of white covered the paving stones. He wanted to warn her that the sidewalk might be slick, if only to have an excuse to take her hand in his. But she was tough and smart. What's more, she'd accuse him of treating her like a damsel in distress—one thing Kansas Colton never would be.

She reached for his hand, lacing her fingers through his. "It might be slick," she said. "I don't want you to fall."

He chuckled quietly.

"What's so funny?" she asked, her words came out in a frozen cloud.

"I was just thinking about offering my hand to you. Since I was pretty sure that you would've yelled at me for being sexist, I didn't."

"I guess that depends," she said, still holding his hand. "Did you want to help me because I'm a woman? Or because you think I need help?"

It was a good question and one he couldn't answer. They took a few steps. "I want to keep you safe."

"Well, I want to keep you healthy." She squeezed his hand tighter. "Maybe we are just looking out for each other."

He hadn't driven his SUV since Sunday morning. It was parked in his assigned space beneath an overhang. Because of the roof, there wasn't much snow on the vehicle. He had the fob in his pocket. From feel alone, he knew which button started the engine. The headlights turned on. A cloud of exhaust billowed out of the tailpipe. All too soon, they reached the SUV. He opened the passenger door. The interior chime began to ding. He let his hand slip from her grip. "I guess we made it safely."

"Thanks for taking care of me," she said before climbing into the passenger seat. He closed the door and rounded the front of the grille. Asher got into the driver's seat. He pulled out of the parking lot and onto the street. The only sound was the roar of the engine and the crunch of the tires on the pavement. Asher didn't speak as he drove, but his silence wasn't from a lack of anything to say.

He'd enjoyed spending the past two days with Kansas. He didn't know how much longer she might be at his house. While he hoped that Scott was caught soon, he'd always want her to stay another day or week or even months.

But how was he supposed to say any of that without seeming creepy? Or, worse yet, needy?

On Shelby's Main Street, he passed the offices for the local paper, where Abby Colton worked. There was Roasters Coffee Shop and Claudia's Boutique. Both businesses were closed, and all the lights were off for the evening. At the end of the block stood the Suite Inn. The inn had originally been a chain motel. But when the company went bankrupt, Lakin Colton and Troy Amos bought the property. They'd spent the past several months fixing up the place. The inside had been renovated and the outside had been given a fresh coat of paint. Trees and windows were decorated with twinkling lights.

"Looks like a popular place to be," said Kansas.

She was right. Most of the parking places were filled. As he pulled into a spot near the back of the lot, he said, "It's great that everyone turned out for Troy and Lakin."

They walked through the dark and the cold. The glass doors opened as they approached. The lobby was filled with light, laughter and music.

After days of being alone with Kansas, the noise and sights were an assault on Asher's senses. He paused at the door.

"Are you feeling okay?" Kansas asked. "You look a little piqued."

Maybe it was the remnants of his concussion, but he

didn't think so. Actually, he knew what it was wrong. He wanted to go back to his house and have Kansas all to himself. "I guess I've just gotten used to being home."

"It's winter." She reached for his hand and gave his palm a squeeze. "It's okay if you want to hibernate."

Troy and Lakin approached. They'd spent months renovating the hotel and now, was their moment to celebrate. Asher was happy to see that the couple was smiling. "Hey, you two," said Troy. He held out his palm for Asher. "Good to see you both."

"It's good to be seen," he said, shaking the other man's hand. "The place looks great, and you both look happy."

"We're booked through the holidays," said Lakin. "And reservations are starting to come in for the summer." She pulled Kansas in for a hug. "We heard what happened. I'm so glad you're safe."

She hugged her cousin back. "I wasn't the one who got shot. It was Mr. Grumpy Bear over there who took a bullet."

"Grumpy Bear?" asked Troy. "What am I missing?"

Asher had to chuckle. "I guess that's my newest nickname. Kansas just said it was okay to hibernate in the winter. I'm supposed to be Grumpy Bear for having to leave my lair."

"Good thing you came here," said Troy. He gestured to the far end of the room. "The only reason a bear leaves his den in the winter is for food. And we have plenty. Help yourself."

Three tables were set along the back wall. Plates, napkins and cutlery sat at one end. Then there were bowls filled with different kinds of salads. Steaming side dishes came next. There were three platters filled with meats—

turkey, ham and roast beef. At the end was an entire table just for desserts.

Kansas's father, Ryan, stood next to the dessert table. He placed a large piece of cake on the plate before looking over his shoulder. Asher wasn't exactly sure what—or who—he was looking for, but he saw Kansas and smiled.

After grabbing a fork for his dessert, he crossed the room. "Honey, you're here. Your mom said you might stop by." He kissed Kansas's cheek. "I'm glad that you did."

"Cake for dinner?" she said, eyeing the chocolate wedge on his plate.

"You know what they say." He cut a piece with the side of his fork before stabbing it with the tines. "Eat dessert first."

He popped a piece into his mouth, chewed and swallowed. Using his fork to point, he said, "This is delicious. Where'd you get it?"

Lakin said, "Roasters started making cakes and cookies."

"They do a fine job," he said. "Everyone should start with dessert." He looked around the room. "I don't know where your mother went, but she's going to want to talk to you."

The door opened again. Dove and Mitchell entered.

"We'll let you find your mom, Kansas. She was over by the tree, last I saw." Lakin pointed to the corner. The large pine tree was decorated with twinkling lights and was impossible to miss. "We have to greet our newest guests."

Troy added, "We'll catch up with you in a bit."

Abby Colton was easy to find. She stood next to the tree and chatted with her sister-in-law, Sasha.

"Hey, Mom," said Kansas. "Hey, Aunt Sasha."

Both women looked up and smiled. The expression was so genuine and filled with love that Asher knew it had been the right decision to come to the party.

"Honey." Abby pulled Kansas in for a tight hug. "How have you been? You look good. You're pale, though. How are you feeling?"

Kansas laughed and held her mom at arm's length. "I'm fine. Good, actually. I might be pale, but it's because we haven't seen the sun in weeks."

Abby hugged her daughter again. "That's true. I'm just worried." Then she looked at Asher. "How are you?" She reached for his hand and squeezed his palm before letting go. "I'd say you look pale, too, but I guess you'd just tell me it's because there's no sun. But I do worry about you. Not just because you've been so good to take care of Kansas. But everything that happened with that explosion. You've been through a lot."

"Considering everything," he said, "I'm doing good." Asher had known that the Colton family was always welcoming. But Abby's concern filled him with a warm emotion. "And while I'm keeping Kansas safe, she's taking care of me, too."

She pursed her lips. "Are the two of you getting along?"

"Mom," Kansas protested. "He's nice enough to let me stay at his place. Just leave it at that, please."

So, the banter between Asher and Kansas had become the stuff of legends? Or maybe Kansas had complained to her mother. That meant Abby had gotten stories firsthand. The second thought burned his cheeks like a quick slap. "I've changed my ways," said Asher. Still, he needed to say more. "I never meant any harm. But it seems like I was more obnoxious than funny."

"I didn't think you were trying to be mean," Abby clarified. "It's just that you two were always—" she pressed her two fists together "—butting heads."

"I guess we were," said Asher. "But we've learned how to get along now."

"Trust me, Mom." Kansas moved closer. Her shoulder brushed against his arm. There was a spark of electricity where they touched. "We're doing fine."

"That's good to hear," said Abby. What else she might've added was cut short by the arrival of Hetty.

"Kansas." She opened her arms for a hug. "I was wondering if you'd make it to the party."

"Thanks to her capable bodyguard," said Abby, "she was able to come out."

"Hi, Asher." Hetty gave him a hug, as well. "How are you doing?"

"We're good," Kansas answered for them both. "But since we're all here, we need to talk about something important. The bridal shower. Dad says the cake from Roasters is good. Maybe we should order one from there."

"It's funny that you brought up the shower," said Abby. "I was just playing around with some invitations on the computer."

"First, we need to pick a date. Then we need to decide on a location," said Kansas.

"I volunteer my house," said Abby before asking, "What date works for you, Hetty?"

She paused a moment to think. Asher took advantage of the silence. "I'm going to get something to eat. Can I grab a plate for anyone?"

"I'll be over in a minute." Kansas smiled at him.

Asher couldn't help it. Whenever she smiled, he had to smile back.

He wandered across the room, greeting people he knew. At the food tables, he took Ryan Colton's advice. Starting with the desserts, he grabbed a small plate from a stack and a fork from a basket. The sheet cake had been precut into squares and he selected one. Using his fork to cut off a slice, he took a bite. The cake itself was moist, light and sweet. The icing was the perfect mix of sugary and sour—cream cheese frosting, most likely. He took another bite. He should take a slice of cake to Kansas. She'd definitely want to serve it at the upcoming bridal shower.

Before he got a chance, he caught a glimpse of Eli walking through the front door. His partner with the ABI greeted Troy with a handshake and Lakin with a hug. Then he waved at Asher and crossed the room. "Hey, man," he said, "how've you been? You and my cousin surviving? What have you been up to?"

The memory of Kansas, bare to the waist straddling Asher, came with a clarity that sent his pulse to the roof. He took another bite of cake to hide his reaction. "Everything's good. It's nice to have her around. I know that everyone keeps praising me, but she's good company." He added, "We decided to make an appearance here for an hour or so. I think it's good for Kansas to be around family and friends." Had there been affection in his voice? The last thing he wanted to do was give away the fact that he was starting to care about Eli's cousin. "Any word on the investigation?"

Eli let out a long breath and rubbed the back of his neck. "Nothing much to report. Aside from the blood trail outside Kansas's house, there were no other clues. I sent samples to the crime lab. The report hasn't come back yet, but we're assuming that the blood belonged to Scott."

Asher nodded and took a bite of cake.

"Obviously, we alerted all medical professionals about Scott and his injury. And just as obviously, he hasn't tried to get medical treatment for the gunshot wound."

"It's possible someone else is helping him." Asher took another bite of cake. It might be the best cake he'd had in his life. "Although with all the media attention, they have to know who they're dealing with."

"Anything and everything's a possibility," said Eli. "We're looking into all angles." He paused. "I miss having you on the team."

The thing was, Asher missed being part of the team, as well. Sure, he was doing his part by keeping Kansas—Scott's ultimate obsession—hidden. And it was true that he was injured and needed time to recover before returning to duty. But it was also a fact that the Scott Montgomery case was his. To have the killer arrested and not be a part of the operation was unthinkable. The cake, as delicious as it had been, sat in his gut like a stone.

Asher knew he should feel festive and happy to be at such a lively gathering. Yet he couldn't help but wonder—where was Scott Montgomery and what was he doing right now?

Chapter Twelve

Scott Montgomery lay in the dark. A sheen of sweat covered his brow and yet, beneath the blankets, he shivered. His whole body ached and his thigh pulsed with the beat of his heart.

He knew that his bullet wound had gotten infected. The thing was, he didn't know how to deal with the poison that was slowly filling his body before he went into septic shock. He couldn't seek medical care. Doctors were obligated to report a gunshot wound. That was assuming he could find a practitioner who didn't watch the news. Or read a newspaper. Or get on social media. And somehow know nothing about what Scott had done.

Even with a fever that made it hard to concentrate, he knew it was an unlikely scenario.

He dared not go online to look for home treatments, either. If the state police had his IP address, they could find him as soon as he got back on the internet.

When he was a boy, his grandmother lived in this cabin. She barely left the woods and always used home remedies to treat ailments. She swore by mixing honey, lemon and vinegar with chamomile tea for a sore throat.

Years later, Scott looked up the old concoction. As

it turns out, his grandmother was onto something. The recipe had analgesic properties, along with a weak antibiotic. He had honey and black tea but nothing else. He recalled once when his grandfather had lost a finger. His grandmother had held a white-hot brand to the stump. She said it was to stop the bleeding and prevent an infection. It had done both and his grandfather was able to use his hand the next evening.

But Scott had been shot three days earlier.

Would the same treatment work for him now?

He pushed up to sitting. Pain shot through his leg and left him nauseous. Through sheer will alone, he stood. For a moment, the floor seemed to undulate, and his vision closed in from the side. He drew in a deep breath and blew it out. His vision returned and the floor was steady. What remained was pain. Throbbing radiated from his thigh to his hip to his stomach to his chest. He shuffled across the floor to the small kitchen. Leaning on the counter, he gulped down air. Sweat dampened his hair and streamed down his cheeks. Using the sleeve of his shirt, he wiped away the perspiration.

He pulled down his pants and stood, shivering, in his underwear. He carefully stepped out of the legs and examined his injured thigh. A bandage, at one time white, was now gray. The flesh around the wound was red, tender and hot.

Not a good sign.

He should have cleaned his leg more often. But the pain had left him woozy for days. He'd done what he could and even that hadn't been enough.

He peeled back the tape. The gauze bandage stuck. He lifted a corner and pulled it free. The first thing he noticed was the smell. It was the sickly sweet scent of something that was rotting. Then he noticed that the entrance wound was crusted with white and yellow pus. The hole itself was bright and red.

If he was going to cauterize the wound, it needed to be cleaned out first. Sealing the hole with all the infection inside would only cause more problems. He hobbled back and forth along the counter, collecting everything he needed. A knife. A bottle of rubbing alcohol. A towel. A clean gauze pad and the last bit of surgical tape. He pulled the small heater next to where he stood. He wedged the knife into the safety mesh and turned up the thermostat to high. The coils began to glow red. Next, Scott wetted the corner of a towel at the taps and gently patted the skin around his injury. He focused on his breath. In through the nose. Out through the mouth.

After he'd cleaned away the dried pus, the flesh was cooler. But he had to do more. Sitting on the floor, he braced his back against the counter. Scott bent his knee, a feat in itself, and brought his thigh closer.

For a moment, he wondered what his grandmother would think about him sitting in his underwear on the floor. Even she, a woman who wasn't comfortable with towns or roads, would have said that Scott was better than sitting around like a dog. But there was no helping what he had to do. Placing his thumb on either side of the hole, he began to squeeze.

The pain was instantaneous and severe. Tears filled his eyes. He bit the inside of his lip to keep from crying out. His teeth cut into his flesh and the coppery taste of blood filled his mouth. The pain was so intense that it brought him back to a time years earlier when he was just a boy. His father was working on a fishing boat, gone for weeks. During those first days, his mother was always the worst. She spent her days in bed. Whenever she rose, the antiseptic stench of booze surrounded her like a fog. She always seemed surprised to find Scott sitting in the living room when she got up, not noticing that he was in the same pajamas from two days earlier. Or that he'd only been eating cereal without milk, because he wasn't allowed to handle a gallon jug on his own.

Then there was the time that his mother forgot about him completely.

She left with friends and didn't come home that night. Or the next. Or the one after that.

There was no cereal in the house. No bread or peanut butter. Nothing other than water at the sink. To this day, he wasn't sure how long she'd been gone when his grandmother arrived. But he still recalled the hunger—deep and burning—and the fear that his mother would never come back. His grandmother helped Scott change his clothes. Then she bundled him into her rusted truck, tucking him in with a blanket because the heater didn't work. She handed him a brown paper bag. Inside was a peanut butter sandwich, a slice of cheese and a bag of chips.

"Go slow," she warned. "If you eat too fast, you'll get sick."

It was her voice that he heard as he squeezed the leg wound. Go slow. Go slow. Pus, yellow and putrid, continued to flow from the injury. He wasn't sure if it would ever end. Then, the first bright red blood came out of the hole. He laughed, blinking away his tears. The pain eased. Leaning against the cabinet, he drew in a cleansing breath.

As much as he hated to admit it, he'd only endured a small amount of the anguish that was to come.

Using the damp towel, he cleaned his leg. Next, he opened the bottle of rubbing alcohol. The scent returned him to the stale air in his mother's room. He drew in a large breath and poured the liquid into the hole on his legs. He wanted to cry out with the agony. But he couldn't break his silence. He didn't know who was around and might hear him yelling.

Instead, he focused on a different memory.

Whenever his father was home from the sea, his mother controlled her drinking. She made dinner every night. Smiled. Laughed. She got out of bed in the morning and even did laundry. Their small house was clean.

How could she be so sweet and loving when his father was around and then completely ignore her son when he was not?

His grandmother said that the booze made his mother sick. But there was more. She saw her son as a burden. She only took care of him when his father was around to praise her mothering skills.

He was eight years old when he started to hate his mother.

He and his father were sitting in the living room. On the TV was a *Where Are They Now?* documentary. It was about the triple homicide that had occurred in a ritzy neighborhood of San Diego. The mother, father and teenage daughter had all been murdered by one of the daughter's admirers. The young man also killed himself.

"Jesus," said his father with a chuckle. "That guy must really have loved that girl. Look at what he did for her."

Back in the kitchen, the wound was as clean as it could get. Now only one thing remained. He held the corner of the towel to grab the knife's handle. Even through the rough fabric, he could feel heat radiating off the blade.

Without thinking, he pressed the hot metal to his wound. The pain was overwhelming. He'd tried so hard to not make a sound. But now, he couldn't help himself.

He screamed as his flesh was seared.

He didn't care if someone heard.

He pulled the blade away. Leaning into the cabinet, he let his eyes close.

He remembered the TV show—the one about the girl who'd been murdered. The documentary showed photos of her—both snapshots and professional pictures from advertisements where she'd been a model. She was stunning. Long dark hair. Bright blue eyes. A perfect nose and rosebud lips. Her complexion was creamy and smooth. She was everything his mother was not.

"That guy must really have loved that girl." His father's voice once again echoed in his mind. "Look at what he did for her."

At eight years old, Scott was confused. How was killing supposed to be the same thing as love? "I don't get it," he said. "He murdered her parents. That's wrong." Although sometimes he wished his mom would die.

"Think about it," said his dad. He lifted a can of beer to his lips and took a long swallow. Smothering a burp behind his hand, he continued. "He was so obsessed with her that he snuck into her house and tried to take her away. The fact that she fought him off and died is her own fault."

Scott looked back to the TV, trying to make sense of what his dad had said. It was obvious that his mother loved to drink. It was just as obvious that she cared nothing for her own son. Was love when something became the singular focus of attention?

It made sense.

More pictures of the victim flashed on the screen. She was in a bathing suit, sitting beside a pool, drinking an orange soda. She was wearing a long green dress, spraying perfume on her neck. There was even a shampoo commercial where she rode a horse on the beach.

In that moment, he fell in love with the murdered girl.

Over the next few years, he learned everything about her that he could.

Her name was Caroline Colton.

Her parents were Edward and Mia. They ran a successful real estate business in Southern California. The man who didn't love her enough was a guy named Jason Stevens—a loser who could only have gotten Caroline's attention by kidnapping her.

By the time he was a teenager, Scott knew he was different. He was smart. Talented. Good-looking—even if it was in a studious way. He could get a girl like Caroline Colton if he wanted. But she was dead.

It really wasn't a surprise when Kansas Colton showed up at his office. And sure, the name Colton isn't exactly unique. But he knew she was from the correct branch of the family tree just by looking at her. She had the same dark hair. The same bright blue eyes. The same rosebud mouth.

It didn't take long for him to find the connection—aunt and niece.

He opened his eyes.

How long had he sat on the floor in a stupor. It might have been minutes. Or hours. Or days.

His leg was still sore, but the worst of the pain was gone. He put on a clean bandage and new pair of sweatpants. Gripping the counter's edge, he pulled himself to his feet. After filling a glass with water from the tap, he drank it in one swallow. His stomach gurgled painfully. He remembered his grandmother's warning. If you eat too fast on an empty stomach, you'll get sick. Scott set the glass aside and found a sleeve of crackers, still in the box.

He took them all to the sofa and sat down. After opening the wrapper, he removed a cracker and nibbled the corner. The fog in his brain thinned, allowing him to think clearly for the first time in days. Chewing slowly, he assessed his situation. He'd lost time with a fever and infection.

It wasn't the worst thing in the world. Certainly, the police had been looking for him. The fact that he hadn't been arrested meant they still didn't know about this cabin.

He ate another cracker, savoring the saltiness as the wafer dissolved in his mouth. Even as an adolescent, he'd known that Caroline Colton was part of his destiny. But Kansas was more than her aunt, who was nothing more than a pretty face. Kansas was dedicated to her job. She never rested when someone was missing and needed to be saved. She'd been his salvation and never knew. Or maybe she did know, and all this time she'd been tormenting him.

After all, he'd come for her. What thanks did he get? A bullet in the leg.

It seemed like it was time to make Kansas pay for all the injuries that she'd caused. He just had to figure out how to hurt her the most.

Kansas sat on the sofa in Asher's living room. She still wore the outfit she'd donned for the grand opening of Suite Inn—minus her boots. Asher had taken a recliner in the corner. *White Christmas* was playing on the TV. The light from the screen flickered in the dark room.

The joy of spending time with her family and friends still filled her chest. She was warmed further by the simple domesticity of watching television with a man. Well, not just any man—but Asher Rafferty.

Leaning back into the cushions, she set her socked feet on the table and sighed.

"You okay?" Asher asked, sitting forward in his chair. Even in the glow from the TV, she could see that his brows were drawn.

His reaction, immediate and concerned, left her unmoored. "Yeah," she said before pausing. "I'm fine. Good, really. I was just thinking that I'm having great night. The party was fun. The food was good." She nodded toward the TV. "This is even my favorite Christmas movie."

"It has been a nice evening. I'm glad that we went. I'm glad that you were able to see your family." He gave her a small smile. Her heart skipped a beat. "That cake really was good."

"Think I should order some for the bridal shower?"

"I think you should order some for breakfast tomorrow."

With a laugh, she turned back to the movie. "Troy and Lakin put in a lot of work on that old motel. The lobby looked great. The tree especially."

"It's not as nice as the tree we decorated."

Matching his teasing tone, she said, "Too bad our tree isn't here, though."

"Yeah, there are a lot of things wrong with this situation. You not getting a Christmas tree is just one of them." He rose from his seat. "I can't believe I'm saying this, but I want something to eat. What about you? You feeling snackish?" He walked through the living room and into the kitchen.

Kansas wasn't hungry. There had been enough food at the party for a small army—and she'd eaten her fill. Still, she followed him into the kitchen. Asher stood at the refrigerator with the door open. He stared at the shelves.

"I guess that nothing really looks good," he said, pushing the door shut.

He turned, running straight into Kansas. She stepped back to get out of his way and lost her footing. Just as she was certain to fall, Asher's strong arms were around her waist. He pulled her into his chest, keeping her upright.

Her heart slammed into her rib cage. She wanted to think it was all because she'd lost her balance. But she knew better. It was because Asher held her. Her palms were pressed against his chest. His touch sent an electric current dancing along her skin. The thing was, she could tell that he felt the connection, too. His pulse thrummed at the base of his throat. His breath came in quick gasps.

The best thing would be to step away. To let the connection between them short-circuit before she did something that couldn't be undone. Yet she remained in his arms.

"You all right?" he asked.

She met his gaze. "I'm fine."

His lips twitched into a smile. "You are definitely fine."

The double entendre was impossible to miss. But she could still walk away if she wanted. The thing was, she didn't want to let him go. She'd ignored the sexual tension that had been building for far too long. In fact, she'd tried to focus solely on Asher as a person, a coworker, a friend. And that friendship made this moment all too important.

The wrong choice could ruin everything.

But the right decision could bring Kansas everything she'd ever wanted.

Without another thought, she reached behind his neck and pulled him to her. She placed her lips on his, kissing him softly.

Asher pressed his forehead into hers. "I can't lie to you, Kansas. I want you so bad it hurts. But I don't want you to do something now that you'll regret later."

Kansas understood his worries. But she also understood a desire that bordered on pain. She wanted him. No, that wasn't right, she needed him. Pulling him closer, she rocked her hips forward until she could feel his hard cock. "Kiss me again."

Letting out a low growl, he claimed her with his mouth. He gripped her rear and lifted her to the counter. Kansas wrapped her legs around his waist, pulling him closer. His hand trailed up the hem of her shirt, his touch traveling from her stomach and to her bra. He slid a finger underneath the cup and stroked her nipple. The sensation left her dizzy. But she wanted more. Pulling her shirt over her head, she tossed it aside. As he kissed her, she unhooked her bra and took that off, as well.

Asher removed his sweater and the shirt underneath. And then he kissed her mouth. Her throat. Her chests. Her breasts. Each sensation was delicious. Kansas was like a starving person at a banquet, and she only wanted to be sated.

She reached between them and unbuttoned the fly of his jeans. "I want you," she said, breathing the words into the kisses.

"Let's go upstairs," he said.

She couldn't wait. "I want you," she said again. "Now."

Asher pulled down the front of his pants, freeing his hard cock. She wiggled out of her pants and underwear. The head of his dick was only inches from being inside of her. She scooted forward, making contact.

"Protection," said Asher. "We need some protection."

"I'm on the pill." Somehow, she was thankful for her painful periods as a high school student that required a prescription for birth control. Although there were more concerns with sex than just getting pregnant. Then again, she knew Asher. She trusted him fully. If she didn't, well, then she shouldn't be on the kitchen counter with him. She kissed him again. "It's okay."

Asher pulled her to the edge of the counter. She held him tighter with her legs and braced herself with her arms. He kissed her once more softly on the lips, and then he entered her fully. He slid back slowly. She looked down to where they were joined and watched him as he moved inside of her. Sliding back, slowly, slowly, almost to the point of pulling out. Then he drove inside of her hard.

She cried out with the pleasure, unable to think or speak, only feel.

"Do you like this?" He lifted one of her legs onto his shoulder.

"Yes," she said, her voice a whisper. He drove into her harder and deeper than before. She thought he would never be inside of her deep enough. "Yes. Yes. Yes."

He slipped his hands between their bodies and found the spot at the top of her sex. He began to rub his thumb in a circle. A wave of pleasure rolled through Kansas. She could feel her climax beginning to build. Lifting her higher and higher. Holding on to his shoulders, she cried out as she came.

Asher pumped into her harder and faster. He leaned forward, pinning her to the counter and moaned. For a moment, Kansas was deaf to every sound except her own racing pulse and Asher's breath in her ear.

"Kansas." The one word was hot on her shoulder. "You're wonderful. Magnificent."

She couldn't recall the last time she'd come so hard and so fast. Maybe it was never. She was exhausted, but she gave him a weak smile. "You're pretty exceptional yourself."

He moved back, sliding out of her. He pulled his jeans up, holding them closed at the fly. "I gotta get cleaned up," he said.

"I'll be here."

She watched him go, leaving the kitchen and heading to the bathroom. As she slipped off the counter and redressed, she had but one thought. The sex was, as he had said, magnificent. But it was foolish to think that after that, they could ever go back to being just friends.

Chapter Thirteen

Asher wasn't completely sure where to go from here. His pulse still raced after his mind-blowing orgasm. Kansas's kisses lingered on his lips. But she was more than just an energetic lover. She was smart. Dedicated. Funny. She was his coworker. She was the younger cousin of his partner, Eli, and therefore, off-limits. At times, Kansas and Asher quarreled, but without question, she always captured his attention.

Standing in the bathroom, Asher stared at his reflection in the mirror. His eyes were clearer than before, and a stupid smile was plastered on his face. After turning on the tap, he ran his hands under the water.

Even if he tried, he couldn't pretend that their tryst never happened. In fact, if he were being honest with himself, he didn't want to go back to whatever they were before.

After turning off the water, he dried his hands. From the bathroom he went straight to the living room. Kansas was sitting on the sofa watching TV. She looked exactly as she had before they had sex. Even though it had only been a few minutes, everything had changed.

"Hey," he said, leaning his shoulder onto the wall.

She looked up from the TV. "Hey."

"Can we talk?" he asked. "About what happened, I mean."

"Sure."

She folded her arms across her chest. He read the gesture as a defensive and protective move. In short, it wasn't a good sign.

He pushed off the wall and sat on the cushion next to her. The need to touch Kansas, to feel her hand in his, was stronger than any hunger he'd know before. Asher pressed his palms onto his thighs to keep from reaching for her. He knew that popular wisdom would dictate that he play it cool. It was obviously what she was doing. The thing was, Kansas wasn't just some random one-night stand. Choosing his words carefully, he said, "I don't want things to be weird between us."

"I'm a big girl," she said before turning to look at the TV. She glanced at him once more and gave him a small smile. "It's not weird, I promise."

The hell it wasn't.

"I don't want to lose you," he said before thinking through what he had said. Well, if he was in for a penny, he was in for a pound. "I won't say I'm sorry that we had sex—because I'm not. But you matter to me. As a person. As a coworker. As a friend."

Kansas stared at him. Her expression was unreadable.

For a long moment, neither of them spoke. The quiet was only broken by Bing Crosby and Danny Kaye's duet. Her silence bore under his skin, leaving him itching and unsettled. He tried to smile and make a joke. "C'mon. I'm not that bad."

"Do you understand what you're saying?" she asked. "We've known each other too long for a get-to-know-you phase. We're beyond the introducing each other to family or friends. We'd go from being Asher and Kansas—Two separate people—" she held up her pointer fingers on each hand as she said their names and moved them so that they stood side by side "—to becoming Asher and Kansas, a couple."

He reached for her hands and placed his lips on the Kansas finger. "I'd be okay with that." He laced his fingers through hers. "What about you?"

"I'd hate to go back to being antagonistic—or worse, truly disliking each other." She shook her head. "Besides, I'm here to keep away from Scott Montgomery and not because we're an item. What happens if we try a relationship and start to loathe each other? Where do I go next?"

Damn it. She was going to turn down his offer for more. Asher tried to tell himself that it didn't matter. He'd been disappointed in love before. Sure, it hurt like hell, but he always recovered. The thing was, he was certain that he'd never get over Kansas Colton. Still, it was her choice to make. But he wasn't about to go down without trying once more. "Asher and Kansas. Kansas and Asher. I think it has a nice ring to it."

The side of her lip twitched into a smile. "You act like we'd be a celebrity couple or something. What would they call us? Kasher? Ansas?"

He couldn't help but laugh. "God, I hope we never get called either."

"Really? I think Kasher has a nice ring to it."

"So—" he laced his fingers through hers "—are we officially an item?"

"For now, we are. But I have a few rules."

She was such an organized person, he wasn't surprised. "And they are?"

"We can be Kansas and Asher, but only with each other and only in this house. That way, if things go south, we won't have to explain anything to people."

"I don't care what people think."

"People like Eli," she said. "I don't want him to feel like he's caught in the middle. Who knows when—or if—Scott will get caught. But you'll go back to work after the New Year and things might be strained if he has to pick a side."

She had a point. "For now, we're Asher and Kansas in this house."

Until now, Asher never knew what he wanted from his life. But taking Kansas as his lover had brought everything into focus. It's like all his choices had led him to this moment and he was truly ready to start living.

KANSAS SNUGGLED NEXT to Asher on the sofa. Lights flickered across the TV with another holiday movie. But her eyelids were too heavy to keep open. She leaned against Asher's chest. The resonance of his heartbeat pulled her closer to sleep. Outside, the wind blew, howling in the trees. Fat snowflakes were caught in the light of a streetlamp. At the bottom of the TV screen, a crawler warned of another winter storm along with high winds.

Right now, they had power. There was plenty of food in the fridge. And there were more than enough Christmas movies to watch. It seemed like the perfect few days to hibernate. And Asher was the perfect person to be with in the middle of a blizzard.

"Hey," Asher whispered. "You awake?"

"Sorta." She reached over her head, stretching out her back and shoulders. There were a series of pops and clicks as her joints loosened and realigned. It had been days since she'd gone to yoga. Who knew how long it would be before she'd make another class. She could always do a practice at home. Maybe Eli would pick up her yoga mat and some workout attire.

"Want to go to bed?"

Kansas heard the longing in his tone and she wasn't as tired anymore. Flipping onto her stomach, she looked up at Asher. The side of his mouth lifted into a smile. How had she ever seen that smirk as smug? Her chest tightened, filling with an emotion that she didn't want to examine too closely.

"Where should I sleep?" she asked, teasing him.

"You can use whichever room you want. But I was hoping you'd want to come with me." He leaned forward and placed his lips on hers. "And as far as sleep, well, I was also hoping we could find something else to do."

"You're pretty cute when you're trying to be seductive."

"Trying? As in, I'm not succeeding?"

She pushed back onto her heels before standing. "I did say that you're cute."

"Cute," he repeated with an exaggerated eye roll. "I guess I'll take my wins where I can get them."

Reaching for her, he pulled himself to his feet. "Kansas and Asher."

"Kasher," she corrected.

He lifted a brow but said nothing.

She gave him a coy smile. "Sit with it for a while. You'll get used to it."

"C'mon," he said, using the remote to turn off the TV. "Let's go to bed."

Kansas's mouth went dry. Sure, it was one thing to have a quickie on the kitchen counter. But it was another thing to spend the whole night sharing a bed. In many ways, sleeping next to him was more intimate than sex.

Holding his palm in hers, she let him lead her up the stairs. With his free hand, he pushed open the door to his bedroom. Light from the hallway stretched across the carpeting and fell in a wedge on the bed. The sheets were rumpled, and a dark blue comforter was balled up at the foot of the mattress. A TV hung on the wall opposite the bed. A chest of drawers stood in the corner. Asher's scent filled the room.

Standing at her back, Asher placed his hands on her shoulders. He kissed her neck. Gooseflesh rose under his lips. "You are so beautiful, Kansas."

She leaned into his chest, letting his words wash over her. Her heart shared a beat with his and for a moment, nothing in the world mattered beyond being with Asher.

He traced her shoulders, and his fingers slid down her arms. He held her hands and she rocked her hips backward, pressing her rear into his pelvis. He was hard, straining against the fabric of his jeans. She wanted him inside her again. She turned to face him and ran her fingers through his hair. For a split second, she was back in the hospital room and watching Asher as he lay unconscious after the explosion. She'd spent hours at his bedside. At the time, she'd told everyone—even herself—that she felt responsible for his accident. After all, he was trying to arrest Scott Montgomery. A man who was killing women because he was obsessed with her. She also told everyone—even herself—that she was worried about Asher because he was coworker. She'd be concerned about any fellow trooper who'd be injured in the line of duty.

But there was more.

She had been in Asher's hospital room because she cared about him personally. It's why she'd left her parents' party when he'd teased her about having feelings for him. He'd been right. At the time, she didn't want to admit to those emotions—even to herself.

Now, everything was different.

Bringing her mouth to his, Kansas tried to communicate everything she felt with a single kiss. But she wanted more. She needed him inside of her. Breathing her words into his mouth, she said, "Take me now."

"I will have you," he said. "But I'm going to take my time."

"Oh yeah," she said, challenging him playfully. "What do you have in mind?"

"Why don't you get on the bed and find out."

Excitement and expectation filled her middle. Turning, she walked to the bed before kneeling on the mattress. She crawled forward, her back arched, to show off her curves.

Asher hummed with satisfaction. "I like the view from here."

Kansas was in the mood to be coquettish and seductive. She looked over her shoulder and gave him a small smile before pulling the band from the ponytail she always wore. She ruffled her hair. "I'm glad you like what you see."

He knelt behind her, his hands on her hips. He rocked his pelvis forward, until his hard cock was pressed into the cleft of her rear. Sure, they were both still dressed. Layers of clothing separated the two. But the anticipation was almost as good as the actual act—almost, but not quite.

He reached between her thighs and traced a line from

the front to the back. His touch sent a shiver of desire down her spine. She sucked in a breath.

"You like that?" he asked.

"Yes."

"What about this?"

He bent behind her, covering her back with his chest and reached around to touch her. Asher placed a palm on each of her breasts. He stroked her nipples through the fabric of her shirt and her bra. It was the faintest of pressure. Just a hint of friction. But it left her wanting more. "Oh, Asher," she said, whispering his name.

He slid his fingers inside one cup of her bra. Asher twisted her nipple. The pleasure bordered on pain. It was such a delicate balance that she feared she'd fall into an abyss and never come out.

"Do you like that?" His breath was hot in her ear.

"Yes." Kansas tried to turn and face Asher. He held her tighter with his arm, keeping her in place.

"Stay here, like this. I want to take you from behind. Do you want that, too?"

There were no lights on in the room. Facing forward, she couldn't see Asher. She could only hear his words and feel his touch. But she did want him, and in every way possible. "Yes."

"Don't look back," he said. He rose from the bed and the mattress shifted beneath her. His footfalls were muffled by the carpeting as he crossed the bedroom floor. He closed the door. The latch engaged with a soft click.

Now, the room was completely dark. The curtains were drawn, cutting out whatever ambient light there was from the storm. Kansas looked over her shoulder, but in the gloom, there was nothing to see.

But she could hear everything. The metallic sound of

teeth unlatching as Asher unzipped his jeans. The soft thump of his pants as they hit the floor. The whisper of cloth on skin as he removed his shirt, socks and underwear.

"Take off your clothes," he said as his voice came out of the darkness.

She did as she was told, rising to her knees and stripping out of her top and her bra. Next, she unfastened the front of her pants and shimmied them over her hips. She flipped onto her back to take off her panties and socks.

"You aren't on your knees anymore," said Asher.

His words left her still for a moment. He was right, but how in the hell did he know? She couldn't see a damn thing.

"I'm not," she said. "I took off my clothes like you said."

"Good." He lifted her foot from the bed and pressed his lips onto her instep. The kiss sent an electric charge up her leg.

"Get back on all fours."

She placed her palms and knees on the bed, getting into position. Once again, the mattress moved as Asher climbed up behind her. He placed one hand on the small of her back, holding her in place. Then, he slid a finger inside of Kansas. He moved it back and forth before adding another and then another. She was stretched in the most intimate way, but she wanted more.

Moving her hips, she took him in deeper and harder. Asher reached around her and found the top of her sex. "I know you like this," he said, while rubbing her.

The force of her orgasm was already building. "Yes," she said. And then, "Harder. Faster."

He licked her back and complied. Kansas's breathing

grew ragged as her climax got closer. Asher's fingers were still inside of her, and now his mouth was on her. He suckled her. Licked her. Kansas was all feelings and sensations and no thought. Her orgasm exploded with the force of a blizzard. She cried out as she came. He removed his fingers and licked her once more.

"Do you still want me?" Asher asked, kissing her hip.

Her legs were heavy. Her arms were wobbly. Her pulse raced and her breath came in short gasps. Now, she was desperate for him to be inside of her, throbbing, as he came. "Yes," she said. "I want you."

Asher entered her in one long stroke. He held on to her hips, keeping her steady as he drove into her from behind. He was in her deep now, deeper than before. The bed rocked, slamming against the wall. She braced her arms on the mattress and felt like a snowflake in the middle of a storm. She had no choice other than to go where the wind sent her. And now, for Asher, she was ready to surrender. He continued to pump inside of her harder and faster. Then he growled and came.

Kansas was exhausted. No, she was more than tired. She was spent. Her arms could no longer hold her weight and she slipped onto the mattress, lying on her stomach. Asher laid down with her, covering her with his body. He kissed her cheek softly. "That was great. You're great."

She was already sleepy. "You're pretty great yourself."

He kissed her. His lips tasted of her own satisfaction. "How'd I get to be so lucky to have you in my bed?"

"I don't know." She tried to think of the punch line for a joke, but her mind was empty.

They lay together, listening to the wind howl. She moved until her head was on a pillow and pulled the blankets over her feet, legs and belly. Asher held her in his arms, and she rested her head on his chest.

True, she couldn't think of any jests about how lucky Asher was to be her lover. But Kansas knew that she was fortunate, as well. The relationship was new, but right now, sleeping in his arms felt perfect.

The wind blew through the trees, and Asher breathed deep. The sounds combined to become Kansas's lullaby. As she drifted off to sleep, she felt as if nothing—and nobody—could keep them apart.

Yet all the reasons she'd listed for them to not get involved were still true. One day soon, all of this would be over. The time they spent in his condo would feel like a dream.

Or maybe she wasn't living in a dream but a nightmare.

After all, the only reason they'd been thrown together was because a killer was on the loose. What would happen if the murderer was never found? She couldn't stay hidden forever.

Would their newfound romance really be able to last?

Chapter Fourteen

Kansas woke to the all too familiar ringtone alerting her to a call from Aquwik. She blinked awake, not sure of her new surroundings. Then she recalled everything from the night before. The sex with Asher in the kitchen. Cuddling on the couch. More sex in his bedroom. And finally, sleeping in his arms. She also knew that her phone was charging in the guest room.

The ringing stopped.

Kansas sat up. Aquwik wouldn't call unless it was important.

"Where are you going?" Asher asked, his voice gravelly with sleep.

"I got a call from work. I need to call them back," she said, slipping out of the bed. After their second round of lovemaking, Kansas hadn't bothered getting dressed. She stood naked in the dark, shuffling her feet on the floor and hoping to find something to wear. Her toe hooked on a piece of cloth. She picked it up. It was Asher's T-shirt. Good enough for what she needed.

She pulled it over her head as the phone began to ring in the other room. She hustled out of the bedroom. The phone sat on a bedside table in the guest room. The screen glowed. It was the only light that was on in the house. She picked up the cell and swiped the call open.

"Hey," she said, the word coming out as a wheeze. "I'm here. What's up?"

"You okay?" he asked. "I sent a ton of texts and called like four times already."

Crap. How had she slept through all those calls? Then again, she knew. She was sated from sex and nearly comatose in sleep. Even now, she was still groggy. "I left the phone plugged in next to my bed and didn't hear it ringing until just a minute ago."

"You left your phone charging next to your bed, but you didn't hear it ring?" Aquwik asked, his tone was confused more than confrontational.

Kansas wanted to groan. How could she have been so stupid to tell the truth? "No, I meant I'd left it plugged in downstairs and didn't hear it in the guest room."

If her coworker found her excuse unreasonable, he didn't question her further. "You know I wouldn't call you if it wasn't an emergency. But we've got a problem."

She listened for a full minute as he told her about the abandoned car that was discovered by state troopers. It was determined that both the driver and passenger had left the vehicle and set off on foot. One SAR team had been called out hours earlier with no luck. Since there were several directions that the couple could have taken, another search and rescue team was needed. He ended with, "I know you're on limited duty for now, but a few people are out sick. The couple who's gone missing is a guy and his pregnant wife. We can handle the search, but I thought you'd want to know in case you want to help."

"You were right to call me." Without thinking, she placed her hand on her middle. Sure, it was unlikely that she got pregnant tonight. But finding the woman became a personal quest. "I don't have a vehicle at Asher's house. Can you pick me up? I'll be ready in five minutes."

"I'm on my way," he said before ending the call.

"So, there's another search and rescue?"

Asher's voice seemed to come from nowhere and she stiffened at the noise. "Yeah," she said, reaching for the bedside lamp. She turned the knob and light spilled into a small puddle on the table and dripped onto the floor.

Standing in the doorway, Asher shaded his eyes. "Damn," he cursed. "That's bright."

The thing was that the light was fairly dim. She'd been around enough people with concussions to know that a sensitivity to light was a common symptom. It's just that he hadn't had the issue recently. "Are you all right?"

"Yeah." He backed into the hallway until he was lost in the shadows. "The light was giving me a headache."

For a moment, Kansas was frozen with indecision. Did she go out on the call or stay and take care of Asher? Then again, there were other people on her team. Asher only had Kansas. Well, when she thought about it that way, there was no question of what to do next. "I won't go," she said. "I'll call Aquwik back."

"Don't call him on my account." Asher was nothing more than a shadowy outline in the dark hallway. "I'll be fine. I am fine."

"You don't look fine to me."

"Trust me," he said, "these headaches come and go. I haven't had one for a while now. But the doctor assured me that it's all part of my healing."

"I wonder what triggered your pain." The moment the words left her mouth, she knew the root cause. There were so many biological changes during sexual intercourse—hormonal, cardiovascular, respiratory. Any one of those could have set off a reaction that ended with sensitivity to light and a headache. "I'm so sorry. I should've thought about your concussion before we did it. Twice."

Asher chuckled. "If having sex with you is what gave me a little bit of a headache, then it was well worth it."

At least he could make a joke. That was a good sign, right? And yet, "I should stay."

"Don't." He paused. "I'm just going to rest, so all you're going to do is watch me sleep." He paused. "Unless you want me to go with you for security."

Honestly, Asher wasn't going to be much help in a fight—not in his current state, anyway. Besides, she'd have Aquwik with her as well as a cadre of other troopers. "I'll be fine," she said, "but what about you?"

"I just need a little more sleep." He stepped back, farther into the shadows.

"As long as you're sure," she said, but she was already moving toward the closet where she'd stored her gear.

"I'm positive," he said, opening the door to his bedroom. "I heard that Aquwik was picking you up. Do you need anything from me?"

"I need you to take care of yourself," she said. "I'll see you when I get back."

"Sounds good." He backed into the bedroom and closed the door.

Kansas wanted to worry about Asher. But her ride was on the way. After collecting her gear and changing her clothing, she was ready. With her go bag slung over her shoulder, she took the stairs down to the first level. A set of headlights cut through the gloom.

Stowing the pack on one shoulder, she opened the front door and stepped outside. Aquwik was waiting in an official state police SUV with the state's seal emblazoned on the door. It was a good thing that he had a SUV, too. Last night's storm had dumped another foot of snow— and that was piled atop the foot from the last blizzard. They would need the powerful engine and the heavy tire tread to make it over the slippery roads.

The walkway was buried. Kansas waded through the drifts, before pulling open the door to the SUV. She tossed her bag onto the floorboard and climbed into the passenger seat. While pulling the door closed, she said, "Thanks for picking me up."

Aquwik put the gearshift into Drive and pulled out of the parking lot. "If you're okay with it, I'll brief you while I drive."

"Of course," said Kansas.

As Aquwik spoke, she listened. She began to form a plan as the miles and minutes slipped away. And yet, she couldn't help but wonder, how was Asher now?

THE THROBBING IN Asher's head lessened with each beat of his heart. Mentally, he chastised himself for not going with Kansas. It was more than just keeping an eye on her. It was the fact that he liked to watch her work. She was a competent leader and a skilled tracker.

Rising from bed, he stood for a moment and waited. There was no dizziness, and the headache from before was quickly receding. Without Kansas in the condo, there was one place he wanted to go. He checked his phone for the time—it was 9:30 a.m.

Honestly, he was surprised that it was so late. Then again, during the darkest days of the year, it was impossible to tell the time without a clock. He quickly showered, changed and ate a small breakfast before heading out the door. In less than an hour, he was pulling up to the curb in front of Kansas's house. Eli's official cruiser was parked in the drive.

He walked up to the front door and knocked before turning the handle and pushing the door open. "Hey," he called out. "It's me. Asher."

Eli appeared at the corner where the hallway and front room connected. He wore a pair of latex gloves. "Hey, man," he said. "It's good to see you. But what are you doing here? Is Kansas with you?"

Asher shook his head, answering the last question first. "She got called out on a search and rescue. From what I gathered, there were several teams out looking for a pair of motorists who wandered away from their car."

Eli's eyes narrowed. "You should have told her to skip the SAR."

How was he supposed to explain that after last night, their relationship had changed? Instead, he asked, "You want me to tell Kansas to skip an emergency? And if I did, do you really think that she'd listen?"

His partner exhaled. "Point taken. But you didn't tell me, what are you doing here?"

He was happy to see Eli. But he hadn't expected to encounter anyone else. Now that he was here—and had to admit to his errand—he hesitated. Still, there was no denying the truth. Nodding toward the Christmas tree, he said, "I came for that."

"What in the hell are you now? The Grinch?"

He gave a quick laugh. "She said that she missed having her tree. I thought since she was out this morning, I could come by and at least get her ornaments."

Eli regarded him for a moment. Finally, he said, "Sounds like you two are getting along pretty well."

"What's that supposed to mean?" Asher immediately regretted saying anything.

"It doesn't mean anything, other than the two of you didn't seem to like each other much. And now you're taking her to parties and picking up the ornaments for her Christmas tree. Tell me the truth, man. Is there something going on between you and my baby cousin?"

"She's hardly a baby," said Asher.

"You didn't answer my question."

"So, what are you doing here?" he asked, changing the subject. "What's going on with the case? Any news about Scott?"

"Whoa." Eli held up both palms. "That's a lot of questions."

Asher shrugged. "It used to be my case, too. Also, Kansas is living in my house for her own safety. I have a right to be curious."

"I wish I had more to tell you. So far, we got a lot of nothing. The tech guys haven't gotten anything off the cameras. Seems like Scott disconnected them remotely."

Asher recalled the moment that Scott broke into the house. Correction, he'd let himself in to the house. From what he said, it was obvious that he'd seen the kiss between Asher and Kansas. "That camera was active while I was here," he said. "He made reference to some of the things that Kansas and I discussed a few hours before he arrived."

"You mentioned that before," said Eli with a nod. "It makes me think that Scott was—and probably is—still close by."

Asher hated to think that the killer was around town. "But you don't know that for a fact. He might've left the area."

"Everything's possible. Including the possibility that he died of his gunshot wounds."

"Possibility," asked Asher, "or hope?"

Eli snorted. "I'd love to get that lucky." He paused a moment before adding, "It is a theory that he left the area for real this time. That could be why we haven't gotten reports of a gunshot wound from any doctors. Although we put the word out through all state police databases in the lower forty-eight."

Obviously, that part of the investigation had led nowhere. Which is why, he was assuming, Eli had returned to the house. "You find anything else here connected to Scott?"

With a shake of his head, Eli said. "Nada, man. The son of a bitch just disappeared again." Eli glanced around the room, as if searching for something that he might have overlooked. His gaze stopped on the Christmas tree. "So, you came to get all the ornaments."

Was it a question or a comment? Asher couldn't tell. Still, there was only one thing to say. "That's right."

"And you aren't going to tell me what's up with you and my cousin?"

"Can't a guy just do a decent thing?"

"I suppose he can. But I'm not sure about you. You've been avoiding my questions since you got here."

He understood why Kansas wanted to keep their relationship a secret—at least for now. Empty boxes were still stacked in the corner. He picked one up and sat it on the coffee table. "You going to help me, or what?"

"Well, since you aren't going to level with me, I guess there's nothing else to do." Eli stripped off his latex gloves and shoved them into his coat pocket. "Let's start packing up those ornaments."

SCOTT MONTGOMERY WOKE covered in sweat. His leg was still sore, but he knew that his fever had finally broken. Cauterizing the bullet hole had been risky, but it had worked. He sat up and let the blankets pool around his waist.

The first thing he noticed was the stench of body odor. It had been days since he'd felt well enough to bathe. Added to the smell of his unwashed flesh, the stink of infection hung in the air. Just the thought of sponging off in the bathroom left him exhausted. But, he couldn't continue to lay on the sofa and he stood. The floor seemed to tilt toward a chasm as his vision dimmed once more, closing in at the edges. Scott held on to the corner of the sofa until the dizziness passed.

That's when his stomach stomach contracted painfully. It was more than hunger—he was close to starving. He remembered those times when his mother forgot to feed him. Anger surged through his veins and he let go of the couch. He needed to eat something and drink something. But first, he wanted to get cleaned up.

He walked slowly to the cramped bathroom. A cabin this remote was lucky to have indoor plumbing and power. But he wasn't fortunate enough to have a shower. He grabbed a thin washcloth and a block of soap. After turning on the tap, he created lather in the cloth before washing his entire body. He rinsed out the cloth and watched the gray water swirl around the drain. He then washed the wound carefully. He'd stored several clean outfits in a suitcase that was shoved into a corner. Scott dressed in a fresh pair of underwear and socks before donning a black pair of sweatpants and a sweatshirt.

Once again, he was exhausted. But he needed to eat. Limping slowly to the kitchen, he put a can of soup into a pot and placed both on the burner. While stirring the soup, he tried to piece together the time since he was shot. It had been Saturday night—no, make that the early hours of Sunday morning—when he'd gone to Kansas's house. But what was it now?

Morning?

Night?

Was it Monday or Tuesday or even later?

He pulled back the curtain and stared into the dark. Light from inside fell on the snowy ground, but it was impossible to tell time from the constantly dark sky.

He let the curtain fall back into place as the savory scent of tomatoes rose from the pot. That's when he heard the voices.

Faint but unmistakable, a man yelled out, "Hello!"

The man's voice was followed by a woman calling, "Hello! Is anybody there?"

"Damn it," said the man. "I swore I saw some light. But now, it's gone."

"Gone?" the woman echoed. "I never saw anything. You're hallucinating. We should've stayed with the car. Someone's probably found the car by now, which means they would've found us."

"I told you, already. I didn't just want to sit around and wait until we froze to death."

As the couple outside bickered, Scott's heart slammed into his chest. It drowned out almost every sound, except for the droning argument outside. Silently, he cursed himself. It had been foolish to look out the window. On a dark night like this, the couple could have seen the light from more than three miles away.

The voices were clear. It meant that the couple was close. Less than a quarter of a mile, if he had to guess.

For a split second, he considered his options.

First, the woman was right. Most likely, their abandoned vehicle had already been located. It meant that the state police had a search and rescue team out looking for them now. It meant something else, as well. If the cops found the couple, they'd be on his doorstep.

He could kill them both and dump their bodies closer to the road. But that would start a whole new investigation and bring more police to the area. Besides, he wasn't in tip-top shape. Scott didn't know if he could take down the man and the woman at the same time.

Shooting them was a possibility. But firing a weapon was loud. The sound could carry damn near a mile. Someone was bound to hear and call the police.

That left Scott with a single option. He could stay in his cabin and hope that the couple wandered away.

The last choice seemed to be the best. He carefully placed the spoon on the counter and turned off the burner. Backing out of the kitchen, he turned off the lamp. The switch caught with a click, plunging him into darkness. He took a step, stumbled, and his hip hit the table. The lamp fell to the ground with a crash.

He froze in his place as his heart thumped against his ribs.

Staring into the dark, he held his breath and listened.

"Did you hear that?" asked the woman.

In the cabin, he silently screamed.

"Hear what?"

"I heard something," said the woman before she shushed the man. After a moment, she said, "Maybe it was just my imagination."

He willed the couple to just go away.

They didn't cooperate. "I think I hear something, too," he said. "Hey!" he yelled. "Hey! Help."

Faint but unmistakable was the sound of barking dogs.

"I hear it," said the woman. "Do you think those are wolves?"

Scott knew better. It was a K-9 unit that being used to find the missing motorists.

The barking got louder. Then he could hear several voices. At first, he couldn't make out anything beyond jumble of noises. Then, the words became clear.

"I found the trail."

"It leads this way."

"I think the tracks are fresh."

Feeling his way through the dark, Scott found the sofa and sank into the cushions. His empty stomach roiled. Bile rose in the back of his throat. He swallowed it down to keep the retching. God, how humiliating it would be for the sound of vomit to give away his hiding place.

"Joyce! Bruce!" a woman called out.

He recognized the voice.

Jesus, was it really her?

She spoke again, confirming what he already knew. "This is Kansas Colton, from the Alaska Department of Public Safety. If you can hear me, call out."

Kansas had actually come to him. It was serendipity. No, it was stronger than mere coincidence. It was fate. He had to see her. Rising from his seat, he felt his way to the door.

The man and woman were screaming.

"Here! Here!"

"We're over here!"

And yet Scott barely heard their words over the buzzing in his ears.

"Stay where you are," said Kansas. "We'll find you."

The search party was getting closer. He could hear the dogs barking as they bounded through the snow. The woman had started crying, her sobs were audible even in the cabin.

"It's okay, babe," the man said.

"I know," she replied. "I'm just so happy."

If Scott wanted to step outside, now was his chance. Of course, he'd have to be careful not to be seen. But any noise he made would be lost in the chaos.

His boots were where he left them on a mat. His coat was hanging on a peg nearby. He put on his outdoor attire in the dark before feeling for the door handle.

"Oh my God," said the woman. "I can see the lights. Hey! We're over here."

"Over here," the man bellowed.

Scott took his chance. He pulled the door open. Cold air stole his breath. He pulled the door closed quietly and quickly. The cabin had an overhang, protecting the porch from the deepest drifts. But several feet of snow covered the ground. He carefully waded into the snowbank.

It was easy to follow the noise of the rescue party as they found the missing couple.

The woman, still crying, said, "I can't believe you found us. *He*—" she emphasized the single word with distaste "—he said that he knew where the road was and that there was a gas station less than a mile away."

"I did know where the road was," said the man, defending himself. "And there is a gas station just a mile away. It's just that I got turned around."

"And then our phones both died because of all this cold," the woman said, continuing the story.

"Well, none of that matters now," Kansas interrupted

diplomatically. "The important thing is that you've been found and we're going to get you somewhere warm and safe." She paused. "The report we received is that you're pregnant, Joyce. Is that correct?"

"We were just coming back from her appointment with the obstetrician when the car crapped out," said the man. What had the man's name been? Oh yeah, Bruce.

The sky was filled with clouds and endless darkness. Scott trudged through the snow. The wound in his leg throbbed with each step. His lungs burned and his pulse raced. Yet, he kept going even as sweat covered his brow, and his side tightened with exertion. The need to see Kansas was stronger than his pain. He watched from the tree line.

"I'd like to put you in a toboggan, Joyce," said Kansas. Her voice was like a song. "We can pull you out of here and get you to a place where a helicopter can pick you up and take you to the hospital for an evaluation. And Bruce, we can help you out in the same way."

Scott kept to the trees as he made his way closer to the voices. Through the limbs, he could see a clearing. The SAR team had set up a single light on a pole and it illuminated the field. There were seven people in the search and rescue party. Two of them held dogs on leads. One of the canines—a large German shepherd—turned to look in his direction.

Scott stepped farther into the shadows and watched as the SAR team unfolded a toboggan made of Gor-Tex and collapsible poles. As they got ready take the stranded couple back to civilization, an idea came to Scott. It was genius and would solve all his problems.

Chapter Fifteen

By the time Kansas returned to Asher's condo, it was already 2:00 p.m. She'd been dropped off at home after a SAR by her coworker, Aquwik, countless times. At her house, nobody was home. Knowing that Asher was waiting made all the difference. For the first time in forever, her pulse raced with excitement about going inside.

"Thanks for the lift," she said, grabbing her bag.

"Anytime," he said. "Although I won't bother you unless it's an emergency. You know that, right?"

"I'm happier working than not," she said, her hand resting on the door handle. "Besides, I'm safe if I'm part of a team."

"I guess that's right," said Aquwik, though he didn't sound convinced. "Anyway, I'm glad that you were there today and that we found those two."

"Those three," she said. "Remember, Joyce was pregnant."

"Then we got an especially good outcome."

Aquwik's use of "good outcome" turned her thoughts back to Asher. She knew life was no fairy tale. Still, she wondered about the next chapter.

She opened the door. A gust of wind swirled past her as she jumped to the ground. "Thanks again for the ride."

She slammed the door closed and Aquwik waved.

Lights on tall posts lit the parking lot and the buildings in the complex. A path had been shoveled to Asher's front door and she walked down the narrow track. She'd seen him open the door enough that she knew the code, but should she just barge in? Knock? Before she had a chance to decide, he opened the door. Light shone on him from behind, surrounding him in a golden halo. He wore a flannel shirt in plaids of wine and rust. Somehow, the colors brought out copper highlights in his hair, mustache and beard. It also turned his eyes to rich and chocolatey shade of brown.

"Hey," she said, breathless at the sight of him.

"Come in." He reached for her hand. "I want to show you something."

In the parking lot, Aquwik gave two quick beeps of his horn. She turned and waved. Then the SUV pulled away. She watched until even his taillights were swallowed by the darkness.

"You want to show me something?" she said, both nervous and excited. "What?"

"Close your eyes," he said. "And keep holding my hand."

Squeezing Asher's fingertips, she closed her eyes. "What's up with all the secrecy?"

"Come with me."

She let him lead her into the house. Once they crossed the threshold, he held on to her shoulders and steered her from behind. She'd taken less than two dozen steps before Asher stopped. "Okay," he said. "Now."

Kansas looked. In front of her was a Christmas tree.

Lights and ornaments hung from every branch and bough. "You bought a Christmas tree?"

That much was obvious. It was also obvious that he'd done it replace the tree she'd left behind.

"It's not just any tree," he said, taking the go bag from her hand. "Look."

Dangling from a hook was an ornament just like hers from the University of Alaska. No wait, it was her ornament. And there was a black-and-white ball from when she played soccer in middle school. There was a picture of her and Spence in a snow globe.

For a moment, she stared, open mouthed at the tree. Then, in a flash, she understood what happened. She closed her mouth and swallowed. Yet, her eyes burned and emotion caught in her throat. "You went to my house and undecorated my tree, then redecorated one here."

Asher gave a quick shrug. "I hope you don't mind. I just wanted to give you back some of the holiday joy you lost."

"I don't know what to say."

"Tell me that you aren't upset."

"Upset? At you?" She shook her head. "I'm not mad. In fact, I love it. This might be the nicest thing anyone has ever done for me." More than this thoughtfulness, Asher had invested a good bit of time. "How long did all of this take you?"

"It wasn't too bad. Plus," he added, "Eli helped."

Now that was a surprise. "He did? How did you arrange that?"

Asher opened his arms, and she stepped into his hug. His embrace had become her favorite place. "When I got to your house, he was looking around for clues that he missed the other night."

Scott Montgomery had become like her shadow. Ever-present. Dark. And yet, somehow, never truly there. Looking up, she met his gaze. "Did he find anything?"

Asher shook his head. "There was nothing. He did ask what I was doing at your place. I told him I'd come for the tree."

"What did he say?"

"At first, he accused me of being a Grinch." Shaking his head, he chuckled. "It was obvious that he thinks there's something going on between us. Hell, he asked me outright if we were together."

"And what did you say?"

"I just kept ignoring his questions."

"That must've been hard," she said, "I mean, Eli is your partner at work."

"Until now, I've always been completely honest with him."

Kansas rested her head on his chest. "I'm sorry you couldn't tell him the truth. It must be hard to lie to your partner about anything."

"I'll always do what you want. But ignoring him didn't do much to appease his suspicions." He held her tighter. "But honestly, I don't think he cared."

"You don't think Eli minded?"

"Not at all."

Had Kansas been wrong all along? Was there a way that she and Asher could openly be a couple? Was now the time to find out?

THE NEXT TWO WEEKS, Kansas lived in bliss. She was still on restricted duty because Scott still hadn't been found but had been called in twice to find people who'd gotten lost outside of Shelby. Asher was still on medical leave, with plans to return to work on January 2.

Just because she wasn't at work didn't mean that she'd gotten bored. With so much extra time, Kansas spent several days with her mother planning the bridal shower for Hetty. They'd sent out invitations and were expecting a large crowd. They'd also made a trip all the way to Anchorage to shop for dresses. There, Hetty had found the perfect bridal gown. Her mother had purchased a full-length dress in ruby red. And most shocking of all, Kansas had actually found a bridesmaid dress that she loved. It was a sheath of emerald-green silk with a scoop neck and short sleeves. Even though she'd hated dresses her whole life, she still felt beautiful when she put it on.

Her mother had gotten all the ingredients for her famous seafood chowder. They'd planned two different kinds of charcuterie. Wine—both red and white—had been purchased. Kansas had even ordered a cake from Roasters and would be picking it up on her way to the party.

Beyond all the plans for the shower, there was the wedding, which would take place on New Year's Eve and would be held on the grounds of RTA. It was the perfect place for her brother and his fiancée to get married. After all, they both loved the company, and working as guides was what brought them together.

Over the weeks that they were together, her relationship with Asher continued to grow. More of Kansas's belongings had been brought from her house to the condo. She had permanently moved from the guest room and now shared the master bedroom with Asher. Every day was a new adventure in domesticity. They cooked together. Cleaned together. Shopped for Christmas gifts online. Asher was still recovering from his concussion and often needed a nap in the afternoon. But each day he was stronger.

Kansas and Asher also made love whenever they felt like it, which happened to be often.

The surveillance equipment Asher ordered finally arrived. Noelle came over and spent an afternoon helping with installation. Now there were three cameras in the condo. One in the living room. One at the back door and one on the front door. The feed went to an app on Asher's phone.

The only dark spot on Kansas's otherwise gleaming life was Scott Montgomery. He hadn't been seen or heard from since he broke into her house three weeks earlier. There were several theories about what had happened to the murderer. The most popular one was that he died of his gunshot wound or an ensuing infection.

While Kansas wouldn't mourn the death of a serial killer, the thought that she'd taken a life weighed on her chest. For the most part, she could ignore the possibility that she was also a killer. But often, at night, when she was alone with her thoughts, it was hard to breathe.

At times like that, Asher held her tight. He placed his hand on her racing heart and told her that everything would be okay. They were together and could handle anything. The thing was, she believed him. As a team, Kansas and Asher were unstoppable. But that brought up another question—one she tried to ignore—what would happen once they were both back at work? Finally, it was the day of the bridal shower. Outside, it was clear and cold. There were no storms in the forecast, which meant that the weather was as close to perfect as anyone in Shelby could hope for at this time of the year. Sitting at the breakfast table, Kansas stared at the to-do list she'd created on her phone.

"I think I've got everything on here," she said before scooping a bite of oatmeal into her mouth. "It looks like there's still a lot for me to get done before this evening."

She had come up with three games. The prize for each winner needed to be wrapped. She still had to put together the favor bags and make mini chocolates that looked like seaplanes and mountains. Dread settled in her stomach. Sure, she'd watched plenty of online videos about how to make the individual candies. But she'd never done it before and was worried they wouldn't turn out right.

"And if you don't," Asher began, "who cares?"

"Who cares? I care. My mom will care. The guests will care. Hetty will care."

He held up his hands in surrender. "All's I'm saying is that this shower is about showing Hetty how much you love her and that you want to share in her happiness. If something's not perfect, it's not the end of the world."

Maybe there was some wisdom in his words. Still, she was nervous and wanted to do everything right. "I guess."

The phone in her hand buzzed. There was one word on the caller ID: Mom.

"I gotta take this," she said to Asher before swiping the call open. "Hey, Mom." Holding the phone to her ear, she rose from the breakfast table and walked into the living room. "I was just going over everything for this evening."

"Actually, I was calling to see if there was anything you needed me to do," said her mother. "The house is clean. The ingredients for the seafood chowder need to be prepped, but that won't take too long."

Turning on the speaker function, Kansas settled onto

the sofa and gazed at the tree. "I still haven't started on making the candies. In theory, it seems easy. But a double boiler to melt the chocolate? I don't have one of those. I saw something that said to use two pots—one that fits inside the other. But still…"

"You can microwave the candies," her mother suggested.

She'd watched a video that had used the same technique. It seemed simple enough, but the comments warned that the chocolate burned easily. "I'm just overthinking this," she said. "I'll be fine."

"Or you can bring all your supplies over here this morning. We can make the candy together."

"I don't want to give you extra work…"

Her mother interrupted with a tsking noise. "I'd love to see you and I'd love the company. Besides," she added, "your vehicle is back at the house. I can come over and get you, then you can drive yourself home."

"That sounds like a great idea," said Kansas. "Give me an hour to get ready."

"See you soon," said her mother. Then she ended the call.

Asher stood in the doorway.

"Hey," she said, "not sure if you heard, but I'm going over to my mom's. She's going to help me make the candy."

"Sounds like a nice time for you both. Do you need me to come with you?"

For the most part, she didn't leave the condo unless Asher was with her. He was still officially her security detail, even though their relationship had taken a decidedly romantic turn. But the longer Scott Montgomery was missing, the more certain she became that he was dead. His body might be buried by the winter's snow and not discovered until spring. Or maybe his remains would never be found.

"You know," she said, "I think I'll be okay."

"You sure about that?" he asked.

Kansas nodded. "I'll text you when Mom and I get to her house."

It wasn't the best safety plan. But for now, it was enough.

An hour later, Kansas stood in her mother's kitchen. The chocolate wafers were in a double boiler and melting slowly. She had several plastic molds set out on the counter waiting to be filled, along with individual tulle baggies for when the candies were ready.

"How have you been?" asked her mother, stirring the chocolate. "I know you weren't pleased to be staying with Asher Rafferty."

A flush crept up Kansas's cheeks. She wanted to tell her mother everything—well, maybe not *everything*. But she did want to share that she and Asher were a couple. Then again, she'd sworn him to secrecy—at least for now—and she couldn't break her own rule. "It's been nice, actually."

"I heard that he went to your house and got your Christmas tree."

Obviously, Eli told her mother about seeing Asher. Well, there was no use denying the truth. "He did."

"And?" her mother coaxed.

"And what? It was a nice gesture."

"Well, that seems more than a little nice to me."

"He's a considerate guy. What else do you want me to say?"

"I'm your mother. I know you." She tapped the spoon on the side of the pot. "I think there's a lot more you can say."

Kansas didn't want to have this conversation with her mom, not yet anyway. She changed the subject. "Is the chocolate ready?"

"Looks like it." Abby lifted the smaller pot filled with melted chocolate out of the larger one that was filled with slowly simmering water. "Get me something to set this on."

Kansas opened the drawer where her mother kept kitchen towels and hot pads. She set a mat on the counter close to where the molds were set. Abby placed the pot down.

He mom began her instructions. "We fill each mold slowly. We don't want air bubbles in our candy. You want to try?"

As a kid, Kansas had little interest in learning how to cook. She picked up the basics from her mother, and it was enough to get her through college and into adulthood. But as she let the chocolate drizzle into the form of a seaplane, she wondered if she'd missed out on something special. "Thanks for helping me out with this, Mom." She scraped the last of chocolate into a form. "You're the best."

"It's easy to be the best with you." Her mother squeezed her shoulder. "Since the molds are full, tap them the counter gently. That'll make sure the backs are even."

Kansas did as her mother instructed. "Now what?"

"Now we wait for them to cool. We can pop them into the fridge and speed things along. Then we start all over and make more." She set a timer on her watch for thirty minutes.

"If we make enough, I'll take some back for Asher."

"I'm sure there will be plenty," said Abby. "Want to help me get everything prepped for the soup?"

"So long as you teach me how to make it."

"I'm happy to have you learn." Her mother pulled out several different kinds of seafood wrapped in white paper from the fridge. "But why have you taken an interest in cooking all of a sudden?"

Kansas knew her reasoning. It was because she'd been staying with Asher for weeks and he was the cook in the couple. Sure, she was always happy to have a warm meal made for her, even if it meant cleaning up afterward. It's just that she liked to idea of wowing him with a fabulous meal. Especially since she knew that he loved her mother's seafood chowder. "I don't know," she lied. Again, heat rose in her cheeks. "I guess I'm just feeling more like an adult and less like a kid."

"Are you sure it doesn't have anything to do with a handsome trooper?"

"Who? Eli?" She made a face, teasing her mother. "That's gross. He's my cousin."

"You know very well that I mean Asher Rafferty. It's obvious that you two have done more than figure out how to get along. You're both fond of each other."

"I guess he has grown on me," said Kansas, still careful not to reveal too much.

"I won't push," said Abby, taking a bag of carrots out of the refrigerator, as well. "But I am your mother. I can tell that he's done more than grow on you."

"Mom! Stop."

Her mother held up her hands in surrender. "I won't say another word." She used a peeler to point at the bag of carrots. "Wash, peel and slice all of those."

As she worked, her mother took a soup pot out of a cabinet and placed it on the stove. She measured a tablespoon of oil and put that in the pot before turning on the burner. She set several stalks of celery in front of Kansas. "You chop that and the veggies into the pot. Once they've sautéed, we'll add more ingredients."

The women worked quietly, the companionable silence only broken by Abby's instructions on the soup. When the timer on her mother's watch beeped, Kansas was surprised that thirty minutes had already passed. "I'll put the candies on a plate. You wash the chocolate out of the smaller pot."

After squirting liquid soap into the pot, she filled it with hot water. "You know, Mom," she began, not really decided what to share with her mother. "You're right."

"I'm always happy to hear that I'm right—it happens so rarely," she joked. Abby Colton was too careful to get much wrong. "But what am I right about?"

"Asher," said Kansas. "He and I have become more than friends."

"Oh, honey. I'm not surprised. But I'm happy to hear that you two have found each other."

"How are you not surprised?" Kansas asked. "We used to bicker all the time."

"Well, I'll admit that the two of you could've been more mature. But it was obvious that you were on each other's minds a lot. To me, it seemed like you were hiding your true feelings behind the antagonism."

That's exactly what Asher had said to her before they kissed for the first time. Had it only been three weeks ago? It felt like months or years—but only in a good way. "I guess a lot of that was happening. We're kind of a couple now." Once she started sharing with her mom, she couldn't stop. "I mean, right now, it's just us. And he's really easy to be around. But he goes back to work after New Year's." After sharing all her fear with her mother, Kansas felt like a washrag that had been rung out. Slumping against the counter, she sighed, "Once he's back at work, I don't know what we should do. Try to keep the relationship a secret? Tell everyone and hope that it works out? End it all before it gets messy?"

Her mom rubbed Kansas's back. "Life is always messy. But what does your heart tell you to do?"

Without question, her heart told her to stay with Asher. It's just that she didn't know where their path would lead. "It's such a small town and a smaller ADPS office. If things go sideways…"

"If things go sideways, as you say, then you and Asher have to renegotiate after the breakup," said her mother. "But, honey, what if things never go sideways? Maybe you should embrace the good that comes your way instead of trying to avoid the bad."

She leaned her head on her mom's shoulder. "Thanks, Mom. That's exactly what I needed to hear."

"Glad I could help. And speaking of help, let's get the rest of the candies made."

As Kansas washed the pot, Abby filled the boiler with water and set it on the stove. "What else do you have on your to-do list?" her mom asked.

"The cake will be ready at four. I'll stop by Roasters on my way back and should get here by half past at the latest." She rinsed all the suds off the pot before drying it with a dish towel.

Her mom started melting another batch of chocolate wafers. The kitchen was filled with the savory scent of sautéed vegetables, salty seafood and sweet candies. The smells blended into the aroma of her home. And while they worked, Kansas knew that her mother had been right. She should embrace the happiness she'd found with Asher and not worry about problems that didn't—and may never—exist.

Yet, if all of that was true, why couldn't she shake the feeling of dread?

Chapter Sixteen

Asher took advantage of Kansas being out of the condo for a few hours and went into town. Shelby was a popular spot during the tourist season. But being this far north, very few people lived in Shelby year-round. It meant that many of the shops, which only catered to travelers, were closed for the season.

But one near the marina was open.

Claudia's Boutique had been a staple of shopping in town for decades, all the way back to the original proprietress, Claudia Bouchard, a shop owner in Montreal who ended up in Shelby after coming west with her prospector husband during the Yukon gold rush at the end of the 1800s.

Legend has it that Claudia, sick of travel, set up a store in Shelby. Her husband continued north, never to be heard from again. Whether it was true or not, Asher didn't know. What he did know is that the store carried all sorts of high-end goods—jewelry, native art, hand-knit scarves and sweaters, along with handmade soaps and specialty knives that were made in Shelby by a Tlingit master bladesmith.

Light from the front window spilled onto the otherwise

dark street that ran parallel to the marina. A set of jingle bells tinkled as Asher opened the door. A fake Christmas tree decorated with crystal ornaments and white lights stood next to the door. The scent of apples and spice filled the shop. William Bouchard, a direct descendant of Claudia, looked up from a display as Asher entered the store.

"Detective Rafferty." William wore a pair of round glasses and plaid bow tie, and always insisted on using everyone's official title. "Happy Holidays. I expected to see you before now. How have you been?"

Asher wasn't about to tell him that Kansas had been staying at his home for her own safety. If her whereabouts, though not necessarily a secret, became common knowledge, then what was the point? "Convalescing," he said, wrapping the side of his head with his knuckles.

"I heard about the explosion." He tutted. "Damn shame that you got hurt and that lunatic got away."

"Damn shame" was an understatement. "It is."

"Well—" William straightened his bowtie "—what brings you into the boutique today?"

"I'm looking for a gift," he said. "Something special."

"As you can see." William opened his arms wide. "We have a whole store filled with special. What exactly are you looking for?"

Asher wanted to get something for Kansas. The question was, what? "I'm not exactly sure," he said, being honest with William. "If it's okay with you, I'll just poke around for a few minutes."

"Can I get you a cup of hot cider while you browse?"

Something hot and sweet sounded perfect. "Yes," said Asher, before remembering his manners. "Please."

"Back in a jiff," William said before disappearing into the back of the store.

Asher walked by each case, glancing at the displays. Nothing caught his eye until he passed one that was filled with jewelry. He knew it was far too early to be thinking of engagement rings, and still, he examined each one through the glass.

William returned and set a paper cup with cider on the counter. "So, you're looking for a gift for a lady."

"I am," he said, before picking up the warm cider. Asher took a drink. It was sweet and spicy and reminded him a little of Kansas.

"Are you thinking of something blingy?"

He was and he wasn't. "I'm not sure that we're at the point in the relationship."

"Tell me about her?" asked William. "What does she like?"

Kansas liked being in the woods. She liked her family and friends. She liked helping find people who were lost. She liked movies with singing and dancing. She liked her scrambled eggs with toast. "Christmas," he said after a moment. "She likes Christmas."

"I have just the thing for you." William walked to the large tree with the twinkling lights.

"I had these imported from a glass blower in Seattle," he said, lifting an ornament from the tree. "He works at the Chihuly Museum of Glass."

Asher had been to the museum, but it had been years earlier. The large sculptures of swirling colored glass made to look like the ocean or a field of flowers had been amazing. And the ornament William held was just as impressive. It was green and brown and blue. "It looks like a mountain range but in abstract."

"That's exactly what the artist had in mind," said William. "This one is called *The Great North*."

The twinkling lights caught the glass and sent rainbows dancing across the floor. In years to come, would Kansas share stories about this ornament. But what would she say? And maybe there was an even more important question, would he be around to hear them all?

"I'll take it." He reached for his wallet. "How much do I owe you?"

"This one is one-seventy-five," said William.

Asher swallowed, shocked at the price. He bit back the urge to ask if William meant 175 US dollars. Obviously, he did. And just as obviously, Kansas Colton was worth an expensive ornament—even if he could have gotten her a flight to Seattle for the same price. He removed a credit card and held it out. "Can you gift-wrap that for me?"

"Of course."

It took only a few minutes for the payment to go through and to get the ornament into a box and wrapped with a red paper. A gold bow was affixed to the top. With his purchase safely in a paper bag with the store's logo on the front, Asher left the store. It was only 12:00 p.m. and still it was dark as midnight. There were no clouds, so the sky was filled with thousands of stars. It was beautiful but cold. The icy air stung his cheeks and burned the inside of his nose with each breath. He walked quickly and carefully back to his SUV and drove home. Back at his condo, Asher placed Kansas's gift under the tree just as the front door opened.

He looked up as she crossed the threshold. Her cheeks were rosy from the cold and her eyes were bright. "Hey," she said. "What's up?"

Asher rose slowly as a headache formed behind his eyes. "I just went out for a bit. Is everything ready for the shower?"

"I still have to pick up the cake, but I'll do that on my way over," she said, unwinding the scarf that was around her neck. She shrugged out of her coat and hung both in the closet. Pointing to the tree, she asked, "Is that a gift?"

Since it was the only present under the branches, it was fairly obvious. "It is," he said, adding quickly, "I went into town and picked up something for you."

"You did?" Her face lit up with a smile. "Can I shake it?"

"Oh, no. No shaking this box."

"Har-har."

"I'm not joking." Somehow, his headache was getting worse. Maybe it was because he hadn't eaten lunch. "You hungry?"

Kansas pressed a hand to her middle. "Ugh. No. There were several candies that didn't look so good. I had to take care of them."

He laughed. "Well, I'm going to make myself a sandwich."

She followed him into the kitchen and leaned against the counter. "Do I get any hints about what's in the box?"

"Not even a little one," he said, removing lunch meat and cheese from the fridge.

She faked a pout.

"You know that Santa is watching," he said while setting everything onto the counter.

She nudged him with her shoulder. "Are you saying that you want me to be a good girl?"

"Well, not too good…"

He put all the fixings on two slices of bread and took a bite. The food turned to sand and ash in his mouth. He choked down everything anyway. Asher had gone too long without eating, that was the only problem. He forced himself to take another bite. This one stuck in his throat. He gagged it down. It churned in his stomach and threatened to come back up. Just when he thought that all the symptoms from the concussion had passed, another one returned.

He set the sandwich on the plate. "You know, I'm not as hungry as I thought."

Her brow tightened with concern. "What's going on?"

"I'm not feeling great." He picked up the lunch meat and cheese. "I'll put this away and then I'm going to rest."

She took everything out of his hands. "I can handle the kitchen," she said, placing everything back into the fridge. Then Kansas removed a glass from the cabinet and filled it with water. She held it out. "Drink this."

He took the glass and drained it in a single swallow. His headache receded a little. Kansas was right, he might be dehydrated. "Thanks," he said, setting it on the counter next to the plate. "But I can pick up my own mess."

True, before Kansas entered his life, he wouldn't have thought twice about leaving a mess in the kitchen if he wanted to grab a quick nap. But since she'd been living with him, he'd found comfort in the order she created.

"Go," she said. "Rest. Feel better. If I'm not here when you wake up, I've gone to pick up the cake and then to my mom's house for the shower."

"What time are you leaving?" he asked.

"A little before four."

It was just after noon right now. "I won't sleep that long," he said, although he wasn't sure if that was true. The headache was getting worse with each beat of his heart. "But wake me up before you go."

"Not gonna happen." Kansas opened the dishwasher

door. "Now, go and take care of yourself." She slipped the glass onto the top rack.

Asher watched Kansas. Her back was to him and yet, he'd memorized her face. He knew the exact blue of her eyes. The rich brown of her hair. The way the right side of her mouth lifted just a bit more than the left when she smiled. As he walked upstairs, the hallway was blessedly dark. Yet he had to wonder how he'd gotten so lucky to have a woman like Kansas in his life.

FOR TWO WEEKS, Scott had been patient and focused. First, he'd stolen an old cell phone from a nearby cabin that was closed for the winter. Once he got the device online, he rented a PO Box from a town farther north. Using the phone, he'd ordered everything he needed and had it shipped to the new address. To keep from being recognized, he let his hair and beard grow before bleaching them both white. The peroxide had burned his skin and given him a headache that lasted for days. But as he drove his car down the snow-covered road, with his packages in the passenger seat, he knew it had all been worth it.

He stopped in front of the cabin and turned off the engine. The air inside the car started to cool. But he didn't want to waste time by going inside. He'd ordered an Orange Box, the kind that switched the caller ID frequency-shift key. He opened the shipping container and removed the device. It was a simple, orange-colored plastic square with several buttons and a small LCD screen. He was familiar enough with the technique from his time with the state police. But to be certain, he read the directions.

It took him only a few minutes, but already the windows had started to fog. Each breath froze into a cloud. Using the buttons on the Orange Box, he entered in all the information. He inhaled. The air was cold, but confidence filled his chest. He sent the text and waited. The message on the LCD screen read, Sending… Sending… Sending… Sent. A moment later a new message appeared: Received. He'd done it. All this perseverance had paid off, but in the end, it would be worth every sacrifice.

KANSAS SAT ON the living room floor atop her yoga mat. Just like Dove taught in class, she was in easy seat—otherwise known as crisscross-applesauce. Her palms were resting on her knees and her gaze was lowered. She inhaled deeply, filling her belly, then her chest, then her throat. She exhaled. Throat. Chest. Belly.

It did nothing to stop the butterflies that flew wildly in her middle. The bridal shower for Hetty was the first time she'd hosted an event. Sure, she'd had weeks to plan and her mother's help. But what if something went wrong?

Like she'd learned at yoga, she let the thought go and returned her attention to her breath. Concerns about the bridal shower returned. Had they made enough favors? Too many?

Inhale. Belly. Chest. Throat.

Exhale. Throat. Belly. Chest.

Her mind continued racing.

What was Kansas going to wear? Sure, much of her clothing had been brought to Asher's condo. But did she have an outfit that would be nice enough?

Inhale. Exhale.

It was obvious that she was too keyed up for mindfulness and meditation. After lifting her gaze, she rolled her shoulders up, back and around. It eased some of her tension. But not enough. Maybe Kansas was anxious because she had too much time between now and the party. Well, she could keep herself busy by deciding what to wear.

Standing, she rolled up her yoga mat and tucked it under her arm. Kansas climbed the stairs to the second story. She paused at the master bedroom. Pressing her ear to the door, she listened. Asher's snores were soft but unmistakable. At least he was getting some rest. Hopefully, when he woke up, he'd feel better.

Kansas entered the guest room, where all her stuff was kept. She set the yoga mat in a corner and opened the closet doors. She scanned her clothes. It wasn't like her to worry too much about how she looked. A pair of jeans and a T-shirt, sweatshirt or sweater was always good enough for her. But recently, she wanted to look as good as she could. What's more, she knew why.

She wanted to be the best version of herself for Asher. And she supposed that desire bled into other parts of her life—like a bridal shower for Hetty.

Pulling a V-neck sweater from the closet, she tossed it onto her bed. As she looked at her bottoms—mostly jeans and a few pairs of chinos—her phone dinged with an incoming text. It was hooked to a charger and sitting on a bedside table. She lifted the device and swiped the message open.

It was from Aquwik.

Sorry to bother you. We have more missing motorists.

He also included the address for a meeting location, not far from where they'd found Bruce and Joyce. What was it about that stretch of road that made people think they could wander away from their car?

His first text was followed by another.

I'm already on-site and cell service is spotty. I can't give you a ride. Sorry.

None of his message came as a surprise. But she had Hetty's shower later. Even if she hadn't been on limited duty, Kansas would have taken a personal day. She sent a quick reply.

It's Hetty's Bridal Shower tonight. I never pass the buck, but you need to find someone else.

The text bubble appeared on her screen as Aquwik sent his reply.

Another team leader is on their way. I just need you to get things organized.

Aquwik was more than capable of organizing a team on his own. Why did he need her?
Another message followed.

It won't take more than an hour.

Well, there was really no reason to refuse her partner's request. Her message back was simple and direct.

On my way.

Her go bag was on the closet's top shelf. She pulled it down and opened the zipper before removing all her gear. As she changed her clothes and put on her base layer, she wondered if she should wake Asher. She also wondered if she should let her mother know that she might be late to the shower.

No. There was no reason to worry Mom now. She still had almost four hours until she needed to pick up the cake. As far as Asher, he really did need his rest. Hopefully, she'd be back before he ever knew she'd been gone.

Dressed and ready to go, she hooked a strap of her bag over her shoulder and took the stairs to the first floor two at a time. Within minutes of getting the text, Kansas left Asher's house.

She drove through the dark, thankful that it wasn't snowing. Although with the clear skies, the temperature was well below freezing. As she turned off the main road, she eased her foot off the gas. She expected to see cars from several different jurisdictions lining the roadway. And yet, there was nothing except a solitary car that was parked nearby. There was no exhaust coming from the tailpipe. No lights on in the interior. No driver behind the wheel.

They couldn't have found the missing person already.

Even if they did, the team would still be assembled.

Putting the gearshift into Park, she pulled her phone out of her pocket. After opening the messaging app, she checked Aquwik's text again. She was in the right place. But where was everyone else?

Using the message to open the contact, Kansas placed a call.

Three tones followed by an automatic message: "You do not have coverage in this area. Please try your call later."

She typed in a text.

Where is everyone?

And hit Send.

The message left her phone with a whoosh. But immediately, red wording appeared above the text bubble: Message Not Sent.

Something wasn't right. Her chest tightened. She drew in a deep breath and made a plan.

She would retrace her route until she found coverage. Then she'd call Aquwik. After tucking her phone into the cupholder between the seats, she reached for the gearshift. Before she could get it out of Park, her door swung open. Outside stood a man with white hair and beard.

For a moment, she couldn't think. Like a computer that needed to be rebooted, her mind went blank.

"Come with me," he said, "and you won't get hurt."

She recognized the voice at once. Her veins filled with icy terror.

"Scott?" she said. Her voice was strong and steady—completely opposite to the terror that gripped her throat. "What are you doing?"

He smiled. It was a slow reptilian expression that turned her stomach. "I thought you would've guessed by now. I'm here for you."

"There's a missing person," she said, warning him. "The team is about to arrive. If you're here when they show up, you'll end up in prison for the rest of your life."

He shook his head, chuckling softly. "You don't believe that. You're a smart woman, Kansas. You know what happened."

The truth was, she did understand. Scott had somehow faked Aquwik's number and lured her here. Well, the thing was, she wasn't going down without a fight. Kansas dropped her foot onto the gas. The engine roared. She shoved the gearshift into Reverse. She was fast, but

Scott was faster. He grabbed her arm. She only saw the glint of the needle before she felt pain in her bicep. Then her hand went numb. The steering wheel slipped from her grasp. The numbness spread. She lost control of her other arm. Her chest. Her torso. Her legs. Kansas could no longer hold herself upright and she slumped to the side, falling out of the open door.

As a cloud of nothingness came to claim her, she had a single thought.

Nobody knows where I am.

Chapter Seventeen

The buzzing of a phone pulled Asher from a deep slumber. Without looking at the screen, he swiped the call open. "Yeah?"

"Asher? Is that you? Thank goodness I finally reached you. It's Abby Colton. I'm trying to find Kansas."

He was immediately awake, and yet her words made no sense. "Find Kansas? What time is it?"

Glancing at his phone, he answered one of his own questions. The time was 4:48 p.m.

Before he'd gone to sleep, she'd told him that she was going to pick up the cake and go to her mother's house. What time had she said she would stop at Roasters, 4:30 p.m.? No, it was 4:00 p.m.

"The bakery called. She never stopped by." He could hear the worry in the woman's voice. "Even before that, I called several times. She never answered."

Asher's heart skipped a beat. Was Kansas missing?

He wouldn't get upset—or upset her mother—until he had all the facts. Rising from the bed, he turned on the bedside lamp. It filled his room with a warm glow. Thankfully, the headache from before was completely gone. "Let me see if she's still here," he said, crossing the floor. "Or if she left a note."

He paused at the door and opened the messaging app on his phone. There was nothing from Kansas. Turning the handle, he stepped into the hallway. All the lights were off. Feeling his way across the hall, he knocked softly on the guest room door.

"Kansas? You in there?"

There was no answer.

Asher let himself into the room and flipped on the overhead light.

A deep blue sweater was lying on the bed. Other than that, there was no sign of Kansas.

"She's not in the guest room," he said to Abby. Leaving the room, he strode down the hall with a renewed purpose he hadn't had since the explosion. "Let me check downstairs."

The main floor was as quiet and dark as the upper level. He turned on every light. There was no written note on the kitchen counter, the dining table or in the living room. He stifled a curse. "She's not here, Abby," he said, before adding. "I don't know where she went."

But he paused. That wasn't exactly true. Actuating the speaker function, he opened his home monitoring app. There was a notification that his front door had opened at 1:12 p.m. He pulled up the video. In it was footage of Kansas leaving through the front door. She was dressed in her bright red SAR jacket. Her go bag was slung over her shoulder.

"Mystery solved. It looks like she was called in to work," he said to Abby. "More than three and half hours ago."

"I'm surprised that she went out today of all days," she said before adding, "and didn't even call to let me know."

It was true that Kansas was dedicated to her job. But it was also true that she was responsible. She wouldn't have gone out on a search and rescue without letting her mother know that she might be late. Something was wrong. The metallic taste of panic coated his tongue. He swallowed, choking down his fear. He had to think like the detective that he was.

"Call all of Kansas's friends. Maybe she stopped by the yoga studio to see Dove. Or maybe she's at RTA with Hetty and Spence. If you hear anything, call me back."

"What are you going to do?"

He opened his contact app and found the number for Aquwik. "I'm going to confirm where Kansas was headed. I'll call you back once I know."

"Thanks for all your help." The sharp edges of anxiety were gone from her voice.

"I'll call you once I know something. You do the same."

Abby thanked him again and ended the call.

Asher immediately called Aquwik. The phone rang twice before he answered.

"Hello," he said. In the background a baby squalled.

"Hey. This is Asher. Am I getting you at a bad time?"

"My wife is getting ready for Hetty's bridal shower, and I need to feed the baby. I'm slower in making the bottle than she wants." He paused a moment, and the crying stopped. "Success," he said. "Now I can hear. What do you need?"

"I was looking for Kansas," he said. "I know you had a search and rescue earlier…"

The other man interrupted. "The team hasn't been called out at all today."

"Are you sure?" Asher brought up the video from the front door. Once again, he watched footage of Kansas going down the walk. "My doorbell cam caught her leaving more than three hours ago. She's got on her red SAR jacket and has her go bag."

"We haven't gotten any calls at all today. While she's on limited duty, I'm the contact person. But maybe someone didn't get the memo to call me. Let me reach out to headquarters in Juneau. I'll call you back."

Asher thanked him and ended the call. He knew that there could be a legitimate explanation for Kansas being incommunicado. But he also knew now was the time to get concerned. He could make calls of his own to the office and find her vehicle by using GPS. But there was someone else he had to contact first.

ELI COLTON WAS still at work. Noelle was going to be at Hetty's bridal shower all evening, so there nothing for him to do other than work. The Scott Montgomery file was open, and papers spilled across the wooden table. Leaning on his elbows, he reread an interview that had been conducted with one of Scott's elementary school teachers. The woman, who was in her upper eighties, still recalled each and every one of her students.

She had clear memories of Scott, a bright but quiet boy. She knew that his family life was difficult. His mother was, as she put it, often sad. Scott's father worked on a fishing boat and left the home for weeks at a time. She mentioned that Scott had written a story about spending time with his grandmother at her cabin in the woods.

He read the report again. And once more.

One of the problems with Scott Montgomery being the perpetrator was that all the investigators with ABI knew him—or so they thought. Eli couldn't count the number of conversations he'd had with Scott over the years. The topics ranged from the professional to the personal. But he was certain that Scott had never mentioned being especially close to a grandmother. And he definitely had never brought up a remote cabin.

Reaching for his laptop, Eli connected with the state police's website. For the purposes of his investigation, he had access to everything associated with Scott Montgomery. The first thing he did was pull up Scott's birth certificate. The father's name was listed as Wilhelm Montgomery.

He then did an internet search. It turned up several news articles from decades earlier. Wilhelm was born and raised in the vicinity. He worked until he was thirty-five years old, when he went to prison for killing a man during a bar fight. At the time, Scott would have been fourteen years old. Subsequently, Wilhelm died in prison when he got into an altercation with the wrong inmate.

The fact that Scott's father had died in prison might seem unrelated. But missing that detail had been sloppy police work. Normally, Asher would have already uncovered that important fact.

Eli's phone began to ring. He picked it up and glanced at the screen. After swiping the call open and turning on the speaker function, he said, "That bump on the head you got must've given you psychic powers or something. I was just thinking about you."

"She's gone," he said. "The bastard has gotten her."

Eli didn't need to ask who he meant. Scott had kidnapped Kansas.

He kept typing on the computer. He had to find out all he could about Wilhelm Montgomery and any link to where Scott might've taken his cousin. "Tell me what you know," he said to Asher.

His partner gave him a rundown of the events, beginning with him being asleep when Kansas left. The video that showed her dressed and ready for a search and rescue, although there were no SARs called in today. There was also the fact that she hadn't been seen or heard from since then. He ended with, "I called the office. They were able to pull the GPS coordinates for her vehicle." He then gave Eli the location.

"But you don't have Scott on video?" he asked, clarifying the points in Asher's story.

"I do not," he said. "But I know it's him. Somehow, he lured her from the house and he has her now."

While Asher spoke, he was able to dig deeper into Wilhelm's past. As it turns out, at the time of his death, he held the deed to a property that had once been owned by Gretchen Montgomery. It was close to where Kansas's car had been found. "I think I know where he's taken her. I'm going to call in backup. Stick close to your phone. I'll reach out as soon as I know something."

"Don't bother with the call," said Asher.

Eli usually understood everything his partner said. But this time, his words made no sense. "What do you mean by that?"

"It means I'm coming with you."

KANSAS'S HEAD ACHED and her mouth was dry. She was lying down. There was rough fabric beneath her cheek. Her eyelids were too heavy to open, and she couldn't recall where she was or what she had been doing. Then the memories came back, rolling over her like an avalanche.

Scott Montgomery had lured her to a secluded spot and then, as she tried to drive away, he'd injected her with something. Her bicep was sore. Without thought, she touched the spot where the needle had gone in.

"So, you're awake. I was wondering when the medication would wear off." Scott's voice came out of the darkness.

Kansas opened her eyes. A single lamp shone down on her face. The light was too bright and black dots began floating in her vision. She screwed her lids shut and pushed up to sitting. She could feel her heartbeat in her skull. Peeling her lids open, she squinted at Scott. He sat on the far end of the sofa. She could barely focus. His face came out of the gloom.

"What have you done?"

"I'd think it would be obvious." He gave her another reptilian grin.

Why had she never noticed that he looked like a snake when he smiled? "Not just drug me and bring me to..."

Her vision had cleared enough to see her surroundings clearly. She sat on a sofa with tweed fabric. She was in a cabin, she guessed by the wooden walls and plank flooring. There were two doors on either side of the room. A kitchen area sat beneath a small window. There was also a folding table and a single chair. A small heater sat beside the sofa. The coils were red, and waves of heat flowed over her bare skin.

Bare skin? That wasn't right.

She now wore a black cocktail dress with long sleeves and a pair of patent leather pumps—just like the other victims. A gaudy ring had been slipped onto the ring finger of her left hand. While she was unconscious, he'd stripped her down to her underwear and then put her in this dress. The thought left her nauseous.

How many nights had she lain awake, racked with guilt over taking Scott's life? She'd been mourning the man who had been her friend. As it turns out, he really was a monster. The irony would have made her laugh, except the situation was deadly serious.

No. She wasn't going to let Scott win. She wasn't going to let him turn her into another victim. If she wanted to survive, she was going to have to fight. She tried to make a fist, but her fingers wouldn't move. Whatever drug he'd given her was still in her system. She needed more time to recover.

She had to do something. But what?

Then she knew. She had to keep him talking.

"Why have you done any of this? You killed all those women. You've kidnapped me." Her last word caught on her fear and grief. If she died here, would anyone ever know what happened? Would her body ever be found? But that thought brought up a new question. "Where are we?"

"You don't need to worry about any of that," said Scott, rising from the sofa. "Are you thirsty? I have champagne."

He walked across the room and removed a bottle from a small fridge. As the mental fog lifted, she could see him clearly. His hair was white. He'd grown a beard and that was white, too. But even more confusing, he wore a dark suit, white shirt and a red tie.

Of course, she'd noticed his new hair color when he'd attacked her at her car. But she asked, "What's up with your new look?"

"Do you like it?" he asked, popping the champagne's

cork. Foam fizzed out of the neck. "It's part of my disguise."

"You look like a demented Santa Clause." It might not be smart to antagonize Scott. But she couldn't help herself.

He glared. "That's not very nice of you."

"I don't think it's nice of you to kidnap people, either." Kansas wiggled her fingers. Her hands were getting stronger. She inhaled deeply. Exhaled fully. More of the stupor lifted. "Or commit murder."

"You don't want to get into an argument with me over proper behavior, Kansas. I saw what you did with Asher Rafferty." He turned to the counter and filled two cups with bubbly wine.

With his back to her, she glanced at the lamp. It was wires and tubing inside a plastic casing. It wasn't heavy and not much help in a fight. She needed to find a weapon. But what?

Scott returned to the sofa, holding mismatched wineglasses filled with champagne. "Here," he said, holding out a glass.

She hadn't been able to see what he was doing when he filled the glasses. Had he added poison to the one he now offered her? Struggling to sit up, she reach for the glass that he hadn't offered. "I'll take this one, if you don't mind."

He gave her a lopsided smile—the same one she used to think was sweet. Now it turned her stomach. "You don't trust me."

"Of course I don't trust you, Scott." Breathless, Kansas slumped back against the sofa. "You drugged me to get me here, remember?"

He took a sip of his wine. "I like that you're still feisty. Most of them cried and begged."

Them. All his other victims. "You didn't have to kill anyone, you know."

He took another sip of champagne, swishing it in his mouth before swallowing. "Yes, I did have to kill them all. What's more, you know that's true."

"I don't know anything of the sort," she said, before asking, "Why?"

"To get your attention. To let you know how much I love you." He took another drink, draining the glass. "You see, when a man loves a woman as much as I love you, he'll do anything for her." His eyes were turning glassy. The roses on his cheeks had begun to bloom. He nodded toward her glass. "Aren't you thirsty?"

Her mouth felt as if it had been packed with cotton. Yet, alcohol wouldn't help to clear her mind. "I don't feel like celebrating." Maybe if Scott were drunk, it would be a fair fight. She lifted her champagne. "You can have my drink, too."

He accepted the glass and downed the bubbly wine in a single swallow. "If I wanted to kill you already," he said. "You'd be dead."

His words sent a chill down her spine. Her feet, once numb, were filling with pinpricks of pain. She hoped that was a sign that the sedative was wearing off. She also hoped that Scott would be less of a threat after two drinks. But she needed more time. She had to keep him talking.

"There's something I've always wondered about this case—even before I knew that you were the Fiancée Killer." She didn't wait for him to respond and continued. "Why the little black dress? Why the fake diamond?"

"Oh, that ring on your finger isn't fake."

She looked down at the large sparkling gem. It was showy and nothing she'd ever choose for herself, but it must've cost a fortune. "Why go through all of this if you're just going to kill me?"

"It's all because of your Aunt Caroline."

Kansas shouldn't have been surprised. It didn't take Eli long to see the similarities in the cases. But she asked, "What does she have to do with anything?"

"Jason Stevens, the man who killed her, was devoted to Caroline Colton. He would do anything for her—including kill her parents, her, himself."

Inside the black pumps, she flexed her feet. "There's a big difference between you and him. He killed my aunt because she fought back when he tried to kidnap her. He wanted them to be together. He accidentally choked her to death while trying to subdue her. After she died, he killed himself. He'd never planned a triple murder and a suicide."

Scott huffed out a breath, nostrils flaring. He was annoyed, she could tell. "What's the point?"

"The point is that Jason might have loved my aunt. And you're right, he was willing to kill so they could be together. But he only planned to murder her parents. Her death was an accident. He only killed himself because she was already dead."

"And…"

"And if he had done things right—if he had been smarter—they would have ended up together." Each word was a lie and tasted sour. But she hoped it was what Scott wanted to hear—and gave her enough time to recover and escape.

He rose from the sofa and refilled one of the glasses

with champagne. "Are you saying that he didn't really love her? Because love is caring about someone so much that you're willing to kill for them. You're willing to die for them."

Without trying, Asher came to mind. What was Kansas willing to do for him?

By now, someone must have noticed that she was missing. There would be clues. Like the video of her leaving the condo. Her vehicle was tracked with GPS. But was it enough? Would someone find her before it was too late?

Chapter Eighteen

Standing next to the kitchen counter, Scott glared at Kansas. His gaze hit her like daggers to the heart. Had she done something that gave away her thoughts? Exhaling, she made her expression neutral.

"You never answered my question," he said, before taking a sip of champagne. "Are you saying that Jason never loved Caroline?"

Jason had ruined her family by taking away grandparents and an aunt that Kansas would never know. While he was bad enough, Scott was worse. He'd killed five women and had destroyed their families, as well. So, no, she didn't think that Jason had loved her aunt. The same way she didn't think Scott cared about her at all.

But she couldn't say that, not if she wanted to survive.

"Of course he loved her," she lied. "It's just too bad he accidentally killed her. I'm sure they would have eventually been happy together."

Scott finished his champagne. That was his third glass. He had to be tipsy by now. "You really think so?"

She nodded her head. The movement loosened tight muscles. Little by little, the tranquillizer was wearing off. But it wasn't fast enough. "I do," she said, continuing to lie.

"What do you think he should've done differently?"

"Well." Kansas sighed, emptying her lungs. She drew in a deep breath and tightened her abs. She also tightened her thighs. The muscles in her legs burned. It was a good feeling—better than the numbness from before. "We don't know exactly what happened. But he probably should have talked to Caroline more. Showed her how much he cared." Of course her aunt freaked out. Jason had just murdered her parents. She'd had no choice but to fight for her life. Unfortunately, she'd lost that battle. But Kansas didn't intend to go down so easily.

"What should he have said to her?" Scott asked.

"He should have told her how much he loved her." Again, Asher's face came to mind. She couldn't let herself be distracted by him—or anyone else. But she did have one regret. She should have embraced the relationship with Asher from the beginning. It was ridiculous to be so worried what people might think.

"I love you, Kansas," said Scott. "I always have. I always will."

Bile rose in the back of her throat. "Oh, Scott," she said, trying not to retch. "I wish you'd told me sooner. Then you wouldn't have committed all those murders, and we wouldn't have to hide."

"I don't care about them," he said, his face twisting into a sneer. "And I don't care that the police are looking for me, either. I wanted you all to myself from the beginning."

He was even more unhinged that she'd thought. She had to get away from him, and fast.

"Can I have a glass of water?" she asked.

Scott nodded toward the sink. "Sure."

"I can't get up," she said. "My legs are useless."

It was another lie. Kansas felt as if she had regained control of her body. The question was, was she strong enough to fight?

He snorted a laugh and turned on the tap. "Yeah, well, that might take a while to get out of your system."

He returned from the sink with a water in a ceramic coffee mug. Kansas accepted the cup and drained the contents. The water revived her even more. "Sit," she said, placing a hand on the cushion next to her. "We need to think about what to do next. Because the police are looking for you and me. They aren't going to stop unless we give them a reason."

He dropped down beside her. "What kind of reasons would they need?"

"We could give them two bodies. One male. One female. Roughly our size. Put them both in this cabin and then burn it to the ground."

He shook his head as she spoke. "That won't work. There are dental records. Besides, fire doesn't destroy DNA—not completely."

Of course, he was an expert in forensics. But Kansas didn't intend to kill anyone or give the police two new corpses. All she wanted was for Scott to be close enough for her to strike. She wrapped her fist around the mug's handle and punched, aiming at the side of Scott's head.

The cup connected with his skull, giving a satisfying crack.

Blood seeped from Scott's hairline. He listed to the side. She might not have knocked him out, but she'd left him stunned.

Kansas lunged forward, racing toward the door. Her

legs were heavy, and she could barely stand in the stupid pumps. After kicking off her shoes, she stumbled across the floor. She unlatched the lock and jerked the door. It didn't budge. That's when she noticed the dead bolt, set in high on the door. What's more, there was no thumb latch, only a keyway. In short, if she didn't have the key, she couldn't open the door. That meant, she was stuck inside the cabin with a killer.

ASHER SAT IN the passenger seat of Eli's official state police vehicle. Lights in the dashboard strobed red and blue and a siren wailed into the night. The speedometer climbed: eighty miles per hour, eighty-five, ninety. Outside the window, the world went by in a blur.

Yet, for him, it wasn't fast enough.

The GPS led them to a desolate road at the edge of nowhere. As he expected, Kansas's car was there. The headlights glowed, cutting through the gloom. Exhaust billowed into a cloud. The driver's side door was open, but the dome light was dark.

Eli slowed as they approached. Before the car rolled to a stop, Asher had unbuckled his seat belt and opened the door. He jumped from the passenger seat. As his feet hit solid ground, he sprinted toward her car. Even without the interior light, he could tell that the vehicle was empty. "She's not here," he said, as the words clawed at his throat.

"Let's check the trunk." Eli stood next to the tailgate. He'd left his car in the middle of the road.

Asher hit the trunk's release button. It unlatched with a click.

"She's not in here, either."

"We both know where she is." Asher turned off the

ignition and closed the car's door. Sure, the car was the scene of a crime. But he wasn't going to waste his time trying to preserve evidence. "Scott has taken her to the cabin."

Like many homes in Alaska, the property owned by Scott's grandparents didn't have a street address. They had a general location. It was about three miles from where they now stood. While en route, they'd called in backup. Several units were on the way, but they had yet to arrive.

A helicopter had been called in from Juneau to conduct an aerial search. The winds were too high for the aircraft to take off. Another one was in preflight in Fairbanks. But it would take an hour to arrive on the scene.

It was time that Asher didn't want to waste.

"We can't just sit here," he said to Eli. "We both know what Scott is going to do."

Asher couldn't bring himself to say the plain truth. Scott planned to murder her and then commit suicide. For a moment, Asher tried to imagine a world without Kansas Colton. The pain and the nothingness sucked him in like a black hole.

"We aren't doing nothing, man," said Eli. "We're waiting for backup."

"They're taking too damn long," he said. "Besides, we've never waited for backup before."

"Yeah," said Eli. "And because of that, you got blown up."

Asher stood taller. "I'm still here and I'm going in after her. Come with me. Don't come with me. It's your call."

"Stop being so stubborn. We've called in the team. They're coming."

That was another thing that bothered Asher. "If Scott

realizes that twenty troopers are coming for him, he's going to kill her right then." Asher's sidearm was secured in a holster at his hip. He removed it and made sure that the gun was fully loaded. It was. He stuck the gun back into the holster and zipped up his coat. "You know that the only way we can save Kansas is to go and get her right now. Just the two of us. Fast and silent."

"You aren't thinking straight. You'll end up dead if you go in without backup."

The thing was, he didn't care. He'd do anything to save Kansas. "If you aren't coming with me, I'll go alone."

"I'll come with you." Eli turned off the engine to his car. Without the lights, it was dark as pitch. "I've always got your back, you know that."

"You're more than a work partner," said Asher, clapping his hand on Eli's shoulder. "You're a true friend. A brother from another mother," he joked.

As soon as he spoke, he knew that his words weren't exactly in jest. He cared about Kansas more than he'd cared about anyone before. One day, would he and Eli actually be family?

Asher couldn't let plans of forever get in the way of what he needed to do now—like saving Kansas. And stopping Scott Montgomery.

Eli held out a backpack. "Take this. It's got water. A flashlight. A GPS. And a walkie-talkie."

It was everything they'd need to go into the woods, traveling light and fast. Asher hooked the straps over his shoulders and pulled them tight. "Let's go."

KANSAS'S HEART HAMMERED against her ribs. She jerked hard on the handle. The door rattled in the frame but didn't budge. She needed the key. But where was it? Before she could decide what to do next, Scott grabbed her from behind.

"Where do you think you're going?" he asked, his breath hot on her ear.

Bile rose in the back of her throat.

He held her around the middle. He pressed her to him tighter and tighter. Forced all the air from her lungs. Kansas wouldn't let him squeeze the life out of her. Shoving her feet against the wall, she knocked them both back.

They hit the floor. The back of her head slammed into Scott's forehead. He cursed as stars exploded in her vision. Rolling to the side, she scrambled to her feet. There, on the counter, next to the bottle of champagne, was a key ring.

She rushed toward the sink. Scott grabbed her foot and pulled up. Kansas came down onto the floor. Her face hit the planks, and her mouth filled with blood.

She flipped to her back as Scott fell on top of her. He reached around her throat, his grip tight. She couldn't help but recognize the cosmic humor that she was going to die in the same way as her Aunt Caroline.

No.

Kansas refused to give up.

Caroline had been seventeen years old. Dead too soon, but she didn't have Kansas's training or experience. Kansas reached up to Scott's face and pressed her thumbs into his eyes. He roared with pain and rocked back.

She didn't know if she'd blinded him or not. She got to her feet and rushed to the counter. Scott was right behind. He grabbed her by the shoulder, trying to pull her back. She stretched out as far as she could. Her fingertips brushed the keys, but she couldn't bring them to her. Marshaling all her strength, she pressed forward. His grip faltered and she fell, hitting the counter. Her fingertips tangled with the fabric of the curtains, pulling them down as she went.

Scott was on her back, pinning her to the floor. His hands went around her throat once more. Kansas couldn't breathe. She clawed at his hands. But his grip was like a vice, strong and unyielding. Every cell in her body screamed in pain. The world began to shrink, closing in from all sides, until only a pinprick of light remained. And then, even that disappeared, and everything went dark. As her consciousness faded, Kansas had only one regret. She never told Asher how she felt.

THE TREES CLOSED in on Asher, blotting out the stars and the sky. The snow was deep this far into the woods, sometimes reaching up to his knees. If he had waited for backup, he would have been able to get a pair of snowshoes or cross-country skis. Either would have made it easier and faster for him. But he'd come too far to turn around now.

"Hold up." Eli removed a GPS from his parka's interior pocket. "I want to check our coordinates." The handheld device illuminated his friend's face from below, giving him a ghoulish appearance. Pointing due south, he said, "Best I can tell, it's about half a mile in that direction."

Removing a bottle of water from his pack, Asher took a long drink. Finding that cabin in the thick forest was akin to looking for a needle in a haystack. He shook his head, clearing away the doubts. That's when he saw it—a spark in the darkness. He stepped to the side and checked again. Without question, there was a light.

"You see that?" Asher pointed through the trees.

"See what?" asked Eli, squinting. And then, "Hell yeah. I see it."

"You think it's him? You think that's Scott's cabin?"

"I think we need to check it out and see."

They both started to walk as quickly as they could through the drifts and toward the light. The trot became a jog. The jog turned into a run. And the run became a sprint. Sweat dripped down Asher's back as he pushed through the snow. His side ached and his head throbbed. He could feel the beat of his heart in his skull as well. It was symptoms of the concussion he knew. But he wasn't going to stop, not now. Not when Kansas might be nearby.

As they got closer to the light, it took on a shape. Square, like a window. The shadowy outline of cabin was also visible. With fifty yards to go, Asher held up his hand for Eli to stop. Leaning in, he whispered, "I'll take the window. You go in through the door."

"Agreed."

At the corner of the cabin, they separated, going to a different wall. Asher pressed his back into the cold wood and held his breath. He listened for the voices or the sound of movement from inside. Somewhere in the woods, snow fell from the bough of a tree with a woosh. Other than that, it was silent.

They'd found a cabin. But were they in the right place?

Slowly, carefully, without making a sound, Asher crept toward the window. As a trooper, he'd conducted raids countless times. But this was different. Kansas might be inside and saving her was more than a job—it was personal.

Drawing in a deep breath, he glanced inside before melting into the shadows. But what he had seen was unbelievable. He brought the image to mind, examining each thing that he'd seen. Kansas lay face down on the floor. She wasn't moving. He wasn't even sure if she drew breath. Next to her, Scott sat on the floor and cried.

Rage and misery filled him with a venom that seeped out from his soul. He wanted to lash out at Scott Montgomery and make him pay for everything he'd done. Sure, Asher understood that he was a state trooper. His job was to find the culpable, not deliver cold justice.

But in that moment, he didn't care.

Kansas had been stolen from him. She was gone before he told her how he felt. Gone before she knew that he loved her.

Asher removed his gun from the holster. He came back to the window and looked inside. Scott was still next to Kansas's body and hadn't notice that he was being watched. Lifting his firearm, Asher lined the sights up with the middle of Scott's forehead. His finger curled around the trigger. And he applied the faintest hint of pressure.

Then he stopped and unwrapped his finger from the trigger.

He couldn't kill a man—even someone like Scott Montgomery—by shooting him in the back. It was his job to catch the killer—not bring on his demise.

Then, he looked at Kansas' body on the floor. His eyes burned and he tried to swallow down his fury. But his anger caught in his throat as the pendulum of his thoughts swung back to where it started.

Asher could still shoot. It would be a justified kill. Scott was still a danger to the community. And keeping the state of Alaska safe was his job.

He could tell himself that his actions wouldn't be

driven by retribution. Even Asher didn't believe himself and yet, he slipped his finger over the trigger once more.

Eli came around the corner. He saw Asher aiming his gun into the cabin and stopped.

"What are you doing?" He hadn't bothered to whisper.

Scott looked up, his eyes wide. For a moment, the two men regarded each other.

Then Scott darted forward. The killer moved out of Asher's sites for an instant as he grabbed a kitchen knife from the counter. Asher lined up the barrel of the gun with Scott's forehead as the other man pressed the blade against her neck. "Drop your gun, Rafferty," he said loud enough to be heard through the glass. "Or I will slit her throat."

"You think I care if you cut a corpse?" Asher's voice trembled with fury. But his arm was strong. His hand was steady. Scott's forehead was still in his crosshairs. He had the shot and could take it if he wanted.

Scott sniffled. "She's not dead. Not yet."

Asher wanted to believe him, but he shouldn't trust a killer.

Through the window, he could see Kansas's eyelids flutter.

Jesus, was she really alive?

"Eli's here with me. Backup is on the way," said Asher. "The only way you survive is by letting Kansas go."

"That's not going to happen." Scott pressed the blade into her neck. A seam of flesh opened and wept blood. "I'm not giving her up. I'm not going to let you have her. We will be together, even if it's in death."

Kansas was alive—but if he didn't act, she wouldn't be much longer. What's more, Scott was armed, and he refused to surrender.

All the reasons Asher had hesitated were gone.

"She's mine," said Scott, "for eternity."

That's when he tightened his finger and pulled the trigger. For Asher, time slowed. He imagined that he could see the bullet as it punched through the glass. Then, it drilled into Scott's forehead before coming out the back. The knife fell and clattered to the floor. The killer's eyes rolled up, showing only the whites. Then Scott fell backward as a red mist colored the floor.

Asher used the barrel of his gun to break away the rest of the glass.

"I'll give you a lift," said Eli, holding out his hands like a step. It was enough that Asher could easily shimmy through the window. He dropped to the floor, kneeling next to Kansas. She was dressed in a black dress and a large ring was on her left hand. It was all part of Scott's delusions. Feeling her neck, he searched for a pulse. It was there, strong and steady. The cut to her throat wasn't deep and the bleeding had stopped. There were fingerprint bruises on her neck consistent with strangulation.

"She's alive." Asher spoke loud enough that Eli could hear him outside. "But we need to get her out of here and to a doctor."

"I'll give our location to the backup."

Asher nodded. "Sounds good, man." Then he thought of something else that needed to be done. "Call your Aunt Abby. She'll want to know that we found Kansas."

"Will do," said Eli before stepping away from the window.

As an investigator, there were several things that Asher should be doing. Since the victim was alive and stable, he should check on the perpetrator and see if he needed care. He should also be examining the cabin for clues.

But Kansas was no ordinary victim. He wasn't going to leave her side, not now at least.

Besides, he knew that Scott was dead. Hell, the back of his head was all over the carpet. There was nothing that could be done for him now—or ever again.

Chapter Nineteen

Cold air blew into the cabin from the broken window. Asher removed his jacket and draped it over Kansas. She moaned and he reached for her hand. "Hey," he said. "It's me. Asher. I'm with you. Eli's here. Backup is on the way."

She squinted at him. "Asher? What happened? Where's Scott?"

He shook his head, not sure how to answer her question. He wasn't sure how much she knew already and how much more to share. Then again, Kansas could handle the truth. "Scott's dead. I shot him when he tried to slit your throat."

Her hand, pale against the dark blue fabric of his coat, touched her neck. "The last thing I remember was being choked. I thought I was going to die." A tear leaked from her eye and snaked down the side of her face until it disappeared into her hair. "I thought I was dead."

He held her hand tighter. He'd thought the same thing, too. His eyes burned with the memory. "You're here. You're safe."

"It's all because of you. It's because you kept me safe, just like you promised."

He lifted her hand to his lips and kissed her palm. "I will always keep you safe."

She touched his cheek. "Asher," she began, "I..."

Whatever else she was going to say was interrupted by banging on the door. "It's Eli. Open up, man. Backup is here."

Asher didn't want to leave Kansas's side. Yet he couldn't ignore his troopers outdoors. He pressed his lips into the heel of her hand. "I'll be right back," he said, rising to his feet.

"Asher."

"Yes?"

"You need a key to open the door," she said, pointing to the small counter. "It's up there, I think."

A set of keys sat next to an empty champagne bottle. He picked up the ring and skirted around Scott's dead body. The killer's eyes were still open. His gaze was already milky as he stared at nothing. At the door, Asher examined the lock. There were only four keys on the ring. He found the right one on the second try. He pulled the door open, and several people rushed in.

Two of the troopers who had come out were also trained as EMTs, and they began to examine Kansas. The other members of the team started to process the cabin, looking for evidence of Scott's many crimes. A sheet was draped over the body. At some point, Asher would be asked to surrender his weapon and answer questions about the shooting. But he really didn't care about the outcome. To save Kansas, he was willing to do almost anything.

Technically, Asher shouldn't even be here. And while there was plenty of work to do—photographs of the crime scene to be taken, fingerprints to be collected, evidence to be gathered—he stood to the side and watched as the EMTs treated Kansas's wounds.

"She'll be okay," said Eli, "thanks to you."

Asher hadn't even noticed his partner coming up to stand beside him. "I hope so."

"Kansas is a tough woman. Hell, she's the youngest in the family but she kept up with everyone when we were kids."

He liked the thought of a free-spirited young Kansas running through the woods. "I'm surprised she wasn't the one in charge."

Eli chuckled. "There was that, too." He reached into his pocket and removed a pair of latex gloves. "Since you're here, you want to help with the search?"

Kansas was being assisted to her feet by the troopers with medical training. Outside, the emergency toboggan was ready to take her back to the rendezvous point. And then, she'd be transported to the medical center in Shelby. It looked like she was in good hands. And sure, he could stay here with Eli and try to piece together the puzzle that had been Scott Montgomery. But there was someplace else he wanted to be.

"Thanks for the offer, man," he said. "But I'm going with Kansas."

Eli dropped a hand on his shoulder. "You take care of yourself. Take care of her, too."

"Actually," said Asher, "we've gotten pretty good at taking care of each other."

His coat had been draped over the back of a chair and he collected it on his way out of the cabin. Kansas was secured in the toboggan by the time he got outside. Poles from the frame were attached to the waist of a trooper who was already on a set of cross-country skis. As he'd noted before, he didn't have his own skis. It would be hard to keep up, but he'd do his damnedest.

He knelt next to the sleigh; only Kansas's face was visible. The rest of her was wrapped up and warm. "How are you?"

"I never thought I'd be riding in one of these things," she said, giving him a wry smile.

"Glad that you still have your sense of humor," he said. "I'm coming with you, although they might have to send out a search and rescue to find me later. I'll be on foot."

"Rafferty," said the trooper on the skis. He slipped off his backpack and tossed it to Asher. "I have snowshoes, if you want to use those."

He unfastened the zipper. Inside was, as promised, a pair of men's snowshoes and a set of telegraphing poles. He still wouldn't be as fast as he would be on skis, but at least he could keep up. "Thanks, man," he said, removing the metal-framed shoes. Then, to Kansas, he said, "I guess I'll be right behind you." He kissed her exposed forehead and rose to his feet.

Asher had kept his promise. Kansas was safe. Scott Montgomery would never hurt anyone again. He should be happy—ecstatic really. But he wasn't and he knew why. The case was over. Did it mean that Kansas would be leaving his life?

ASHER SAT IN the waiting room of the only medical facility in Shelby. A TV hung on the wall. A holiday baking show was playing, but the sound was turned down. He held a cup of coffee and stared at the floor. He'd stayed with Kansas all the way through the woods. An ambulance was waiting to transport her to the medical center when they arrived at the rendezvous point, and he'd ridden with her to the small hospital. As soon as they arrived, Kansas had been taken back to an exam room. Then he'd called her mother and filled her in on what he could. The Colton family was on their way. In reality, he'd been waiting less than twenty minutes. But to Asher, who had nothing to do but worry, it seemed like an eternity.

The door opened. Abby and Ryan Colton crossed the threshold. Spence and Hetty were right behind them. Self-doubt was a foreign feeling for Asher, but as Kansas's family approached, his guts twisted with apprehension. Would they blame him for what happened?

After all, it had been his job to protect Kansas.

He rose to his feet as they approached.

Abby pulled him into a hug. "We heard what you did. That was very brave of you," she said. "How are you?"

"I'm okay." During his career as a law enforcement officer, Asher hadn't killed anyone before. Eventually, he'd have to deal with his feelings about taking a life—even though the shooting had been justified. For now, he would think about other things. Like the fact that the Coltons really were nice people. They were obviously worried about their daughter and sister, but they cared enough to ask about him, as well. "Kansas is being examined right now. I'm not sure when she'll be back. I was told to wait here. The staff might give you more information since you're her family."

"I'll see if I can find someone who knows something," said Abby.

Hetty followed. "I'll go with you."

Both women left through the same door they'd just entered. It left Asher alone with Kansas's dad, Ryan, and her brother, Spence. "I'm sorry about what happened to Kansas," Asher began.

Ryan stopped him with a lifted palm. "You were the one who rescued my daughter," he said. "I'll always be grateful."

Asher knew that Kansas was getting the medical care she needed. But he also knew that he hadn't said enough to her dad. In a big way, he was responsible for Scott getting his hands on her. "I was sleeping when she left. If I'd been awake, maybe things would have been different."

"They would have been different for sure," said Spence. Then he quickly added, "But the outcome might've been worse. If you had told my mom that she got called out for a SAR, nobody would've worried. Hell, we might not be worried now."

Asher hadn't thought about it that way. He felt as if he'd just set down a boulder that he'd been carrying. He was exhausted. Sore. But also free of a heavy burden. "Thanks, man," he said.

"For what?" Spence asked.

Before Asher could explain how he felt, an orderly entered the waiting room.

The man held a tablet computer. After checking the screen, he asked, "Is there an Asher Rafferty in here?"

Lifting his hand, he said, "That's me."

"The provider is with Kansas Colton," he said. "She wants you to come to her room and get all of her discharge orders."

Obviously, Kansas didn't know that her parents had arrived. That's why she had asked for him. "Her dad's right here." Asher placed a hand on Ryan's shoulder. "And her mom's around here somewhere."

The orderly looked at his computer again. "It says that I'm supposed to get you. That's all I can tell you right now."

"I'll straighten this out," said Asher, "and be right back to get you."

"Or maybe she wants you with her." Spence dropped into the chair that Asher had just vacated. "But either way, we'll hang out here until you come back."

Asher followed the orderly. The medical center in Shelby was small. There were six or seven patient rooms on one side of a hallway and urgent care exam rooms on the other. The orderly stopped in front of one of the urgent care rooms. "She's in there."

The door was partially open, but Asher knocked before crossing the threshold.

The room was small, containing only a sink and a narrow counter, along with an exam table—covered in paper—and metal chair in the corner. Kansas sat on the table, dressed in scrubs and rubber shower shoes. "They took the dress and shoes away as evidence," she said by way of greeting.

Another woman, also dressed in scrubs, stood next to the table. She held a tablet computer and several sheets of paper. "You must be Mr. Rafferty," she said, extending a hand for him to shake. As he gripped the woman's palm, she continued, "I'm Linda Douglas, a nurse practitioner."

"It's nice to meet you," he said. "Kansas's parents are in the waiting room. I can get them if you want."

"You stay," said Kansas. "We can talk to them when we're done here."

We. Asher and Kansas. Kansas and Asher. "Kasher," he said, giving her a wink. "You're right, it has grown on me."

"Told ya."

Linda held out the stack of pages for Asher. "These are all the discharge instructions. Physically, Kansas is fine. But she's been through a lot—which I understand you know already. There are no restrictions, although I don't want her to be alone for the next few days or operating a vehicle. We need to make sure that there are no side effects from the sedative that was injected into her system. I've also recommended counseling. Mental health is also health care, and I want Kansas to be able to process everything that happened to her in a safe space."

"I can keep her safe," he said. "But there are a few people who want to see her now—namely her parents and brother."

"If Linda says I can go, I'm ready."

"You take care of yourself, okay?" said the NP.

Asher offered Kansas his hand. "Let's go and see your folks."

She placed her palm in his. Together, they walked into the hallway and toward whatever their future held.

Kansas entered the waiting room at the medical center in Shelby. Her mother, father, brother and future sister-in-law were huddled in a group talking quietly.

"Hey," she said. Her voice was loud in the quiet room. "Are you having a family meeting without me?"

They all looked in her direction.

"Honey," said her mother, coming at her with open arms. "We were so worried about you."

Kansas had to let go of Asher's hand to get a hug. One day, she would tell her mother all about what happened in the cabin when she was a captive. But for now, she said, "I'm here. I'm alive. That's all that matters."

Her father wrapped his arms around Kansas, as well. "My little girl," he said, his voice thick with emotion. It was so unlike her father to cry that Kansas's eyes began to burn.

Hetty and Spence joined in the group hug. "Sis," said her brother. "I don't know what I would do without you."

"Let's hope that you never have to find out," she said. And then to Hetty, "I'm so sorry about ruining your bridal shower."

"I'm not," said Hetty. "All I care about is that you're back where you belong."

"We should reschedule," Kansas suggested. But when? Christmas was in three days. After that, there was less than a week until the wedding. "Maybe everyone could come by tomorrow? We can do lunch at noon. After all, Mom's house is ready. The chowder is made. We can call Roasters and pick up the cake in the morning."

"Honey," said her mom, "are you sure that you'll be feeling up to all that?"

Kansas had survived Scott Montgomery's twisted obsession. But she was ready to do more than merely endure. She was ready to live, to thrive, to grow, to love.

She glanced over her shoulder. Asher was standing at the side of the room. She understood that he was giving her time with her family. The thing was, over the past three weeks, he'd become part of her family, too.

"Hey," she called out. "Why are you ignoring group hug time?"

He smiled. "It seems to me like it was a family thing."

"It is," she said, opening an arm and making room for Asher. "Now get over here."

Asher stepped into the circle and wrapped his arm around her waist. She leaned into his chest. In this one room, in this one embrace, were the people Kansas cared about the most. For a single moment, her life was perfect.

"Asher," said her mother, "we all owe you such a debt for taking care of Kansas."

He said, "Just so you know, I would do anything for her."

Kansas's eyes started burning with more unshed tears. The last thing she wanted to do was ruin the moment by crying. "All right," she said, her tone jovial. "We have to break up this love fest before security kicks us out."

Everyone chuckled and the group hug was over.

"It's late," said Abby. "It's time for us to all go home."

Reaching for Asher's hand, she said, "I'll see you in the morning. Is it okay if I come over at ten? I'll send an email tonight to let everyone know about the new time for the shower."

Her mother drew her brows together. "What do you mean that you'll see us in the morning? Aren't you coming home with your father and me? I don't think it's a good idea for you to be alone after what happened."

She squeezed Asher's hand tighter. "I won't be alone, I promise."

"Kansas…" her mother began.

"Abby," said her dad. "Just let her be. She's a grown woman, not a child."

Kansas let go of Asher long enough to give her mother a tight hug. "I'll see you tomorrow, okay?"

Her mom rubbed her back. "I'll see you in the morning."

Holding Asher's hand once more, she walked out of the waiting room and into a new day.

Chapter Twenty

As far as Kansas was concerned, the bridal shower was a huge success. Hetty received lots of different gifts, like towels, sheets, baking dishes and an outdoor sign that read, Colton Family, along with the date of their wedding. Beyond the gifts, the food was good. Even though the cake was picked up a day late, it was still moist and delicious. Everyone loved the bag of homemade chocolates. But the best part of all was spending an afternoon with family and friends.

After all the guests had left, it was just Kansas, her mom and Hetty. They sat in the living room. A pile of presents sat in the corner.

"I can't thank you enough for the party," said Hetty. "You know me, I'm not really a girly girl. But today has been special."

"I'm glad that we could have the bridal shower," said Abby.

"Yeah, even if it was a day late," Kansas added.

"Nobody minded having the shower a day late," said Hetty. "Especially since you were here."

Outside, a car door slammed.

Kansas sat up taller and her pulse started to race. Sure,

she knew that Montgomery was in the morgue. He wasn't going to bother her or anyone else ever again. But the kidnapping had left her jumpy. As the front door opened, she promised herself that she would definitely call the therapist.

Her father entered the house first. He was followed by Spence and Asher. She knew that the three men had been together at RTA and setting up for the wedding. She liked that her father and brother had include Asher in their plans.

"I figured it was a safe time to come home without interrupting the festivities," said her dad. He took a seat on the sofa next to her mother and placed a kiss on her cheek. "How'd it go?"

"Everyone had a great time. So that counts as a success," said her mom.

Spence stood near the corner, examining the gifts. He held up the sign. Smiling wide, he said, "I like this. We can hang it outside the house."

"I think that'll be perfect," said Hetty, rising to her feet.

Kansas stood, as well. Aside from the pile of presents in the corner, there was also a pile of dishes in the kitchen. "I'll start cleaning up," she said. "That way Hetty can show Spence everything."

"You stay and rest," said her father. "We chatted. Since you all put on the shower, we decided to be the cleanup crew."

"If that's the case," said Abby. "I'll get us all some coffee and we can keep chatting. I think there's more cake left. Anyone want a slice?"

"If you mean the cake from Roasters, I'll take some," said her dad. "The cleanup can wait."

"I'll make the coffee and get the cake," said Spence. "Everyone is working hard for me and Hetty. It's the least I can do."

"I'll help," said Kansas, following her brother into the kitchen.

Spence removed a bag of coffee from the cabinet, along with a filter. Fitting the paper into the filter basket, he said, "I can take care of all this by myself, you know."

"I know," said Kansas, setting a stack of plates next to the sheet cake. "Can't I just help my big brother?" But there was more helping Spence than just being nice. "Besides, I'm curious. What do you think of Asher?"

"Asher is great," said her brother, adding water to the reservoir. The pot began to hiss, and the first drops of coffee fell into the pot. "The question is, what do you think of him?"

"I think he's pretty great, too."

"He must feel the same way," said Spence. "In fact, I think he's serious about you."

Kansas tried to act cool. She set a piece of cake on a plate. "Why do you say that?"

"Well, he spent his afternoon helping us. I've always liked him. He's Eli's work partner. But that's not something you do for a casual friend. He was there because of you."

She liked Asher. But there was more than simply liking him. She cared about him. They were good together—at least when nobody else was around. But Scott was gone. There was no reason for her to stay at his house any longer. Sure, the NP had told her not to be alone. But obviously, Kansas could stay with her parents. The thing was, she wanted to be with Asher.

"How many people are you planning to feed?" Spence asked.

Kansas looked down at the counter. She'd plated ten slices of cake. "I guess I was preoccupied," she said with a quiet laugh.

"Are you thinking about what happened to Scott?"

She shook her head. "Not him. Asher."

Their mother kept a serving tray in one of the kitchen cabinets. Spence found it and set it on the counter. He set six plates with cake on the platter, along with napkins and forks. "If you like Asher so much that you get distracted while cutting cake, then maybe you should see where this road takes you."

"Are you getting all poetic on me because you're getting married?" She nudged her brother and then winked to show that she was teasing.

"I've always had a thing for Hetty," he said, pouring the pot of coffee into a carafe. "But when I thought I'd lost her—when I thought that hitman had killed her—I was sick. No, more than sick, I was gutted. Once we found her, I knew what I had to do and proposed." He held up his hands before she got a chance to argue. "I'm not saying that you have to marry Asher. But if you care for him, which I know you do, you need to go for it. Grab whatever happiness you can find in life. Because we aren't guaranteed anything beyond today, and I don't want you to have any regrets."

"Thanks for saying all of that. You've given me a lot to think about."

He patted her shoulder. "Let's get all this out to the living room. Dad's been talking about the cake all afternoon."

With Kansas carrying the tray and Spence holding the coffee and a stack of Styrofoam cups that she'd bought for the party, they entered the living room. It might have been her imagination, but all the conversation stopped as she approached.

"Okay," she said, setting the tray on the coffee table. "That's awkward. What were you talking about that I can't hear? Or are you keeping secrets from Spence?"

Her mother said, "Asher was just telling us about a special present he bought for you."

In all the excitement, she'd forgotten about the gift. "Oh yeah, it's the one I can't shake."

"You definitely can't shake that present," said her father, reaching for a piece of cake.

"So, tomorrow is December twenty-third. It means Christmas Eve is the day after tomorrow. Then Christmas day," said her mother, although everyone already knew. "What are your plans for the holiday, Asher?"

"Usually," he said, grabbing a slice of cake, "I go to California and visit my parents. This year, I wasn't sure where I'd be with the case and the recovery. So I haven't made any plans."

"You have to celebrate with us," said her mom. "We have a big Colton family dinner on Christmas Eve at Will and Sasha's. In the morning, we have breakfast here. There's plenty of food and laughs. We hope you can join us."

He glanced up at Kansas. Was he looking for her permission?

Well, there was nobody else she wanted to be with her for the holidays. "I'd like it if you can come, too."

"I guess it's settled," he said. "I'll be here."

EVERY CHRISTMAS EVE that Kansas could remember, she'd been at her Aunt Sasha and Uncle Will's house for the Colton family celebration. For the most part, it was all about the food. There was prime rib, venison sausage, poached salmon, four kinds of salads—garden, fruit, Caesar and pasta. There were side dishes—mashed potatoes, yams, cranberry sauce, green bean casserole and creamed spinach. There were also more desserts than she could count.

Beyond all the food, her favorite part of Christmas Eve was being with everyone. She had to admit that her family had grown since last year. Sixteen people were crammed around a table meant for ten. She didn't mind being so close. For her, it was part of the fun.

As dishes and platters were passed, Uncle Will stood. Clinking a spoon against his wineglass, he said, "Can I have your attention?"

Everyone stopped talking and looked up at Will. "First, I want to thank you all for sharing this night with us. Christmas means many things to many people. But for us Coltons, it's all about family. It's about being there for each other. Supporting each other. Keeping each other safe."

Asher sat at her left. She glanced at him and smiled. Their relationship embodied all her family ideals. She liked that.

Her uncle continued, "We have a lot of new people with us this evening. And one thing we always do is share what we are thankful for this year. I'd like to start." He lifted his glass higher. "I'm thankful for every one of you at this table." He looked at his wife. "Sasha."

"Same," she said, reaching for her husband's hand. "And I'm especially grateful to be married to a wonderful man like Will."

"What about you, Ryan?" Will asked, "What are you thankful for?"

"After your speech, I feel bad saying that I'm thankful for the desserts." Everyone laughed. "I'm thankful that after months of worrying, our community and our family is safe again."

"I'll drink to that," said Eli. He lifted a glass of wine and took a sip.

"Abby?" Uncle Will coaxed.

"I'm like all of you, thankful for family. Friends. Safety. But I'm especially thankful that I'll be getting a new daughter soon." She reached out to squeeze Hetty's hand.

"Eli? What are you thankful for?" Uncle Will asked.

"I'm thankful that Noelle is back in my life and is here with us today."

Noelle spoke next. "I'm sad for the reason that I came back to Alaska. But I'm thankful that you all have been so warm and welcoming."

Parker said, "Well, I'm thankful for a few things. First, RTA is doing well. We already have several trips booked for next year. I'm thankful that we're going to be hosting Spence and Hetty's wedding in a week. And I'm thankful that every day when I go into the office, I get to work with the love of my life, Genna."

"I'm thankful for a job that I love and that I get to help grow a business with the man I love, as well." Genna kissed Parker on the cheek.

As if it were planned, all the cousins said, "Aww," at the same time.

Lakin sat next to Genna. "Wow," she said. "This has been a big year. I'm thankful that I finally found out about my birth mother." Lakin had been abandoned at a local grocery store when she was just three years old. There was no trace of who had left her behind. Soon after, she was adopted by Will and Sasha. As it turns out, Lakin's mother had left her so she could escape an abusive relationship—one that eventually took her mom's life. "I'm so grateful that Troy and I finally opened Suite Inn."

Troy said, "I'm like Genna, thankful to be running a business with the woman I love. I'm also thankful that my kid sister, Hetty, is marrying Spence, who's a great guy. And Hetty's getting a great family in the process."

"At least you know that you like the in-laws," Kansas joked.

"That is true," he said with a laugh.

Mitchell was the next one to speak. "I'm like my mom and dad. I'm thankful for everyone here and I'm especially thankful that Dove is a part of my life."

"Thank you all for welcoming me into your house and your hearts," said Dove. "I'm thankful for the support you've given me after the death of my father and the opening of my business."

Hetty said, "I'm just thankful that soon it'll be official, and I get to marry my soulmate. I'll go from being Hetty Amos to Hetty Amos-Colton."

Spence kissed the back of Hetty's hand. "I bet everyone can guess what I'm thankful for."

Asher was next. "Like you all know, Eli's my partner at ABI. With the type of work we do, we've become tight over the years. He's my brother from another mother. But I appreciate that you all have included me in your family celebration." He lifted his glass. "Cheers."

Eli lifted his own glass. "Or maybe one day we will really be related."

"Good job," said Parker. "Way to be subtle and put pressure on Kansas and Asher."

"We prefer to go by Kasher," he said. Then he winked

at Kansas before looking at Eli. "If you don't like it now, wait a little bit. It'll grown on you."

Now it was her turn. Kansas had never been nervous in front of her family. But butterflies flitted around in her belly as she tried to find the words she wanted to say. "Well, for starters, I'm just thankful to be here. I'm thankful for everyone who worked hard to find me when I was lost and brought me back home." Sure, there were lots of people who worked on the Fiancée Killer case. But Asher was the only one who came to mind. "I'm thankful to put petty arguments in the past and I'm ready to move into the future."

She looked around the table, at the faces of her family, her friend and the man she… Well, she wasn't ready to put a name on how she felt about Asher. Her eyes burned. Even after everything she'd been through, Kansas hadn't cried once. Yet a tear leaked down the side of her face. She wiped it away with her shoulder. "I just love you guys so much. I really am grateful to be here with you all."

Her speech was followed by a round of applause.

Dinner was followed by a gift exchange and holiday charades. The festivities wrapped up by 11:00 p.m.

"Everyone needs to be in bed and asleep by midnight," her Uncle Will advised. "Since we're so close to the North Pole, Santa gets here first. If you're awake, he won't stop."

It was the same warning he gave every year, even though they'd all quit believing in St. Nick years before. But it was getting late and everyone started collecting their coats. Kansas and Asher had ridden together to the party and would be leaving together, as well. She still hadn't moved back to her own home and knew that a conversation about living arrangements needed to happen. But it could wait until after Christmas.

After slipping on her coat, she pulled her gloves out of her pocket. Her phone tumbled out as well, hitting the ground. The screen glowed. She'd missed seven calls. Her stomach sank to her shoes. Should she be out on a search and rescue?

She picked up her phone and checked the transcription of a voicemail. Then she read it a second time. Luckily, she hadn't missed anything work-related, but still, the calls had been important.

"Hey, everyone," she said, raising her voice to be heard over the din of people saying their goodbyes. "I got a call. It concerns us all. It's something you'll want to hear."

She opened her voicemail and turned on the speaker function.

"Ms. Colton, this is Shauna Billings. I'm a producer from Cable News Central." CNC was a twenty-four-hour news channel known for being fair, impartial and widely watched. "I saw some reports from the Alaska Department of Public Safety about your kidnapping and noticed a striking resemblance to what happened to your Aunt Caroline almost thirty years ago. I'd like to talk to you about your experience and how this is related to your family history."

The message ended and the room was silent.

Parker was the first person to speak. "How dare that woman call you! And on Christmas Eve of all times."

Kansas understood some of her cousin's anger. In fact, she felt a good bit of it herself. But being mad wouldn't change the truth. "The media has gotten ahold of the story. It's going to come out. The question is simple. What do we—as a family—plan to about it?"

Her father and uncle exchanged a glance. After another moment of silence, her dad said, "When Caroline and our parents were murdered, we lost more than our family. We lost our sense of security, as well. Many of you all hadn't been born yet, and Eli is probably the only one who remembers much—if anything."

"I remember Grandma and Grandpa. They had a big pool in the backyard and Aunt Caroline used to push me around on the floatie. I also remember that day." Like shades had been drawn across a window, Eli's face became dark and empty. "It was the worst day of my life."

"It was the worst day for all of us," said Aunt Sasha. "It's why we decided to sell everything, start a foundation and move up here. We were trying to outrun our past. But it caught up to us and Kansas almost lost her life."

"We have to ask ourselves if we want to keep running," said Abby.

Kansas knew what she wanted. She'd never met her grandparents or her aunt. They were real to her—but only in the way that characters in a book become real. Sure, their story had become her story. But there was more. "I don't want to hide the truth of our family anymore," she said. "I know that people still miss them, but it was because we tried to hide our identity that Scott was able to get away with so many murders."

"That's not fair," said Parker. "Scott had his own set of problems, and those had nothing to do with our family."

He was right, and still she wondered out loud, "But if investigators knew, would they have connected the dots sooner?"

"We can't answer that question," said Eli. "But I agree that it's time we embrace our past—as hard as it will be. But we've got each other. We'll get through this. All we have to do is believe."

Believe. Their family motto.

"I believe in our family," said Kansas.

Her brother echoed, "Believe."

"Believe."

"Believe."

Even Parker said, "Believe."

"It's settled then," said Kansas. "I'll call the producer back on the twenty-sixth and see what happens next."

Soon after, everyone left. Kansas and Asher had plans to go to her parents' house the next day. Spence and Hetty would stop by after they spent the morning with her family.

The ride to the condo was unremarkable, and Asher parked in his assigned spot. The sky was an inky black, and the air was so cold that it burned the inside of her nose each time she drew a breath. Together, they walked from the vehicle to the front door. Asher entered the door code and pushed down on the handle. Kansas crossed the threshold. They'd left the lights on the tree even though they'd been gone. The living room was bathed in warm golden glow.

His condo, where she had been a temporary guest at the beginning of the month, had become a home. After hanging up his coat, Asher checked his phone for the time. "It's five till midnight," he said. "I guess that's close enough to Christmas to give you this." He knelt in front of the tree and grabbed the mystery gift. "You can open it now if you want."

"Are you sure I can't shake it?" she asked, teasing.

"Please don't."

Kansas took off her own coat and sat on the sofa. He handed her the box. It was a small square, wrapped in red paper. The seam was secured with a gold foil tag with two words in script: *Claudia's Boutique.*

She thought about making a joke about the gift being fancy since it came from such an expensive store, but she didn't want to ruin the moment. She tore through the tag and unwrapped the paper. The box was a simple cube, giving away nothing of what was inside. She opened it. It was filled with creamy tissue paper.

"Be careful when you take it out," said Asher.

Kansas removed the paper. There was something solid in the folds. Setting it on her lap, she opened it up. A stylized mountain peak done in glass caught the twinkling lights from the tree.

"This is the perfect ornament. The perfect gift. Thank you so much."

"I'm glad you like it," he said, scooting closer.

"Like it." She put her hand in his. "I love it."

He laced his fingers through hers, knitting them together. "When I saw you lying on the floor of that cabin, not moving, I didn't even think that you were breathing. Well, it felt like the world had ended. But I knew I loved you even before I thought I lost you. I think I've loved you all along."

"I love you, too," she said with more certainty than she'd ever felt before.

He placed her lips on hers and everything was right in the world.

"I want to find a place for this ornament on the tree," she said, rising from the sofa.

Asher stood, as well. "What about there?" He pointed to one of the upper branches. "Right by the star."

She handed him the glass ball. "You hang it for me."

"Don't you want to put your ornament on your tree?"

"It's our tree," she said.

As Asher hung the mountain range in glass on one

of the boughs, Kansas glanced at her watch. The time changed from 11:59 p.m. to 12:00 midnight, making it Christmas Day.

"Merry Christmas," she said.

Asher stood at her side, admiring their tree. "Merry Christmas, Kansas. I hope this is the first of many we spend together."

She knew this was just the beginning of their happily ever after.

Epilogue

It was New Year's Eve, and the grounds of Rough Terrain Adventures had been decorated for Spence and Hetty's wedding. The ceremony was taking place outside. The ground had been shoveled and was now free of snow. Several heaters were set up around the perimeter to chase away the chill. Chairs had been set up in rows and most of the seats were filled. Asher sat in the front row next to Kansas's dad.

He would have been fine with a seat in the back. But it seemed as though the Coltons had adopted him as one of their own. And in all honesty, he was fine with being a part of the family.

Hetty and Spence stood at the altar under an arbor of evergreen boughs and fairy lights. They were flanked by Troy, Hetty's brother and the best man. Kansas was the maid of honor. The ceremony was officiated by Mitchell Colton. It made sense. After all, he was the lawyer in the family.

Mitchell began, "I want to thank everyone for being here. We have all come to this beautiful place to witness two people pledge themselves to one another. Hetty and Spence have known each other for years, and friendship is the best place to start a life together. But more than pledging to be faithful to each other, to honoring each other, to loving each other in sickness and in health, they are bringing their two families together to create something new. That's why I was so happy to see that Spence and Hetty had chosen Troy and Kansas as their witnesses and attendants. By choosing these specific people, they're bringing together two halves to make a new whole."

Asher tried to listen to what Mitchell had to say, but he was too focused on Kansas. She stood next to the bride and held Hetty's bouquet. For the ceremony, Kansas wore a forest-green dress that skimmed the floor and had short sleeves. The fabric shimmered and skimmed the curves of her body. Her dark hair was pulled into a sleek ponytail that cascaded down her back. Her eyes shone in the twinkling lights. She was radiant and the most beautiful woman he'd ever seen.

"And now," Mitchell announced, "by the laws vested in me by the state of Alaska, I pronounce you husband and wife. Spence, you may kiss your bride."

Hetty grabbed Spencer by the lapels and pulled him in for a kiss.

Then Mitchell said, "Or, Hetty, you can kiss your husband."

That remark earned Mitchell a chuckle from the audience. The kiss got a round of applause and whistles.

Music began playing and everyone stood as the couple receded down the aisle. Troy and Kansas followed. Next in line were the parents and siblings of the bride and groom. Asher was part of that group.

The reception was held inside the offices of RTA. All the equipment had been cleared out of the large area used to store gear and meet with clients. A bar had been set up in one corner, along with a table for presents or cards. There was a temporary wooden dance floor in the middle of the large space, and tables were set around it.

Parker was in charge of the music and was also serving as emcee for the event. After all the guests were gathered, he said, "I'd like to welcome the newlyweds, Mr. and Mrs. Amos-Colton, to the dance floor for their first official dance."

Hetty and Amos swayed to a song as Kansas stood on the other side of the room with her parents, Troy, and Mr. and Mrs. Amos. Sure, the newlyweds were cute, singing to each other and sharing a kiss. But really, Asher could only watch Kansas.

Parker announced, "The happy couple would like to invite the wedding party and their parents to join them on the dance floor."

Asher expected for Kansas to dance with her new brother-in-law, Troy. But instead, she came up to him. Holding out her hand, she asked, "Can I have this dance?"

"I'd love to," he said, reaching for her palm.

They moved to the middle of the dance floor. Troy had grabbed Lakin, and both sets of parents were already dancing. Kansas wrapped her arms around his neck, and he placed his hands on her hips. Now it was his turn to sing the lyrics to Kansas. Sure, everyone in town was at the wedding. The thing was, he was proud to be with her and happy that finally the world knew they were a couple.

"So," she asked, smiling at him, "what did you think of the wedding?"

"I thought you were beautiful," he said.

She batted him playfully on the shoulder. "What did you think about the vows?"

What vows? "Honestly, you were the only thing I could see up at the altar."

"Really?" Color crept into her cheeks. "I'm not sure what to say."

"Say that you'll move in with me," he said. In a few days, she'd be back in the office. Asher was expected back at work, as well. They were about to return to their normal lives. But he didn't want their time together to end.

"Are you sure that's what you want?" she asked. "It's a big step. Besides, even if I move back to my house, we can keep dating."

"I want more from you than just dating." He continued, "I love it when I wake up next to you," he said. "I love that you make lists on your phone and look at them over breakfast. I love that you can get ready for a SAR in less than five minutes. I love the way my house feels warmer when you're inside. I love holding you at night as I fall asleep. And I love waking in the morning with you at my side—starting the day with you all over again."

"It is New Year's Eve," she said, "the perfect time to start something new."

"Is that a yes?" he asked.

"It is." She kissed him again. "There's nobody I'd rather be with than you."

* * * * *

COMING SOON!

We really hope you enjoyed reading this book.
If you're looking for more romance
be sure to head to the shops when
new books are available on

Thursday 15th January

To see which titles are coming soon, please visit
millsandboon.co.uk/nextmonth

MILLS & BOON

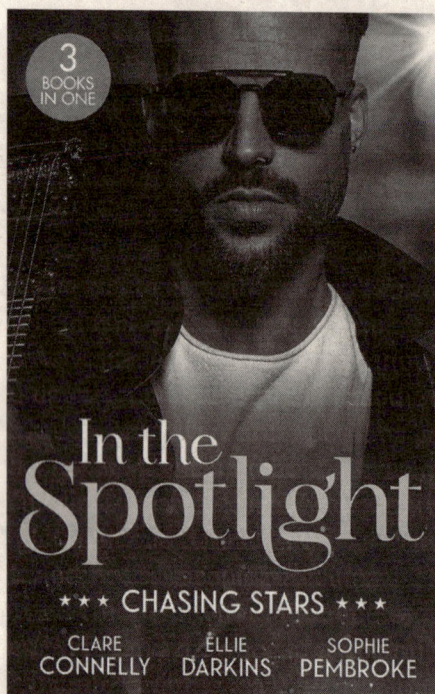